significant

others

significant others

zoë eisenberg

mira

Recycling programs
for this product may
not exist in your area.

ISBN-13: 978-0-7783-6966-0

Significant Others

For questions and comments about the quality of this book, please contact us at
CustomerService@Harlequin.com.

TM is a trademark of Harlequin Enterprises ULC.

Mira
22 Adelaide St. West, 41st Floor
Toronto, Ontario M5H 4E3, Canada
BookClubbish.com

Printed in U.S.A.

significant

others

1

J

That morning I woke to the sound of retching. At first, I thought the noise had followed me out of my sleep. Some shadow of a dream I'd already forgotten, but no. It was there in the room. A violent, choked sputter followed by the slick slop of release.

Through the cracked bathroom door I glimpsed the bare bottoms of Ren's feet. Ten toes neatly rowed atop the pearly tiles. She'd developed an obvious intolerance to alcohol toward the end of our twenties. A single drink made her empty herself completely the next morning.

This didn't stop her.

In bed, I rolled toward the open window and listened to the ocean breathing until the toilet flushed and the faucet hissed.

When the mattress gave to her weight I spoke without turning. "Why don't you puke in your own bathroom?"

"Yours is cleaner."

Not anymore. Her foot landed cold against my calf. I shifted, close enough to study the freckles cinnamoned across the bridge of her nose. The skin around her eyes was swollen and her breath carried Listerine and the bland antiseptic odor of vodka.

"Hi," she said. Her smile was apologetic. She was always apologetic when she drank too much. As if apologizing to me and apologizing to herself were the same. I resisted the urge to smooth the dark, ruffled line of her left eyebrow.

"Did you leave your car again?"

She screwed one eye shut in reluctant admission and then, seeing my face, poked me beneath the covers as if reminding me not to judge her and said: "Will you come? Tonight?"

I turned onto my back.

Above me, the cracks in the ceiling were familiar little friends.

"Please." Her voice went low. I knew if I looked at her, her bottom lip would be stuck out the way it always is when she wants something. "You haven't been in months."

Actually, I hadn't been to Crazy Palms in over a year. I didn't correct her. Instead I asked if she was teaching later though I knew she was. "Don't change the subject. Theo's down to go. I asked."

When I turned she was facing away from me. Her shoulder flashed bare beneath her camisole. I inched closer. Blew a long draft against her skin. On the inhale, I could smell cocoa butter. Salt, too. Even fresh from a shower, Ren always smelled of salt. The kind that speckled the glass on our windows, the ones that faced the sea.

"Please?" Her voice was already clotting with incoming sleep.

I didn't answer. Just blew again on her back. Tiny huffy puffs of warm air until her breath went deep and throaty.

6:15 a.m. and Theo was already in the kitchen separating egg whites. Headphones on. Shoulders swaying. He moved like his sister, bones in easy communication, driven by a tempo that was inaudible, unavailable, to me.

He nodded in greeting. There was an interesting zigzag design shaved into the side of his head that hadn't been there yesterday.

As I poured myself coffee the jangle of Sookie's collar began. I turned just as she charged inside through the open sliders, face one large smear of smile. Her tail helicoptered as I rubbed her back, her solid body wriggling between my legs.

I loved this. Mornings in the kitchen, the room a bright warm bulb in the center of the house. It was the main reason we bought the place. The lanai was mid-rot, the roof on its way out, but the kitchen. A center island stretched its length like a runway. Mango cabinets. The space was crafted. Cultivated. Someone had loved it.

"But we don't cook," Ren objected when I first showed it to her.

She was right. Before Theo came, the kitchen was just storage space for cereal boxes. Still. Much of the land along Kalaniana'ole was flagged for homesteads, so listings without a blood quantum requirement didn't come up often. I felt guilty for being so excited about this, but comforted myself with thoughts of how at least I was born here, would live in the house, was not some twenty-six-year-old software developer flying in from the continent, buying the place sight unseen with plans for a vacation rental.

We made an offer that afternoon, taking the auntie by surprise.

She'd just meant to hire me.

The night we closed, Ren popped a bottle of mid-range champagne and danced around our living room in an oversized tee and knee socks. We were twenty-five then. Living in a little two-bedroom by the golf course. Our third spot since graduation. Ren was already teaching at the gym twice a week, a cross between dance hall and kickboxing. *Kickjam*, I'd joked, and it stuck. I was studying for my broker's license and Theo had still been in LA trying to make it as a DJ. He didn't like when we brought that up now.

I carried my coffee over to the sliders. Out in the yard, liliko'i vines choked the chain-link fence with fat purple flowers like something full of poison and in the back corner sat that sad mound of mulch. Six feet high at least. Higher than the fence. Delivered last summer with the idea of building up a garden. Months later it lay quilted with vines and weeds. A lone, pregnant mound of earth. Sookie liked to roost atop it. Queen of the yard. All tongue and teeth.

"Eggs?" Theo's headphones were down, bass bleeding out around his neck. I shook my head. My window was closing—even in April, the sun would punish by seven.

Sookie whined as I moved for my sneakers. She had many virtues. Patience was never one of them. "Hair's new," I said to Theo as I laced up.

"You like?"

"Sure…"

He held a jar of mayonnaise and an uneasy smile. "What?"

"Nothing, just…" I shrugged. "Forty is coming no matter what."

"Yeah, hey, don't forget to run into traffic."

I laughed, popped out the door and then swung my head back in. "You mind driving separate? I have a doctor's appointment."

Theo nodded, licking mayo off a butter knife.

Out on Kalaniana'ole, we ran right. Past the beach parks and run-down motels, their roofs blanketed with rust, all of it outdated. Like they got left behind somehow.

Our feet pounded a familiar heartbeat along the worn pavement. To our left, the ocean frothed. Tourists would clog the road come noon, smelling of reef-safe sunscreen and looking both ways before they jaywalked.

We ran to where the road skidded out, then took the slim dirt path to the Queen's Bath. The too-blue lagoon always looked a bit fake. Like a movie set. One and a half miles there. One hundred squats under the old manele tree as Sookie snacked on dirt or dog shit or the occasional coconut. One and a half miles back.

I focused on my breathing. Smooth and controlled.

I'd be home by seven thirty. The early hour hid me from harsh sun, which would feel good on my bare skin but would burn badly if I didn't protect myself. This had always seemed cruel.

How something that felt so lovely could do so much damage if I let it.

That day I had a nine o'clock appointment with a moon-faced couple on the freshman side of their twenties. They fidgeted across the desk as I ran through it all, slowing on the bit about *a house they could grow in* and smiling with practiced warmth. I told them not to decide now. To go home and think about it.

I watched their eyes meet.

It was always easier with a couple. They thought they had a language of their own. The darting gaze. The lift of an eyebrow. Like teenagers in the back of a car. But the way they communicated was easy, and I was fluent.

They were not going home to think about it.

She nodded, just a minor dip of the chin. He reached for the pen.

After they left I took a lap around the office, found Ku'ulei by Lisa's desk laughing at something on her computer screen. "Kayson got into my lipstick," Lisa said when she saw me, moving aside to offer up her screen. I leaned in enough to be polite.

The child looked directly into the camera. His chin was smeared in waxy clownish red and his nose appeared to be full of snot. "Cute," I said, and Lisa laughed.

She was always doing that. The laugh thing. I couldn't tell if it was off-putting or endearing to clients. Ku'ulei checked her phone.

I imagined their relief as I turned to leave.

Kim's desk sat sentry to the double doors that swung out into the parking lot. She'd been my very first hire. I could never bring myself to call her from my office though she called my office from her desk all the time. She minimized something on her desktop when she saw me coming and I pretended not to notice. Made small talk about the rain before asking about my messages. Reminded her to schedule a call with the guy who ran our WordPress site and another with Lorna, who kept our books.

I made sure to smile before I moved away.

At exactly ten o'clock I dialed the house and imagined the phone ringing on the wall of the kitchen. Once. Twice. Three times. Then I hung up.

Theo walked by my office door, Lava Java cup in hand. Late technically, but it didn't matter. His numbers ran double what the others managed. I knew he'd kill if he could commit. That'd been the risk with him but by the time I took it, it was as much for Theo as it was for Ren. When I'd first shown her our house, I'd tried to imagine how I'd show it to a client. A young couple maybe. The house was perfect for a young couple. *And the third bedroom could be an office...* I'd trail off then. A dramatic pause— *or a nursery.* Time to smile. Feign casual. *You never know.*

But that afternoon, standing with Ren in our future kitchen, tile floors glossy as the white of an eyeball, I hesitated. *And the third bedroom could be a room to stretch in. Or space for an older brother in the midst of a nervous breakdown. You never know.*

I didn't have a script for us. I'd never needed one.

We met our freshman year through a dorm assignment. One hundred and ninety feet of twinned space. Two school-issued desks. Blue nylon mattresses.

The halves remained identical for fifteen minutes until Ren showed up and exploded color. Bright scarves over the mirror. Windowsill dotted with competition trophies. Books she'd never read lined up spine-out along the floor.

Ren found it radical I'd never left the state. "But you've been on a plane, right?" Once, two hours earlier, from Honolulu to Hilo. Her mouth popped open then shut itself.

She was the most beautiful girl I had ever seen.

It took us two weeks to understand the room assignment was likely based on some sort of familial algorithm. Or rather, a lack thereof.

Ren was six when her parents' car flipped over a meridian on their way home from a conference in DC. Theo was ten. They'd been asleep at their grandmother's in Fairfax. They never went home again.

She told me about it that first October. Just before midnight. Each of us hemmed into our skinny beds. I said nothing. Just let her go on. Then, with a rustle of sheets, she appeared next to me looking long and dark in the yellow-green haze from the sodium streetlights. Instinctively I scooted toward the wall so she could climb in. It was the first time I could remember sharing a bed with another person. I lay awake with her breath on the back of my neck and felt safe.

That Thanksgiving I flew to Virginia and stayed in a cavernous blue bedroom in her grandmother's house. I'd been shocked to walk through the front door and realize the whole place smelled of her. Or, that she smelled of it.

I sat on a wooden stool in the kitchen and watched her grandmother make shrimp callaloo and tea from dried hibiscus, her hands two lively birds at the ends of her wrists.

I was unprepared for the fall weather, which Ren found ridiculous. Virginia was mild, she'd said. We spent most of that week huddled on the couch watching *Law & Order: Special Victims Unit* and eating Ritz crackers. I'd never had a Ritz cracker before. Ren found this ridiculous, too.

By the new year, if one of us arrived somewhere without the other, friends and classmates would ask why. As if the presence of only one of us created a hole in the shape of the other. This became a running joke whenever we left the room alone.

Where's Jess? she would ask, tying a shoe.

Where's Ren? I would echo.

She was the first person I spoke to in the morning and the last person I spoke to at night. She felt like a gift for which I had no one to thank.

R

You can tell a lot about someone by the front of their refrigerator, and ours went like this: a photo of me and Jess in cap and gown on graduation day, smiling under a banyan tree, me looking into the camera, Jess looking at me. One of Sookie as a pup, her head too big for her body, her legs all gangly, and then a third, Jess and me on our lanai the day we closed, arms around each other, a play on the cheesy homeowner shot that ended up looking natural, the irony lost somewhere. There was the promotional magnet with Jess's face on it and, pinned beneath, the more mundane: our grocery list written on Paradise Property stationery—eggs, dog food, salad dressing, coffee. I picked up a pen and added "OJ," with a little heart for effect.

That spring, the surface of my life had grown a scuzzy film of predictability, like water left to stagnate, each day like the day before it, and some translation of the one that would follow, calculable as the telemarketing robot that called the house three mornings a week, always at ten on the dot, always from a private number, three rings and then silence. While it was jarring to routinely have my sanctuary of sleep cleaved by the shriek of the phone, I could hardly hate the spambot, which usually saved me from oversleeping. Even so, it never failed to kick the morning off with a hostile headache. Or maybe that was the vodka.

Back in my own room, I yanked a hoodie and mismatched socks from a rumpled mound on the floor, found my phone on the nightstand with three percent battery and no alarm set. I held my fingers to the bridge of my nose to relieve the mounting pressure in my skull, then sniffed around for something passable to wear, grateful Jess wasn't there to witness, although she mostly kept out of my room. Theo, too. They couldn't even stand in the doorway without straightening something. I unearthed a stiff pair of jeans and tossed them onto the bed for my shift later, already tired from the thought of it. I used to find Crazy Palms exciting—the tips obviously, and the crowd—but at some point, the place started feeling like a time loop, some vortex I'd stumbled into at twenty-two and was still stuck in more than a decade later, serving the same faces the same overpriced drinks like a boozy Bill Murray in that movie about Groundhog Day. Each time I walked through the door I felt a familiar weight drop onto my shoulders and it took at least one vodka Coke to lift it. Sometimes two. I could blame it on the cheesy decor or the sunburned tourists or the terrible Marley covers but in reality it was this: there's nothing more cliché than a middle-aged bartender.

It irritated Jess when I talked about this.

"There's nothing wrong with *bartending*," she'd say, always with some thread of disdain that negated the very statement she'd just made, "and you're not *middle-aged*." It was true, we weren't quite, but there were changes happening while I slept, a slack to my face that hadn't been there a year or two earlier, the skin below my eyebrows drifting towards my lids. "Stop that," Jess would say when she caught me pulling at my hairline.

Back when she still drank, she'd bring in clients and I'd feed them liliko‘i margaritas rimmed with caviar-colored li hing and never let them pay for anything. She came in so much that ChaCha thought we were a couple. We got that a lot after college, although never during. If we looked anything alike, I'm sure we'd have gotten sisters, as if there was nothing in between.

My problem was not necessarily that I wanted to do something different. The problem was that I had come to feel as if I were waiting for something, but I could never quite figure out what.

Studio C at Ralphie's had low ceilings and a long wall of mirrors that Odessa labored over twice a week with Windex, and as I looked into them I focused on pulling energy from the women behind me, a slippery concept that only worked if I didn't think too hard about it. The more energy I called in from the bodies around me, the more I had to push out, front back, left right, hips swinging, that zing that kept us all present, daily drudgery forgotten, eyes bright, smiles genuine.

I hollered instruction at the faces behind me. I'd never needed a microphone. The women shadowed me in unison, shoulders rolling, hair flying brown, black, gray, gold. Front and center, Barb became a tornado of trembling flesh and black Lycra, three times a week for the last thirteen years, seventy-eight now, and proud. I smiled and she smiled back and as we got low, I thought: if you haven't seen a grandma go all dance hall, you haven't seen shit.

After class I followed Mei out so Ryan would see me busy with someone else, walking half a step behind her, nodding along as she talked about her mother, *she calls and leaves a voice mail and then texts to tell me she's left a voice mail, all while she knows I'm on the way home, will literally see her in forty-five seconds*, not really listening, just feeling Ryan's eyes on me and the predictable zipper of electricity that opened along the front of my body. It was a game I played, one I only won if I refused to notice him, though of course in reality I noticed him all the time. It wasn't his fault, this weird attraction repulsion thing. Whenever we did speak, he was inhumanly nice, never any leer behind the eyes, a true smile, and real questions about how I was doing, and that jawline—oh god that jawline. We matched on an app once and I was so mortified I deleted my account.

Off-screen, he stood statuesque behind the juice bar three days a week looking so good it made me uncomfortable. He was a parody of himself, that was part of the problem, the overgrown white boy gym rat surfer, living for a decent set of waves, the random string of day jobs, the refusal to acknowledge the passing of time. The island was perfect for that. Not that I could talk, which of course was also part of the problem. Mei was still speaking about her mother. *It's like every time I open my Insta-gram she's sent me forty baby animal videos, and I try to encourage her to—* As we moved past Ryan's counter, I touched Mei's elbow to remind him we were close, that I was well-liked, tipping my head back to laugh over nothing, his torso in my periphery, all shoulders and chest above a fat stack of carrots. My laughter echoed against the gym's tin walls and Mei laughed back, and I felt a dizzying rush then, knowing he could see me so happy and in charge.

The locker room smelled of bleach and coconut body wash. I had nothing in there, only went in because Mei had, *what bothers me most is it's like, in thirty years I'll basically be her,* but I ducked into a stall anyway for tampons, single serve, housed in their own individual cardboard apartments. I shoved a fistful into my duf-fel and didn't feel bad about it. I paid for my own health insur-ance, and besides, Jess and I both used them. We'd been on the same cycle since I got off the pill and she never asked where I got them, which of course meant she knew. On the back of the toilet sat a wrapped roll of toilet paper and I grabbed that as well.

Ryan was gone by the time I was back on the floor, and I felt that familiar, psychotic double edge of disappointment and re-lief. Near the exit I paused to peer into the glass fishbowl of a room where keiki played with sticky blocks, *Moana* playing on loop while their moms firmed and toned, a UH student in the corner scrolling her phone, glancing up every now and then to make sure no one was choking. Ralphie once caught a woman dropping her three-year-old and leaving for work, cashing in on childcare for the low cost of $19.99 a month. He only realized when the woman had car trouble and failed to come back before close, the college girls gone home, just Ralphie and the little one waiting in the empty gym with Odessa and the cleaning crew. He revoked the woman's membership and I'd felt bad when I heard about it. She probably bought her own health insurance, too.

Through the glass, I watched a baby in a bubblegum-colored

onesie crawl across the floor at gastropod speed, pudgy fingers working the soft foam tiles, diaper suspiciously soggy, and felt the urge to enter the room and pick the child up, to press it to my body. Just the idea sent a surge through my body, something like a hunger pain. I could not pinpoint it, a time, an exact moment, when my body awoke from a sort of maternal hibernation and said: now.

"Maybe we should adopt," I'd said to Jess last spring. She'd been reading in bed and tipped her magazine down on her lap. "What else am I doing?"

I rolled my eyes then, belittling myself before she had a chance to. I didn't know how to communicate what I really meant, which seemed to be: I want to surrender myself to the care and development of something helpless, something that needs me. I want a reason to hold myself to higher functioning. Jess had stared at me for a moment as if to make sure I was joking before returning to her article on rapid ʻōhiʻa death, or Hawaiʻi's alarming dependence on imported food, or whatever depressing exposé she'd invested herself in to "relax."

Inside the keiki corner, two moms queued at the sign-in station, infants dripping from their hips. Both the women seemed younger than me, and I wished I didn't notice. I tried looking down at my feet, imagining them as a collection of bones and ligaments, something that could exist on any mammal, but it didn't help the way it normally did.

My bag was stuffed with stolen tampons.

It was not what I thought thirty-six would look like.

2

J

I'd seen Dr. Mirin every April since I was eighteen. Her office was always cruelly cold, and overhead a cartoon pineapple was taped to the ceiling wearing sunglasses, with a thought bubble that read *life's a beach*.

I'd been looking at it once a year for eighteen years.

Six apartments. One house. Four presidents.

Through it all, the pineapple still clung to the doctor's ceiling.

"Scoot forward a bit," Mirin said from the other side of my paper gown. I did, and was punished by a kiss of metal so impossibly cold it felt pulled from the freezer. To distract myself I picked a space to walk through in my mind. Our first apartment after graduation. A one-bedroom that looked out onto the parking lot of a Zippy's. Ren had been with that boyfriend then.

The Fighter. We called him that for months.

The name was a sort of code between us.

As if we were the real unit and he was the plus-one.

MMA, he'd correct when I called it boxing, which I did just to watch his mouth make a tight little gash. Nohea was his actual name. They'd taken the bedroom.

I felt a pinch then and clenched my teeth against the gritty scrape of dry cotton against my cervix. "Almost, almost," and then, "done." Mirin pushed herself back in her chair. Snapped her gloves off. Scratched a note on her clipboard.

Her hair was almost completely silvered. I squeezed my knees together and tried not think about what would happen when she retired. I could list on a few fingers the folks who'd enjoyed her annual view.

She looked up. "So. Jess. What's new?"

I made a low noise. Something agreeable. I wanted her to leave so I could get back into my underwear.

Her smile hung tight, and I knew what was coming. "I see you still haven't followed up on that referral."

I made another noncommittal noise. In truth I couldn't even imagine it. Freezing bits of myself. Storing them in some walk-in freezer alongside the intimate scraps of strangers. Women that drove by me as I jogged with Sookie. Clients, even. I could unknowingly show them a house while our eggs sat side by side like little biological popsicles.

Dr. Mirin pushed her clipboard away and dropped her gloves in the trash. At the door, she paused. "You know, by thirty-six, the average woman has a fifteen to twenty percent chance of conception per ovulation. And the numbers only drop from there."

She left me to get my clothes on.

These appointments used to be entirely different. Birth control, birth control, birth control. I wasn't on it, and it drove her mad. *Low-hormone. Options. Once a day like a vitamin. Just in case of accidents.* As if I could get pregnant from taking a turn too fast on 130.

Somewhere around twenty-five she switched tactics. "Seeing anyone?" she'd say, lubing up a finger. I always said no, which was always the truth other than those few months with Frank, and those felt so inconsequential I often forgot about them. That was before we moved to Kalaniana'ole and I was still running laps at the high school. Six a.m. when the track was empty.

We passed each other three days a week.

Faces slick.

Shirts breading our sticky backs.

Eventually he started talking to me while I stretched by the bleachers. Asked me out. Put his tongue in my mouth inside his Prius. I was still drinking then so it had been easier. He was divorced, and there'd been an empty photo frame on his dresser, and as he moved above me I would stare at it and wonder what had once been inside. We'd carried on for six or seven weeks and then it stopped and I hadn't felt anything about it. Actually, I hadn't really noticed it stopped until a few weeks went by and I realized I hadn't heard from him.

I'd never thought to reach out myself.

"They broke up and she didn't even notice," Ren teased me whenever it came up, and Theo would say something like, "I believe it."

The few times I'd stayed at his house I'd been unable to sleep. I lay there listening to the unfamiliar rhythm of his breathing thinking *who are you? Why am I here?*

Ren thought this was probably why I never actually got to know Frank. Because I was too fixated on how I didn't already know him. But I didn't *want* to know him. It was an effort I didn't have time for.

When I turned thirty Mirin shifted her angle as if she'd been counting up. Twenty-seven, Twenty-eight, Twenty-nine, *Do you want to be a mother, Jess?*

It was all I could do not to laugh.

I was working eighty-hour weeks. Had just hired Ku'ulei and put my face on two dozen bus stops. I had managed somehow to avoid the apocryphal belief that motherhood was the ultimate purpose. And yet.

When I pictured myself at fifty, I always saw a family. A crowded dinner table. Conversation tuned to a domestic static. A paradox, I knew.

Ren was on her yoga mat in the living room when I got home. Cheek pressed to kneecap while Theo folded laundry with a surgeon's precision. The house was warm and smelled of garlic from whatever he'd made for dinner, and immediately the day slid from my back like butter.

"Did Mirin guilt you about your expiring ovaries?"

I hung my keys on their hook. "Oh, did she ever."

Ren got the same annual lecture. She knew.

The couch wheezed as I sat, a wire biting hungrily into my lower back. The sofa was ancient, purchased ten years ago and secondhand even then. I ran a hand over its pilled arm. "When will you let me get rid of this junk-piece?" I asked.

"Don't call her that." Ren's nose was tucked to her knee, and she stared at me with only one eye.

"You've got attachment issues."

"And you're allergic to sentiment. Or maybe you have no conscience."

"Maybe," I said. It was hard to know if you have a conscience if it's never really been tested. I watched Theo tug a pillowcase from his pile in three sharp yanks and swallowed the urge to ask about his Reeds Island listing. We tried not to talk shop at home, which just meant that we waited for Ren to leave. Like it didn't count if there wasn't a witness.

"Do my back?" Ren scooted so the slender bottle of her waist faced me, an inch of smooth skin winking above her jeans. I lifted my socked feet to her body and pushed gently.

We looked into it once. Freezing our eggs. Two years ago, Mirin'd freaked Ren into considering it until she saw the price tag. Twelve thousand for hormones and extraction. Another eight hundred for storage. *Annually.*

"Eight hundred dollars for freezer space?! Can't I store them myself?"

I'd laughed at that. Our eggs wedged between an ice cube tray and a bag of frozen mangos. I didn't know what they'd look like, so I'd imagined them fused together. A pair. Like gecko eggs.

Beside us, Theo struggled with a fitted sheet, brows meeting above the bridge of his nose in a mannerism that mirrored Ren's so exactly it'd been jarring the first time I'd seen it. As if he were wearing her face.

The clock over the stove read ten of seven. "When's your shift start?"

Ren glanced toward the kitchen. "Fuck." She hopped up and zipped her jeans.

I heard the tinkling of her keys.

At the door, she stopped. "You're coming later, right?"

I grunted.

I'd hoped she'd forgotten.

The tacky tropical decor. The noisy UH kids marauding in to spill beer on the sad little dance floor. We were them once.

Maybe Ren was right. Maybe I was allergic to sentiment.

The door banged hard behind her. When I turned, Theo was looking at me. "What?"

"It wouldn't kill you to let her be late."

I sighed. "She's late all the time."

"Yeah, well, it wouldn't kill you to *let* her be. See what a consequence is." He gave me his back then. Headed for the hallway with the empty laundry basket glommed to his hip like a toddler.

We'd been at Crazy Palms all of ten minutes when Theo went to the bathroom and didn't come back. It took me another ten before I spotted him in the opposite corner with a waifish blond, avoiding my eye and gesticulating the way he did when he found someone sexually attractive.

I thought about Sookie curled on the couch at home. Envy rose in my throat like bile. Theo's fingers fluttered, and I decided I would leave him to call a rideshare if he didn't look at me within the next three minutes. Maybe two.

It had been raining when we came in. My umbrella dripped onto the floor as I stood in the corner nursing a soda water with lime.

Above me, a fritzing neon sign shaped like a palm tree pulsed a sickly green light in irregular, stuttering beats. As if it had an arrhythmia.

The place was packed. Bikini ties wormed from the necks of tank tops in rows so thick that Ren was barely visible behind the bar. The dance floor, however, was still empty. A gaping corral in the center of it all. If it stayed that way much longer, Ren's boss would send her out to hype it up.

This had always made me uncomfortable. It felt entirely problematic, meaning sexist, and no, it didn't matter that it was Cha-Cha's idea. But Ren swore her tips tripled on the nights she danced a song or two, grabbing a tourist to tag along. Besides, she would remind me, the dancing was the whole reason Cha-Cha offered to train her behind the bar in the first place.

Theo was still pretending I wasn't in his line of sight, and I glanced back at the bar, hoping to catch Ren's eye so we could bookmark his companion for later discussion. She'd be able to see the blond's face and I was betting he had a mustache. Theo'd been going through a mustache phase that spring.

But she didn't look at me, and there was a telltale floridity to her face that told me she was on her second drink. This worried me, not only because she had to get home safely or because she'd make herself sick, but because she always drank more when she was feeling sorry for herself.

I was feeling sorry for myself too, but only because it felt unfair to be alone in a corner when I was the only one who hadn't wanted to come out at all.

"This light seems to be having a seizure," a voice said then, and I looked up.

His head was a good foot above mine, and his hair was the color of a rusty nail. I hadn't seen him sidle up and had no idea how long he'd been standing there.

I considered giving him a *fuck-off* kind of smile. One that said: *I'm smiling in case you're a murderer but if you're not please go away.* But there was an apology in his eyes. Like he understood the role he was playing—strange man at the bar—and was actually sorry about it.

It was this look that made me change my mind.

"I think it has an arrhythmia," I half shouted.

He smiled a crooked smile. As if one half of his face had given up. "Oh, are you a doctor?"

"I don't have to be a doctor to know what an arrhythmia is."

He laughed. There was a wash of gray at his temples, and when I looked down to calibrate his social standing based on his footwear, I saw he wore those hideous chunky sandals tourists seemed to find necessary. I placed him somewhere between forty and forty-five. "Quincy," he said, and held out a hand.

I took it. "Where are you from?"

"Oh, what, it's that obvious?"

I shrugged and he waited, his smile tilted down as if to meet me.

"Your shoes," I said.

"What? What's wrong with Tevas?"

"Nothing." I twisted my mouth up into a teasing shape. "If you're a tourist. Midwest?"

He tipped his head toward the ceiling and laughed again, a big roaring laugh that showed off the great white trunk of his throat.

To my surprise, I flushed.

It felt as if I'd won some sort of game.

This was unusual for me. Normally I hated the specific falsity of this kind of exchange. At work my transactions were contractually agreed on. Here, in these kinds of situations, you had to pretend you weren't aware of your own currency even as you passed it back and forth.

But there was some quality about him that put me at ease. A friendly sincerity too genuine to seem desperate. He leaned toward me and said, "Missoula," and then, "Montana."

For a moment I'd forgotten I'd asked him the question at all. I rested my umbrella against the wall. "And what do you do in Missoula, Montana?"

He told me he taught, and when I asked what subject, he responded biology. Then, as if changing his mind: botany.

"What year?"

"University."

"You're a professor then?"

"Technically, yes." He said this almost reluctantly. As if his accomplishments were more embarrassing than his sandals. The sleeves of his shirt were pushed up and there was some sort of floral tattoo traveling up one of his forearms. A vine with small purple flowers, disjointedly delicate for his size.

I glanced over at Theo. He was still talking to the twiggy blond. His hands hovered stupidly around his face. I would let him take a car home.

"So," Quincy was saying, "this place is kind of awful, isn't it?"

I felt myself bristle. Though I hated Crazy Palms, it felt as if he had offered a critique of my family. One that only I had the right to make. I heard my voice contract as I said, thinly, "It's not so bad."

He looked at me then. A long, hard look. As if he didn't believe me. "So, you just what? Come here to stand alone in corners?"

Between my ribs, something clenched. I knew if I mentioned why I was there, he'd turn to look. He was taller. He could easily pick Ren out behind the bar.

It felt like a betrayal somehow. The opening of a door that I wanted shut.

Quincy's smile held, easy and expectant, and before I could respond, a clap began. I turned and there she was.

Palms to knees in the center of the dance floor, her smile contagious.

Attention shifted and the crowd became an audience.

Their clap moved like language from front to back until everyone was in on it. I watched as she plucked an older guy with a dumb-looking goatee from the crowd. Pulled him into her circle. Spun him around. Owned him, despite the five inches he had on her.

Quincy clapped along beside me, and across the room I found Theo looking directly at me, at us, and I realized, *now*.

I nodded toward the door and didn't wait for his response.

Out in the rain I realized I'd left my umbrella.

I didn't turn around.

Theo's drunken state announced itself as soon as he got in the car. His head bobbled atop his neck. "Seat belt," I prompted.

The rain came harder as I pulled out of the lot.

I squinted at the road in front of me.

"You get that guy's number?" His tone was teasing. I ignored it.

"What guy?"

"That ogre-y one you were talking to."

Theo loved to point out tall men, especially if they were straight. Some sort of vertical insecurity of his own. I thought of the wide expanse of Quincy's neck.

"Well?" I could tell he already knew the answer. That he just wanted to make me say it. Ren liked to say we butted heads because we're so similar. I never quite saw it. Maybe that was her point.

"He was just a tourist." I said this though I knew that for

Theo, someone being a tourist was a good thing. It meant they would leave. Through the rain-streaked windshield, downtown glittered like a Christmas tree knocked on its side.

We continued in silence. Theo had his head tipped back and his eyes closed. The clock read nine fifteen.

Just before we reached our intersection, he murmured my name. It came out singsong. Three distinct syllables, *Jess-ahhh-meen*, and I understood he was even drunker than I'd thought. "I know why you didn't get his number."

I felt my shoulders inch toward my ears. "Oh?"

"Yeah."

We were stopped at the intersection, the light red. To my right, two filthy bare feet jutted from the shadow of an awning. The sight of them made me crave the dry warmth of my own bed. I waited for Theo to push further and when he didn't, I glanced over and saw he really had fallen asleep, his head against the window and his breath fogging the glass.

The light blinked green. I accelerated down the empty street. Eventually our house appeared, and I triggered my turn signal though there was no one else on the road.

In the carport I killed the engine but didn't move.

Just listened to the coqui frogs and Theo's heavy, rhythmic breath. Grateful for the familiarity of the darkness around me.

Then I got out of the car and quietly let myself inside.

R

The band was shit but they got me moving, a grimacing "Valerie" cover, the woman at the mic in a ratty felt vest. It didn't matter, of course. I took the floor from vacant to packed in half a song. Goatee dude had better rhythm than I'd guessed, but when I tried to grab his eye, he looked off by my ear, then above my head. Eye contact seemed to be a hard thing for some men to understand. I told that to Jess one time and she'd snorted and said, *maybe it's just you they have a hard time looking at.*

When the song ended I let Goatee loose, scanning faces for Jess before locking on to the first person that made solid eye contact, a noodley white dude a few folks back, rocking his body side to side, just missing the beat. He'd ordered a water with his beer, tipped me a five, and as I tugged him to the center of the floor he said *oh, alright* as if I were bullying him. "You'll regret it though," he added with a laugh, his face red, his body all disco fingers and dad hips, but with a goofy confidence, as if he knew what he looked like and had made peace with it. When he lifted his hands to his face to vogue, I laughed a real laugh, none of that for-your-money business I do behind the bar. "I warned you," he said, smiling.

"You did."

We didn't talk anymore after that, and when the song ended, I lifted my hand in a vague farewell gesture and turned away before he could return it.

I wanted another drink but was already two down. Three would mean calling a ride and I didn't want to face Jess if I left my car again. I relieved ChaCha from behind the bar, set a round of Cuervo shots for a couple UH guys and scanned the room twice. No Jess. The blond that Theo'd been talking to reunited with the group he'd come in with. I felt stung then, over their lack of goodbye, and glanced again at the exit, where the neon silhouetted Kekoa's athletic frame. He'd been working here as long as I had, had started me smoking those few years I'd made a habit of it, and we'd probably spent a cumulative two hundred hours standing out front, two chimneys talking shit. Jess was always telling me he was in love with me, but she was always telling me everyone was in love with me, and Kekoa had already been with Marcie for years at that point, though back then it was before the kids. Now they had two kids under three and he never stayed after closing anymore, had warm bodies in beds to return to. The knowledge that his life had changed so wildly while mine had stayed the same made me feel itchy and hot.

I poured a draft for a local dude in a sovereignty tee and stared at my forearm, imagining the blood pulsing below the thin layer of flesh, the mycelial network of veins communicating with my organs. Jess said it was our education system that left me feeling this way, and maybe she wasn't wrong. I'd always done well in school, As and Bs that led to more As and Bs, progress directly linked to how hard I worked, easy to quantify in semesters and then years—sophomore, junior, senior. But now, Jess pointed out, how hard I worked didn't seem correlated to progress, and there were no GPAs to tell me if I was succeeding, no semesters to count off, and without warning I'm thirty-six and bewildered as to how or when that happened. Above me mold bloomed in familiar floral patterns by the air-conditioning unit, and I wondered how many more Fridays I would spend with them.

"Hey," someone shouted.

It was disco dude, standing on the other side of the bar. Off the floor I could see he was older than I'd first thought, though not in a bad way.

"Hey yourself."

He leaned onto the bar. "They pay you to dance with us, don't they?"

"They do."

"Incredible," he said, smiling as he shook his head. He put a twenty down and ordered a bourbon.

He was skinny, but his teeth were straight, and his body was so large that if I stood behind him I would probably disappear completely, and this appealed to me. I poured him a double, and then, smiling with eyes that meant open for business, I poured one for myself. Surprise splashed across his face, and I felt a tiny thrill between the ribs. I'd always liked being the best thing that happened to someone's evening, it filled me with a specific sort of energy, like a balloon inflating inside of me, pumping my arteries with oxygen until I felt almost invincible. We raised our glasses, threw them back, the bourbon smooth and clean. Immediately I felt lighter. Disco dude clunked his glass on the bar, and I leaned in further than I needed to while I retrieved it. As I did this I thought about Ryan, standing behind a totally different bar, one I couldn't lean across because that bar held no bourbon, and because that bar was well-lit, and because if I leaned too far across that bar and things didn't work out, there he'd be, three days a week, and so I'd rather walk by him pretending something could happen than let it happen and end up disappointed.

That strategy didn't actually work, of course. I was disappointed anyway. I thought about the mold on the ceiling. I thought about Jess leaving without saying goodbye. I poured two more doubles and watched this strange man smile.

The ride home was a blur, the city gone to sleep outside my window, the dark-sky streetlights glowing their weird alien green onto my face, which was almost entirely numb, and suddenly I was opening the front door, the rideshare backing out of the driveway, and I had no idea who had called it, but hoped it had been him. We banged a bit into the doorframe and in the dark I could see Sookie, a black mass on the couch watching us uncertainly. The floor shifted and I grabbed on to his arm, *shhhh.* I laughed, my body rubbering, his hand on my lower back, a thumb on the skin between my shirt and jeans. A little shiver moved down down down, down the hall I traced one hand along the wall to steady myself, his finger through my belt loop and oh, the height of him, his body a small tree, the way he let me lead us, none of that macho bullshit.

"What?" he whispered into the dark.

I laughed again, suffocated it with my palm, bumped against the wall. Don't wake Jess and Theo. Or do. They left without saying goodbye. My bedroom door closed, and the lights stayed off as I peeled away my shirt, stepped out of my jeans, three feet of space between us so that he could watch, which he did, because I wanted him to, which he knew. I had to stand on tiptoe to kiss him, to move his hand where I wanted it, his tongue in my mouth and his fingers cold and his voice asking something like *is this okay*, and mine saying something like *yes, yes.* I was untangling sheets before I realized he still had all his clothes on and this made me laugh because I was nearly naked and he laughed and we laughed maybe too loud and I quieted him, *shhhhissss,* but this made us laugh harder as I unbuttoned his shirt, so many buttons, one then another then another, his mouth on mine between each like punctuation, and on his face, something like surprise, like gratitude, which of course was why I chose him.

We were down and he was above me with a gentle pressure, his mouth pillowy with lips women would pay for and my underwear sliding away like a dream. He asked something again and I said *yes, the box, in the drawer, bedside table,* the window open as moonlight crept in over his shoulder and into me, where he moved and I inhaled sharply and felt the pad of his thumb on my lips then inside my mouth where it tasted of salt and earth and then gone, down, touching me until some sort of syllable pushed past my lips and white light slunk in around the edges of my vision and I closed my eyes and watched it fracture like lightning. I pressed my hand against his chest and when my eyes opened, I saw a shadowed web of vines starting at the center of him and running down his arms, little flowers, round purple blooms that surprised me so much I laughed and he laughed, and then his rhythm changed and need shot through my body and my laughter went quiet and that hot white lightning was again behind my eyelids.

Is that good? His voice came low and close and somehow familiar.

It's good, I said, or think I said, and things got bright, bright, brighter.

3

J

In the morning I woke early and sat at the kitchen table in a slant of sunlight drinking coffee and reading an article about the evolution of the word *bitch*.

Theo'd been up before me, was already out on the lanai cleaning the glass sliders with a red bucket at his feet. "A glutton for punishment," Ren would say about his habit of fighting a hangover with a cleaning spree. But it wasn't punishment. He enjoyed it. Taking something dirty and turning it clean again. A clear task with a measurable outcome. A reset button.

He had said nothing about waking up in the car.

The shadow of his hand swooped birdlike across the page of my magazine, and down the hall, Ren's door creaked. Probably on her way to heave last night's shift into a toilet bowl.

There was a showing later. A retired couple downsizing. Soon I'd have to shower. Get dressed. But not yet.

I was at the coffeepot watching liquid move from carafe to cup in a little brown fountain when a throat cleared behind me and a man's voice said, "Oh, wow."

I pivoted so quickly that coffee continued its arc all over the clean tile.

He stood in the jaw of the kitchen door wearing a white undershirt, one hand in the pocket of his jeans, his button-up slung over one shoulder like a bath towel.

"Jess, right?" Coffee, warm and wet, soaked into the bottom of my slippers as he smiled that lopsided smile. It occurred to me that maybe I should be scared, but before the thought could even complete itself, he said his name with his hand placed below his left collarbone and then, "I think I met your roommate."

Something popped in the center of my chest.

A compact blow like a truck backfiring.

"Oh," my mouth said, *oh*, just as Theo and his red bucket walked through the sliders with Sookie in tow. Wriggling with joy, she barreled excitedly into Quincy's shin.

"Well, hello," he laughed, leaning down to ruffle the fur on her flank.

Theo looked to me for an answer to this unexpected presence. Wide-eyed. Like perhaps he'd misjudged something.

"Aren't you a handsome guy, huh?" Quincy told Sookie. "What's your name?" He asked this straight to her face as if she might answer.

"Sookie," I said. "She's a she." It was the first full sentence I'd managed.

"Right." He smiled almost sheepishly. "Of course." He straightened and extended a hand to Theo, introducing himself.

Their palms met with a meaty *thwap*. Then Quincy pointed his thumb toward the hall and said, "I came in last night with your roommate."

"Ren?"

"Yeah."

"She's my sister."

He had to know that. They looked exactly alike.

But Quincy just laughed and said, "Man, awkward," with a self-deprecating wince. As if he wanted us to know that he not only understood the situation but was surrendering to its discomfort. I busied myself by placing my soggy slippers in a plastic bag and pulling the mop from the closet by the fridge.

"Here," Theo said to me, sliding his bucket forward, soapy guts sloshing. The sharp scent of vinegar and peppermint slithered up my nostrils and coated my mouth. He turned back to Quincy. "You were at Crazy?"

"Yeah." Quincy gave Sookie another pat. "Interesting spot."

Theo snorted. "That's kind." He nodded at me. "Jess hates it, too."

Quincy studied me then with a knowing smile. It was unsettling, that look. It insinuated something. I wasn't sure what and I didn't like it.

"So do you always follow women home from bars then?" I heard myself asking.

Theo's mouth opened but Quincy just looked at me. "Only sometimes," he said, tugging on his earlobe. "When they invite me."

Tension bloomed. Theo broke it with a joke about wishing he could offer Quincy a cup of coffee, motioning to the mess at my feet. I watched the dark liquid soak into the cotton fibers of the mop and wondered if it would stain.

I do not remember how Quincy said goodbye or if I looked at him while we made this exchange. Somehow, he exited, and after he was gone, Theo and I stood there staring stupidly at the door as if he might walk back through it.

Only Sookie moved. Bumbling back outside.

Those friendly hands already forgotten.

"Well, that was weird," Theo said finally. "Kind of goofy. Very boy-band-on-vacation." I could feel him watching me.

"*Ogre-y* was the word you used last night."

"Wow. Drunk Theo's an ass."

I drove the mop across the floor again and thought about the look Quincy'd given me when Theo'd said I hated the bar. As if we were co-conspirators.

As if we suddenly shared a secret.

The floor shone by the time Ren's bedroom door croaked open, a sound so specific it may as well have been a word. I kept my back to the hall. Ran the mop repeatedly around the white belly of the stove until I heard her say, "Morning."

She stood with one foot flamingoed up against her opposite thigh, wearing the same ratty university tee that I did.

I wondered with strange embarrassment if Quincy noticed the congruency, then realized she may not have had it on when he left.

"Nice shirt," she said, opening the cereal cabinet.

Theo grinned smugly at his sister as she hoisted herself onto the counter, sat there poking her hand inside her Cheerios box. I could feel him delightedly holding our knowledge high above her, deciding when and how to smash it over her head. I avoided his eye. I did not want to be an accomplice.

He plucked an apple from the blue bowl on the counter. "So," he started, tossing the fruit hand to hand. "Since when'd you start taking tourists home?"

"Right," Ren said. "That."

Theo crunched viciously into his fruit. Little flecks of flesh flew. "D'you know your fuckboy tried to pick Jess up first?"

Ren scoffed. "That was *not* a fuckboy. That—" She looked at me then, a handful of Cheerios halfway to her mouth. "Wait, really?"

I shrugged. I could've told her, no, not really. I could've told her how we just talked for ten minutes, maybe less. Instead, I said, "Was that safe? I mean, he knows where you live now." The floor was clean but I ran the mop over it again. "He could be murdering college students in Missoula, for all we know."

Ren gave me a blank look and I was hit with a bouncy spring

of satisfaction. "That's where he's *from*." I could feel Theo watching but went on anyway. "He's a *biology* professor."

Theo hooted. "Of course he is."

Ren looked down into her cereal box as if something interesting was inside of it. "He was gone when I woke up."

I thought of how casually Quincy's shirt had been slung over his shoulder. "What an asshole," I said, and left the room.

I wasn't sure why I was so thrown. It was hardly the first time Ren had brought someone home, though it had been years.

The older we got, the more our house became a sanctuary where strangers were rarely invited to sleep. When required, Theo and Ren slept out. Ren dropped me pins in case she showed up murdered, whereas Theo had toured the beds of half the hotel rooms in Hilo.

In college, sometimes boys would come by to see Ren after dinner or walk with us back to the dorms following a party like it was normal. Like they walked with us every night.

When the lights went out, they got into Ren's bed and I'd turn toward the wall with my iPod, the volume up a little higher than usual. In the morning they would leave, and we would dissect the details from our separate beds, our bodies curled toward one another like closed parentheses.

I rarely had my own details to dissect. Jonathan Umali, once, in his dorm room sophomore year. It only happened because he felt so familiar.

Like he could have been a cousin.

That made sense to me but weirded Ren out, and either way, I hadn't enjoyed it. The slick slap slap rhythm. Later, with Frank, I stared at the ceiling ignoring the bacterial tang of his breath and thinking how there should have been a pineapple poster pinned up there.

Asha had been the one to hang around longest. Junior year she came to the first meeting of some social science club I'd joined.

Sat in the back with her sleeves cut off.

Afterward she'd stopped me on the pretense of borrowing a used copy of *The Selfish Gene* that Ren had bought me for my birthday.

For two months we spent Tuesday and Thursday evenings in my room while Ren rehearsed her winter showcase. Eventually she'd come home and make a cup of noodles on our dorm-illegal hot plate and chat with Asha about movies I hadn't seen or music I didn't listen to and I would be confused and frustrated as to when Ren had watched or listened to these things herself.

Sometimes it felt like Asha had more to say to Ren than to me, and only later did I realize that was just Asha's way of showing me she cared about me.

I liked her body more than any of the men I'd been with.

She made a habit of standing us nude in front of my mirror to study our shapes side by side.

Hers was much sleeker, almost aquatic.

She was an excellent swimmer and it was obvious why.

You looked at her body and imagined it wet.

Mine was rounder, more solid. Though I was also a strong swimmer, when you placed me next to Asha you might look at my body and decide it would sink.

I didn't think about my body then. I guess I still don't. But she did.

She said complimentary things about parts of me I had never thought of, like my collarbones or the fine dark down on the backs of my thighs. In bed, she would bring her mouth to these places and tell me how much she enjoyed them.

After it was over I realized I liked the way she liked me more than I had ever liked her.

And always, when given the choice, I preferred to spend my time with Ren. This posed problems. The last time Asha came to my room she told me Ren and I had *codependency issues*.

She drifted away after that. I'd see her around campus and

try not to think about her hands or what her teeth looked like up close. Glistening morsels of bone.

In the bathroom I brushed my own teeth and listened to Ren and Theo move around the kitchen. The toaster popping. Plates being put away.

I brushed and thought about how the only thing Quincy had asked me was whether or not I was a doctor. The rest of the time he spent talking about himself. I wondered how many women he'd approached before he got what he was looking for, and I felt acutely frustrated.

I was usually better at reading people. When I spat into the sink my saliva shone pink with blood.

R

Jess had to return me to my car for the second day in a row, which was embarrassing enough without the Quincy thing. I spent most of the drive with my hand out the window, enjoying the air between my fingers, until she asked me to roll the window up, *please*. She drove staring straight ahead with her back one rigid line, the radio tuned to an HPR piece on the protests, the issue all the way up to the Supreme Court now.

It'd been awkward, earlier in the kitchen. I could tell she'd wanted me to see that she knew more about Quincy than I did, that it'd made her feel better somehow, but I wasn't really sure about what or why, since it was hardly surprising. If you left Jess in a room with anyone for five minutes she'd leave knowing their birthday and the names of their children, their favorite place for brunch, where they got their teeth cleaned. It was part of her job, to collect details from strangers and then use them to imitate intimacy. This skill had bought us our house.

When we pulled into the lot there she was, my old white Corolla with her battered fender, and I felt the same pulse of guilt I always got when I abandoned her overnight, as if I'd wronged her somehow. The bar looked different in daylight, vulnerable almost, and I thought of how Quincy had taken his pants off before his shirt, which had felt backward somehow, had made me laugh. I felt an urge, suddenly, to share this bit with Jess. She'd often kept quiet in the mornings after I'd been with someone, waiting until I voluntarily shared some little thing, a way they'd moved or a thing they'd said, and then everything would be normal again. I didn't share it, though, just thanked her for the ride, wished her luck with her showing, though I knew Jess didn't believe in luck. She believed in hard work. I'd once pointed out how that perspective could be patronizing to anyone who worked hard yet remained unlucky, and she'd coughed and looked at me as if those people didn't exist.

My car was pleasantly warm. I sat inside it with the windows closed and the engine off as Jess drove out of the lot, enjoying the animal heat that crawled up the back of my shirt. I replayed her strange behavior and thought about the time, four years earlier, when Theo'd had a short-lived fling with a man named Stefan who worked as a graphic designer and brewed craft beer.

Though Theo employed the apps with near obsession, his flings rarely turned into actual relationships, probably because he refused to sleep next to anyone. He thought waking up together was too intimate. Fucking, according to him, was not. Stefan had been his last actual boyfriend, and he'd found my relationship with Jess ripe for endless needling. At first he accused us of suffering from an internalized homophobia that blocked us from, as he put it, enjoying each other sexually, and when I pointed out that Jess had enjoyed other women sexually, he moved on to refer to us as *queerplatonic*.

To this, Jess had said, *Isn't that just friendship?*

Stefan had shrugged and said, *Not at thirty-two.*

College had been full of friendships like ours, when it was natural, normal, to wear each other's clothes, to do one another's eyeliner with stoic concentration as warm breath washed over our faces in comforting waves. It was only later that we seemed to mystify people, as if the normalcy of our specific kind of closeness had an expiration date, like milk. It felt bizarre to me that it would be more socially acceptable to live by myself in some shitty rented apartment because I could never afford to own alone, swiping around for a stranger on the internet, hoping they might take me to dinner, that they might be sane enough for me to risk going home with, that we might build something half as stable as what I already had.

Jess's romantic relationships were with people who pursued her aggressively, who were convenient, easy, who required no effort, as if it didn't occur to her to desire anyone of her own volition. She just agreed with their choice of her and then agreed again when they changed their minds.

I just don't get it, ChaCha'd said once. *You're both perfectly datable.* The conversation had begun around my disinterest in Kekoa, who actually probably had been half in love with me at some point early on, Marcie or no Marcie. Of course, I'd told Jess what ChaCha said, and this became a refrain.

Perfectly datable, whenever she caught me frowning at my own face in the mirror. *Perfectly datable*, when I would emerge from my room in an outfit I was unsure of. We sometimes joked we were lucky to have lost our moms early, the result being that neither of us had anyone to disappoint with our perpetual singledom. Those jokes were heavier, not because we didn't mean them, but because we did.

When I got home I went straight to my room, lay on my bed and googled *Quincy, Missoula, Montana, biology professor.* He popped up right away. A social page, a staff directory, a university video channel, his face big and round on every third or fourth thumbnail. I felt relief then, knowing he was a real person, not some psychopath like Jess had suggested, understanding fully my relief was absurd. Psychopaths could have YouTube channels, too.

I scrolled through the thumbnails without clicking any, three or four dozen with titles like *Getting Rid of Spider Mites* and *Ants in Your Plants.* I switched over to his Facebook, flicked through his photos. He posted semi-frequently, and I was able to track his movements over the last week in a way that made me feel oddly guilty. There were the iconic red bridges at Liliʻuokalani Park, a selfie at the Kīlauea Iki trailhead, his brow shining, a bandanna tied around his head, and there, from last night, a poorly lit photo of the mushroom burger at Ono's, recognizable from its square plate, the signature housemade pickle.

So, he was the type of person to post pictures of his food to the internet. Jess would have laughed if she'd seen that. I went back further, passing my finger over the page and watching years tick off, until I stopped on what was clearly a wedding album. A lump hibernated in my throat as I swiped through several shots of Quincy kissing a petite redhead in a low-backed white dress beneath a flowered arbor. The photos were dated twelve years old, his relationship status unlisted. I moved up again through his feed, closer and closer to the present, watching the redhead appear less and less and, finally, not at all.

I slid my phone underneath my pillow, thought again about the awkwardness in the kitchen, in the car, Theo's smug face, how Jess had called Quincy an asshole before she left the room. In truth I *was* bothered Quincy hadn't said goodbye, not even a note, but more than that, I was bothered by how bothered I was. I had no interest in hearing from him again, and really, any sort of goodbye would have been unbearable, the witnessing of each other's naked bodies without the comforting blanket of alcohol. But this meant that while I didn't care about hearing from him, I *did* care that he clearly felt the same way about me. This embarrassed me. Was that the kind of person I was? The kind who wants to be wanted for the sake of wanting alone? How small. I brought my hand high in front of my face and tried to pretend it belonged to someone else.

I had class in an hour, knew I should shower, get ready, but I felt glued to the bed, to the ache of my injustice over having been dismissed, over the dysfunction of my own behavior. Inevitably I thought about Ryan from the gym, and the real reason it was hard for me to see him and act like a rational human being: we went out once, a month or so back, right before I saw his name on the apps and deleted myself in a panic. He'd taken me for sushi and sake at a spot by the mall I'd never been to. He knew the menu, was kind to our waiter, asked me a lot of questions and didn't try to touch me at all when we said goodbye.

I'd have let him if he had, and maybe everything would have been different, but he didn't, just told me he'd had a nice time and waited with a smile and a final wave for me to pull safely out of the parking lot. The next morning I'd woken to a text reading *I had fun with you*. I stared at it for several hours before sending him a string of emojis: Pineapple, sushi roll, smiley face. An excruciating hour later, he'd emphasized the message with a heart. If I pulled up his contact on my phone, that was still the last thing we'd said to each other, and I couldn't bring myself to delete the thread even though it made me want to disappear whenever I looked at it. I wasn't even sure why I did that, the emoji thing. I didn't even use them that often.

Mei liked Ryan, I knew, was always stopping for juice after class just to flirt with him. He flirted back, but in a way that seemed almost kind, like he was humoring a middle-aged woman, though Mei was younger than me and noticeably cute, with bangs and big owly eyes. I never told her about our sushi date and had convinced myself this was because we weren't that good of friends. In actuality, the hidden information seemed to add an interesting layer to our dynamic, or perhaps it was *the* most interesting thing about our dynamic, and the only time I ever felt truly comfortable around Ryan was when she was there, and he was complimenting her earrings, then smiling at me when she went to dig out her wallet to pay for her nine-dollar vegetable juice, her cheeks colored with the pleasure she derived from his attention, oblivious that maybe the attention was for someone else's benefit entirely.

Maybe I was a small person after all.

After dinner, Jess set gecko traps by pouring an inch of orange juice into Ball jars and leaving them around the kitchen. In the morning, she would release them into the yard. I loved them, their Christmas-colored bodies, the savage way they chased each other up and down the walls, their rubbery little feet and loud orange stippling, the animatronic way they rotated their heads to get a better look at us. But they shit everywhere and Jess wouldn't have it. "Like birds," she complained, scrubbing a crust of black-brown excrement from a doorjamb.

That night I decided to fall asleep in her room so I didn't have to lie alone thinking about how Quincy hadn't left me his phone number and how I wouldn't have called him if he had.

"I feel like an oily puddle," I told Jess as I climbed in bed.

She was sitting up under the covers with an issue of *The Atlantic* propped up on her knees. "Mmm," she said without looking at me.

"Like I'm growing bacteria."

She flipped a page and said nothing. She probably wouldn't have noticed if I vomited into her lap. I peeled back the sheets and stared down at my thigh, bare beneath my bed tee. When I felt this way I would try to visualize my body as if it weren't capable of thoughts or feeling. I found if I imagined myself not as a person who could make choices and decisions but instead as an assembly of tissue and organ, I felt better. You couldn't quite blame a vertical gob of muscle and veins for its lack of accomplishment. For taking a stranger home just to prove it could make something, anything, happen. Jess began talking about some article she was reading about mining the Mariana Trench, starting in the middle of a thought as if I'd somehow read the same thing, or more accurately, as if she were speaking to herself. I had nothing to contribute so I continued to look at my thigh as she spoke, trying to imagine it as a marbled cut of meat, not so different from what you could buy from the butcher's counter, until my breath seemed to slow and tension lifted from my shoulders and back.

"More people have been to the moon," she said, straightening her legs. "It's like, two scientists and James Cameron."

"*Titanic* guy's been to the moon?"

"No, the *trench*. And guess what he found down there?"

"Plastic?"

She frowned. "How'd you know that?"

I shrugged, picking at an ingrown hair near my knee. Jess's investment in these issues had always seemed intimidating, not only because she cared about things I couldn't muster the energy for, but for the way she could compartmentalize those feelings when she needed to. During the last election I'd seen her smother herself to cater to conservative clients in a way that was both disheartening and impressive. Theo'd become more like that too, both of them changing faces like sweaters if it helped them sell houses.

Theo hadn't always held that chameleonlike quality. That was a learned behavior, although he had always cared about his image. The first time I went to visit him in California, he picked me up from LAX in a brand-new car, a black Audi shining on the curb like wet ink, and when I saw it I thought: *he made it*.

I don't think I even knew what that meant, to *make it*, but that was what I thought, sixteen to his twenty, because it was exactly what he had wanted me to think. It was only later that I learned he'd been leasing the car for way more than he could afford, which was part of the problem. The money. We'd each gotten quite a bit when we hit eighteen, what with our trust and the life insurance. It was meant for college, but at some point, Theo realized he could stop using it for school and just use it to live. He dropped out right before his junior year, which was much harder on our grandmother than if he'd skipped college altogether, and she never quite forgave herself for not setting things up differently. My trust got me all the way through school and a few years after, and when she died and a little more came in, I'd used that to help Jess put a down payment on the house. All of that had made sense to me, probably because Jess had been there to make sure it made sense, but Theo didn't have a Jess, so he blew through his by twenty-one, then waited tables until he was twenty-eight, trying to make the DJ thing take off before eventually crash-landing in Hilo, fried from a decade of partying, of breathing exhaust fumes off the highway, of wolfing uppers to stay out later and longer, of living for a dream that never really panned out. His apartment had been a shithole, but his car, a promise. I could just never quite figure out to who.

"Are you upset he didn't say goodbye?" I realized Jess had been studying me for who knows how long.

"Who?"

She leveled me with a pointed stare. I thought then about telling her how I'd googled Quincy, how I'd looked through his wedding photos, maybe even pulling up his feed right there in bed so we could watch a video together. We'd laugh about it, and I'd feel better. But her gaze was hard, so I just pinched the inner flesh of my leg and watched it blush. "He's not exactly your type," she said after a moment. "Although, I guess he *is* an asshole, so."

I didn't like that insinuation, but I also couldn't argue with it. Nohea once threw a potted orchid at the wall of our old apartment, and I remembered feeling sorry for the little white flowers as I cupped spilled dirt around their naked roots. I knew Jess was waiting for me to respond, would likely keep pushing until I did, so finally I said, "I think we both got what we were expecting to get from the exchange."

"Well," she said. "That's democratic of you." She returned to her magazine then, and I looked back down at my thigh and imagined it covered in plastic and tucked into a bed of Styrofoam next to the burger patties in the meat case at Safeway.

4

J

I've always liked money. I liked to talk about it, and think about it.

I liked to log in to my bank and look at the numbers there.

I felt a deep personal satisfaction when those numbers grew.

This fixation might be similar to how a certain kind of woman feels about dieting. The perception of control that springs from monitoring the food you put into your mouth and its direct correlation to the numbers reflected on a scale or the hug of your jeans.

To me, monitoring money seemed much more practical than monitoring caloric intake. Money was what bought you the calories, after all.

When I was nine my auntie Clem showed me how to balance her checkbook. Watching her line up numbers in their straight columns gave me a serene sense of equilibrium, the kind I got when floating on my back at Waipahu Beach.

I'd been living with Clem for four years at that point. She wasn't my real aunt but a friend my mother had met through a program for alcoholics that didn't work out well for either of them, but arguably worse for my mother. Clem never had kids, had never been married far as I knew. Every couple weeks she'd have some friends over, three or four aunties from the FCCH, who came with Tupperware heaving with lumpia or pork adobo, who would go through all the ice in the freezer and run out for more, who by the end of the night were speaking so loud it could qualify as screaming. Maybe I just felt this way because I never knew what they were saying, had never spoken Tagalog, though their occasional glances to my corner of the living room or hurried snatches of my mother's name told me they were talking about me.

Secretly I would pretend I understood them, that they were praising me, talking about how clever I was.

Of course, I didn't really, had never understood the language because my mother hadn't either.

At Clem's I slept in a walk-in closet she'd converted into a bedroom by cramming a twin mattress inside. There, I lay awake listening to the rats fight in the ceiling. Clem's sclera were stained a pus-yellow and every night we watched reruns of *The Golden Girls* in two worn recliners while she drank a tumbler filled so high with vodka it looked like a glass of water.

What I liked about balancing Clem's checkbook was that there was always a right answer. I found this deeply comforting. Clem worked as a bookkeeper for a small string of L&Ls and when she was happy with what I'd done with her checking, she showed me how she kept the convenience store books, rewarding me with garlic shrimp or day-old musubi.

When I was fourteen I got a job clearing dishes at a hotel luau. My supervisor was a rot-toothed man people called Mano who paid me eight dollars an hour under the table in cash. I dutifully logged what I made in tidy square print in a blue-lined notebook that I kept with my earnings in a Skechers box.

When the box was full Clem helped me open a bank account, and by sixteen I'd saved enough for a tired Nissan Altima with a

cracked fender and two hundred thousand miles on the odom-
eter. The car's front seat was marred by waxy burns from errant
cigarette embers and it smelled like smoke and fried food, but to
me it was a sanctuary synonymous with the word *independence*.

I even liked the high mileage.

It made me proud to drive something that had been so many
places.

I picked up a second job working the register at one of the L&Ls.

I bought myself my own musubi.

The numbers in my bank account ticked up.

Each additional digit heightened my sense of personhood and
by the time I left for freshman year I understood firmly that
the more wealth I amassed the more freedom I would have to
do whatever I liked.

Despite this, I was bothered by what this mindset did when
held universally.

I resented the noisy, sun-charred luau guests even as their
picked-over plates put gas in my beloved car. I hated watching
the faces of our mountains grow acned by high-rises, yet I loved
to line up all of the things I owned and look at them.

By then I understood that military, tourism and real estate
were our sole viable industries, and that all of the Indigenous
practices that once made the islands a functional ecosystem had
been dismantled.

I knew these things, and I cared about these things, but I felt
I had no personal way to impact them. More than that, I also
benefited. I sipped the juice being squeezed from our resources.
This duality between my ideals and my behavior posed a problem, which I solved by not thinking about it.

Clem died of cirrhosis halfway through my junior year of
college.

Over a long weekend, I flew back to Oʻahu and packed up her
house.

Ren offered to come.

I thought of her grandmother's airy, flower-strewn home in

Fairfax, and then of Clem's house with its black mold and the rats in the walls.

I told Ren no.

Though Clem had lived in her home for twenty years, it was owned by a family in California, and her death had inspired them to finally sell it.

I was stacking secondhand Precious Moments figurines into boxes when their real estate agent came to show the house to a white couple in their midforties. The selling agent carried an expensive-looking handbag, and from one room over I listened to her speak excitedly about the potential of the home Clem had died in.

The agent's shoes were the same shiny black as her purse and she kept them on inside, even though she was local, and I wondered then if she was softening her *T*s, stripping the incisive *V* sound from her *W*s, the way I would later learn to do with certain clients.

When she was done with the couple she drove off in an SUV that certainly did not have two hundred thousand miles on it, and I understood for the first time that you could make money selling something that belonged to someone else.

Toward the end of May the attention in our house was centered entirely around Theo's fortieth birthday party. I'd felt good the week leading up to it. Had scrubbed the house until it smelled of vinegar and peppermint oil. But two days out my chest began to fill with bees.

There were a few reasons for my building unease. I'd tried and failed at getting a guest list from Theo. When he pitched the idea of a party, I'd assumed it would be for the office. Maybe some of his clients. A dozen folks at most.

But Kim had begged off, then Lisa and Ku'ulei.

Blaming kids. Early morning activities. A lack of childcare.

When Theo insisted we order a keg, my nerves doubled.

When I overheard him inviting the Lava Java barista as we picked up coffees for our end-of-week meeting, they tripled.

"You invited the *barista*?" I hissed as soon as we were out in the lot, dodging puddles all the way to Theo's lime-green hatchback. The rain was on a break but overhead the clouds loomed aggressively.

"Roggie? Yeah."

"*Roggie?* Is he even old enough to drink?"

I saw then with rapid clarity our house frat party—trashed. The smash crash of a lamp as it fell. Vomit crusting over in the driveway. I had an ache in my lower back that told me my period was on its way, and I wanted the day to be over. Theo sighed as he slid his cardboard tray on the car's wet roof. He'd just finished a round of Crest whitening strips and his teeth were nearly phosphorescent. "We can't have a party without people, Jess."

"But the *barista*?"

"You're such a snob." Theo swung his door open and got in.

At the office I asked Lisa to hang back after our meeting and watched without surprise as she glanced pointedly at Kuʻulei.

I liked Lisa. I did.

It was why she was still with us despite her mediocre performance.

I also knew it was hard for her. She was divorced, and though her mother had moved in to help with childcare, she struggled. There was often an inch of gray at her hairline before she made it to the salon.

When we were alone I asked her about her client touches, how much attention she was giving to prospecting, and she laughed.

"Sorry," she said, "it's just funny we call it that. Prospecting, I mean. It always reminds me of gold."

"No, yeah," I said. "It should."

After I sent her on her way, I imagined her walking past Kuʻulei's desk and rolling her eyes. I'd never actually seen them do this but had the feeling they did. I could easily picture the two of them up late in a dim kitchen taking down a bottle of sweet white wine and complaining about me.

This used to bother me, but then I thought: unity between team members generally increases sales. If their unity had to be against me, then so be it.

Over my desk hung a framed photo of our house on Kalaniana'ole. It blew Theo's mind when he found out Ren and I co-owned. "But won't that be messy when one of you moves out?" he'd asked when I wasn't around.

We'd laughed at that.

He'd been living with us for a couple months.

Had somehow assumed the place was mine. He wasn't paying rent yet, but he used his SNAP to cook. Poached eggs with hollandaise. French toast and fried plantains and jerk chicken, their grandmother's recipes.

He cleaned, too. Stayed up all night so when Ren and I woke the kitchen grout gleamed white as his own teeth. But he slept late. Watched too much TV. There were days his eyes never opened more than halfway. I knew it wasn't laziness. I'd seen the way he cleaned a set of louvered windows.

One night after dinner I sat him down and said: "You get your real estate license, I'll hire you." He had the personality for it. All those years promoting himself had turned him into a performer. Or maybe he'd always been that way. "I'll even pay for your courses."

He'd just shrugged. Put his headphones back on.

Three days later I was in the kitchen picking through the *Tribune* when he sat down across from me. Folded his hands on the table and cleared his throat. "Tell me how it works."

"What?"

"You. What you do."

So I did, as Theo plucked at the scruff on his chin like he does when he's thinking.

When I finished, he nodded. "I got it. You're the pimp."

"I didn't invent the system."

He laughed. "But you're gonna milk it." He got up then. Hooted all the way down the hall. He was licensed only six weeks when he had his first close. Two retired psychologists from the Midwest. Three bedrooms. Oceanfront.

His commission was upward of twelve grand.

He never laughed at the system again.

At my desk I drafted an email to a selling agent and then read through it to remove any softening qualifiers or hedging language.

I stood and closed my office door.

When I sat back down, I checked Quincy's pages.

I'd been doing this most mornings for almost a month.

He posted frequently and it hadn't been hard to find him.

The Facebook page and some sort of college-run video channel. A dozen or so clips of him walking around a greenhouse talking about dirt.

I'd watched every one of them in my office with the door closed.

He spoke into the camera with the same easy candor he'd used in the bar and, later, in the kitchen.

As if everyone he spoke to was already a friend.

It comforted me somehow, to watch those videos.

I hadn't told Ren about them.

This also comforted me, though I couldn't articulate why.

I watched a few, clicking through to various points without really digesting anything. When the clock hit ten, I called the house phone, let it ring three times, and hung up.

R

The afternoon of Theo's party I went with Jess to pick up the cake. It was a Saturday, the sidewalk hot as the hood of a car, the cake box heavy as we moved down bayfront. My mouth tasted like metal, I'd forgotten my sunglasses, and with no free hand to shield my face I was forced to squint against the violent sun. At midday, the island wore a deep, brilliant blue, the color a regional trademark, something about the way the sun reflected off the lava rock. It was one of the first things I noticed when I landed here, the shade so precise, so familiar, a déjà vu kind of color, like it was returning to me from a dream.

Recycling bin blue, Jess said when I met her, flat and matter-of-fact. It was one of the first things she ever said to me, already in the dorm when I'd arrived with my two huge suitcases, my nervous chatter about the color of the sky. She'd picked the bed away from the window, leaving the best space for me. It was one of the first things I noticed about her. *Recycling bin blue*. I'd felt like an idiot for not recognizing it.

Up ahead on the sidewalk, she moved like she always did, with no hesitation, as if pulled by an invisible string. She looked back at me, her hair swinging over the top of her shoulder, and said, "Hurry up. The frosting will melt." She'd called the bakery three times that morning to verify the pickup time, to change the color of the piping, to double-check the spelling of Theo's name. I quickened my pace, my heel grinding painfully into the back of my shoe. We ducked quickly toward the road to bypass a family of five spread thoughtlessly across the sidewalk, their sunburned faces peeling, oblivious to everyone as they made their way to lunch, shopping, a snorkel excursion. At times, living here felt like working at an amusement park, existing solely to help everyone else ride the roller coasters. Jess scolded me when I shared this observation, spat facts I already knew about the defilement of the islands' culture and resources, but still I often felt this way; I just never mentioned it again.

She had parallel parked in the shadow of a malnourished palm. I slid the cake box onto the back seat and pulled off my shoes and socks. My feet looked swollen, and already a blister raged on the back of my left heel. I peeled off a tender sliver of skin as Jess cranked the AC on high. I rolled the window down to deposit my cells onto the hot pavement and immediately she told me to roll it up, leaning into the back to prop open the cake box, *Happy 40th Birthday Theo!* written in neon-orange frosting. It was jarring, Theo turning forty, not only for what it meant for him, but what it meant for me. I closed the window as Jess tilted the AC vent toward her face, her eyes closed, the air blasting so hard that stray hairs danced around her forehead like those inflatable men outside used car dealerships. "How many people do you think are coming?" she asked.

I squeezed my foot, watched the blood retreat, then released my hold to watch it return in a blooming, aggressive purple. "We don't know that many people."

"Do you think I ordered enough pizza?"

"I'm sure."

"Should I call and add a few more?" I could feel her anxiety pulsing out like some sort of electric force field.

I pulled my sweaty sock back on. "Jess."

"I mean with the keg we really should make sure we have enough pizza, yeah?"

"*Jess.*"

She looked over at me. "What?"

"It's just a birthday party. It'll be fine."

She looked away, straight ahead at the convertible parked in front of us with its top rolled back. "I know."

"Say it."

"Say what?"

"It'll be fine."

She tipped her head back onto the leather and closed her eyes. "It will be fine."

I closed my eyes too, sat listening to the ocean move in and out like breath, like we were housed inside someone else's body. After a moment I said: "I wonder if people like living by the water because it sounds like being in the womb. Like we remember it somehow."

She opened her eyes then, turned around and checked the cake again. Her fixation, I knew, was an extension of her own unease, a single facet she could exert control over, her way of coping with a situation she did not enjoy but tolerated because she loved us. That was the thing about Jess. Her rigidity came from a place of deep, intense devotion. I reached over and gave her hand a squeeze. The random metallic taste lingered in my mouth, my body aching with exhaustion despite the nine hours I clocked last night. If we went straight home, I might be able to get a nap in. As if she knew what I was thinking, Jess gave me a soft smile, released my hand, and shifted us into gear.

5

J

The strangers began arriving around ten, their cars creeping down Kalaniana'ole like a funeral procession. By eleven, our house was infested. From the lanai I watched a man in a neon tank piss on a fern in a blackened corner of the yard, his body swaying like palm fronds.

Inside I recognized no one. My chest vibrated painfully. I found Theo in the living room talking to some skinny kid with long hair the color of dying leaves. I touched Theo's back and he turned.

His eyes were glassy.

"Who are all these people?" I strained my voice. A Grimes song shrieked from the surround sound.

"All these who people?" He smirked, then looked away. Over his shoulder, the mousy kid looked at me with a surprising note of apology.

I shoved back through a narrow forest of people. I needed to change my tampon but the thought of forcing my way to my bedroom felt arduous. In the kitchen I dug under the sink for a trash bag then moved to the center island, the granite swampy with greasy napkins and empty pizza boxes.

I began filling the bag with sticky cups and folded paper plates. Beside me, two tanned men discussed a class they were taking at the university.

A tight knot of resentment formed inside of me.

I thought of the cake, still in the fridge.

It had been expensive.

There was no way I was feeding it to this army of strangers.

I looked to the man closest to me and asked him how he knew Theo.

His left eyebrow was pierced and the skin looked infected. "Sorry, what?"

"Theo," I repeated. "How do you know him?" His expression remained blank. "Theo Kelly?" He shook his head as if he didn't understand the question. "You're at his birthday party."

His inflamed brow reached for his hairline. "This is a birthday party?"

I lifted my hand to my chest and pressed down to calm myself as I told him, *yes.*

"Oh, weird," he said, looking to his friend again. "We just saw the wet post."

"Which one is he?" the friend asked, craning his head around the room.

"Wait, sorry. You saw the what?"

"The post," pierced kid said. "On wet?" Sensing my confusion, he wiped a hand on his jeans and pulled out his phone. Swiped around. Faced it toward me.

The screen was so bright it hurt, and I squinted. *HOUSE PARTY*, the post read in all caps. *SINGLES ONLY.* Below was a photo of Theo's abs glinting in his bedroom mirror and our address. *WHET*, read the app banner in a rainbow sans serif.

I felt as if my chest was about to explode.

In the living room I grabbed Ren's elbow and marched her

toward my bedroom. "What?" she asked, wrenching her arm away. "Ow, Jess, what?"

I was too angry to speak.

When I opened the door two men sprang apart on my bed. One wiped at his mouth. The duvet beneath him lay wrinkled.

"Out!" I ordered. "Get out." The beardless one scowled unattractively. I steeled my voice. "Get. Out."

"I'm parked up front," the bearded man said to the other in a low grumble. I looked pointedly away as one readjusted himself at the beltline.

As they passed us the beardless guy muttered, "Pushy fucking dykes."

My mouth opened to the slam of my own door.

Ren giggled. She looked more than a bit drunk.

I stalked into the bathroom and splashed water on my face. "Did you know Theo posted this on some app?"

She appeared over my shoulder in the mirror. She was wearing a shiny sort of lip gloss that made her mouth look like glass. "Really?"

"I think it's a sex app."

Ren snorted. "A *sex* app?"

I could hear myself. I sounded old. I couldn't help it. "He posted our *address*."

Ren gazed at her own reflection, then touched her tongue and used her spit to smooth one curl, then another. "What an idiot."

"So you didn't know?"

She seemed to startle. "Of course not." She blinked once, twice, as if making sure I was serious. "Obviously I'd have told you."

There was an easing in my sternum then. A release of grip. I lowered myself onto the lip of the tub. The porcelain was cool against my calves.

I tried not to think about the sections of floor growing sticky with beer.

The red cups Easter egging beneath the furniture.

She'd have told me, I thought, and watched Ren dab her finger into her mouth.

R

By three, the keg lay defeated on its side in the yard, red cups polka-dotting the shy grass, the coquis chanting in sharp unison. They were invasive but I loved them anyway, for the predictability of their soundtrack, for how they reminded me of the summer cicadas in Virginia. I stood alone in the backyard calling the dog's name. Theo'd disappeared around two and I hadn't seen Jess since she dragged me into her bedroom hours earlier. I hadn't seen the dog in twice that time.

I yelled for her again, cocked my head, held my breath. Nothing returned to me except the distant ocean, the rhythmic chirp of the frogs. I hollered her name yet again as the night pulsed around me. My feet hurt, my bed called, and my mouth still tasted like I'd been sucking on a dime, but I couldn't bear leaving her out all night. I worked the yard's perimeter, making singsong nonsense noises, no real words, just soothing tones, until I neared our looming pile of mulch and heard the chime of collar tags. A blunt snout poked out from behind the shadowed dune, then her eyes, wide with caution. From two feet away I could see her tremble. I dropped to a squat and opened my arms, let her creep into them, her big, muscled body quivering, the mushroom of her nose wet against my neck.

Up in the house she circled her bed twice and flopped down with a pacified sigh. The wreckage in the kitchen alone was enough to give Jess an aneurism. Theo too, although he wouldn't dare say anything this time. Hunger complained sharply from my center. It'd been hours since I'd inhaled a gluey slice of pizza. I pulled Jess's forgotten cake box from the fridge, snagged two forks from the dishwasher, then hit the lights.

In the dark of her bedroom, I made out the gentle slope of Jess's shoulder. She stirred when I sat, smiling softly, eyes closed. There'd always been a specific softness to Jess when she edged in or out of sleep, something cottony she refused to reveal when conscious. "Wakey wakey," I whispered.

Her eyelids fluttered and I saw her face close, a garage door drawing down. She rubbed an eye with a balled fist. "What time is it?"

"Time for cake." I flicked the light by the bed, and she shielded her eyes with a forearm.

"Did everyone leave?"

"Uh-huh." I flipped back the cardboard lid and wedged a fork directly into the center of it, brought it to my mouth. It was good—rich, dense, sweet but not cloying. I took another bite, then offered Jess a fork. She ignored it.

"I can't believe he invited all those strangers."

"Can't you though?"

She slumped back into the pillows. "He could have asked."

"You'd have said no."

"I wanted him to have a good time." She said that last bit as if reminding herself.

"He *did* have a good time."

Her shoulders sank. "I guess it's over now anyway."

"There you go. Futility is good for you."

She accepted the fork this time, leaning over the box for crumb control, our legs touching beneath the covers. She took a bite and made a low, guttural moan of approval.

"Right?" We ate in silence, addressing the cake from the center out, which felt just a little bit wicked. The dark shrouded the details of her bedroom, and sitting there in the middle of the night with a cake to ourselves, it felt like we could have been in any of our rooms over the past two decades, the dorm with its thin walls, our one-bedroom by the high school the year I'd been with Nohea. The spaces changed but we remained the same, shoulder to shoulder, the door shut to the rest of the world, and for all the frustration I felt with my own stagnancy, my life a cup of tea grown cold, always, there was this.

6

J

It was still dark when I woke, and beside me, Ren's breath was soft. Peeling the covers back, I was hit with the bready smell of our bodies. I stepped over the cake box, propped open on the floor.

Just the rind left. Frosting gone stiff.

I pulled on a sports bra and shorts and eased myself quietly down the hall. Tiptoeing through the living room, I was grateful for the dark. If I'd looked around, metered the aftermath, any chance of a run would evaporate.

Outside, the sky was a perfect cobalt. A lone truck flew by too fast, surfboard tucked into the bed, its driver's mind already out on open water. A cramp had taken residence in my lower belly, my body speaking to the ghostly eye of the moon overhead. If I didn't run during this part of it, my mood soured and I found it hard to focus. The endorphins mellowed things.

My feet struck the same old comforting rhythm.

One. Then the other. Sookie glanced up every few beats to check in.

We were at our squat station under the manele tree when the sun made its entrance, a furious blush spreading overhead. Sweat rivered down to my belly button and the anger I'd felt toward Theo last night drained in one steady glut like water from a tub.

I felt clean and hollow.

I savored the prospect of the mile-plus home.

A hot shower and time spent cleaning slowly.

All three of us with nowhere to be.

It'd been a while since we had a day like that.

A Christmas kind of day.

I was in the shower when the door opened and Ren lifted the toilet lid to vomit.

The room was thick with steam. She heaved again. "I'm telling you, you're allergic." The flush of the toilet brought an assault of frigid water. I yelped and backed out of the spray.

"Sorry," I heard Ren say. I waited for the water to warm again before I moved back into it. Reached for the shampoo. Began a lather.

After my shower I took the last tampon from our little white basket beneath the sink. My limbs felt rubbery and well-worked. Ren was lying on my bed with her knees pulled to her center.

I climbed into an old pair of underwear and caught my reflection in the mirror. My breasts were swollen, and I looked quickly away. "I just used the last tampon," I told her. "Should I go get some or do you have more?" I rummaged in my dresser for something cozy and oversized, settling on a soft tee from a company fundraiser we'd done years ago. Lupus or leukemia or something. Ren was up on her elbows watching me. "You know. The ones you steal from the gym."

Her lips parted.

"What? You think I don't know where they come from?" Sometimes her naivety shocked me. She'd been bringing those tampons home for nearly a decade. I smiled to signal I wasn't judging her. She searched my face with a look of panic. "What?"

Her eyes went big like two full moons.

"What?" I asked again.

She shook her head.

A bladed quiet crept into the room then, and instinctively I put my hand to my throat.

When I returned from the pharmacy Ren stood in the living room wearing a look of unanticipated composure. "Okay, I got six different kinds, I wasn't sure." I dumped my haul onto the coffee table.

Six pastel boxes. The contents of a fateful Easter basket.

The static behind my breastbone had become so savage I worried if I stopped moving, I might somehow combust. I paced around the couch like Sookie looking for a spot to sleep.

Ren stood still and said nothing. Red cups loitered around her feet and I felt a sharp longing for the day that had been taken from me. One where the most difficult thing to tackle was a series of domestic tasks.

The righting of our own chaos.

Finally, she sank into the battered sofa and held my gaze with wide, wet eyes. It felt as if my chest was a hive someone had whacked with a stick. "You could just be late," I said.

When she didn't respond I reached into the colorful pile of boxes and grabbed one at random. Held it out.

She looked at me but did not move.

We stared at each other. Breathing in turns.

Ren sat on the toilet with the thin plastic reader eclipsed between her thighs. The bathroom was still balmy from my shower. I flipped over the empty pink box and reread the instructions. I had always loved instructions. A comforting list of trackable, manageable things. Pee on the stick. Wait fifteen minutes. One line, not. Two lines…

The bees in my chest hummed terrifically. It felt as if I might die.

Ren flushed the toilet and I said, "Didn't you use a condom?"

"Of course we did. I mean. I think we did. I know I thought about it, at least."

I sighed, dropping the box back onto the counter.

"That's not very helpful right now."

"Sorry."

Ren laid a square of toilet paper on the sink. Placed the plastic reader on top of it.

"We have to wait fifteen minutes," I said, and she nodded.

Fifteen minutes later we were back in the living room and for some reason I expected it to look different. Ren stood at the window as I picked a red cup off the floor.

Then another. Another.

Followed them around as if they might lead me somewhere.

Ren's silence made my body fizz even harder.

When I had two dozen cups stacked into one another like nesting dolls I balanced them on the coffee table and sat. I was grateful then for the sofa's familiar frame. Its constant state of tatter. I'd never admit it, of course. I'd spent too long campaigning for its removal.

"I want to keep it" is what she finally said.

The information did not shock me.

It felt like something I already knew. Like someone reading me my own phone number.

Outside, two fat robins argued at the base of the driveway. She turned from the window then. Her face was so familiar it was like looking at my own. Without speaking, I asked her if she was sure, and she nodded yes. The electricity in my sternum made it difficult to breathe.

"It's not that different, really, from what Mirin wanted us to do," she was saying.

"Harvest our eggs?"

"The sperm donor."

I had never really considered that part of the plan. What

would have happened *after* freezing the eggs. When it came time to use them. I'd never thought about it because I'd never really wanted to freeze them in the first place. That was Ren.

Ren and the wistful way she ogled babies in lines at Safeway.

The way she examined her body in the mirror.

Pulling and pinching and lamenting the passing of time.

How had I never realized this before? I knew the answer, of course. It was because I had never been interested and it never truly occurred to me she could feel something different.

My mind beetled to Quincy, standing in our kitchen in his undershirt. I pushed the image away but Ren seemed to follow it.

Her voice came small like a little girl's. "No one tells the sperm donor if they've been chosen. Do they?"

I didn't actually know the answer to this, but I wanted to harmonize so I shook my head and told her no, no one tells the sperm donor. I felt dizzy. Winded.

She sat and sank her hands into her hair. She looked at me. I knew the look. It was the one she gave me when she wanted something.

I closed my eyes then and imagined a house with two hallways.

One was familiar and full of furniture and down at the end I could hear the voice of someone I knew. The other passage was empty. Barren. A sterile new-build still smelling of paint.

I opened my eyes. Ren was still watching me.

"I'll help, of course." My face was warm, and I put my hand there. "Whatever you need. We can do it together. Like with Sookie." Then, hearing myself, "Except, not a dog, obviously."

She laughed, scrunched her eyes shut, and when she opened them again, they shone. Moisture slipped down the side of her face as she nodded. She did not wipe it away.

I smiled. She smiled wider. My chest eased, the bees disbanded, and the relief was so staggering I laughed.

Theo walked in then, yawning, a pillow crease still running along his cheek. "Holy shit, this room."

Ren's back was to him. He couldn't see her shiny face.

The anger I'd felt toward him the night before no longer existed and Ren's eyes stayed on mine as she said, "We're having a baby."

Hearing this sent a shock down my center and I realized she was speaking only to me. "Yeah." Theo walked into the kitchen. "Me, too."

Ren looked away from me then. She moved after Theo, and I followed. At the counter, he poured coffee into two mugs. "For real," Ren said to her brother's back. "I'm pregnant."

Theo's shoulders drew inward. He turned slowly. "Serious?"

Ren nodded. Theo scanned both of our faces for a punch line, and then he seemed to deflate. He pushed his coffee away as if it could do nothing for him now.

I watched the tendons in Ren's neck pull tight.

"That goofy-ass fuckboy?"

"Please stop calling him that." I was surprised by the anger in Ren's voice.

"And you're gonna…"

"Have it. Jess is going to help."

Theo's gaze landed on me and hardened.

Before I could speak, a voice sounded from behind us. "Morning," it said with a healthy degree of uncertainty, as if it wasn't convinced.

The skinny kid with all that hair stood in the entry to the kitchen in the exact spot Quincy had stood a month earlier. Between the hair on his head and the hair on his face he looked like a young Jesus, not sure how he fit inside the tension he'd walked into.

Theo introduced this man to us as Taylor. He seemed no older than twenty-two. Theo slid him a cup of coffee across the island. "Milk?" he asked with something surprisingly close to affection on his face. Ren looked at me with an arched brow, her eyes asking *are you seeing this*, and I pinched my lips together to let her know *yes, I am seeing this*, and in that moment I knew without a doubt that everything would be fine.

R

We came up with a plan. I would finally quit the bar and take a leave from the gym. We'd set a crib up in my room, and eventually we'd renovate the carport into an additional bed and bath. There was childcare at Ralphie's whenever I decided to start teaching again, and Jess would open up a joint savings account, start a college fund. We would do what so many others before us had done. We would expand.

Four days after Theo's party we went to see Dr. Mirin, and I spent most of the drive over squeezing my knees together to stop them from trembling. I couldn't remember the last time I'd wanted something so badly. It was the last week of May and so humid the air seemed to lick at my face as we walked across the hot parking lot. Jess had made the appointment, had taken part of the afternoon off, had explained to Mirin that we'd used a sperm donor, even sat in that low chair in the corner during the exam part because I asked if she could, gauzy blue paper spread between my knees, my socked feet stuck in those stirrups, and when I craned to look at her, holding her purse atop her lap like a little dog, I felt childish for how comforted I was by her presence.

When Mirin left the room for my test results I quietly got back into my shorts. Overhead, a cartoon pineapple had been taped to the ceiling, the edges yellowed as if it had been there a long time, though I'd never noticed it before. Over Jess's shoulder the blinds were drawn against the bright midday sun, the entire room glowing in a tempered golden light.

"Well, you're definitely pregnant," Mirin said as she came back in. "Congratulations." I hadn't realized I'd been holding my breath until I released it, and when I turned to Jess she smiled in a dazed way, her eyelids fluttering like two dying moths.

Mirin moved to the sink, ran the faucet, started a lather up to her elbows. "I'd put you just under five weeks. Sound right?"

I nodded. Then, realizing she couldn't see me, told her yes, that was right.

She turned off the tap and shook water from her hands. "Right now, the embryo is the size of a sunflower seed. I'll want to set you up with an ultrasound appointment for about six weeks from now. You can see Claire on your way out to schedule that." A paper towel rustled softly between her palms. "In the interim, let's get the donor's medical history over." I winced, thinking of Quincy's body on mine. Mirin used the heel of her boot to jam down the lever of the trash can. "Should I have Claire put in a request with the clinic?"

"Is that really necessary?" Jess asked.

Mirin had her clipboard and was flipping pages. She spoke without looking up. "It's just standard procedure."

"For what?" Jess's voice was needley, but when I turned, she smiled reassuringly.

Mirin did look up then. "Oh, in case of any preexisting conditions." She smiled. "I'm sure he's in good standing, that's the beauty of a donor, but I'd still like to have his records, should there be any family history, hypertension, diabetes, you know." Mirin pushed her glasses up her nose, her pen hovering. "Did you use FIHC? I can have Claire give them a call. Easiest way."

I could feel Jess winding up, so I cut in quickly. "Actually, the whole thing was pretty…" I searched for the word. "Unofficial."

Mirin's pen lowered slowly. "Ah," she said, and when I glanced at Jess she was staring at the window as if she could somehow see through the blinds.

I rolled my window down as we drove out of the parking lot. I stuck my hand out, caught the air moving through my fingers like water. Five weeks, proof beyond that little piss reader, its piddly twin blue lines, so seemingly innocuous, so utterly life-changing. A wave took off in my stomach then, an excitement I hadn't allowed myself to feel yet, even though the bag on the back seat rattled with prenatal vitamins. Jess had bought those.

Beside me, her jaw was set. "Well, that was outrageous, huh?"

"What was?"

"The sperm donor thing."

"Was it? I don't know, we're likely in for years of that." I'd agreed to sub a jazz class in an hour and wished I hadn't, longing instead to spend the afternoon lounging and thinking about the sunflower seeding in my center.

"But from our *doctor*? Maybe we should find someone else." Her voice was brittle with indignation on my behalf and I felt my chest puddle.

"I don't know, I like Mirin," I said. "She was just trying to figure us out." I leafed through the paperwork we'd been sent home with, stopping on the section for the baby's father: name, age, occupation, ethnic background, preceding health conditions. I didn't even remember the color of Quincy's eyes. I thought of his face grinning in all of those video thumbnails. I still hadn't watched any of them. That morning a blonde woman had tagged him in a photo on some wooded trail, holding a mountain bike high above his head and smiling. *Bike buddy*, the woman had written, with a heart emoji, and when I clicked on her page it was set to private. I folded the paperwork and dropped it into the back seat.

Out the window, clouds stretched across the sky like cataracts.

I was carrying life, I was carrying life, I was carrying life— and for once I had something going on that was larger than myself. I was so distracted by these thoughts as I walked into the gym that for the first time in two years, I found myself face-to-face with Ryan without organizing my expression into something cool and aloof. I corrected this immediately, zipping on past with a brief nod, his mouth opening like he might say something, his skin shining a deep wheat-gold as he lined tiny paper sample cups along the front of his counter. As I rushed off with his eyes on my back I realized with a crushing finality: this would likely stop as soon as I started showing.

This understanding was rapidly replaced with the more aggressive realization that I was not sure when I would have to stop teaching, that I should've asked Dr. Mirin, and that I would definitely have to stop bartending sooner rather than later. A pregnant bartender would be obscene. The plan Jess and I had come up with had been loose at best, and these obvious details began to hit one after another, an unfortunate procession of mental fender benders: How would I continue to pay my part of the mortgage until I could come back to work, and when exactly would this be? I waited for that dreaded heaviness to settle on my shoulders, but felt only the soft, chilly stream of the air-conditioning vents pumping away overhead. Things would be fine, I told myself. Things would be fine. I was carrying life.

In the locker room Mei told me I looked tense. She worked as a massage therapist at one of the hotels and was interested in holistic health, hadn't eaten meat since she was twelve, and carried opinions about the benefits of alkalized water. She lived with her mother, had never moved out, but somehow this didn't carry the connotation of failure the way it did where I was from. Instead it meant filial devotion. We didn't have that much in common but she'd been taking my class for years, and was always complimenting my hair or my skin or my clothes, even when they were the same leggings I'd been wearing every other week for months. *You're holding it in your neck*, she was saying. *That actually says a lot about you, you know. Where you carry your stress.*

Taylor's car was in the drive when I got home. He'd been in and out since the party, smoking skinny hand-rolled cigarettes on the lanai, slicing a star fruit in the kitchen, juice puddling on the cutting board. Though he seemed resistant to speaking about himself without being prompted, through Jess's careful dissection we'd learned that he was in the second year of a graduate program in social work, that he'd done his undergraduate out here, too. It had been years since Theo'd seen someone seriously, and while I couldn't tell if this would be serious yet, so far it was at least consistent.

They were shirtless in the kitchen, their faces specifically dewed, and I had no doubt about how they'd been using their time with the house to themselves.

"So?" Theo prompted when he saw me, opening the freezer.

"It's definitely happening." I shook the bottle of vitamins out of the pharmacy bag. "But we shouldn't, you know, tell anyone for another month or so. Just in case."

Theo said nothing, just cracked ice from the neat domiciles of their trays with a homicidal twist, like the snap of a spine. The liberated cubes splashed freely into a pitcher of cooled tea, and I used my teeth to peel the plastic off the pill bottle as the silence in the room became weighted. Taylor must have felt it too, because he leaned back against the sink as if removing himself physically from the tension snaking between Theo and me. I thought again of the sunflower seed and imagined it nestled in a pile of pillows for safety.

"You're sure about this?" Theo asked, sliding a knife through a lemon. I felt my body tense. "You know it's going to be…" He trailed off.

"Hard?" My voice was thin and coppery.

"Right."

"Of course I know that."

Theo stirred tea with a long wooden spoon. I could tell by the pinched, focused look on his face he wasn't finished yet and I counted down from ten, nine, eight, seven, six: "So, like.

Legally, how will it be set up? A hanai situation or something more established?"

We hadn't really talked about it, the legalities, but I knew admitting that to Theo would feed his assumption that I was underprepared, and although he was right—I was underprepared, how could I possibly be prepared—I didn't want to give him the satisfaction, so I shrugged as if I found his question uninteresting.

"And what about fuckboy?"

"Will you *please* stop calling him that?" I shot Taylor a look of exasperation, and he returned it with a timorous smile as Theo moved toward the sink.

"Fine, when are you going to tell him?"

I removed the puff of cotton from my prenatals, put a vitamin on my tongue, and swallowed it dry. Enough time lapsed that Theo stopped stirring and looked at me. "You *are* going to tell him."

"He's not even on island. He's essentially a stranger."

"Strangers deserve to know when they've accidentally impregnated another stranger, don't you think?"

"Well, I don't even know how to reach him." This was a lie and I covered it by pretending to read the back of the vitamin bottle.

"Have you tried, gee, I don't know, the internet?"

"Theo." I put the vitamins down. "I'm excited. Can you please let me be excited?"

He blinked then, looked away. My jaw ached and I realized I'd been clenching it. I rubbed at the hinges as Theo dropped lemon slices into the pitcher of tea, *plunk plunk plunk*, the only sound in the room that didn't come from our lungs.

Sensing safety, Taylor stepped forward again. "Well, I think it's really cool."

"Thank you, Taylor."

His smile widened and I felt a pang of tenderness, like I should hug him, or at least tell him I liked him already, that he didn't have to try so hard. Theo grabbed a trio of glasses from the drying rack, metered iced tea into each of them and slid one toward me. An olive branch. The tea was cold and bitter with citrus rinds and tannin, ice clattering like pocket change against the side of the glass, and as I took a sip, that old weight settled back onto my shoulders with surprising force, that inexplicable heaviness I hadn't felt since Jess got back from her run and I realized I was late. I was further surprised when my mind flashed, with sovereign determination, to Quincy.

7

J

The first week of June I started showing condos to an old client named Tatia Chen. We'd worked together four years earlier when I'd helped her hunt down what she imagined to be her retirement home, her husband and his weak chin trailing behind.

For other people divorce was usually considered a bad thing. For me it meant a change in housing.

He was keeping the condo and now she seemed set on getting a near-identical one. Oceanfront. Appliances still in their wrapping. Hallways the color of bone.

It seemed weird to me. Like she was trying to simply reset her life without him in it. Maybe this was the point.

She stood over my shoulder as I fiddled with the lockbox of a two-bedroom unit. Door open, we were hit with the comforting smell of bleach. "Carpet? Who installs carpet out here?"

"New, at least."

Tatia wrinkled her nose. She carried with her the brisk efficiency normally encountered in a medical facility. "What a *sand* trap," she said, stepping further into the hall.

"You could always rip it out."

When we rounded the corner into the living room, she inhaled like she'd stepped on something sharp. The view. A rectangular portrait of sea framed on either side by the gentle shag of coconut palms. It was the focal point of the entire apartment.

"Who could get tired of *that*," she murmured.

Clearly someone had. The owners of this particular unit had been transplants who stayed three years then returned to the Pacific Northwest. This was not abnormal.

They'd likely had no knowledge of the rain.

Of the two-hour drive to the closest white sand beach.

No one had lived in this particular unit for over nine months, and I could feel it. The placid emptiness held by vacant houses. Homes with owners who have already abandoned them. A ghostlike feeling. Like you've crossed into some other dimension.

Like the time you spent there doesn't count.

In the master bath, Tatia stared long and hard at the sinks.

Two of them. Jack and Jill.

She pressed a hand to her mouth and I wondered if she was reminded of the last time we did this together. How she'd done all the talking. How when we went through the paperwork she signed first. Offered him the pen like an afterthought.

From somewhere else in the condo came the lonely drip of a faucet. I told her to take a minute, then retreated quietly. Lisa liked to joke we should all be gifted honorary therapy degrees. She wasn't wrong.

In the living room I stepped out onto the narrow lanai to meet that four-hundred-thousand-dollar view. The water was choppy despite the clear sky overhead. The island was disingenuous that way. It loved to misrepresent itself.

Though I'd stopped regularly checking Quincy's social media, after the new developments I found myself pulling up his pages again. A blonde woman made an appearance in several photos. Riding bikes and eating tacos. Posting snapshots of the two of them in someone's garden. It amazed me somehow that he could be existing elsewhere.

Carrying on normally.

Clueless that an ocean away he had created a life.

A life that other people would tend to.

I'd never lived in a house with a child.

Neither had Ren.

My mind started to drift then to the rest of the afternoon—I had contracts to go over back at the office and I wanted to stop by Kinkado's before they closed to get a crib for Ren. A gift.

Now was the time. Before she thought of it. If it were up to her, she'd head to Target or worse—Walmart.

Still. I'd let Tatia make the move to leave.

I resisted the overwhelming urge to glance at my watch.

The disappointment on Ren's face was unanticipated. A swift kick to the stomach.

We stood in the driveway, the trunk of my SUV gaping, the crib swaddled inside like the cargo it would soon carry. Koa wood with a butter-yellow sleeping pad. A front panel that slid down with a satisfying little sigh.

My own disappointment declared itself from somewhere behind my ribs. "You don't like it?"

This hadn't even occurred to me as a possibility.

The crib was the nicest one they had.

Worth more than Ren's car.

"No, no, I do, of course I like it." She pressed the toe of her shoe against the asphalt. "It's just…" I waited. Pushed against the slap of rejection. "I kind of would have liked to help pick it out."

Of course. The obviousness of my error was glaring. I rubbed at the back of my neck. "I guess I was thinking, like, a present."

"No, I know." She reached out and held the back of her hand to the smooth wood as if taking its temperature. "Just. I want to make these kinds of decisions, too."

"I can take it back." I gripped the top of the trunk as if to close it and she held her hand out to stop me.

"Are you kidding?" She smiled then. "It's gorgeous. I was just saying, you know, for future reference." In the evening sun the wood shone as if it were wet. "Gorgeous," she said again, and knocked her hip softly against mine.

Four days later, Theo called us into the living room. He was watching *Top Chef* with his feet draped over the side of the couch and I was surprised not to see Taylor beside him. His presence had been so frequent I asked Theo if maybe he thought they were moving a bit fast, to which he'd replied, *I'm forty now, remember? I have to date in dog years.*

Taylor was twenty-four. What were Ren and I doing at twenty-four? Not moving in with forty-year-olds.

Still, I liked how infatuated they clearly were, their hurried tether reminding me of our old college habit of asking after the other.

Where is Ren?

Where is Jess?

Where is Taylor?

Ren was late for work, and as Theo and I waited for her to emerge from her room there was an odd agitation to his movements. A strain in the way he stared straight ahead. As if he were purposely avoiding my gaze.

"Hey, Ren?" he called again.

She appeared then, elbows working for the holes of her turtleneck like some modern dance piece. *Woman Wears Sweater.* Finally, her face emerged from the neckline. "What?"

Theo looked from me to his sister as Ren fluffed her hair to its full height. "I wanted to talk to you both about—" He stopped. Ren had turned and walked back into her room. "Hey!"

"I'm listening," she called.

Theo sighed. "This is important."

After a moment Ren reappeared with her head tilted to one side. An earring flashed between her fingers like a fishing lure.

Theo cleared his throat. "I just wanted to tell you that, uh, with the recent developments it's, uh." He swallowed. "I started looking at houses. Like. Seriously looking."

Ren glanced at me before turning back to her brother. "You're moving out?"

"I mean, it'll take some time to find a place but hopefully before the, uh." He nodded at Ren. "The baby's done."

Done. Like pregnancy was a home renovation project.

"You're gonna need my room, yeah?"

Ren frowned. "Not right away."

"We're going to renovate the carport," I said.

"This way, you won't have to."

A hollow opened up behind my breastbone.

Theo, always up before me.

Coffee already made.

The careful way he folds the towels.

The constant drift of Big Wild or Suuns playing from his bedroom.

I started asking about price range and Ren trailed back into her room as Theo and I buried ourselves in budget. Bed and bath counts. There was a stiffness to the way he answered my questions. He seemed to be using as few words as possible.

As we talked, I pictured Ren in her room. Blotting her lipstick on those thin cotton rounds that overflowed from her trash can. She'd be upset by this. I wanted to go in there to check on her but something about Theo's odd behavior kept me on the couch.

Ren said goodbye at the door and snatched her keys off their hook. Together, Theo and I listened to her clomp down the lanai. The slam of her car door. The growl of her engine turning.

"So have you applied for an FHA?" I asked. Sookie wandered over to bury her head in my lap.

He didn't answer me for a long moment, long enough to let

the question lapse, and when he spoke his voice came so quiet it was almost a whisper. "Are you sure this is a good idea?"

I sighed dramatically.

Theo angled his body so he was facing me fully. "Really, though, do you even want a kid?"

"I want a family, of course I do."

"You don't need a kid for that."

I thought of the emails stacked up on my phone.

The calls I had to return. The other things I could be doing. "Look, this is hardly a novel concept at this point—"

"That's not what I mean. I just want to make sure your motives are straight."

My chest began to fizz like a soda bottle someone shook then opened. "What does that even mean, my *motives*?"

He looked toward the door Ren had just exited through. "I think this is some grab at keeping her."

"*Keeping* her?"

"Whatever. You know what I mean."

"Obviously, I don't." I stood then, moved to turn on the overhead fan but it was on already. I sat back down.

Theo tugged at his chin. "Look. Ren is either too oblivious or too attached to the convenience of you supporting her—"

"I don't *support* her—"

"*Please*. She's barely contributed anything since she emptied her trust into your down payment."

"*Our* down payment, which she did so we'd have *equal* stakes. The exact opposite of me *supporting* her." My voice was high and uneven and the sound of it made me cringe. I stopped. Reset myself. "She pays a third every month, same as you."

Theo coughed. "And her car insurance? Groceries?"

"Why does that matter?" I said, and he laughed, a tight incredulous knot of sound. It was a laugh Ren used often and it felt like a betrayal somehow to hear it turned against me. "Ren's not a child. She can make her own decisions."

"Can she? Cause you seem pretty good at making them for her."
It hung there between us.

Our sheer inability to understand each other in the moment.

"Would this be easier for you if we were sleeping together?"
I asked.

"*Don't* you sleep together?"

I gave him a hard look and he folded his arms. I could see
him as a teenager then. Pouting in his bedroom. Then he said:
"A baby isn't some bill you can split, Jess."

I started to say something like *why not?* but stopped, because I
knew on some level it would be false. That due to genetics and
the labor Ren was already undertaking, she would of course always have more claim. There was also, I knew, some truth to
what Theo was saying. Though he seemed intent on villainiz-
ing me, he was right that raising a kid with Ren would cement
something between us. This child could only bring us closer.

"Listen," I started, softening my voice. Hearing the change
in tone, Theo uncrossed his arms. I willed the words to emerge
steady and controlled. The way they would if I were talking to
a client. "This is actually smart. I mean, we've already lived together longer than most marriages last." My palms were moist,
and I wiped them against the arm of the couch. "We don't run
the risk of waking up and deciding we don't like each other
anymore."

Theo shook his head. "What you're saying is idealistic and
naive. Which, honestly, is unlike you."

"Okay, well, I think you're being reductive. So. Here we are."

He picked a piece of dog hair off the leg of his Levis. Deposited it onto the floor. "And what happens when one of you
meets someone?" The way he said *one of you* clearly indicated
that he meant Ren.

"Then we'll explain the situation."

"And what about not telling what's-his-name? Don't you
think that's morally fucked?"

I shrugged. "I never knew my dad."

"But that was his decision, no?"

"I wouldn't know."

I became tired then. Unbearably tired. Why should I have to explain this to Theo? Why should I have to explain anything to anyone at all?

On the wall in the kitchen the clock ticked slowly, and I felt inexplicably as if a countdown had begun, but to what, I didn't know.

R

My shift at Crazy felt three times longer than usual, noisy and hot and unbearably sober. I knew being able to drink on shift made the place more tolerable, but I hadn't noticed just how much it made time move, blending the crude edges of everything into softer shapes before delivering me kindly to the end of the evening.

Embarrassingly, it hadn't occurred to me that Theo would want to move out. I thought we'd just add a kid to the mix and everything else would stay the way it was, the three of us acting like the makeshift little family we were, and I couldn't tell if my assumption had been selfish or naive or a bit of both, so I spent most of my shift trying to visualize the tiny bones that made up the fingers in my hands. Just before ten I took a short break outside with Kekoa, who still held his pack of cigarettes out to me every time though it had been several years since I quit. He was fighting with Marcie again, he told me. He'd slept in his truck last night, parked out in his own driveway.

Came back inside for breakfast so keiki would not suspect. He exhaled, dragon-like, through his nostrils, and I imagined what that would feel like, to creep back inside your own house like a stranger. *Marcie just stay in her room while I'm cooking. Breakfast is my time anyway.*

I liked that picture, Kekoa making his kids eggs or frozen waffles, everyone sleepy and mussed. He would be excited for me, I knew that somehow, although I wasn't sure when I should tell him. Mei, too. I wasn't supposed to be telling people yet, but there was always a fine line between your people, the ones you tell everything to immediately, and other people, the ones who would have to wait. I didn't know which one of those people Mei was, or Kekoa, or how those decisions were made anyway.

The house was dark when I got home, Sookie in her spot on the couch. I washed my face and slunk softly into Jess's room, moving on my toes to keep the floorboards from creaking, but as I slid in next to her, she asked me how my shift was with no rasp to her voice, no trace of sleep. She'd been waiting for me.

I told her it was fine, sheets cool and clean on my bare feet as I punched a pillow into a more comfortable shape. I couldn't see Jess's face fully but could tell somehow that her eyes were open. "Do you really think Theo will move out, or was he just being dramatic?"

From the dark she said, "I don't know. But after you left he told me I'm in love with you."

I gave a single pop of laughter. "Aren't you in love with me though?"

She jabbed me and I caught her finger in my palm and gave it a cursory squeeze. When I let it go she added, "He thinks I'm the reason you want to do this."

"Oh, and what, I have nothing to do with it?"

"That's what I said."

I thought of Theo's strained half silence in the kitchen, how he'd told me it was going to be hard. It would be less hard with Jess, of course, which he knew. Theo loved to point out all the things Jess did for me, paying my parking tickets, making sure I voted, but he never liked to look at how much she'd also done for him.

She was quiet on the other side of the bed, but it was the loaded kind of quiet, like she was waiting for me to say something. I wanted to tell her then how I'd been looking at Quincy's page, how the videos made me anxious, and I wasn't sure why. I was still too chicken to watch any of them, but I looked almost every day for new ones. It was compulsive, the constant checking, the scrolling through thumbnails, his big white face frozen in the center of the frames. It was simpler with his Facebook, the photos safer somehow, as if by watching him move and talk and laugh he would become more real, his presence more difficult to dismiss. Somehow, I sensed that bringing Quincy up then would be taken as a betrayal, so instead I said, "Do you want me to talk to him?"

"No." She sighed, rolling over. "He'll get over it."

We were quiet for a moment and then I said, "Maybe he won't move out. Maybe he's just making a statement."

Jess didn't answer and we lay in silence, just the collective sound of our breath and the ocean rolling across the street and the gentle purr of the overhead fan leading us slowly toward sleep.

Two days later Theo and I drove over to Waiānuenue Falls and hiked the hundred steps up, Sookie tugging at her leash, our hands gripping the worn metal railing, rust raised along the edges like mold. Already I'd come to understand that days like this were quite literally numbered, and Theo seemed to understand it, too.

At the top of the falls we followed the stream up, passed a group of UH kids floating in one of the shallow pools, a six-pack bobbing in the water beside them, their loud voices laced with the familiar slur of inebriation. I grimaced at the memory of the four cups of beer I'd had at Theo's party, the vodka sodas on shift, and the graphic images in those books Jess brought home, stillborns with bodies shrunken and withered. Dr. Mirin said I probably didn't have to worry, but I placed my palm on my stomach as if that might help.

We followed the narrow dirt path into the trees where lush banyans loomed overhead like a circus tent. Theo grabbed a low-hanging branch, did a couple pull-ups before hoisting himself into the foliage. I tethered Sookie to a gnarled root and made my way over to a bundle of twisted vertical branches ribboning skyward, climbing with more caution than I might have a month ago. Theo found a firm perch and I scooted over until I sat beside him. Around us, roots as thick as refrigerators dropped from branches to meet the ground, creating an elaborate multi-trunk network of support as their arms grew longer, and heavier.

Theo asked me then if I remembered a trip we took to Lake

Gaston when we were children. We didn't often talk about the time when our parents were alive, so his question disarmed me. I turned to study the familiar shape of his ear. On the ground below, Sookie looked up, following the sound of our voices, and wagged her tail.

"Barely," I told him. I'd just turned six, and all I could bring up were random sensory details, disconnected fragments, my hands stained with mulberries and my feet caked in that good continental dirt. "Why?"

"Dad tried to teach me how to fish."

The image of Theo fishing unironically felt almost impossible. "How'd that go?"

"Terribly. I caught this sad little sunfish and when I realized we'd put a hook through its lip I sort of lost it. Just wailing, right there on the dock in front of all these grizzled old fishermen."

"Of course," I laughed. "Then what?"

Theo brushed an ant from his leg. "Then nothing. He packed up our stuff and took me to that corner store, bought me a Dr. Pepper."

"Scandalous." Our parents never let us drink soda, and I wondered vaguely what kind of parent I would be, as if it was something that just happened and not a series of linked decisions. I tilted my face to catch the brindled light. "I wish I had been there."

"I doubt I'd have let myself cry if you were."

"Obviously."

"I think about it a lot though. That trip." Theo's smile dropped then, his face settling into seriousness, and I realized the trap I'd walked right into. "I think it's really fucked up not to tell Quincy, Ren."

I sighed then. I could hear my own petulance. It was funny how we reverted to these roles, the bratty younger sister, the protective older brother. But it wasn't my fault; Theo was a crocodile once he got his jaws on something, although at least he'd used Quincy's name. "Why? In case he wants to fly out to take the kid fishing?"

"You're, like, abducting his genes."

I made a hot, indignant sound, like a dog's bark. That morning, Quincy'd posted a photo of his breakfast, eggs and bacon in a smiley face on his plate. I'd checked the photo twice. "Look," I said. "Sperm donors aren't told if their sample has been chosen—"

"Sperm donors *choose* to be sperm donors, Ren."

"So does any dude who sticks their dick in any woman, ever. There's always a chance. And Quincy took it." My brother rolled his eyes but said nothing, and it hit me how he'd probably never had to think about that chance. Other chances, sure, but not that one. He'd never had some young oblivious girlfriend. By eleven, his bedroom was already covered in Marky Mark posters. He'd always had himself figured out. I let the thought pass, too eager to rush into the opening his hesitation had created. "*He's* the one who snuck off in the morning. *He's* the one who left without a way to get in touch. I think we spoke fourteen words to each other the entire night. I don't feel bad about this, Theo. I'm sorry that you do, but it's my decision."

He rolled his head like one giant eye.

"And you know what," I went on, "while we're here, I really don't appreciate you accusing Jess of baby trapping me."

"Now, that's not what I said."

"Close to it."

"Do you have any idea how expensive a baby is, Ren?"

"Don't change the subject."

"It's the same subject."

I pressed my thumbs into my eye sockets and rubbed. "What are you saying, then?" When he didn't answer I added, "I'm thirty-six, Theo."

"Yeah, I know."

"Okay, well, obviously this isn't the situation I'd imagined for myself, but it's not a bad one either."

"No, I know." He picked a loose piece of bark off the tree limb, rolled it around between his fingers, and when he spoke again his tone had dropped, had lost its edge, was soft, almost pleading. "I just want to make sure you've thought this through."

"I have. And I'd really like your support on it. It would mean a lot to me." I swallowed. "Please."

I was shocked to see a shine move across my brother's eyes then. He nodded stiffly and looked away. Staring down at his knees, he nodded again, then released his scrap of bark, and together we watched it fall to the ground.

8

J

June carried in a new type of normal. In the evenings I'd make a pot of tea and sit with Ren on the couch spitting out random bits of information from the baby books.

We were particularly taken with the industry's habit of comparing fetal sizes to produce. "At eight weeks," I read, flipping a page, "your baby is the size of a grape."

Ren made a face and removed her thumbnail from her teeth. "And then?"

"Kumquat."

"Disturbing."

"For real. I never realized how esculent a fetus could be."

Theo'd calmed down, too. He seemed apologetic, or, as apologetic as Theo could allow himself to be. He showed up at the office with malasadas for the team. Spent a Sunday making banana bread.

His apologies often came in food form.

One evening he brought home a book for *labor companions*, which I suppose was the closest thing he could find to a book for me. And Taylor helped diffuse things. He lived in a rental downtown with five other graduate students. In the afternoons and evenings he worked as a server at an overpriced Italian restaurant with signage reading *ITALIAN RESTAURANT* so that tourists would know exactly what it was. On his nights off he sat with Theo and watched *The Great British Bake Off* or suffered through a thousand-piece puzzle of Waipio Valley they'd started on the coffee table. They were in that stage of cathexis where some piece of their bodies had to be touching at all times. A knee or a wrist or a foot. It was hard to be irritated at Theo with Taylor around.

I wondered if Theo knew that.

We celebrated Ku'ulei's birthday at the office with lunch brought in from Bay Cafe, and in the afternoon her son Ioane sent her a bouquet of fat, happy sunflowers and a pakalana pīkake lei.

I showed more condos to Tatia Chen. We'd toured a dozen by then and I could tell that the process would be long.

The spaces we looked at were near-identical and yet she found different things wrong with each of them. Not enough parking. Poor air circulation.

Whenever this happened I thought of that first day and how she'd stared at those dual sinks in the bathroom with her hand to her mouth as if to silence herself.

At the end of the month hundreds of protesters gathered on the mountain to block access to the telescope construction site. They rolled large rocks across the road. They chained themselves to a cattle guard.

Thirty-eight kūpuna were arrested. We watched coverage on the TV, the elders being loaded into police cruisers, their faces set stoically, reminding me of Clem, her dark hair gone silver, how small she'd been by the end.

While this was happening, I started looking at houses with Theo. He didn't need me there.

He'd invited me along in reparation and I was glad. His list of must-haves was manageable. A short drive to the office. Two bedrooms. "One for me and one for the Little, on weekends with *the godfather*," he said. His new excitement was endearing even if it was based more on vanity than anything else.

We found one promising listing right away.

Wood floors and walls the color of an aloe plant, rooms gutted of furniture.

In the living room, muted light penetrated gauzy white curtains and dust particles floated like plankton. But the kitchen was a deal-breaker. A slim galley. A crack of a room. I tapped a knuckle against the wall that fenced it from the dining area. "Could knock this out. Open it up."

Theo shut a cabinet with his nose scrunched.

Seated on the edge of the tub in the hall bathroom, I turned the tap on just to give myself something to do. Hot water ran neatly over my fingers. I could hear Theo creaking around the house. Touring closets. Checking for signs of termites.

It could easily take another six or seven months to find the right space.

He could still be in the house when the baby came.

We planned to clear half of Ren's room just in case. Move the crib in. A changing table. It was unsettling, the way it could take Theo longer to find a home than the human body to create life.

She was just beginning to show. The softest curve beneath the belly button. She'd be one of those women who only looks pregnant from the side. Like someone shoved a beach ball under her tank top.

"Having a bath?"

Theo stood in the doorway.

I looked down and saw that I'd let the bathtub fill halfway.

I hadn't even realized the drain was shut.

Warm water cuddled up my forearm as I pulled the stopper. "Well?"

He shrugged. "Needs more room for tiny feet."

R

July brought the blister beetles. They swarmed inside at night, following the light, creating intricate patterns on the walls like something from a horror film. Jess and Theo became obsessive, inspecting the screens for holes, scraping the dead bugs off the floors and windowsills every morning. On the Fourth came fireworks and traffic jams and sovereignty protests, homemade signs dotting the highway reading *Not Our Independence Day* or bearing the stenciled, pensive face of Liliʻuokalani with her signature choker, her butterfly hairpin.

The month also dispatched a gush of morning sickness that woke me hours earlier than normal and tethered me to the toilet. Jess would come back from her run and bring me saltines or chilled glasses of seltzer, set them on the sink where they'd leave crumbs or puddles of condensation. Luckily, the quease faded by ten and I was able to keep my teaching schedule, although the bar shifts had begun to feel particularly draining. Or maybe that was just pregnancy itself. I had a hard time telling what was what, and it really didn't seem to matter. I was tired and sore, constipated and cranky, full of crackers and bubbly water. I had to pee all the time, a phantom urge, an internal pressure like someone had set a heavy book on my bladder, but when I got to the toilet there was rarely anything to deliver.

Theo calmed after our talk in the banyan trees. I'd asked him to be the baby's godfather in an unofficial, nonreligious way, and he peacocked around the house afterward, marbling the words around in his mouth, trying the phrase on with different inflections, *God*father, God*father*, and doing a terrible Brando impression.

At week ten, with clearance from Mirin, I went through the motions of telling the people I needed to tell; there weren't many, which didn't do wonders for my self-esteem, just Cha-

Cha, who would now need to find a permanent replacement, and then Ralphie, who had to find a sub until I could return. This was doable, I knew. Odessa was off for three months when her twins were born and then right back to the mirrors, but it wasn't guaranteed, and the lack of security made me nervous. As I sat across from him in his tiny office I was irritated at my own unease, at the way my armpits insisted on smelling like a freshly cut onion, at how aware of this odor I was as I told him.

Ralphie carried the unmistakable heft of a former body-builder, the wide neck and once-muscled chest softened by age into a dormant sort of bulge. He hulked. His office seemed shrink-wrapped around him. I imagined him waiting outside the gym with that child, the one whose mother cashed in on free babysitting, the sodium lights washing their faces an un-fortunate snot-gray, the kid soggy-diapered and solemn, shift-ing self-consciously in the presence of such a large specimen of stranger. "Due in February," I finished, and watched his eyes dart, uncaged, to my stomach.

"Hey hey," he said after a beat, slapping a thigh. "That's some good news, yeah?"

I told him it was, that I could teach into my second trimes-ter but would need to take some time after, that maybe Kealani could cover my classes for a few months. I worked to keep my tone stentorian, to remove any trace of inflection from the end of my sentences, like Jess had coached—*tell him the plan, don't ask.*

I watched as he absently reached for his one cauliflowered ear, pinched and puckered like something regurgitated. Nohea had one too, though not as severe. The gym had been a point of contention when we split. Noh'd been training there longer than I'd been teaching but in the end, my paycheck won.

"Kealani, can do, sounds good," he said, and I tried to swal-low the tremor of possession I felt when I thought of the bouncy twenty-two-year-old taking over my studio time. What if her attendance was better? What if they kept her on? I looked at my pointer finger in my lap and imagined the thin rod of bone as Ralphie assured me *can can, whatever I needed*.

"Hey!" he said, straightening. "How 'bout if you started one a, a *whatchamacallit*." I looked at the expectancy in his face, as if I could pull any thread of meaning from that. "Class for other hāpai kine, yeah?"

"Maternity kickjam?"

"That!" Ralphie put his big feet on the desk and then, as if remembering himself, swung them back down. "We get lots of hāpai wāhine in the gym, you know."

I did know. I'd begun to see them more often, or, more specifically, I'd begun to notice them, like how I started seeing white Corollas all over the road after I got mine. Women pumping milk in the locker room, moving their swollen bodies carefully between the strange, torture-looking weight machines. One woman, Bridget, tall with lanky chestnut-colored hair, still took my class even though she had to be somewhere in her third trimester. She did a modified version of everything, of course, and I liked to watch her belly move in the mirror. I imagined a whole sea of bellies dropping low. It was actually not a bad idea. I could create routines with less impact, less bounce. Across from me, Ralphie rubbed one massive shoulder and grinned.

I'd been thinking a lot that week about Theo's story, our dad and that failed fishing trip, the conciliatory gas station soda. I didn't have many memories of our father, just shards of sensation, his wide, rough hands, and the weighted, safe feeling of being in his presence. This made me think of Quincy, off in Montana posting photos of his breakfast on the internet. His child would never find a weighted safety in his presence. This was the reason Theo had shared that story with me, and it made me furious, how well he knew me.

I was out in the gym lot unlocking my car when Ryan's four-door pickup pulled into the empty spot beside me, rust red with a surfboard tethered to the roof, "Santeria" swelling through the windows. I tried to duck into the safety of my car but he was too fast, already out on the pavement with his engine off saying *hey, stranger*, his keys jangling en route to his pocket. I had managed to get inside the vehicle, but my door was still open, and I couldn't decide whether to stay where I was or get back out, so I remained seated and let him lean down, his palm on the roof, his body blocking the glare of the sun. "How you been?" he asked, his face wide and golden, the start of a five-o'clock shadow on his jawline.

"Fine, good. Summer and all." It felt insipid even as I said it, *summer and all*, but he just smiled and nodded, friendly little crow's feet hugging the corners of his eyes.

"So, uh…" He ran a finger across the top of my car and when he pulled it back, the pad was black with grime and he seemed embarrassed, looking around as if he didn't know what to do with it before finally wiping it on his jeans. "I've been meaning to talk to you," he said, glancing up at me almost shyly as my entire rib cage dropped into my stomach. "I thought we had a good time together, when we…" He paused, struggling. "You know, that night. But it kind of feels like you've been avoiding me."

The night we went out his shirt had been so crisp it had clearly just been ironed, and I'd thought about that throughout dinner, the image of him pressing his clothes before he saw me. He blinked once, twice, his eyelashes impossibly long.

"God, no, sorry," I said finally, removing my thumbnail from my mouth. "It's not that." My face felt feverish. "I'm actually, I'm pregnant?" I hated myself immediately, both for the inflection, the question of it, but also because the excuse was relatively new and had nothing to do with the way I had, yes, absolutely, been avoiding him.

His gaze seemed to stutter. "Wow," he said, and there it was, the sprinted gaze to the belly as his smile reestablished itself. "That's great, Ren. Right *on*." If there was disappointment there, he was good at hiding it. "When are you due?"

"First week of February."

"Aquarius. Like Oprah."

I laughed at this, a genuine laugh.

He smiled wider. "Well, in that case, maybe we can have a playdate sometime." I paused, trying to sift through the words for meaning and he caught it, tilting his head to the side. "My daughter's eighteen months."

"Really?"

"Yeah. Grace." His face visibly brightened on the name. "Shocker, right?"

I winced over my own transparency, the obvious incredulousness in my face. Clearly the image I had of Ryan, blasting unironic college rock, adding creatine to carrot juice for a living, it didn't line up with a kid in the picture.

I glanced back at his truck and sure enough, I could make out the nubby gray top of a car seat. "She lives with her mom, mostly."

I nodded dumbly. How had I sat through an entire meal with this man without stumbling across the fact he's a father? I thought again of how Jess found out more about Quincy in five *minutes* in a noisy bar than I learned during the evening I spent undressing him.

My silence had extended awkwardly by that point and Ryan glanced toward the gym. "Well, I gotta head in but…" His eyes caught mine. "Congrats, Ren."

"Thank you."

He started to turn away and then stopped. "Hey, you should teach a maternity class."

I laughed. "Man, Ralphie said the same thing."

"Really? Shit." Ryan snapped his fingers. "Every time I get a good idea, someone beats me to it. You ever feel like that?"

"All the time," I said, although it wasn't true, because I never had any good ideas. He turned then, and I closed my car door but didn't start the engine. In my rearview, I watched him swing open the gym's tinted glass door and disappear.

9

J

On the second Tuesday of July we sat in a small dark room while a stranger sent sound waves into Ren's uterus to make an image of her child.

At first, I didn't think much of it.

It looked like every other ultrasound image I'd seen on TV.

An alien glob of tissue and organs. Its head too large. A tadpole.

But when the technician asked if we'd like to hear the heartbeat my throat forgot its capacity for moisture. The noise, when it started, was like sitting inside a car wash and Ren looked at me with an expression of such wonder I pretended to cough into my shoulder.

They sent us home with a shiny printed image. "What a little bean," Ren said in the parking lot, tracing her finger along the glossy outline of the baby's skull.

I felt oddly removed from the situation. As if I were walking behind us.

"The size of a mushroom," I said, trying to climb back inside my own body.

★ ★ ★

That night Theo made korma and naan, which he puffed in a skillet on the stove as Ren worked her way through a glass of orange-flavored Metamucil and I read her an article about a South American species of cuckoo that raised its young in large family units.

"The greater anis," I read projected dramatically, "form genetically unrelated coparenting groups that stay together for over a decade."

"Well, we're already on decade two," said Ren. Her skin had a luminous sort of glow to it, as if she'd just stepped out of a bath.

At the counter, Taylor minced piles of cilantro and mint, his knife making a neat, methodical percussion.

"Together," I continued, "they choose a site and build a nest in organized, cooperative efforts. The females lay eggs at the same time in such a fashion that they are unable to recognize any individual egg, so care is delivered democratically and all duties are shared."

"Mmm," Ren murmured, "all duties shared. I like that." Her glass was empty and orange granules sugared the bottom and sides. "Hey," she said, looking up. "What about Ayla?"

"Blech. Too *Clan of the Cave Bear.*" We had just started doing the name thing. Maggie. Sadie. Anna. It felt more like a game than anything. I held the magazine up so Ren could see a photo of the bird.

She frowned. "Looks like a crow."

I examined the photo again.

Theo rotated a piece of naan in his pan and said, "Is one of the crows asexual?"

"Hey."

"Jess is not *asexual*," Ren said.

"Thank you," I said in full agreement.

Her mouth curved upward. "Maybe just *aromantic.*"

I kicked her below the table and she asked, "What about Lola?"

"That's only cute until high school. You don't see many *Lola*s in the workforce."

Ren rolled her eyes. "Of course you're thinking about *hire-ability*."

"Also," Theo said, "you'd be plaguing her with a lifetime of Kinks references."

"What if it's a boy?" Taylor asked, stroking the skin above his lip. He'd shaved his mustache and the bare patch was jarring, like he'd knocked out his two front teeth.

"It's *not* going be a *boy*," Ren said.

Theo turned at the stove. "Intuitively, or definitively?"

"Both. My heart rate is super fast, the doctor said, plus my skin is super oily, and both of those things mean it will be a girl."

Theo raised an eyebrow. "The doctor said that?"

"She said my heart rate is fast."

Theo looked to Taylor. "Her methods are *super* scientific."

Ren flicked her middle finger in her brother's direction.

I picked the magazine back up. "We're doing the gender reveal at eighteen weeks, so we'll find out soon enough."

Ren pushed her glass away. "I don't need that. I already know."

I said to Theo, *"We're convinced."*

Ren smiled at me then, and I smiled back. The kitchen smelled of nutmeg and cumin and over my shoulder the ultrasound image was pinned to the fridge like an art project.

R

Ten days into July, I got a text message from Mei congratulating me about my pregnancy. I knew this meant Ryan had told her, that they'd spoken about me when I wasn't around, and I wasn't sure how to feel about it. I thanked her, and in return she sent me a long, neatly punctuated paragraph about the toxicity of high mercury diets during pregnancy.

That week, Theo asked Taylor to move in with him whenever he found a place. They'd been seeing each other for two months. We were eating in my favorite Thai restaurant when Theo told us, the one next to Kalākaua Park with the purple linens and gold elephants stenciled on the walls, and the news had ruined my meal, not because of anything to do with Theo and Taylor living together, but because it made it harder for me to ignore that Theo was, in fact, leaving. I spent the rest of the meal moving things across my plate as conversation shifted around me.

When we got home Jess and I rearranged my room to make space for the crib. This had been our plan for the evening, though the announcement at dinner made the task feel irrelevant. We did it anyway.

"But way to rush things, right?" I picked up a rumpled pair of jeans from my floor and hung them over the back of a chair, whispering though my bedroom door was shut.

Jess brushed her hands on the legs of her pants. "How long were you with Nohea before he moved in?"

I turned away. "He never moved in." Even with my back to Jess I could feel the roll of her eyes. Technically, Noh had lived with his parents the year we were together, but it was true that his toiletries had invaded the bathroom by week six.

Jess helped move my bookshelf over by the bed, and I pressed the weight of my body against it, hoping it would slide with ease, but it was heavier than I'd imagined, sturdy as a wall against the determined press of my shoulder.

"Pregnancy hernias are real, you know," Jess said. "Pull the books out first."

I sighed, tugging books from the shelves and letting them thwap onto the floor, where Jess immediately righted them into a sensible tower. She'd wanted me to ditch the bookshelf altogether, pointing out that half of its shelves were missing. "But half *aren't* missing," I'd countered, and that had been the end of it. Together we stripped the unit of its bound residents, some owned for decades and still unread. When the shelves were clear, Jess scooted the piece toward the bed as I sat on the floor and picked up a used copy of *Woman, An Intimate Geography*, shuffling pages, scanning, landing on chapter four. "The Evolution of the Clitoris." I thickened my voice. "'Ask most women how big their clitoris is, or how big the average clitoris is, and they probably won't know where to begin or what units to talk about. Inches, centimeters, millimeters, parking meters?'"

"Centimeters," Jess said with seriousness.

I glanced up at her and smiled until she looked away. "Oh! Look here, it says…" I cleared my throat. "'The clitoris' fetal growth is complete by the twenty-seventh week of gestation.'" I dropped the book on the floor. "That's before lungs, I think. Priorities are nice and straight."

Jess pointedly moved the book onto the bottom of one of her piles, then left the room and returned with a broom. The bald patch of floor where the shelves had been contained a dusty nest of dog hair and the odd button. While she swept, I moved to my nightstand, also strewn with various pocket flotsam, a five-month-old gas receipt, a pile of change that was inexplicably sticky, my favorite plum lipstick missing its cap, a lemongrass candle melted down to a nub.

"But really." I used my thumbnail to scrape away the stiff,

crayony pool of yellow wax. "Don't you think he might just be making a statement?"

Jess swept her pile of dust and dog hair into a dustpan. "I doubt it. I just don't think he wants to be here when we're all crying at three a.m. and the trash is overflowing with diapers."

She was right, I knew. Theo wanted the fun uncle duties, trips to the beach, shave ice stops, lychee picking, soda from gas stations. He wouldn't want the brutal, exhausting reality of it. That was for us. I plucked a pair of oversized sunglasses from my nightstand, slid them on, let the room darken around me. Propped against the base of my bedside lamp where the glasses had been I noticed a small green square of cardstock I did not recognize. I pushed the glasses up onto my head and picked the square up as the color in the room righted itself. The paper had a scrawl of cramped writing on it. *Don't b a stranger*, it read. I scanned my brain for the source of the note, a memory submerged—slipped across the bar perhaps?

I flipped it over and my breath caught.

Quincy Jones, PhD
Biological Science
University of Montana

There was a number there, an email address, a fucking PO box. Around me, the room seemed to spin, Quincy on the dance floor, his hips tipping this way and that, his neat pile of clothes on my bedroom floor, the bare flash of his thighs, blinding white, his Facebook page congesting my search history, the videos I didn't have the guts to watch. *Don't b a stranger*. The missing *e* in be. My legs went wobbly, and I sat slowly on the bed, picturing him in my room that morning, searching through his pockets for a pen as I slept, clueless to him, to his departure, to his DNA burrowing deep inside me. Don't b a stranger don't b a stranger don't b a stranger don't b a— I lifted my hand to the back of my neck and found it damp.

Jess's voice reached me as if from underwater. "I was thinking crib to the left, changing table to the right. Thoughts?"

I opened the drawer to my nightstand and shoved the card in. Jess stood in the center of the cleared stretch of floor, hands empty at her sides, her face swarming with the sincerity of her question. I was hit with a throb of affection so tender I nearly gasped. The way these things mattered to her, where we placed the crib, a crib that was likely going to move again before we even used it, everything so carefully planned. And the crib itself—I'd never had such a nice piece of furniture as an adult. Things like that never seemed to belong to me.

"The left is good." I looked down at my stomach and tried to imagine something alien inside of it—mushroom, kumquat, grape, a small soon-to-be-breathing creature that looked just like a man I slept with and never spoke to again.

When I looked back up, Jess was standing in the left corner, looking at the ceiling. "Do you want to get one of those mobiles? For her to look at? I think it's supposed to be good for brain development."

I let her questions drift around me, numb me, nodding when she wanted me to, yes, a mobile. Stars and moons sounded nice. Yes, yellow, let's paint the room a soft yellow, more butter than daisy, sure. I handed her the reins. I was happy to.

10

J

Mid–July I took a random Friday morning off to take Ren lychee picking. It was a tradition, and all of our traditions felt sacred that summer.

We went early, just before nine, and the orchard was eerily empty.

Just us and the gentle chatter of the honeycreepers flitting through the trees.

Fruit dripped from branches in vibrant jeweled clusters, and beside me, Ren's hair was knotted high on her head, revealing the soft brown nape of her neck.

I watched her pluck a plump fruit roughly the size and shape of an eyeball and jam a thumb into its skin. Juice spurted as she peeled back the exocarp to expose an orb of translucent flesh. She popped it into her mouth, jaw working around the pit.

She'd been distant for a few days. Quieter.

Ever since the night Theo'd announced his plans to live with Taylor.

On the ride over I'd asked her twice if everything was alright.

"Don't helicopter," she'd said the second time.

The fruit between my fingers was too soft and when I threw it, it gave a satisfying splat against her shoulder.

Her mouth made a surprised little O, but only for a breath.

Then she plucked a lychee dangling shoulder level and chucked it at me.

I ducked. Darted around the thick hedge. Emerged a row over.

Ren hustled after me, a handful of fruit whizzing in my direction.

I moved deeper into the orchard. A labyrinth of fluffy green leaf and red drupe.

Her laughter followed.

I was moving further from her, tossing fruit over my shoulder, when I heard her call my name. "Wait," she laughed. "Stop. I have to pee."

I slowed, my lungs pushing. "Again?"

She stood in the middle of the grassy lane with her shoulders heaving. She'd peed thirty minutes earlier in a porta potty at the farm's front store. Afterward I'd made her sanitize her hands.

We found a patch of tall grass and I held sentinel while she squatted behind me. The rustle of her jeggings. The hiss of her release. "Do you think this is the right thing?" she asked.

"Pissing in public?" A bee zipped by and instinctively I leaned in the other direction.

"Not telling Quincy." Her voice was nearly a whisper.

I looked at her.

"Hey!" she said, swatting.

I turned back.

Quincy.

The more real the idea of the baby became, the less real he seemed. I'd stopped checking his pages again. I'd stopped thinking about him at all.

"No one tells the donor," I said.

"Yeah." She came out from behind me, wiping her hands along the tops of her thighs. "I know. You're right." She paused, then said it again, quieter this time. "You're right."

R

A tropical storm was announced the third Wednesday of July. Jess texted me about it just before noon as I stood in the kitchen, spooning full-fat cottage cheese from the carton with the fridge open, cooling the back of my neck with frosty air, and I'd dismissed it as nothing serious, just another finger on the clenched fist of her constant worry. We got storm warnings all the time, although since we moved to Kalaniana'ole I'd become a bit more attentive, considering that our house was level with the sea. Even so, I didn't give it much thought until the sky darkened on my way to class and, when I got there, found that half of the women had stayed home.

But even half-full, the maternity class was better attended than my old one, sometimes as many as thirty women crammed into the narrow space. It turned out we were the only maternity dance class on the island, and Jess had called some former client who worked at the *Tribune*, and by the second week there was a wait list. Women who didn't even belong to the gym had joined just so they could sign up. Ralphie was thrilled. They showed up early, lined up single-file by the door, their midsections in various stages of bulge and their chatter filling the gym like birdsong. We warmed up slow, stretching our hamstrings, our backs, then got to it. There was more laughter than ever, hands on our thighs, hips switching, the bulb of our bellies undulating, this crush of women, our smiles broad, our bodies mere months away from multiplying.

Class was a welcome distraction from a particular piece of cardstock tucked into my nightstand. I'd pulled it out a dozen times since I'd found it, turning it over in my hands, telling myself I should march into Jess's room, pretend I'd just discovered it, and deliver it as if it belonged to her. But I hadn't done that, and so I felt guilty.

Guilty with Jess in the lychee orchard, guilty when I let her read me things out of the baby books before bed, guilty when she fell asleep before me, her breath a heavy thing on the other side of the bed, guilty when I thought of Quincy leaving that same bed to search the swamp of my room for a pen, and finally, guilty at how my stomach swelled while he was off in Montana posting photos of his new girlfriend to the internet with a moronic cluelessness that I had thrust upon him. I tried to imagine my body as a mound of meat without any sentience, but since I'd found that I was pregnant the trick had stopped being as effective, possibly because for once I was excited that my body belonged to me, that there were so many things I could do with it.

The wind had picked up by the time class let out, the palms lining bayfront bowing dangerously on the drive home, the sky an ominous sheet of slate. The radio buzzed, station to station, tropical storm Zane holding strong at a category four. I thought Jess or Theo might have come home early to board up the windows but no, the driveway lay empty when I pulled in, the windows bare. Upstairs, Sookie hunkered below the kitchen table, tail between her legs. I pulled her storm vest from the hall closet, Velcroed it around her broad chest, her nose cool against my neck as she shook. She followed me into Jess's bathroom, crouched by the side of the tub as I showered, turning the water hot to cut the chilled air.

In my room, the wind howled as I wrapped myself in a blanket, my hair soaking the shoulders of my shirt. Out my window the ocean roiled, and still no Jess or Theo. I thought about doing something useful, heading under the house to pull out the boards for the windows, but it always felt ridiculous, preparing for the storm. Should the island decide she's done with us, boarded windows wouldn't do shit. Of course, the preparation at least made us feel better. Our very own thunder vest.

I found my laptop in the living room and sat, Sookie curled against me, the shiver of her body moving through the old brown couch. The rain began for real then, not slow but all at once, as if someone overhead had pulled a release chain. The tin roof roared, the dog trembled, and I pulled up Quincy's video feed and forced myself to do what I'd been avoiding. I chose a clip at random, clicked Play, and there he was—that goofy, uneven smile, talking into a shaky camera. Sound muted, I watched him peer into a raised bed of dirt, talking as he scooped up a fistful of earth and held it toward the camera, so close that I could see the mud caking his fingernails. I unmuted the video, pumping up the volume to combat the pounding rain overhead.

"—and really, what we've got here is black gold. You gotta start with good dirt, folks—"

I hit Mute again. His voice was deeper than I remembered it, although I wasn't sure I really did remember it, so in actuality, he sounded like a stranger. I watched as he dumped the soil back into the bed, his lips moving soundlessly, which felt appropriate, as if it acknowledged that I was a voyeur, that I was watching in secret.

When he lifted more dirt toward the camera, I turned the volume back on. "And here you'll find the culprit of all that good good." The camera inched closer to reveal a worm in his palm, its slick noodled body crumbed with earth. "The earthworm in its natural habitat." He spoke that bit with a terrible Irwin impression, more British than anything. He went on, dropping the accent and talking directly into the camera, talking directly, it seemed, to me. "Why are these guys key to good dirt? The answer is in…" He paused, a playful smile curling. "Their poop."

I stopped the video then and studied the smear of earth along the bridge of his nose. It was a good nose, strong but not beaky, and his eyes, with their peculiar red-brown color. I stared into them and thought, *my baby will look like you*, and also, *you are a stranger*. As if sensing my disturbance, Sookie squirmed closer, nudged her head beneath my hand. I stroked the dog and stared at Quincy's face until his features pulled apart. I imagined him without skin, his head just a skull without eyeballs or hair, and felt a little bit better. I minimized the video then, clicked over to his page, scrolled through his feed, scanning for bits I'd missed, until I saw it and stopped breathing.

The post was dated two days prior. *Big news*, it read, as the room around me went quiet. *I've been offered an adjunct position at the University of Hawai'i, Hilo, and it looks like I'm taking it. While I'll always have love for Zootown, I'll be kicking off the fall semester in paradise, so hit me up for hikes or drinks (hikes and drinks? Hrinks? Drikes?) before then.*

The blood in my ears beat louder than the rain above my head. I began maneuvering through the comments, names and words and congratulations, so absorbed in this that underneath the thunder of the rain, I didn't hear Jess's car in the drive, or her feet on the lanai steps, or anything at all until her key slipped into the lock.

11

J

Ren sat on the couch wearing a look of panic.

My ankles were soaked, and as I bent over to roll up my pants I asked if she was alright.

She didn't answer. Just closed her laptop and pushed it onto the coffee table. Sookie was curled beside her. I could see the dog shaking from four feet away.

The storm had upgraded half an hour before I left the office. Hurricane Zane. The name too perfect to have been anything less. Lisa had left early, her car stuffed with bottled water and cans of soup. And she lived mauka side.

Here, we had the water level to worry about.

A paradise tax.

Dampness had tunneled into my bones and settled. "Tea?" I asked. "And then we can do the boards?" I squeezed Ren's shoulder as I passed.

In the kitchen, an open window had sent a spray of rain across the tile. I slid it shut. Put the kettle on. Threw a rag on the floor and mopped up the moisture using my bare foot.

Ren wandered in then, Sookie trailing, tail tucked. "Where's Theo?"

"Taylor's, I think. How was class?"

Before she could answer a gust of wind hurled itself against the house, its old bones howling an eerie, ghostlike moan that sent Sookie bolting beneath the table.

As the kitchen filled with jasmine steam, we hunkered out on the front lanai, me powering the drill, Ren holding the boards. There was a carelessness to her movements. Her mind clearly elsewhere. I kept glancing at her drawn face until she caught me. Offered a smile. It wasn't like her to be spooked by storms.

With the windows covered, the living room felt dark and den-like.

The moist air seemed to pull a musk from the couch.

An earthy smell. Like the sofa was sporing.

I lifted an old cushion. "We really should get rid of this thing."

"Will you get rid of me when I'm old?"

"If you're covered in black mold, then yeah." I watched her face for a smile, but her mouth retained its shape. Her hand moved from dog to sofa. She petted them as if they were one and the same.

Lightning cracked then. Close. Sookie whined and Ren jumped, one hand flying to her center. "She moved!"

"Really?" I sat up so abruptly that tea sloshed from my mug. "Isn't it early for that?"

She blinked, both hands on her center. "I think..." Her eyes popped open, a smile splitting her face. "Here! Feel!" She grabbed my hand and placed it on the soft cotton of her shirt, a shirt that was actually my shirt. The firm rind of her stomach radiated a warmth that spread up my arms and into my face.

I waited. A tightness grew in my rib cage until I realized I was holding my breath and let it go just as lightning cracked again. Ren gasped. Her eyes shone.

"Again?"

She nodded and I was hit with a wave of disappointment.

I'd felt nothing but the heat of her body.

"It's like...like...bird wings." Her voice was saturated with breathy wonder.

"Fluttering." I'd read this in the books.

I wedged myself between the dog and the back of the couch and lay down, cheek resting on the roundest spot of Ren's stomach.

Twenty minutes passed, maybe more.

We listened to the rain, us and Sookie on the old brown couch as Ren felt her baby move, the hurricane coming toward us off the water. We couldn't see it, what with the windows boarded up. Still. We knew it was coming. That there was nothing we could do but sit together, brace ourselves for impact, and hope that the damage was minimal.

R

I spent six days binge-watching his videos before I decided to message him on Facebook. I came up with a million things he might say, pacing around the living room, Jess and Theo at work, the house to myself. I wrote the message out on my phone and then stopped before sending, filed some potential reactions in my head, came up with appropriate responses, fortified my bones against their impending weight. It'd been almost four months, and I was well aware that to Quincy I might be nothing but a blackout blip, a hazy memory of skin and sheets. Maybe he did that kind of thing all the time, traveling to exotic islands and going home with locals and leaving business cards with bouncy little messages before slinking home to those small brown bottles of beer, to blondes in wide hats, to twelve-year-old wedding albums. I deleted my message, then wrote it out again almost exactly the same, deleted it, shortened it, then shortened it again. I hit Send. *Hey* was all it said.

I tossed the phone on the couch, as if distancing myself would somehow make a difference, but almost immediately my screen lit up, not with any of the replies I had braced myself for but with an incoming call. I stared, frozen, hands hovering uselessly, at Quincy's name on my screen. Who even calls on Messenger? I hadn't even considered that as an option. My breath abandoned my body but I forced myself to lift the phone to my face, because I knew somehow if I didn't answer then, I never would.

"Ren?!" He said it with a laugh, as if he were pleased, entertained even, his voice now familiar not from our singular evening together but from his videos, because by then I'd watched all of them, had seen most two or even three times. I realized as I listened to my own name leave his mouth that I'd hoped he wouldn't answer my message. That he'd leave it on Read, that I'd see his green light blinking whenever he was online and feel

validated over the inarguable proof that he was, indeed, an asshole, thus eradicating any sense of guilt or obligation. That way,
if I ran into him on the street years later with a child that looked
like a cross between the two of us, all blame would be negated,
because I had tried. That's what I'd wanted to happen. Wasn't it?

"Yeah, hi," I said, watching myself talk in the mirror by the
front door, as if to prove that this was indeed happening. I looked
at myself and remembered that yesterday, Jess came home with
two identical car seats, one for each of us, and when I told her
it felt a bit premature, she'd responded *car seats reduce the risk of
fatal injury for infants under one year old by seventy-one percent.* From
a zillion miles away I heard Quincy take a breath and say:

"How's paradise?"

"A bit soaked right now actually."

"Right. I thought of you when I saw that report. Zane, right?
Everything okay over there?" He had thought of me. He had
seen the news and thought of me.

"Oh yeah, we're good," I said. "We're used to soggy weather."

It went as well as it could have. Of course it did, because all
we did was talk about the weather, his work, my work, and
when he said he was headed back this way I pretended the information was new, my eyes on my own reflection as I lied,
surprised to see my face make its usual shapes, no sign of dishonesty anywhere. I was going to tell him, truly I was, but when
he asked if he could see me when he got on island, all inten-
tion fled. Actually, what he said was, *It'd be nice to see you again
if you're down. Or whatever.*

I told him I was down, *or whatever.* I would tell him in person,
I decided. I was showing so there'd be no way I could avoid it,
would literally have it written all over me. He arrived in two
weeks, he said, and I was grateful for the slight buffer. I'd have
space to tell Jess. There was plenty of time, I assured myself, but
already a little seed of uncertainty had sprouted in my center,
and I placed my hand there as if to smother it.

12

J

The first week of August I took Tatia to yet another condo, this one on the third floor of a worn complex right at the end of Kalaniana'ole. I knew by then she wouldn't be buying any of these units, but I kept taking her to see them because she kept sending them to me.

I watched her open the refrigerator and look inside.

At that point, she'd opened seven identical fridges and I knew if I didn't nudge her in a different direction, I'd be forced to spend another stack of Sundays watching her peer inside empty appliances as if they might have an answer for her.

Still. It was important to guide her gently.

To let her think she was leading herself.

I leaned back against the counter. "Do you think maybe all of these are too…" I paused for effect. "Similar?"

She clicked the fridge shut. Her lipstick was the color of jam and had feathered into the fine lines around her mouth. "Similar?"

I shrugged like the thought was only half-cooked. "They all have the same feel, don't you think?"

Same exact floor plan as your ex, I did not say.

She'd signed her divorce papers a week earlier and called me afterward to tell me about it. On and on and on. "Jamie, that's my oldest, she's asked me to join a Telehealth with her and her therapist. Her therapist! Can you imagine? She's twenty-nine, for Christ's sake, seems to blame me, because I was the one who left. As if it could be one person's fault. As if it's not, absolutely always, an alchemy." I kept waiting for the discussion to reveal its relevance, and after we hung up, I realized she might not have had anyone else to call.

Tatia blinked slowly around as if seeing the space for the first time.

The blanched walls. The pineapple-shaped lamps.

A high-end domestic pocket decorated in hotel leftovers.

"Yeah…" She patted her chin with one index finger. Her fingernails matched her lipstick. "Maybe what I need is something different."

I said something like, "Mmm."

"Something less…sterile." She swept into the living room. "Something with character. Personality! Not so…" She stopped by a navy armchair and waved a hand in dismissal. "Fuddy-duddy."

I smiled gamely. Character meant unique. Often older. But Tatia was not the fixer-upper type. I'd seen her appreciation for shrink-wrapped appliances.

"Nothing that needs too much work," she said on cue. I grabbed my purse off the counter and herded us toward the door. "I mean really," she said as we exited the unit. "Who installs carpeting in a beachfront?"

In the parking lot my SUV chirped a friendly hello.

For safety reasons I didn't typically drive clients around. But Tatia liked that kind of thing and there was nothing threatening about her. If anything, I found her oddly comforting.

As I slid into the car she glanced twice into the back seat, and I remembered.

The car seat, still buckled in. Soft mint-green with tags still dangling. I'd installed it last night to see how it fit and had forgotten to take it back out.

Tatia examined me as I started the car. I could sense the cogs of her brain grinding out an angle. Strategizing her approach. "I didn't know you had kids, Jess," she said finally, lowering her visor to peer at herself in the mirror.

"I don't," I started, then stopped. A strange sensation washed over me then. A compulsive sort of internal pressure. "Well. Almost," I heard myself say.

A mongoose rushed across the road in front of us then, but I didn't slow or swerve. In my periphery I saw Tatia eye my stomach. "No," I backtracked. "Not me. A friend of mine is carrying. It's…something we're doing together."

Tatia studied me for another second, then gave an abrupt slap of her hands. "Jess! That is so exciting!"

"Is it?"

She scoffed. "Of course it is!"

I never talked about myself at work. I let myself dissolve there. Ren called it hiding. She was probably right.

But Tatia's interest made me feel taller. Like I took up more room. Obviously, she was right. It was exciting. Things were changing. Ren and I were creating change. I felt a prickling down my arms and legs.

"I'm glad it's much easier these days, it seems," Tatia was saying, touching up her lipstick. "You know my daughter Jamie is a lesbian. Although I can't see her having children. She can't even remember to get a pap."

Tatia laughed at herself and I smiled because she wanted me to.

"We aren't a couple though," I said. "We're going to coparent."

Tatia seemed to freeze. "Really?"

I nodded. Waited.

A moment of silence and then, "That's incredible, Jess." Her tone had taken a hushed, serious dip. As if we were talking about money. "And the father?"

"Sperm donor." I had not spoken to anyone about this outside the house or doctor's office. I felt light. I floated off the seat.

"Ha!" Tatia clapped again. "And your friend? Is she in real estate, too?"

"Ren? No. She tends bar at Crazy Palms."

"Oh, I love that place."

I suppressed a smile. Imagined Ren serving Tatia and the coterie of radiologists at her clinic overpriced margaritas at happy hour.

Tatia's blouse rustled against the leather as she turned toward me. "You know, you're a surprising person."

"Am I?"

"You are. That's a good thing."

I let myself smile then. Up ahead the view of the mountain was clear. A craggy peak capped in snow. I drove us toward it and thought how if you weren't looking hard enough, if you didn't know better, you could mistake it for a cloud.

R

Time was not the problem with telling Jess, it turned out. The problem was that I was a coward. Jess was terrifying when she was angry, and I didn't feel like being frightened. I was sleeping in my own room every night now, which was easy to blame on the night sweats, on the way I tossed and turned and mutilated the bedding. Even so, Jess would tiptoe into my room in the mornings to leave me mugs of tea while I lay there, pretending to be asleep, listening to the careful way she entered and exited on the tips of her toes, my room filling with the fragrant steam of her kindness.

I started going into Crazy a couple hours early too, played it off like I was stockpiling hours before I left, but half the time I didn't even clock in, just sat around talking story with Kekoa. This was what I was doing a full week after that phone call, early to my shift with a shitty, pounding headache establishing itself between my eye sockets. I hadn't slept at all, the sound of the overhead fan unusually irritating as my mind rotated the same facts over and over: Quincy was going to arrive in ten days, and I still hadn't told Jess.

Kekoa's face was tinted a sickly green from the neon overhead. He'd settled things down with Marcie, he told me, but now she was pushing for them to get married, which she did at the resolution of every argument, leaning into the leverage she carried in the wake of whatever he'd done to fuck up. Their power dynamic interested me, the way they took turns, their domestic seesaw. I liked listening to it, had been doing it for a decade, soothing myself with the familiarity of their ups and downs, like an aural soap opera. I'd only met Marcie twice and she'd been cool to me each time, but still I felt as if I knew her well, a character in a comfort show I'd watched a hundred times. In truth I didn't quite understand why he wouldn't just marry her.

"I don't like the institutions involved" is what Kekoa said, tapping his cigarette into the five-gallon bucket of sand that acted as an ashtray.

"That how she feels about it?"

Kekoa lifted his thick shoulders. "Who knows."

"I think *you* know."

He laughed, exhaling smoke. "Should you even be out here?" He nodded at my stomach, which had become more noticeable than I'd have liked for fifteen weeks. I was hoping to keep my shifts until I hit six months, but I wasn't so sure anymore.

"Probably not." I slid off my stool then, moved for the bar's heavy doors. "Just marry her. Then she'll have to campaign for something else."

ChaCha was behind the bar wearing earrings shaped like martini glasses, and as I stashed my purse, she gave me a hard, tight-lipped smile, her articulation of warmth. I had no idea how old she was, fifty or seventy, I couldn't tell, she had spent her formative years baking herself on beaches, her skin taking on the appearance of a leather handbag. We'd met at the gym, she'd been a regular in my class before she recruited me. I was certain ChaCha wasn't her real name, but had no idea what it was.

Three girls in clingy nylon came in then, looking so young it made me question Kekoa's judgment, and when I glanced outside he was staring at his phone, probably in the middle of one of his hours-long text arguments with Marcie, digital spars that ferreted him from one end of his shift to the other in the same way my watered-down vodka sodas used to.

My mind went back to Jess—I knew I needed to tell her, had needed to days ago, that the longer I waited the worse it would be, that I was actively watching myself make a mistake, orchestrating then observing my own destruction. I'd also made the mistake of telling Theo. Somehow, I'd thought it would be a comfort, since he'd been the one pushing me to contact Quincy in the first place, and I guess I was hoping for an ally. This made it super frustrating when he chastised me instead.

"Wait, you *told* him?" We'd been in the kitchen, Jess still at work, Theo frying chicken cutlets, the room smelling of hot oil.

"I didn't tell him *yet*," I said. "I'm going to when he gets here."

"Because he's coming back."

"Right."

"To live?"

"Apparently."

"And Jess doesn't know?"

I didn't answer him, just stared at his pan where hot fat sizzled and popped.

He let out a long descending whistle. "Good freaking luck."

She was in bed when I got home, her room dark and cool, and when I climbed under the covers, she gave a little sigh and rolled over onto her back. I studied her that way for a moment, then said her name softly. When she didn't stir, I touched her shoulder and said it again, watched as her eyes opened slowly. "Hi," I said. "I'm going to turn on the light."

I switched on the bedside lamp, and she flinched, shielding her face, sitting up. "Is everything alright?"

I noticed the *Birthing Partner* book Theo'd bought lying face down on her nightstand, splayed to an open page, and a savage guilt bit into me. *Like ripping off a Band-Aid*, I thought. "So, look, I spoke to Quincy."

Confusion passed over Jess's face, and then something else. "Wait...what?" She drew her legs to her chest, pushing the covers back as if she meant to get up and then pausing, the bald crown of both knees visible in the warm light. "When?"

"Last week."

She shook her head as if this was something she could refuse. "How?"

"Facebook."

"Like, he just, messaged you?"

"Uh-huh." I buried myself deeper into her bedding.

She was silent a moment. "Why didn't you tell me?"

"I did. I am." And then: "I was worried you'd be mad at me."

"I wouldn't be *mad*." Her voice twisted sharply beneath the very anger she renounced. She exhaled and stared up at the ceiling. "But…why?"

"Why what?"

"Why would he message you?"

"We did sleep together, you remember."

"Yeah, but why now?"

I hesitated briefly. "I guess because he's coming back?"

"Back here?" She did get out of bed then, moved over to her dresser and studied me from across the room, arms folded.

"He took a temp job at UH."

"He's *moving* here?" When I didn't respond Jess clamped her eyes shut. "When?"

I focused on the bare skin of her knees. "Next week."

She was quiet and when I finally lifted my gaze she asked, "And…?"

"I figured I would tell him in person."

"Jesus, Ren." She let out a long breath. "And then what?"

"And then, I don't know."

"You should have told me."

"I know, I'm sorry, Theo said the same—"

"You told *Theo*?"

Jess's cheeks had gone red, as if someone had pinched them. "Look, I know, it's not what we talked about."

"It's not even a little bit what we talked about." She ran a frustrated hand through her hair. "I just don't understand." Her tone betrayed her though. She did understand. She just didn't like it. "I mean, it's actually sort of messed up."

"What? Why?"

"It's just a little *convenient*, that he moves here and suddenly you tell him." I felt abruptly disoriented. As if my ears were full of water. "It's going to make you seem like you're trying to get something out of him," Jess was saying. She made an indignant clucking noise. "He probably won't even believe it's his."

I could feel my throat thickening. I stared at Jess's bedside table with its neat line of items, ChapStick, lotion, tissue box. "Well, what if he wants to be involved?"

Jess laughed then. "Come on, Ren. He didn't even wake you up to say goodbye after he fucked you."

I felt my nails biting into my palms as my hands curled themselves into fists. "He left me a note, actually." In my periphery, Jess looked up. "I just didn't find it until a bit ago."

She was silent for a long moment. "When?"

"When what?"

"When did you find it?"

"I don't know. The night we put the crib in, I guess."

"You *guess*? Why didn't you tell me?"

"I knew you'd be mad."

"I wouldn't have been mad! I'm mad now, yeah, because you lied about it."

"I didn't lie about it. I just didn't tell you right away." She laughed again and I swung myself out of her bed. "Look," I said, moving toward the door. "If he tells me to fuck off then who cares, we'll be right back to where we are now, okay? It barely even matters."

"Where are you going?"

When I faced her, Jess held one hand flat on her chest. "My room." I switched the bedside lamp off then and left her standing alone in the dark.

13

J

The second Saturday in August I helped Theo host an open house for one of his higher-ends. The place was ridiculous.

Opalescent floors.

A curling staircase.

Standing inside it offered the impression you had wandered into a giant seashell.

Normally I might fawn over a house like this but instead I felt ill. My chest had not stopped humming since the evening prior, when Ren came into my room to tell me she'd spoken to Quincy. Though we'd been at the open house an hour, so far all I'd managed to do was set out bottles of water and whine.

"I just can't see anything good coming out of this," I said for the tenth time, fanning out a stack of one-sheets by the front door.

"Well, what's the worst-case scenario?"

"Honestly?"

"Yes, Jess, honestly."

I shuffled Theo's flyers into an orderly pile, then splayed them out again.

"Worst case. He wants the baby, he and Ren fall in love and move to Montana."

Theo looked at me for a long moment before sighing in such a placating fashion I had the urge to pinch him. "Okay. And the best case?"

I smoothed a crease on the front of my pants. "He wants nothing to do with the baby. Maybe he makes her cry. Then we can trash him for the next eighteen years."

"You're being so selfish it's almost impressive."

If only I hadn't stopped checking his social media. Then I'd have been ahead of this. I'd have seen his post. I'd have known what was coming. "I just have a horrible feeling about it all."

"Please, do yourself a favor and relax."

Theo telling me to relax always had the opposite effect. My body buzzed angrily. I felt like a large piece of machinery.

I couldn't remember the last time Ren and I had anything resembling an argument. That morning I'd thought about going into her room to wake her up. Maybe apologize. But her door was closed, and I couldn't seem to make myself open it.

The moment Quincy saw her, he'd know.

Maybe not that it was his but some sort of mental math would be done immediately and he'd realize—with panic?—that it could be.

I thought about the hope in her voice when she said, *what if he wants to be involved?* The indignation when she told me he left a note after all.

The pleasure over proving me wrong.

Still. If he did take the trouble to look her up. To reach out.

Then she was right, I knew, in telling him.

I recognized this and still.

I felt as if I'd lost at something.

A game I didn't realize we were playing until it was over.

★ ★ ★

At home I found her in her bed with the shades drawn and the TV on mute.

She didn't turn when I came in, but I could tell she was awake. I lay beside her on top of the covers. I waited, hoping she'd speak, and when she didn't, I moved closer.

I'd meant to tell her that I was sorry. That she was right to tell him. Instead what I said was: "I found him online."

She rolled toward me. Her eyelids were raw and red. "Did you see his YouTube?"

"God, yeah."

"Did you watch the one on worm shit?"

"I feel like they were all on worm shit?"

Ren laughed and my entire body gave with relief. "Black gold!" She imitated Quincy's crow so precisely I understood immediately that she had spent many hours watching those videos.

I chose not to comment on that.

Instead, I watched her face closely as I said, "I think he has a girlfriend."

She just nodded. "With the bikes? Yeah, I saw that."

"This will be a lovely surprise for her."

Ren laughed again. "Poor thing."

I slipped my body into her bedding. The sheets were dirty, but her mattress was soft. "When are you going to see him?"

"He's going to call when he gets here."

"Great."

She reached over and took my hand then. I could feel her pulse in my own palm. "I don't need him around," she said. "So you know."

It felt then like someone had reached into my chest and squeezed whatever it was they found in there.

Ren heard from Quincy again the third week of August and he showed up in our driveway two days later in one of those massive Jeeps they rent to tourists.

Boxy and bright and violently red.

I watched from the front window as he pulled in.

Checked his teeth in his rearview mirror.

There was so much static above my rib cage I had to put both hands there and press. Outside, the finches were engaged in a lively, raucous chatter.

"Well?"

Ren stood by the door with her hair braided and her purse over one shoulder. At sixteen weeks, there was a noticeable mound south of her belly button, and she'd put on that hyaline lipstick that made her mouth look wet.

"You look good," I told her, and she pulled a face that suggested she didn't believe me.

From the window I watched her dark head bob down the lanai steps. By then, Quincy was out of the Jeep, kicking mindlessly at the asphalt like a kid at a bus stop.

When he saw her he straightened, a half-formed smile frozen on his face. I watched as reality hit him in real time. His hand stuck at his shoulder in a wave.

It was almost comical.

Or it would be, if it were happening to someone else.

He said something I couldn't hear, and she must've responded because there was a pause, and then his face seemed to brighten.

No flash of anger.

No narrowing of the eyes.

The buzzing in my chest intensified as hope drained.

Hope of his dismissal. Of Ren coming right back inside.

We could call him names.

We could tear him apart.

We could go back to the original plan.

They spoke with three feet of space between them, Quincy's face open, eyes wide, head nodding, hand pulling at an earlobe. He seemed to be blinking more than was necessary. Then he opened the passenger door, hovering as she climbed up and in, one hand near her back, not quite touching.

It told me everything, that hand.

There would be no more original plan.

I let the curtain fall closed. The living room was still and quiet and a little too warm. Outside came the start of an engine. The rumble of the Jeep backing out. Then nothing but the birds.

My eyes roved around the room, looking. For what? Everything was in its rightful place. The squat stack of *Architectural Digests*, slightly fanned on the coffee table. The thick navy blanket on the back of our armchair, folded into thirds. Even the doorknob shone.

A couch spring dug into my lower back. I stood. Turned to look at the relic. Dumpy. Old.

It did not belong.

I moved to the front door and opened it. Looked back and forth between the doorframe and the bones of the sofa. From her bed in the corner, Sookie lifted her head to watch me move to the couch, yank off all the cushions, grab the arm closest to the door, and pull.

I was sweating by the time I got the thing outside and onto the top landing, standing on its end, a full two feet taller than me. Upside down its springs were exposed to the open air, furred with rust.

I counted fourteen steps to the driveway.

Pressing my back to the house I wiggled down. At the bottom of the steps I looked up. On the landing above, the upright couch was a bizarre domestic statue, faded to a drab Tootsie Roll brown.

Beneath the house I found an old swatch of carpet rolled in on itself. The malodor of mold shot into my nose, and I stifled a sneeze as I pulled the fouled rug out.

Hauled it up the steps. Unrolled it along the stairs.

Slowly, evenly, I tipped the sofa onto its side so its front end rested on the fabric. Then I got behind and pushed.

Watching that sofa slide down those stairs was the most satisfying thing I'd done in years. It thudded along with each step and the noise in my chest quieted and I felt buoyant. Giddy almost. It hit the driveway in a cloud of dust and dog hair.

I stared at it for a solid minute.

Hands on my hips. Ribs heaving.

From there it was push-pull, push-pull as I scrambled from one side to the other. I tugged until my arms ached and then pressed my back into the armrest to push until my legs burned.

When the couch was finally settled on the curb, I ran back into the living room for the cushions. Carried them outside to lay them out in their rightful place.

In the afternoon sun, the couch looked even worse. The fabric had worn away along its arms and back, and what was left underneath had a dark black sheen. Like skin.

Upstairs, the seven-foot stretch of floor where the couch once sat was covered in a half inch of dust and little lost bits of life. A penny. A tortoiseshell button. A dried-up gummy bear.

I pulled out the vacuum.

Savored the satisfying little pings and tings as I sucked it all up and away.

When the space was clear I evaluated my work.

Half of the living room looked naked. I stared at it and imagined Ren riding in Quincy's Jeep with one hand out the window, letting all the warm air in. He wouldn't ask her to roll it up. He wouldn't mind.

I turned toward the door.

At the curb, I sat on the couch and tried not to think.

Had they gone to dinner? Somewhere to sit? Waiānuenue Falls, maybe. Ren liked to hike up to the back into the banyan trees. Were they there discussing the future while ancient branches waved overhead like arms?

I sat on the couch for nearly an hour while the sun drooped

slowly toward the ocean. I sat until Theo pulled up in his lime-green toaster of a vehicle.

He gave me and the couch a good once-over, then leaned out the window and said, "That bad, huh?"

R

He was not mad. He looked almost amused, leaning coolly against his massive Jeep, more army vehicle than the tourist rental it's used as. *Whoa*, he'd said, and I laughed at that. The perfection of that response: *Whoa*. I told him briefly about how Jess and I planned to coparent, how we co-owned the house, how we'd done everything together since college, and if he thought it was strange, it didn't show. It was just after four, and we drove along the coast, plastic cups of boba in the cupholders, window down, radio on, Bruce Springsteen singing to us about being born in the USA. I wondered if Quincy liked that song, if he thought I did, or if he was even aware it was playing at all. When we reached the four-way intersection I told him to hang a right, toward the water. The lot was half-full, a handful of pickups, a couple kids splashing through an outdoor shower, a shave ice truck with no customers, its driver visible in the window, cheek propped on one balled fist, scrolling a phone. We parked facing the water, got out and leaned against the hood, sipping tapioca beads through fat straws. Quincy cleared his throat but said nothing.

"So," I started, breaking the tension.

"So," he parroted. In front of us, a surfer bobbed, his dark head a black buoy.

"Are you mad?"

"What? Mad? No." Quincy turned to me, his face open and earnest. "I am..." He searched for the word. "Surprised. I mean, I was not expecting... I don't know *what* I was expecting but not this. But." He shook his head. "It's cool."

"Cool?"

He winced. "I don't know! It's a lot." There was a smile behind this, which was a relief. I chewed a gummy boba pearl and let it slide down my throat. "I guess, I mean..." He sighed. "I always wanted this to happen, when I was younger, but then it didn't, when it should have. I just thought it would be, you know…" He smiled an uneven smile. "With someone whose last name I know."

"You're telling me."

"Fair."

I thought about those wedding photos on his page and wondered if that's what he meant by *when it should have happened*.

In front of us, the surfer caught his wave, rode it toward the shore, and I thought about an alternate universe where this was our second date, our first, technically, as the last one certainly didn't count. But this didn't feel like a date. There was none of that swollen anticipation. In fact, now that the stress of telling him was over I felt at ease, as if my body could register the piece of him that was already growing inside me and flagged him safe as such. "It's Kelly."

Quincy squinted at me.

"My last name."

"Right." He dropped one long arm to his side. "Mine's Jones."

"I know. It's on your card."

"Right. Well, there's no relation."

"No relation?"

"Quincy Jones."

I blinked at him.

"The producer?" Then, off my blank look, "Frank Sinatra? Michael Jackson?"

I shook my head.

"No? Jesus, Ren, what, do you live on an actual rock?"

I laughed and looked back to the water, watched our surfer as he paddled out again. I felt relieved that Quincy hadn't asked if I was sure the baby was his, seeing as I'd surely be offended if he had, though the question was fair.

"So, uh." He cleared his throat, and for a moment I thought my relief had been premature. "Is it too early to know if it's a boy or a girl?"

"We're going to find out in a few weeks, but I think it's a girl. According to the baby books, she's currently the size of a navel orange."

"Whoa." Quincy smiled. Him and his *whoas*.

We watched the surfer take down a wave, then another. I asked when he started teaching. *Two weeks. Nursery Management and Orchidology. We are, after all, on the orchid island.* He spoke with the goofy candor I recognized easily from his videos, and I felt embarrassed then, over how many times I'd watched them.

"Are you still at the bar?"

"For now. And I started a maternity dance class over at the gym I teach at."

"Yeah? I didn't know you taught."

"For a long time. I mean, not the maternity class, I'm about four weeks into that."

"Makes sense."

"Does it?"

"Yeah. My sister has a couple kids, and with baby two, she was really late, and her doctor had her dance around to induce labor. Apparently, it's good for that. Get the blood flowing down to, uh...help with the..." Quincy's cheeks pinked up and I smiled. "Yeah." He pulled at his ear. "I'm just gonna shut up now."

It felt easy, too easy, and I wished Jess was there with us. It would be simpler than rehashing every moment later the way she'd want me to. Around us, dusk was beginning its descent, and toward the horizon, the surfer began to paddle back in. I snuck a look at Quincy, his face in silhouette. "Look, I don't like, expect anything from you, so you know."

Quincy cocked his head. "No?"

"No. Honestly, I wasn't planning on even telling you. But then I guess, I thought, that was kinda messed up."

"Just kinda."

I thought about the woman on his page then, how the news might impact her, a ripple effect. I looked back out to the water. "Jess and I, we've got it covered, and Theo, that's my brother—"

"Right, I met him."

"Yeah. He's gonna help out, too. So, you don't need to like, *be the dad*. I'm not expecting that."

Quincy nodded slowly.

In front of us, the surfer emerged from the waves, board pinched under a muscled arm, his body a sharp V from shoulders to thin hips. He shook water from his hair like a dog.

"What if I want to?"

I turned. "Want to what?"

Quincy met my gaze and held it, his eyes shining their peculiar red-brown, his expression suddenly serious. "Be the dad."

I felt like I was floating as we pulled back onto Kalaniana'ole. It was easy, he was easy, and everything would be fine. But as we neared the house I saw her, our old brown couch, forlorn on the curb, cushions askew.

"Shit," I said under my breath.

"Hmm?" Quincy asked.

I shook my head. The relief I'd felt seconds ago evaporated. It'd been dumb of me, I realized, to think the hard part was over. Quincy killed the engine and hopped out, hurried over to my door, but I was already down on the pavement.

"Well..." He opened his arms as if to hug me and then stopped, stepped back, and raised one hand for a high five. The slap of our palms cut the tension and I laughed, and he laughed too, and over his shoulder I caught a movement in the window, just a flicker of curtain, then stillness.

14

J

"He's coming for *dinner*?" Theo stopped midstride beside an overstuffed sectional. We were at Kinkado's looking for a new couch, my head aching beneath the fluorescents. I'd been up until four trying to count the rotations of the ceiling fan even though I knew from previous experience it was not possible.

"On Tuesday. I assume Ren has volunteered you to cook."

The air in the showroom was slightly too cold and around us the scattered living room arrangements lent the feeling that we were in an apartment building without walls.

"Want me to poison his spaghetti?" Theo walked backward, facing me, his fingers trailing down the back of a cream cabriole. "I'll do it. I look great in orange."

It was almost nine. The store would close soon but we'd come anyway. Ren was at the bar and being inside the house agitated me.

I felt flimsy and hollow and buzzy.

An upside-down paper cup with a fly trapped inside.

Theo flumped down on a parakeet-green midcentury with

jabby, angular Eiffel legs. The only other person in the store was the woman behind the counter. College-age with a narrow face and those oversized glasses with translucent frames everyone was wearing. Probably not even prescription.

I sank in beside Theo and plucked absently at the upholstery.

The last time I'd been in there, it was for the koa crib. That trip came with an entirely different feeling, and I wished I could return to it.

"So," Theo said, "how much involvement does he want?"

"I'm not sure exactly, but apparently he wants to have a *presence*."

"Huh."

"Yeah."

Theo laced his hands behind his head. "Is he going to pay for things?"

"I don't know if they've talked about that."

"Knowing Ren, probably not."

I frowned. I was both comforted by Theo's obvious attempt at alliance and also irritated on Ren's behalf.

Of course, he was right. They probably had not talked about money. I hated that I didn't know what they'd talked about. I felt like I was back in school and excluded from my normal lunch table.

I knew if I'd asked Ren, she'd have invited me to come along. But I hadn't wanted to ask. I wanted her to invite me all on her own.

I knew this was manipulative.

I didn't like the things I knew.

We migrated to a low-lying sectional that could easily fit twenty. Theo lay the full length of his body out and crossed his ankles in a position of such leisure that the girl behind the counter gave us a choleric glare. This normally would have irritated me in a *Pretty Woman* kind of way but I couldn't muster the energy for indignation.

"Did he say anything about custody?"

"Doubtful." I scratched my nail over the ribbed surface of the couch so it made a satisfying little zip-zip noise. "I think he has a girlfriend."

"Yeah, you already told me that."

I had? I stood, moved us over to an L-shaped chesterfield. Black leather with a matching ottoman. The material felt soothing on the backs of my legs.

I wondered what it might cost.

Somehow the idea of dropping a few thousand felt satisfying. Productive, even.

I let myself think about this without looking at the price tag.

"Well, you know what they say." Theo cleared his throat in an exaggerated, showy sort of way. *"You can't always get what you wantttt."* He sang it at full volume. Head tipped back. Eyes closed.

"Do not."

The counter girl scowled as I tossed a slippery leather pillow in Theo's direction. He blocked it with his forearm so that it catapulted over the back of the couch onto the floor, then he lifted an imaginary microphone to his face. *"No, you can't always get what you wannnttt."*

He was doing this to embarrass me and though I was embarrassed I resolved not to show it. The counter girl's nostrils flared.

Theo continued, thrashing his head, eyes closed. He finished that final line about getting what you need with a winding slam on the air guitar, then opened his eyes and flashed a smarmy smile.

"Thanks for that."

"No problem."

"I like this one," I said.

He ran his hand along the couch's tufted back. "Me, too. It has good juju. Let's get matching ones."

This idea appealed to me, if only to see the shock on the counter girl's face.

I flipped over the tag. *The Lola*, it read.

I exhaled sharply through my nose. Of course.

The Tuesday Quincy was scheduled for dinner I decided to reorganize the storage room at the office.

There were other things I could have been doing.

I needed to schedule a listing appointment for Tatia Chen.

I needed to look over a contract for Ku'ulei and two for Theo.

Instead, I spent six hours in the storage room. I pulled all the boxes off the shelves. Old papers we weren't legally allowed to destroy yet. I moved these around until Kim came in to ask me if she could help. If I wanted her to do it.

I shook my head no, but an hour later, she came back and asked again. This time she stayed in the doorway watching me and frowning until I told her I had it, *thank you*, with my eyebrows lifted so she knew I was telling her to leave.

The previous evening, Ren had come into my room to sleep, her hair wet and smelling strongly of coconut shampoo. It'd been just after 10:30 and the windows were open, but everything felt hot and sticky. It hadn't rained in weeks. We lay quiet on our backs with our faces pointed at the ceiling. After a while I said, "So, do you like Quincy, then?"

"Like him?"

I waited for her to admit she understood.

"No. I don't *like* him," she said finally. "But I think he is interesting, and it seems like he's, you know..." She searched. "A good person."

"Based on that one interaction."

"Right."

"Because you don't really remember the other one."

She sighed. "Right."

By four the storage room was entirely reorganized. I felt a small yank of satisfaction as I stood in the center of the neatly stacked boxes.

When I checked my phone, I saw that Ren had sent a photo of her and Sookie. I could tell from the background they were curled up together on Sookie's bed beneath the kitchen table. Under the photo, Ren had written, *come home, we miss you.*

On the way home I stopped at Safeway to get bread and a bottle of wine. Theo and Taylor would drink it, if no one else.

I got a bottle of nonalcoholic too, so Ren could feel like she was participating. Then, for no real reason I understood, I added a single-serving box of Albariño to the cart.

This I drank on the way home. Hugged between my thighs while I drove. Like a juice box. I'd never done anything like it and I tried not to think too much about it. I couldn't remember the last time I'd had alcohol of any kind.

I thought of my auntie Clem and her goblets of vodka.

Outside, the sky was just beginning to pink.

Inside, everything felt soft and slippery.

R

The new couch arrived at five o'clock. I watched from the kitchen as Jess showed the men from Kinkado's where to put it. It was a big black thing, shiny as a new car, and when the delivery guys left, the backs of their shirts inky with sweat, the whole room smelled of fresh leather. The couch made the house look like it belonged to a different type of person, someone who invited friends with dangly earrings over for book club and served them drinks in glasses with spindly necks. I imagined the couch covered in baby toys and dog hair, but when Jess caught my eye I smiled reassuringly. She was nervous, I could tell. We all were. Quincy was due in twenty minutes. Theo had changed the menu four times.

We sat around the kitchen waiting, Theo at the stove arguing with Jess about genetically modified corn, onions hissing in the pan like rain, Taylor rolling a cigarette at the table. Protests had broken out on Kaua'i over a patch of cornfields linked to a spike in birth defects and Jess was taking it personally. She insisted this concern was on my behalf, though we lived on a different island, and nowhere near a cornfield. "It's gotten out of hand, what they're doing," Jess was saying.

"I don't know," Taylor said, "what about the golden rice thing?"

Jess gave him a long look. "The problem is not the GMOs, it's the *herbicides*," she said finally, as if bored, returning her gaze to her phone and scrolling. "Anyway. Where do you think those fields are located? Not by the hotels or high-ends, that's for sure."

Taylor stepped out to smoke after that, Theo saying something about class warfare, dumping tomatoes into the skillet, where they sizzled angrily. I always liked listening to Theo and Jess argue, although *argue* wasn't necessarily the right term for it. It was more *seeing who could be louder*. From out in the drive came the slam of a car door and everyone stopped talking, the room filling with our collective breathing and the gentle bubble of Theo's sauce as it reached a simmer.

I waited for him at the top of the lanai steps, the grass below blond with drought. He'd dressed up, hair slicked back, a blue shirt buttoned all the way up, and as he leaned into the back seat of his Jeep, I tried to imagine him in front of a closet deciding what to wear. He emerged with a large paper bag, and seeing me, he waved, a compact motion first, and then a broader, sweeping fan, his lopsided smile growing wide as he moved toward the house, his stride nearly a bound.

The first thing out of his bag was a petite elephant-shaped pillow. It was meant for a very small head but looked a bit like a dog toy, and from the floor, Sookie wagged. "Honestly it was the first thing I saw in Target's baby department," he said as I closed the door. "Have you been? It is overwhelming." Quincy did indeed look overwhelmed, holding his brown bag like a life vest in our living room, which smelled like car upholstery.

I jockeyed us toward the kitchen as Quincy continued to unearth items from his bag, magic trick–style, a bottle of red wine, a box of chocolate crackers, a pineapple so fragrant my mouth watered immediately. Taylor was at the sink lathering cigarette smoke from his fingers, and Theo wiped his palms on the front of his jeans before extending for a shake. "Nice to see you, man," and then, "Way to knock up my sister."

"My pleasure," Quincy said, and most of us laughed. When we quieted, Jess looked up from her phone with a wintry gaze.

"Hello," she said.

I glanced to Theo, who gave me a meaningful look. *Buckle up*, it said. "Hey, Jess," Quincy said, tucking his hands into his pockets and bouncing on the balls of his feet, and then, nodding past the back slider: "Is that Timor bamboo?"

We stepped out back, and Sookie romped in circles as Quincy ran one finger up a stalk of the black bamboo that grew in clumps around our catchment tank. "You need a lot of rain for this stuff, but it's incredible," he said.

"Isn't it invasive?" Jess asked this in an accusatory way, as if Quincy was the one who had planted it.

"It is, yes," he said, and then, motioning toward our mulch pile, "Making some beds?" He asked this directly of Jess and it became clear he already knew which one of us he needed to win over.

Jess frowned. "Not really."

She was purposely being difficult, I could tell, strategizing, angling—but at what? I wandered off then, pretending to be interested in something near the fence. With no one to perform for, she'd be forced to make some semblance of reasonable conversation. I plucked at a curly liliko'i vine running along the chain-link, its greedy tendrils searching, and thought about how earlier that day I'd stood at the juice counter as Ryan and Mei talked about some high-protein diet trend, *LDL triglycerides body mass legumes*, and I wondered how they'd react if I told them I mostly ate toast and cereal and whatever my older brother made me for dinner. Ryan and Mei had much more in common than I had with either of them, they both surfed and took excellent care of their bodies, and the fact that I hoped they never dated despite seemingly being a good fit made me feel like an asshole, probably because I was one. When I turned back, Jess was saying, "It's fine, really."

"I'm serious." Quincy was tilting his big head to the side. "It's no big deal."

"What's no big deal?"

Quincy twisted toward me. "I thought I'd grab you some starts from the university so you can build a few beds out." Over his shoulder, Jess gave me a daggered look, which I pretended not to notice.

"Really?"

"Sure. We have hundreds just sitting in pots." Quincy moved

toward our mulch pile. "They'd love to get their roots into some of this." He reached his hand into the mulch and peeled a layer back, revealing darker earth beneath.

"That'd be great," I said, turning to Jess and smiling falsely. "Wouldn't that be great?"

After all that back-and-forth about the menu, Theo'd settled on puttanesca, and as I aimed a fork at my mouth I wondered if he'd purposely chosen a dish that was awkward to eat. He was quibbling with Jess over which wine to open, the zinfandel she'd bought to go with dinner or the bottle Quincy'd given as a gift, and after deciding on the zin Theo turned to Quincy. "All of this and she doesn't even drink."

"I don't *not drink*."

Theo looked at her. "I think it's safe to say you don't drink."

"That makes me sound like I had a problem." She looked to Quincy. "I do drink, I just prefer not to."

Theo poured wine into a glass and handed it to Taylor. "She can't stand even a temporary loss of control."

"Har har," Jess said dryly, then, to Quincy, "I stopped drinking because of how it makes me feel afterward." She picked her fork up then put it back down. I thought about, but of course did not mention, her family history with alcohol. "Ren pukes the next morning from a single glass of something. Actually that's what was happening when we realized she was pregnant."

I looked at her sharply. Then, to Quincy: "I didn't know I was pregnant, obviously."

Quincy held his hands up, palms out.

"Don't worry," Jess said. "Our doctor thinks it's *probably* fine." I stared at her. It seemed she was purposely trying to make me look irresponsible. Taylor asked a polite question then about where Quincy was living, and Quincy began talking about the roommate he'd found on Craigslist who had some questionable hygiene practices. Taylor commiserated about his own roommates, also unearthed on the internet, and as the conversation found a comfortable rhythm I thought maybe we'd dodged it, whatever awkwardness Jess had seemed intent on maintaining.

Then Jess turned to Quincy. "So, you have a girlfriend?" She was cutting up her spaghetti, something I had never seen her do before, and I resisted the urge to kick her underneath the table. Quincy just smiled like he did not understand the question, and Jess pressed on. "On your page."

"Ah," Quincy said.

"Well? Does *she* know about your incoming progeny?"

"Jess," Theo said in warning.

"What, it's fine." Jess looked at me then as if to gauge that it was indeed fine. I had no idea what my face was doing but it must have satisfied her because she shifted away and said, "See, it's fine. We're getting to know each other, that's why he's here, right? So we can all get to know each other?"

Theo opened his mouth to object, but Quincy raised a hand. "She's right, it's fine." He looked to me before turning back to Jess. "I don't have a girlfriend. I was seeing someone earlier in the summer but we didn't want a distance thing, so." Quincy shrugged.

Jess made a noise like what Quincy had said was particularly interesting. When Quincy returned his gaze to his plate, I knocked my knee against hers and she looked at me, eyes wide like *what?* Across the table, Taylor smiled at Theo in a reassuring way that made me desperately wish Jess was in that sort of mood.

"I think it's really cool, what you're doing, just so you know," Quincy said then, using a spoon to cradle spaghetti around his fork.

"*Cool?*" Jess's voice dipped dangerously.

Across from me, Theo slowly moved his napkin across his mouth.

"Yeah, you know. It's very progressive."

I winced, but Jess just pushed a piece of hair out of her face.

"Well, we've been living together longer than most marriages last, plus, we have Theo."

"Jess thinks the nuclear family is a by-product of industrialism," Theo clarified.

This seemed to interest Quincy. "Do you really?"

Jess waved her fork dismissively, but I could feel her winding up. "Industrialism, capitalism, sure."

Quincy sat back in his chair. "How so?"

"I mean, when manufacturing became an industry, people had to move away from their extended families to participate. This was normalized through the idea of the self-sufficient nuclear family which, let's be real, hasn't worked since the fifties, and even then, it only really worked when the woman stayed home or could afford to hire help or both." Jess brought a forkful of spaghetti toward her face, then stopped. "So families became more isolated, the wealth gap widened, and here we are."

"Yes, here we are," Theo said.

Quincy smiled. "I didn't pin you for a Marxist, Jess. Aren't you in real estate?"

This made Jess snort happily. "Aren't you *divorced*?"

"Jess—" Theo started, but Quincy shook his head.

"It's alright, it's alright, I *am* divorced. How does that correlate?"

Jess waved her fork in the air as if to say, *How do you think?* I stared at the side of her face. We hadn't talked about Quincy's wedding photos, and her awareness of them meant she'd likely creeped as far back as I had, which surprised me.

"You don't believe in marriage?" Quincy asked.

"Do *you*?"

"Sure. If there's proper communication, and honesty."

Jess smiled. "So which one of those was lacking for you?"

Theo closed his eyes and shook his head slowly, but this reaction only seemed to please Jess, who smiled wider.

Quincy looked at her for a moment, and when he spoke his voice was disarmingly earnest. "A little of both, I'd say." I felt mollified then, almost proud, that he hadn't let her cow him into a corner. That he'd proven he could hold his own. "Anyway," he started again, "you don't necessarily need to be married to get divorced. Not in the emotional sense of it, at least."

Jess looked up then, the expression on her face unreadable. After a moment she asked: "Are your parents still together?"

"They are," Quincy said. "Yours?"

"They're dead. So are Ren's."

Quincy paused, fork halfway to his open mouth.

"Jess," Theo said, quieter this time.

Silence gaped around us and after a moment, Quincy said, "I'm really sorry to hear that." His voice was low and still, and I stared at my plate just in case he was looking at me.

"Oh, it's fine," Jess said. "That's not really my point."

I wanted to ask Jess what exactly her point *was*, but instead I just looked at my spaghetti, the sauce splattered across my plate like gore.

Later, I walked Quincy out, leaning against the railing on the front lanai as he thanked me for having him. The sun was just starting to set and everything behind him was washed in a dark, bruised purple. He moved as if to leave, and then stopped. "Hey so, about Tavi." I stared at him blankly as if I didn't know he was referring to the woman on his page whose profile I had clicked on a dozen times even though it was set to private. "That's, um, the woman I was seeing."

"Please, it's fine. I don't expect you not to date."

"You don't." He looked relieved, and I couldn't decide how I wanted to feel about it.

"No," I said. "That was just Jess being a bulldog."

He smiled. "She's protective. I think it's sweet."

I laughed. "That's very kind of you."

There was a long moment then, and I thought he might say

something else, but he just smiled almost sleepily. "Good night, then," he said finally, and turned to walk evenly down the steps.

Back in the kitchen, Taylor and I finished cleaning up while Theo answered emails, and after I brushed my teeth and changed into sweats, I found Jess on her bed with her eyes closed and the lights still on. She didn't open them as she asked, "How'd you think that went?"

"Which part? The part where you asked Quincy about his failed marriage or the part where you told him our parents are dead."

"Well, it did fail and they are dead. Roll over. You're not supposed to be on your back."

I sighed. "Can you open a window?"

I listened to her feet thud on the hardwood, one and then the other. There was an urgency to the quiet that fell between us then, a fullness I'd learned to identify somehow, a silence unlike our normal silences, a silence that meant something was coming. "So," she started. "How involved is he going to be?"

I rolled onto my back again. "I don't know yet, but he seems open to playing it however we want."

I almost mentioned the money thing then, how during that first afternoon he'd shuffled his feet awkwardly and said: "I'm happy to help with the, uh. With the financial side of things. If you need." I'd tried to play it noncommittal, but it was a relief. Money was weird with me and Jess, because I'd had it growing up and she hadn't, but now she had it and I didn't. It was the most gaping difference between us; my income trickled in through tips and minor hourly wages, whereas Jess's came in big fat hunks, yet we still tried to pretend we were equal, as if the very act of pretending would balance us.

Beside me, Jess shifted. "I think he likes you. Roll *over*."

I did. "You think everyone likes me." In college, Jess was constantly telling me about people who liked me, friends of ours usually, but sometimes boys who never talked to me at all.

"I can't see you with him though."

"No," I agreed. "It's weird, like we fast-forwarded through all of the stages of a relationship already. Now we're at amicable divorcés." Getting to know someone while you carried their child was a lot of pressure, it turned out, and I was mollified at the lack of spark between us, but even as I thought that, I felt a familiar shadow of disappointment, a familiarity that made me squirmy, the sanctuary I seemed to find in letting myself down.

"Has he even asked you if you're sure it's his?"

I shook my head.

"Don't you think that's weird?"

"I think it's trusting."

"Okay, but don't you think *that's* weird? I mean, he's taking this entirely too easy."

She was right about that, it did seem incredibly easy, his acceptance of the pregnancy, his willingness to do whatever it was I asked, and even though it felt like there was nothing between us, I had a sense that if I were to make some move, he would let me do that, too.

Jess rubbed at her nose. "Maybe he's a sociopath."

"Jess."

"What? Don't you think there has to be a catch?"

I reached over to pick at a loose thread on the sleeve of her shirt. "Can you do something for me?"

"I do a lot of things for you." I waited, winding the thread around my thumb. "Sorry. What."

"Can you promise you'll try?"

"Try what?"

"With Quincy. Just try."

She held my gaze, and something softened there, a subtle shift, like how the shadows in a room change slowly as the afternoon extends. "There has to be a catch."

15

J

"So," Tatia said as she got into my car. "I was thinking." Her hair was shorter than the last time I'd seen her, shorn to her head like a helmet, and in the midmorning sun the makeup on her face shone a bit lighter than her complexion.

"Oh yeah?" I switched my blinker on to pull us out of the lot.

"Yes," she said, then stopped.

Despite two cups of coffee the day had a dense mental fog over it, my vision dark around the edges. As if someone had applied a filter.

That morning I'd returned home from my run to a friend request from Quincy.

I hadn't responded to it yet.

Just let it hover there in the corner of my screen.

Its presence felt caustic somehow.

I didn't want to touch it.

I had not behaved well at dinner. I knew this. I wasn't sure why. An urge to shock Quincy, maybe? He seemed so unflappable. Like nothing could faze him.

No matter what I said.

No matter what Ren said.

No matter who was having whose baby.

Quincy would just smile that crooked smile and give one of those sheepish, dopey shrugs. As if nothing he did had any impact on the people around him.

"You and your friend," Tatia started again. "What you're doing."

I felt a cold slap like I'd been plunged into ice water. I'd forgotten our conversation about the car seat, and her rash commentary on my personal life felt entirely intrusive though I knew I'd done it to myself. That moment of unexpected oversharing. I regretted it so severely my chest began to buzz.

"I think you should write a book about it."

I let out a noisy puff of air. My seat belt felt too tight.

"I'm serious." Tatia folded her sunglasses into her purse. "I really think you're onto something. Other women might want to follow suit."

"They are, I think. Or, we are."

"Well. I've never heard of anyone doing it. Not platonically, I mean. I have a friend who works for Simon and Schuster, you know. I'd be happy to make an introduction."

"Neither of us write."

Tatia waved her hand. "So you get a ghostwriter, that's what everyone does. You remember those teenagers who did the same thing? A whole flock of them."

"The pregnancy pact." I did remember that.

"*They* wrote a book about it."

I was in high school when that happened, that group of girls who all got pregnant at the same time. It had felt relevant because we had been close in age. Even then I could see the comfort in it. A stupid decision, yes, but a stupid decision made en masse.

I had imagined them raising their kids together. The girls becoming mothers in unison. Their children born into a pack like those South African crows. Shared duties. A dozen small bodies universally tended to.

It had seemed almost fun.

Later, though, I'd read there was no pact. That the girls weren't even friends. They'd all gotten knocked up after some sort of prom. A coincidence. The only thing collective was how uninformed they were about birth control.

I didn't mention this to Tatia. She flipped down the visor and checked her lipstick, a pale iridescent pink. "Well, think it over and let me know."

I didn't answer. Just nodded and drove us north.

R

The last Sunday in August Quincy arrived with a monster truck stuffed with palms, three types of hibiscus, yellow bamboo, fertilizer, a wheelbarrow, four shovels, two pitchforks, and a heaping pile of cinder soil. Jess was the first to see him, sitting by the window with a cup of black coffee. "Um, Ren," she'd called. It was early, just after eight, and I was in the kitchen, fresh from the shower, furiously digging my way through a bowl of cereal, my wet hair leaving dark circles on the shoulders of my T-shirt. I'd wandered in then with my Cheerios and my spoon to see Quincy unloading hibiscus cuttings onto the drive. "Whose truck is that?" Jess asked, but I didn't answer, and together we watched Quincy hop from the truck bed and squint up at the house. Spotting us in the window, he waved. Beside me, Jess groaned.

It took three hours just to spread the beds, Theo and Taylor hauling cinder as Jess and Quincy hovered around me, making me feel more like a child myself than someone carrying one. "I can handle a wheelbarrow," I protested as Jess tried to intercept me and a load of cinder. It actually felt good, pushing all that earth around. Quincy sprang across the yard, placing plants where he thought they should go, spouting information, his face bright as he explained the proper amount of shade and sun as if any of us would remember it.

Taylor had given up smoking last week and it made him shifty, almost irritable. I watched as he transferred himself into the shade to wipe his forehead, a toothpick protruding from the gentlest scowl I'd ever seen.

Quincy'd hooked a speaker up to his phone and we listened to an HPR piece about the use of sonar mapping to track and predict seismic activity. Jess was quiet but not combative, less steel to her silence, and I was able to relax. Just before noon, as

Quincy was showing us how to tie orchids to the trunk of our mango tree, Jess said, "Would you like me to film you? Maybe you can add it to your oeuvre."

Quincy groaned. "Jesus, you've seen those?"

"Seen what?" asked Theo.

But Jess didn't respond, just smirked and walked into the house.

"What?" Theo repeated. "Seen what?"

We broke for lunch, Theo bringing out turkey sandwiches and a bowl of crinkle cut potato chips, and while we ate, Quincy pulled up pictures of his sister's kids, three boys, rusty-headed and freckled. They swarmed all over Quincy in the photos, draping themselves around his neck and back, and he passed the phone as if trying to prove to us that children liked him, that he was capable. Jess never rejoined us, and it was nearly three by the time the mulch pile had been demolished, the plants rehomed.

Afterward, I walked Quincy and a wheelbarrow full of shovels out to his truck, a colossal thing he borrowed from the university. Clouds had moved in overhead and the breeze caught the sweat on the back of my neck. My feet hurt, my back ached, but I felt oddly satisfied. Quincy unlatched the back of his truck. "That was fun, huh?"

I fiddled with the hem of my shirt and thanked him, and he shrugged the way he always did, as if nothing could ever be taken seriously. He loaded the wheelbarrow into the bed with a grunt then stopped, threw a glance up at the house, and turned to me with a look I couldn't quite read. "What?" I asked.

"Nothing." He touched his earlobe. "Actually, something. Why did you wait four months to write me?"

I looked at him, unsure of how exactly I should phrase it, which he must have interpreted as me trying to be kind, because he scrunched one eye shut as if bracing himself. "Honestly?" I sighed. "I didn't find your card until then."

He drew his head back. "Seriously?"

"Yeah."

"Jesus. You must've thought I was such an asshole."

"It's fine."

"No wonder Jess hates me."

"She doesn't hate you."

Quincy gave me that lopsided smirk. "She doesn't like me."

"She does, she just teases."

"Yes, well, orcas tease seals. I don't think it's because they like them."

I laughed at that, and Quincy smiled, opening the door of his truck. "Funny though. Technically, I met Jess before I met you."

"So I've heard."

"Great," he said, rolling his eyes at himself as he climbed into the vehicle. "Oh," he called, then leaned out through the open window with two orchid stems, long and acicular and dripping with orange flowers the size of my thumbnail. *"Ascocentrum,"* he said, holding them out. "Here." I took the delicate cuttings, brought them to my nose, but the smell was faint, barely there at all. "Give one to Jess, will ya?" he called before he backed out.

I found her in the kitchen cleaning out the fridge, bottles of condiments scattered along the countertops, condensation puddling around them like sweat. I filled an old Ball jar with water and tucked the orchid stems inside, their flowers small and bright. I placed them on the counter and watched Jess pull an old head of lettuce out of the fridge, its plastic bag gone slimy, and toss it into the sink.

"What was that all about?" I asked.

Jess pulled her head from the fridge. She held a hot-pink sponge in one hand and wiped a piece of hair off her forehead with the other. "All what about?"

I took a seat on one of the island stools, picked up a near-empty jar of olives, just two single green orbs floating in brine, and twisted its slippery top. I placed an olive on my tongue, rolled it around, letting the salt shock my taste buds, and from down the hall I could hear Taylor laughing. I'd never heard Taylor laugh directly, only from behind Theo's closed door, and it made me wonder how they interacted when no one was watching. If he was a different person completely. I looked at Jess's back, her right elbow motoring back and forth with focused effort as she scrubbed at something I couldn't see. "You said you were going to try."

"I am trying." Her voice echoed from the hollow of the refrigerator's mouth.

I paused, thinking maybe she'd turn around, but she didn't. "Try harder," I said to her back. Then I got up and went into my room, leaving the empty olive jar open on the island behind me.

16

J

September marked the arrival of avocado season.

They browned in boxes at the ends of driveways with *FREE* Sharpied crudely across the front and dropped from the trees along our running path where Sookie found them and carried them home, tucked into her mouth like dinosaur eggs.

The AC at the office broke and the heat was unbearable, even with the windows open and fans jammed into every outlet. Tatia Chen sent me the contact of her friend at the publishing house and a *Salon* article about other nonromantic pairs and triads who were coparenting.

I scrolled through the article, looking at the photos. Smiling men and women with chunky glasses and edgy haircuts in places like Park Slope and Los Feliz. I forwarded the piece to Ren.

I didn't look at the publisher's website.

During Friday's morning meeting I tried to ply the team with cold brew and mochi to distract from the fact that the conference room felt like a sauna but no one paid attention, the air slowly steaming our brains and the caffeine and sugar making us jittery.

Next to me, Kuʻulei fanned her face with a manila envelope. Even I kept losing my train of thought. "Remember," I sighed, inflection rising to signal I was wrapping up. Belongings were marshaled on cue. Pens clicked and chairs creaked. "What we do is incredibly personal." No one listened but I went on anyway. "Your clients are inviting you inside their life. It's intimate." Across the table Theo gave me a weighted look, nodding past me with his chin. I followed his gaze as I finished with, "It's like seeing them naked."

That last word phlegmed itself to the back of my throat.

Quincy was there in the hall, leaning against a cubicle with his ankles crossed.

He smiled that stupid slanted smile and removed one hand from his pocket to give me a two-fingered wave.

I turned back to Theo, who smirked knowingly.

My body began to carbonate.

I left my door open and pointed Quincy toward one of the chairs across from my desk. I wanted to ask him what he was doing here but instead I apologized about the heat and he just sort of shrugged as if he hadn't noticed.

He wore a plain gray shirt with the sleeves pushed up and as I sat across from him I realized with a sudden, swift impact why he was there. Theo's knowing look. It was so staggeringly obvious I took a quick inhale at my oversight. He'd even complained about his rental situation at dinner. It was embarrassing, to have missed such an obvious opening.

But of course I'd missed it; it was not an opening I wanted to fill.

I felt an intense pressure from my center and pressed my hand there to self-soothe.

"So," Quincy started, leaning forward. "Did I overdo it with the plants?" His gaze was light, almost teasing, and I wondered if he'd rehearsed this. An icebreaker.

"Maybe a bit."

"Typical." He rolled his eyes as if to say, *See, I don't like me either.*

I didn't want to ask him why he was here.

I would not make it easy for him.

I glanced at the screen of my computer to let him know there were other things I could be doing.

"Well," he started again, "it looks like I'm gonna be sticking around for a while." He smiled then and when I didn't smile back, he gave a shrug. "So, I was thinking you could help me find a house."

"Oh," I said, as if I were surprised. I woke my computer with a shake of my mouse. "I'm actually not taking new clients right now." This was not true. "But Lisa Hiraoka, she's one of my top producing agents, I am sure she'd be thrilled to—"

"No offense but I'd rather work with you."

I let my gaze drift back to him and settle. "Does Ren know you're here?"

He smiled again, this time in a sad sort of way. Like I'd disappointed him somehow. Of course she knew. He'd have asked her. I thought of her in the kitchen telling me to try harder.

"Look." He leaned forward, and instinctively I pressed my back against my chair. "I get it. You don't know me. I'm some asshole who got drunk and knocked your family up."

He looked me directly in the face as he said that.

My tongue seemed to tumefy in my mouth.

He watched my face as if waiting for me to agree or disagree. When I didn't do either he said: "But you should know that this situation is huge for me, too."

I remembered how I'd seen him check his teeth in his rearview mirror when he came to pick Ren up and imagined him saying that line over and over as he drove across town in his rental. *You should know that this situation is huge for me, too.*

I worked to keep my face completely still.

Theo passed by us, talking into his phone. I listened enviously to his voice as it drifted away, then the heavy swing of the front door as he let the morning swallow him in its easy sunshine.

Quincy was watching my face closely.

I thought again about Ren in the kitchen asking me to try harder.

How she left her empty olive jar on the counter for me to clean up.

I looked past Quincy, out the open window, where the sky shone a traitorous blue.

R

After class I watched one of my students greet her husband as he waited patiently outside, two compostable cups of juice in hand, and when his wife walked out the studio door his face opened into a smile so sincere that I felt a deep bodily loss, as if someone had plucked out an organ.

When the room emptied, I took my phone off airplane and was hit immediately with two missed calls from Jess and a string of angry messages. My body ran cold. I'd almost forgotten. We'd been together in the living room yesterday evening when Quincy'd called, Jess answering emails while I watched some show about housewives who decided to rob a grocery store. I left the room when I saw his name light up, as if I somehow knew the call would be private, even though there was no reason for me to assume that.

Who was that?

Just Mei.

She calls you?

I knew I should have told her, but I also knew she'd have figured out a way to say no. Of course, he'd also specifically asked me not to tell her, but that was an excuse, and I knew it. Any other time I'd have told her about it anyway and made her swear to pretend I hadn't. There in the studio, I stared at a thread of accusatory question marks on the screen, then put my phone back in my bag without responding.

Behind the juice counter, Ryan pushed a carrot through that big red machine of his. His T-shirt was luminously white, with creases on the sleeves like he'd slid it out from its plastic and onto his body.

"Carrot ginger?" he asked when he saw me. His attention had changed since my pregnancy was revealed, the looks he gave me suddenly lacking subtext, or at least they seemed to.

I knew I should head to the house, let Sookie out, take a shower before my muscles stiffened, answer Jess's messages. Instead, I sat down on a narrow metal stool, folded my hands on top of the counter and told him yes, sure, carrot ginger sounded nice.

It seemed to take forever for Jess to come home, and when the door opened just after five and Theo walked in I'd been surprised, as if I somehow forgot he lived there.

"What?" he said when he saw me.

"What do you mean *what*?" I was on the couch in a pair of sweatpants suffering through terrible indigestion.

"You have a weird look on your face."

I flopped back into the sofa. "I thought you might be Jess and she's mad at me."

"Ah." He hung his keys. "Does it have something to do with Quincy showing up at the office?"

"It does." I had responded to her messages eventually, after I'd showered and taken Sookie for a walk. I'd told her we could talk about it when she got home and she hadn't answered, probably so she could ensure I would sit around waiting for her. I followed Theo into the kitchen, where he pulled a bag of brown rice from the cabinet.

"Where's Taylor?"

"Work."

Theo put rice on to boil and started deveining a bag of shrimp while I chopped carrots into tiny pieces and told him about Quincy calling, how I hadn't told Jess about it. We stood back-to-back, him at the sink and me at the island, and the position offered a strange sensation, as if we were not actually in the same space, which somehow made talking easier, likely because I couldn't see him judging me. "Since when has she ever been mad about someone sending her business?"

"I think she's mad because she doesn't feel like you're a team anymore."

I frowned. "Well, why can't we all be a team?"

"I don't know. Why can't you?"

I looked at my pile of carrots and thought about thirteen weeks earlier, when Theo stood in the same spot and told me this was going to be hard. I'd assumed he meant the whole raising a child thing, but as I set my knife down, I realized how naive that assumption had been.

Jess came in twenty minutes later as I shook up a jar of oil and vinegar for salad, and when we heard the front door open Theo turned and met my gaze.

17

J

"I mean, there are some perks to it." Behind the steering wheel, Theo's voice was flat with disinterest. It had rained, and we were stuck behind a city bus that farted exhaust with every stop.

"Like what?"

Theo let out the tiniest exhalation. I could sense he was tired of talking about this, but I couldn't seem to drop it. Every time I brought it up, I felt a release of pressure like the hiss of a kettle before it begins to scream.

"For starters, Ren wants you to do it so, there's that."

We were on our way to a three-bedroom by the university. It was the first property he was really interested in and technically it wasn't even on the market yet. This put us in a good position if he wanted to make an offer and lent electric excitement to the air.

Except I wasn't excited.

Mostly I just looked out the window and complained.

Theo was still talking. "And don't you want a say in how the kid is gonna live part-time?"

I blinked. Somehow, I hadn't thought about that.

The baby staying with Quincy.

Surely a baby couldn't do that.

At what age would that be safe? Two? Four?

I felt my shoulders inch toward my ears and rolled them back down.

The listing had wide windows and a bushy coppice of palms.

Inside it smelled of yeast and bleach and the furniture was poorly staged. Still. I could tell Theo liked it by the speed with which he moved around.

The place was built into a hill so the ground level was technically the upper floor, with the master bed and bath, kitchen, and living room. Downstairs were another two bedrooms, a full bath, and an outdated kitchenette that opened onto a yard with a little slate patio.

The kitchenette was in desperate need. I studied a cracked cabinet and imagined myself doing this with Quincy. Walking through the quiet stillness of empty spaces. Opening closets.

It felt like a violation.

I'd tried to explain this to Ren when I got home last night, but she'd just commented on my commission. We had our ultrasound appointment later and things were still tense.

It felt like I was watching her move further and further away from me.

I wanted to say all of this to Theo, but instead I tapped my fist on the counter and said, "You could renovate this. Rent it to a couple UH kids."

He walked to the bathroom and stuck his head in. "I could rent it to UH kids now."

I wrinkled my nose. "Smells like old beer."

"That'd probably be a draw."

R

"We put an offer in," Jess said, stripping off her raincoat, Theo stepping around her.

"An offer?" I repeated stupidly.

"Betsy says the seller is real motivated," Theo replied. "We could know as soon as tomorrow." He called Taylor then, wandered off to his room, his voice rising from the other side of the house. Jess was looking at a stack of mail. She was looking at her fingernails. She was looking anywhere but at me.

That morning I'd stayed in bed until well after eleven googling *heartburn, second trimester,* and reading about chewing sugarless gum and eating almonds, glancing up at the koa crib in the corner, a stubborn reminder of Jess's kindness, of my lack thereof. I probably should have given her a heads-up about Quincy. Maybe in some way I had felt like punishing her. Suddenly I felt as if she were instead punishing me.

We drove to the ultrasound in combative silence. On the side of the highway, a knot of pigs tore up the grass with their noses, and as I looked at them I thought, just because Theo'd put an offer in didn't mean he'd actually get the house, but this line of thinking made me feel ashamed, considering how excited he'd seemed. I should want him to have the things that he wanted, I told myself. That was what support meant.

Our technician was different than the last time, a broad woman with a nice smile and wide, callused hands. I lay on my back in the cramped dark space, cold gel on my abdomen giving me chicken skin. We watched the little alien body light up on the screen, and then the technician pivoted to us with her lovely white teeth and said, "Congratulations. It's a boy." I looked to Jess in panic and the woman's smile ossified. "See there," she said, pointing to a small nub on the screen that didn't look much different from the other small nubs.

I don't remember the rest of the appointment. All I could think was *boy, boy, boy, boy, boy.* I thought this while I folded myself back into my clothes and as we crossed the parking lot, oily pools of rainwater punctuating the pavement with their Technicolored skin. *Boy, boy, boy.* I felt embarrassed, over how certain I'd been for absolutely no reason at all that it would be a girl. Jess didn't mention any of that, which was kind of her. This new information seemed to have broken the tension between us, or at least rearranged it so we could see its lack of importance in the face of recent developments. The folder pinned beneath her arm held a new photo of the baby's alien-bean body, which felt entirely different now that we knew he was a *he.* I'd felt certain it would be a girl because I'd wanted it to be a girl, and now that want shamed me. I should be happy the baby was healthy. That was what mattered. Out in the car, we sat for a moment before I tilted my head back, buttoned my eyes closed and said, "Of course it's a boy." Of course it is.

Theo was gone when we got back to the house, and I sat in the living room while Jess fed Sookie and let her out. When she came back in, she'd changed into a pair of plaid pajama bottoms, her hair pushed away from her face with a cotton headband, and the combination of the two made her look much younger, like the Jess I knew in college, padding around the dorm room in an earlier edition of the ratty gray house slippers she still wore. She asked how I was feeling in a soft, gentle tone, and I understood that I had been forgiven. When I told her about my indigestion, she offered to draw me a bath. I didn't think that was a solution for indigestion, but seeing as I was freshly redeemed I liked the idea of being taken care of, so I said yes and she left the room.

A few minutes later I drifted into her bathroom carrying half an avocado and a fork. She was perched on the side of her tub scooping salt into the pummeling water, and though her back was to me, she somehow sensed I was there because she immediately started talking. "If the seller accepts, Theo could be out of here in a month," she said, straining over the water as it beat against the tub. "Do you want to repaint in there before we move the crib?" *In there* of course meant Theo's room. I looked down at the avocado in my hand, its pit exposed. "We could go blue now if you wanted, though I sort of feel like we should be beyond that."

A familiar pressure built at the back of my throat. I tried to look at myself in the mirror, but the glass was jacketed in steam and refused to bare my reflection, as if I suddenly did not exist. I popped the pit out of my avocado and mashed the soft flesh with my fork. At some point Jess turned off the tap.

"Are you okay?" she asked.

"Yeah, fine." My voice stuck in my throat, and I didn't turn, afraid if I met her gaze I would begin to weep. I'd never been much of a crier and was surprised by the urge. I used the side of my hand to swipe a clear patch of glass on the mirror and focused on spreading the avocado across my face, covering my skin in thick green pulp. Jess left the tub then and hugged me from behind, her chin hooked over my shoulder as a heavy, dooming heat collected behind my eyes.

"Are you upset it's a boy?" Her voice was gentle, soothing, my favorite edition of her.

I shook my head. "No. Well. Yes. It's not that. It's just. I thought it would take longer, with Theo, you know? To find something?" I could feel Jess's breath on my neck. I began to cry. "It just feels like so much? All at once?"

Jess gently lifted the avocado skin from my hands and placed it on the counter. "It is, I know," she said, and the sweetness of her tone, the way it felt so good to be held, made me cry harder, my body shuddering as she squeezed tighter, her mouth pressed against my shoulder.

"Oh god," I laughed, wiping at my eyes. "Please don't ever tell him I'm crying about this."

★ ★ ★

Quincy came for dinner again and this time, he insisted on cooking. Taylor was working so it was just the four of us, and I sat in the kitchen as Quincy made baked macaroni and cheese from scratch, watching in half horror as he sank an entire stick of butter and most of a brick of sharp cheddar into the dish, which came out of the oven crisped and golden and delicious. I wasn't quite sure who he was trying to impress, all of us most likely, but it ended up being Theo, who made obscene noises while he ate, pausing to make comments like, "Man, you're going to make us all fat."

Jess had been surprisingly pleasant all evening and I looked at her then, expecting her to reprimand Theo for being phobic, but she just looked up from her plate and said, "Everything that feels good should be good for you."

Quincy had been predictably excited about the gender reveal. I'd told him over the phone, bundled in a towel on Jess's bed as she drained the tub in the bathroom. *That's great*, then backtracking, turning it into a question. *Of course*, I'd told him. *Of course*.

"So, Quincy Jones," Theo said then. "Quite a name to live into."

Quincy sighed. "I know. Especially for someone so embarrassingly white."

I turned to Jess. "Did you know who that is?"

"Of course," she said. "Did you not?"

I shook my head as Theo said: "Did your parents do that intentionally?"

"Surprisingly, no. They are also embarrassingly white." I held my plate up then so Jess could pile another serving of macaroni onto it as Quincy put his fork down and asked, "Hey so, can I ask, what's up with the telescopes?"

Oh fuck. I froze. Across from me, Theo caught my eye, sucking his lips into his mouth. We both looked to Jess, bracing for impact.

"What about them?" Her voice was dangerously measured. A smile there. A trap.

"I mean, what's the issue? Aren't there already like a dozen up there?"

Jess clasped her hands below her chin. "Don't they have reservations in Montana?"

"Ah," Quincy said. "So, it's political."

"Of course it's political."

Quincy nodded, then said, "Okay, I get the land thing, I do, but for the sake of scientific progress, we're talking about a major setback, I mean, years of—"

"Western oppression?" Jess cut in. "Two *decades* of gross mismanagement of the *thirteen* telescopes already up there? *That's* what we're talking about. No one is against the *science*. And don't give me any bullshit about job creation, because we all know they're going to *import* all of the top-tier positions—" she paused so this landed with Quincy the way she meant it to "—and hire locally for janitors."

Quincy ticked his head to the side, a half smile on his face.

"You know who manages the project, don't you?" Theo asked.

Quincy shook his head.

Theo glanced at Jess as if passing her the baton. "The university," she said, with a palpable degree of complacency.

"Ah." Quincy raised his eyebrows. "They certainly didn't mention that during orientation."

I braced myself again for whatever snarky response Jess would inevitably come out with, but she just lifted her shoulders and let them drop, and I understood then that she was trying, in her own way, to temper her outburst, was managing herself on my behalf, and I felt a gust of affection so overwhelming I brought my empty fork into my mouth and pressed my tongue against its smooth metal barbs as silence hung between us, seasoned only with the satisfying clink of cutlery on plates.

18

J

Fall greets the island quietly. Daylight contracts. On the second Tuesday of September Theo's offer was accepted on the house by the university. His close was set for mid-October, and when I told Ren her face folded in like the wing of a small bird.

That week, Quincy emailed over his list of needs and wants, which I let sit in my inbox for over an hour before opening it. They turned out to be pretty minimal. Needs: two or three bedrooms. Good light. A yard.

His want list contained only one thing, an ocean view, and afterward he'd written *ha!* in parentheses as if to belittle his own desire.

I wondered if he was purposely trying not to be difficult.

The first place we looked at was dated, but the family had young children so things felt as if they had been staged specifically for us. A bedroom painted blue. A basket of Legos tucked beneath the coffee table.

Quincy walked around it with a particular bounce.

Like he'd had several shots of espresso.

"My folks are gonna come out in March," he said, touching a set of window blinds. "My mom's like, totally stoked. You'd think she'd be grandmothered out already, what with my sister's kids. Maybe there's no such thing."

"Well. They'll be the only set of grandparents, so enthusiasm is probably a good thing."

His face clouded with embarrassment then and I felt almost bad. We stood in the living room in a narrow bed of sunlight. It was the first time we'd really been alone together other than the day in my office and oddly I felt almost comforted.

To engage with him in a situation I had long ago mastered.

A transaction I understood.

It was much easier than looking at him across the kitchen table and wondering what he was doing there. As I was thinking this he said, "I feel like I always say the wrong thing with you." He watched my face carefully as he spoke.

I couldn't place what wrong things he could be referencing so after a moment I said, "I think we're all just doing our best given the situation."

Quincy smiled. He walked past me then.

In the hall, he opened a shallow linen closet.

Stuck his head in briefly, then closed it.

Moved further toward the bedrooms and disappeared.

"Hey," he called from somewhere else. "Do you really think the nuclear family is just a feeder for capitalism?"

His voice led me down a narrow hallway. "I think almost every aspect of modern American life is just a feeder for capitalism."

I found him standing in the middle of the master bedroom, low-ceilinged and dark. He said, "You mean like mortgaging a house I can't afford?"

I laughed despite myself. "At least houses have use value *and* exchange value."

"At least." He moved to the small window and looked out. "It's good we're doing this together, then."

"What, signing you up for two decades of debt?"

"Taking on the man with a variety of options for free child-care."

"Right, well. You weren't in the original plan, sorry to say."

"So I've been told."

"What *have* you been told?" I tried to keep my tone light, though my curiosity was abruptly inflamed.

Quincy held my gaze longer than he needed to. "Just that the two of you had it covered. That I could come along if I liked."

I felt relief then. Like the night of Theo's party when Ren had turned away from her own reflection to say *of course I'd have told you. Of course.*

Quincy left the window, sat on the edge of the bed and gave it a jounce as if testing the mattress. "I mean, I was honestly surprised when Ren messaged me. It'd been so long since I'd seen her, I thought, that was that, you know?"

I had been leaning my head against the doorframe but pulled myself up straight. "Wait, sorry. *She* messaged *you?*" The ease I'd felt seconds ago was immediately replaced with that familiar, thrashing hum.

He stopped bouncing. "Yeah…why?"

When I got home the living room floor was flooded with books, magazines, movies. As if our entertainment center had exploded.

"How'd it go?" Ren called from the center of the mess, her back to the door, Sookie beside her. At the sight of me, the dog's tail metronomed against the wood. Ren wore a T-shirt with the neck cut out and it draped down over one shoulder. The exposed patch of skin made her look childlike, somehow. Vulnerable.

I hung my keys on their hook, looked at Ren's bare shoulder and said, "Why did you lie about messaging Quincy?"

She straightened but didn't turn. Sensing tension, Sookie's ears pricked up to form two singular quotation marks around her head.

I moved to the couch and sat.

Ren still hadn't turned to face me.

She fingered the dog-eared corner of an old Philip Roth I didn't know we owned. When she spoke, her voice was careful and quiet. "Because I knew you'd get mad."

"But I was already mad." I shifted to the floor beside her. Picked up a dusty *Architectural Digest*. Rolled it up and tapped it gently against her knee. "You can tell me things, you know. If I get mad, then we'll deal with it."

She nodded and her eyes met mine and held on, her mouth twisting. She was relieved, I could see. After a moment she broke her gaze. "I should have just told you when I found his note."

"I still haven't seen it."

"His note?"

She was off the floor then.

Gone a moment and then back with a small green slip in her hand.

His business card was a trendy square shape.

On the back he'd written *Don't b a stranger*.

I thought of Quincy in that empty kitchen telling me he always said the wrong thing.

"Romantic," I said, handing the card back. She laughed and it felt good, both of us laughing. "I wish you could have seen him today. He seemed so nervous. Excited. He'll probably be a really great dad." Ren glanced at me quickly, her eyes round and suddenly slick, and for a moment I thought she might cry but she didn't. Just rubbed the tip of her nose. I unrolled the magazine I was holding, the issue almost ten years old. "So, what's happening here?"

"Since Theo's leaving, I thought it'd be a good time to inventory our stuff."

"Does this mean we can get rid of things?"

"Yes but—" She lifted the magazine gently from my hand. As if it were fragile. Or I was. "Not these. They might be worth something."

I laughed. Picked up another issue. "No one wants decade-old issues of *Arch Digest*, I assure you."

She grabbed the magazine out of my hand and whacked me gently on the thigh. "What do you know?" She smiled. "You don't know anything."

R

I gave my two weeks' to ChaCha the final week of September. It was early technically, but I was exhausted, and even though the bar top hid my stomach from certain angles, the idea of working much longer felt uncomfortable in every sense of the word. ChaCha smiled sadly when I told her, a smear of mascara under one eye, and said, "Well, we had a good run, didn't we?" as if I were an assassin who'd just been mortally wounded. Kekoa, too, took it like he knew it was coming, which of course he probably did, sitting outside on the edge of his stool, looking out into the drizzly street.

"We'll see each other round, yeah?" he said, flicking away a cigarette butt, and I nodded even though I wasn't sure if we would.

Forty minutes later, I turned from a bachelorette party to find Quincy smiling at me from the other side of the bar top. "This feels familiar," he said, rapping his knuckles on the stained wood. "Maybe I should carve our initials. Commemorate it."

"I think we did a pretty good job commemorating it."

"Fair."

I was surprised by how comforted I was to see him. I got out a fresh glass, poured him an IPA. "So, I gave my two weeks' notice."

"I know. Jess told me. How's it feel?"

"Terrifying."

"What?" Quincy wiped a shine of beer from his upper lip. "Why?"

"What do you mean *why*? This is my cash cow."

Quincy's face drifted into a look of surprise then, as if this hadn't occurred to him.

"What, you think I work here for fun?" I remembered Jess's comment at dinner about the telescope project importing all their higher-ups, and what she'd meant about Quincy as she said it.

"I don't know, maybe. It has a vibe."

"It sure does." I caught Kekoa watching us from his post by the door then, though he looked away as soon as our eyes met, and I thought about how the floor here was always sticky even freshly washed, how the neon signs never quite worked, the ceilings low, the cover bands cringey. I felt a specific tug of sadness then, an acute nostalgia, like a memory of standing in a place you loved for the last time, which was disorienting, because I hadn't left yet.

At night, Jess continued to narrate details about my pregnancy from the baby books, her voice laced with a special sarcasm, as if she wasn't taking any of it seriously, although I knew she was, because it was her idea to read them. Things between us had normalized, or, gotten as normal as they could be considering how un-normal everything was, but we'd stopped arguing and there was nothing left for me to avoid telling her because she knew everything, had stopped tensing every time Quincy came up in conversation.

"Oh, here's a good bit: while your baby is still receiving the majority of its nourishment from your placenta, it has started to ingest—and even breathe—trace amounts of your amniotic fluid." Jess flopped the book down onto her lap and looked at me. "What a little parasite."

I smiled. I had a mug of sleepy-time tea cradled in my lap, and Jess's room felt cool with the window open and the ceiling fan on. I sipped my tea slowly as she told me how my baby's spleen was producing blood cells, how it had developed bone marrow, and at some point, my tea gone, I lay down and closed my eyes and fell asleep to her telling me more about what was happening inside me.

In the morning we woke early and went across the street, a Saturday, the day still too young for tourists, just local families staking claim on the grass with plastic tables and canopied tents, their kids shrieking toward the break with bare feet. I'd never been much of a swimmer; I liked to wade in and stand. Usually

Jess teased me about this, she could swim miles if she wanted, but that day she stood next to me in her navy one-piece, the sun buttering our shoulders as the water lapped around my belly like a large animal.

I'd been thinking about money. Or, more accurately, I'd been *anxious* about money, a dilation of the brief conversation I'd had with Quincy at the bar. I knew Jess planned to help, and Quincy had offered, but what did help mean—how much and how often? It wasn't only money I worried about but my time, and the understanding it would soon be given one singular focus, and who would I become when I gave it all away like that? What would I do with myself? I told this to Jess, and she slapped at the water, sending disciplinary spray in my direction. "Something tells me you're going to be pretty busy."

"No, I know, but that's what I mean."

Jess had recently brought home a pamphlet about school districts and day cares, which was alarming. I hadn't expected to have to think about those things before the baby arrived, but apparently there were interviews, wait lists, not only for the day cares, but the pediatricians. The number of things I didn't know to think about only underscored the smallness of my own world, the meager tunnel I had created for myself, an earthworm burrowing to and from the gym and bar and home and back and nowhere else, oblivious to the expanse that existed outside the safety of my own sad little passage. I looked down at the bowling ball of my stomach protruding from my bikini bottom and thought how this was the most interesting thing that had ever happened to me, and even though I was genuinely excited about it, it also made me sad, because it was such an ordinary phenomenon. An everyday miracle. Something that had been happening to billions of women for billions of years.

Jess must have sensed something shifting in my brain because she reached out and grabbed my wrist gently, swung our arms back and forth between us. "Don't worry," she said again. "We'll figure it out."

19

J

It was Quincy who suggested we all go camping.

He liked the idea of sleeping out on the beach. "We don't have those in Montaner," he'd said in a mocking hillbilly twang before dropping back to normal. "Not real ones, anyway."

We were looking at a property in a subdivision twenty minutes from town.

A slab house grafted onto a thick slice of freshly poured concrete.

We stood together in the backyard, which was mostly gravel and had almost no mature plants.

"You'll have to run it by the boss."

"Funny. I thought I was."

We'd begun messaging frequently. Mostly about houses.

He'd send me listings he liked with a joke or a reference to the baby. Which bedroom would be the nursery or if the kitchen sink was big enough for bathing. "I doubt she'll trust you to babysit when it's still kitchen sink–sized," I'd written.

"I don't think a father watching his child really falls under the definition of *babysitting*," he sent back. "Even in a nonnuclear anticapitalist formation."

One morning I snapped a photo of Ren's belly as she poured herself a bowl of Cheerios and sent it to him. "Good morning from your progeny."

It became a thing.

"Show me my baby," he'd write, and if I was home, I'd sneak a picture of Ren's stomach and send it.

Most of our interactions centered around Ren. Or a literal offshoot of Ren.

It was the same when we were looking at houses.

Were the stairs safe?

Did the yard have room for a swing set?

Quincy had built one for his sister's kids and was excited to do it again.

He suggested we plan a shower for Ren.

This embarrassed me because I hadn't thought of it.

It also embarrassed me because I had no real interest in planning a shower, which was likely why I hadn't thought of it. I'd been to exactly one baby shower, for Lisa when Kayson was born. There were no men allowed and we sat around awkwardly watching Lisa open gifts. Later we ate cupcakes dyed blue and played a stupid game where we taped a paper plate to our foreheads and tried to draw babies on them. All of this while her husband drank beer by himself in the garage. I was not the least bit surprised when they divorced.

I told Quincy this and he laughed. "It won't be anything like that. Theo can make a cool playlist and I can develop a drink that describes Ren's personality."

"What kind of drink would that be?"

Quincy closed one eye as if he were thinking hard. "Something fresh and light, but with a fun twist."

"It should be a martini. She's been eating olives by the jar lately."

"I don't think Ren's salty enough to be an olive."

"You would know," I said, and watched his face go a little pink.

We decided the shower would work best as a surprise.

Later he emailed me an article titled "Twenty Best Baby Shower Games" with the note "Jesus, these sound awful." The list included sampling varieties of baby food and guessing the prices of baby items like a maternity-themed *The Price Is Right*.

He followed that one with a list of his own game ideas: writing down common baby-care questions and trying to think of the worst possible bits of parenting advice for them. Pregnant Twister, where you ask guests to wear a fake belly and pretzel themselves up for sport.

"Is that meant to make us empathize?" I asked.

"Honestly I just want to wear the belly."

Having our interactions rotate exclusively around Ren or the baby relieved immense pressure.

Like having a difficult conversation while driving.

The movement of the road a welcome diversion.

A joint focal point.

Something soothing to look at so we could distract ourselves from what was actually happening.

R

I'd sort of thought Theo would say no to the idea, what with only a few weeks before his move, but he seemed to view the camping trip as tandem to the move itself somehow, one last household activity, the closing of a chapter, a celebration of his departure. He took charge of the food, and I aired two sturdy old tents out in the driveway while Quincy made reservations at a spot on the southern end of the island, a campsite with toilets, hot showers, and dolphins that occasionally swam in the bay at sunrise, but it was Jess who surprised me the most by taking the entire weekend off.

She'd made a reservation at a doggie day care she recommended to clients, and Thursday night we sat on the floor with Sookie between us showing her photos of the place and telling her in calm, soothing tones how much she'd like it, with other pups to play with and big soft beds for sleeping, a show for the dog that was really reassurance to us.

Quincy arrived on Friday afternoon in his new car, a chunky white Honda Element that wasn't actually new but was new to him. He'd finally let go of the rental Jeep, and I felt dented over the loss of it. The vehicle had become almost synonymous with his presence, and seeing it reminded me of that day in August when it first pulled into the drive, and I walked down the stairs to change his life.

I rode shotgun while Quincy drove, a coconut-scented air freshener wobbling from the rearview mirror. In the back, Taylor had wedged himself between Theo and Jess, who spent most of the drive complaining from either side about Hawai'i's reliance on imported food.

"For fuck's sake," said Theo, "we ship our cows to the mainland to be slaughtered and sent back."

Quincy glanced in the rearview mirror. "That can't be true."

"Google it, man."

"Yeah, google it, man," I echoed, and Theo kicked at the back of my seat.

We neared the beach just before sunset, winding our way down a two-mile road so steep it felt like we were descending to the end of the world. "Whoa," Quincy kept saying as he navigated. Even his air freshener trembled. To our right, a few fat cows milled around a fenced pasture and, to our left, a jarring drop-off, just the ocean and its endless, overwhelming blue. At the bottom we crawled slowly through a row of wind-washed houses, their wide lanais stuffed with broken furniture. It was just before six and the light was doing its golden hour thing, everything it touched looking a bit royal.

"Whoa," Quincy said again.

The beach itself was a quarter-mile strip of blond sand, nothing like the dark pebbled shoulders on our side of the island, and Quincy signed in while the rest of us unpacked the car and staked out a spot. Jess wouldn't let me carry anything more than my own backpack and bedding. "Pregnancy hernia," she said when I tried to lift a cooler from the trunk of the car.

Returning from the check-in station, Quincy watched her walk off before turning to me, his brows drawn. "Is that a thing?"

We chose a spot right on the edge of the beach, a row of outrigger canoes resting in the sand nearby. There were just a handful of others there, a group of college kids spread noisily over the center and a young mother with a toddler and an older woman, obviously her own mother—she resembled the younger woman so closely it was like looking into her future. When I passed them on my way to the bathroom the younger one caught my eye and smiled, her girl moving slowly through the sand at her feet, and a lightness spread through my limbs, a ball of joy so acute it felt as if I could press it tightly to my chest.

When I returned from the bathroom, Jess was unfolding the spidery legs of our tent. Quincy had brought a Frisbee, and after the tents were set up, the three of us threw it back and forth as Theo got dinner going, Taylor plucking at his little brown ukulele.

"Do you sing?" Jess asked him, spinning the Frisbee toward Quincy without looking at him.

"Only when Theo makes me."

"Too bad."

Taylor smiled. "You wouldn't say that if you heard it."

I'd never seen Jess play Frisbee before, she usually rolled her eyes at any suggestion of group activity, but she stood with her feet in the sand and tossed the orange disc back and forth without a trace of irony. Between throws I scanned the waterline for the rolling backs of dolphins but saw nothing but whitecaps, which caught the light and threw it back out at us like a million tiny mirrors.

The game disbanded, and I popped into my tent to grab a sweater, then sat in the sand with my arms wrapped around myself, listening to Taylor's ukulele and trying not to think about anything worrisome—like childbirth, or how I might pay my bills—but attempting to avoid those thoughts only kept them front and center, a wound in my mouth I couldn't stop tonguing, and Quincy must somehow have picked up on my frequency because he zipped himself out of his tent, sat next to me, and said: "So I was thinking, about what you said about work." It took me a moment to place the reference, our conversation at the bar. "They're actually expanding the dance program at the university next year," he was saying. "I don't know if you have an interest, but I'd be happy to make an introduction."

I looked away. The air around me was cool and glittery, and I could smell the charcoal from someone else's grill. "I highly doubt I'm qualified."

"No?"

Actually I didn't know what type of qualification you needed, but before I could ask, Jess called out, "Ren is uncomfortable with upward mobility." I turned to see her a few feet back, slicing limes at a picnic table.

"I'm not," I said. Jess looked at Quincy and rolled her eyes and I felt oddly comforted, the two of them ganging up on me, a new united front. "I just don't think the university would hire me."

"Well, they hired me."

"How devastating for your YouTube career," Jess said. This tease was not dissimilar to the one she'd used the day we'd built our garden beds, but her tone was entirely different, more shove and less blade, and I was struck by how time could take the same words and make them mean something else.

Quincy groaned. "The kids in my class did those, I swear."

"Black gold," I crowed, the same way I had to Jess months ago, and Quincy covered his face with his hands.

Theo'd used one of the park's cinder block grills to heat chili and cook potatoes in foil. We ate facing the sunset, which was much more of a spectacle than it ever was on our side of the island, and next to me, Quincy wiped his chin with the back of his hand and said, "Whoa," and I thought: *This could be the shape of our family.*

J

There was no service at the beach. This meant I had to forward calls and texts to Kim for two full days, which made my chest all tight and swarmy.

Outside that, the trip was smooth and soft and surprisingly pleasant.

That first morning I woke early to run, sneaking past Ren as she slept on her side with one fist curled in front of her face.

No one else was out yet, the horizon threaded pink and gold. I checked the coast for dolphins or whales but saw nothing.

I ran hard along packed sand strewn with bits of things the ocean had left and would later reclaim. Seaweed snarls. Broken shells. Plastic.

I pushed past flats of black lava rock where salt water gathered in low pools.

Past the little beachfront bungalows, families asleep inside.

Past a pack of hairless dogs who sniffed the feet of a battered grill with coals still softly smoking.

Past an auntie in a worn purple muumuu sipping coffee on a sagging lanai. Her face was deeply grooved, and she didn't look at me at all as I crossed. She sat like a statue. A deity.

I'd been put in charge of the guest list for Ren's shower. So far it read Quincy, Theo, Taylor, Ren's boss from the bar, that bouncer who had a crush on her, and me. Making this list of the important people in Ren's life was a weird exercise because mostly when I thought about people important to Ren, I thought only about myself.

Eventually the sand gave way to a rocky break, and I turned back. As I neared the campsite, I noticed a familiar silhouette crouched on the lava with his elbows resting atop his knees. I ran the back of my hand along my hairline to clear it of flyaways as I approached.

When I was just a few feet away he lifted his face. "Well," said Quincy, "aren't you a masochist."

From his hunkered position I got a rare look at the top of his head where the hair swirled at his crown. The perspective was strangely intimate. I wiped my palms on my shorts.

"I thought I was the first one up," he said.

"You thought wrong."

"I'm used to that." He smiled then and I became aware of how covered in sweat I was. He didn't seem to notice. Just nodded into the small pool by his side. "These are incredible, no?"

I looked down. The pool was still and empty. Nothing but the sun's flirtatious glitter along the surface, shadows yawning around the edges. I glanced with question to Quincy. "Incredible how?"

Quincy nodded his head to the side as if to suggest I should get down on his level.

I did. Squatted next to him and gave the water a good long stare. I was close enough to hear the gristle knuckling between his shoulders as he lifted his arms overhead, his gaze focused on the hollow basin.

"Is this some sort of meditation?"

"Shh."

I sighed, my quads burning in fiery protest. Then, just as I thought about standing again, everything began to move.

First a squat black crab darted from a rocky crevice.

Then another one.

Another.

My eyes adjusted and I realized with a start that they were everywhere.

A dozen crabs. Two dozen maybe. They scuttled left and right through the shifting shadows. I saw, too, that what I'd mistaken for the reflection of the sun was a pod of tiny fish, their silvery bodies catching light and throwing it back in such a fashion you couldn't even tell they were there.

I took a tight sip of air and Quincy laughed. "Right?"

I felt stupid then. My shock so obvious. I watched the crabs scurry, the fish dash, everything that had seemed one way a moment ago now completely different.

I stood then and the pool again appeared empty.

I squatted and stared, and as my eyes adjusted, things began to dance.

I stood and it ceased. Just a bare puddle again.

I felt disoriented. Drunk.

"Magic," I said.

"Attention," he corrected me, and I started to laugh until I saw the thin straight line of his mouth. "Do you like David Foster Wallace?"

"Sometimes." I didn't want to admit I had no clue who that was.

"Sometimes," he echoed. "Well, he has this story about these two fish swimming along in the ocean. Young fish. Adolescent, in their punk preteen fish stage, you know." Quincy picked up a smooth pebble. "So, they're swimming along one day, and they pass an older fish coming in the opposite direction, and they nod at him to be polite, cause, they're not bad fish-kids, they know how to interact with their elders. So the older fish nods back and says, 'Morning, boys. How's the water?'" Here he made his voice go thick, and I thought this must be how he entertained his college kids. He continued, "So, the two young fish just nod politely and swim on, but when they're far enough away, one looks over at the other and goes, 'What the hell is water?'"

"Cute."

"Ah." He smiled. "My one true ambition." His eye caught mine then and there was a disorienting swoop in my center.

We watched the pool for a while longer, then stood in wordless agreement and walked in silence toward our campsite.

Inside our tent, Ren slept in the same position I'd left her in, a single fist still guarding her face. I tried to change into my bathing suit as quietly as possible. This was difficult as the tent wasn't tall enough to stand in and my body was covered in sweat. I lay on my back and wiggled out of my damp sports bra. My nylon shorts.

My swimsuit was rolled halfway up my torso when Ren
stirred. "What time is it?" she asked. Her voice was rough and
pulpy.

"I have no idea." My phone was stuffed inside my bag on
airplane mode. Thinking about this made my chest go tight
again, and I wondered if I should drive to the top of the hill to
check in with Kim.

Ren smiled. "How nice." She stretched her arms overhead
and gave a sigh, and I let thoughts of calling Kim slip away. Ren
started to untangle her hair, occasionally snapping off tiny knots
which she discarded on the floor of the tent.

I wanted to take her to the little tide pool and show her its
special sort of magic. I wanted to tell her Quincy's story about
the fish. How serious he'd looked when he said *Attention.*

Instead, I unzipped the tent.

I'd hoped the dolphins would make an appearance, or a whale,
but when I scanned the horizon line for their rolling presence,
I found nothing.

In the ocean, I wore an old pair of goggles Theo'd found beneath the house, and when I opened my eyes everything was a
dark blue-green like looking through a beer bottle.

I swam and thought about the puddle of water filled with secret life that wasn't so secret if you knew how to look.

Side to side I pulled myself across the bay, and when I stopped to
look back at the shore there was Ren with her ankles in the water.

Even from a distance I could see the swell of her stomach.

She held a bright red coffee mug in one hand and lifted the
other to wave.

20

R

Theo moved out on the second Sunday of October. Quincy came to help pack boxes into a rented U-Haul, and I spent the afternoon trying not to cry. I didn't know why I was so upset, considering that I liked his new place and was excited for him, for Taylor, excited too about setting up a nursery in his old room, but even so, as Quincy and Theo crab-walked a dresser downstairs, I had to squeeze my eyes shut in stubborn defiance.

Under the house, Taylor crouched down to tie fabric around the legs of a chair, a stripe of cherry-red boxers peeking from above his faded jeans, the shiny fabric catching the afternoon light. I wouldn't have pinned him for a silk underwear kind of guy, which showed how much I knew. I taped up another box then, this one containing a set of pans I was pretty sure were a Christmas gift Theo had given to Jess, but I said nothing. Let him have the good cookware. He was the one who used it. I'd miss that most of all, I realized, and then felt embarrassed over my own selfishness. But it wasn't just that I liked having someone cook for me; food was the affection my brother knew how to give, and it was something that always made me feel cared for. I watched Taylor toss his hair from his eyes and imagined the two of them having dinner alone in their new kitchen, or a barbecue on the big patio out back. Good for them, I told myself, though it didn't feel good at all.

I squatted low, knees on either side of the box of cookware, *KITCHEN* on the side in Taylor's looping cursive, and lifted. I'd taken only two steps before Quincy said my name, his feet slapping the pavement as he approached. "Lemme get that," he called, arms already extended.

"I can carry a box," I objected, twisting away from his reach.

Jess walked by then with a floor lamp. "Here. Trade." She put the lamp down and took my box with a firm tug before looking at Quincy, who nodded in approval.

"Pregnancy hernia," he said.

I rolled my eyes in mock exasperation, but Quincy just smiled and watched Jess walk the box off toward the truck. Once she'd disappeared, he turned back to me and asked if I'd thought any more about the UH job.

I looked away. "Oh, I don't know. Even if I was qualified, I doubt they'd even consider me, given my state."

"That would be discrimination, wouldn't it?" Quincy massaged his elbow with his opposite hand. "And besides. The expansion isn't happening until next fall, and you're an alumna, right? That'd give you an edge, I'm sure."

I hesitated, rubbing my hand along the crest of my stomach. It was Jess who had brought up the qualifications. I'd never taught at an institution, and it'd been a decade since I'd even got my teaching certificate, which it turned out I hadn't even needed for Ralphie's.

"Just let me put your name in."

I fidgeted, pressing my thumbnail into the pad of my pointer finger. I wondered again if Quincy was thinking about Jess's comment about the university and the telescopes, about how they always imported their better-paid positions. If he felt guilty for being imported himself and was trying to give back in a way. I could have reminded him that I was also imported, but didn't. In truth the idea of teaching was exciting, but I didn't want him to know that, because it felt like cracking my ribs open and showing him something wet and pink and internal. "You sure you're comfortable with that level of nepotism?"

"Please, there's nothing wrong with a little of that. Right, Theo?" Quincy called. "Isn't that how you got your job?"

"What?" Theo dropped down from the truck and came toward us, wiping his hands on his jeans.

"Nepotism. Isn't that how you got the job with Jess at Paradise?"

"Psh. I got the job because of my excellent salesmanship." Theo flashed his teeth. "Also, because Jess is low-key in love with my sister."

Quincy laughed. "Well. Who wouldn't be?"

I felt my face flush then and hid it by untangling the cord of the lamp Jess had left me with. When Theo walked off again Quincy took a step toward me. "Look," he said, voice low. "It's just putting your name in, okay? Please?"

Alright, I told him, turning. *Alright.*

J

Theo gone, Ren and I spent an afternoon transforming his room into the nursery. We stationed the crib beneath the largest window. Assembled the changing table. Leaned paintings against the wall to mark where we hoped to hang them.

At first this felt enjoyable. Soothing.

Then a weird thing happened.

Once the room was ordered, I stopped wanting to go inside it.

When I did, I was overcome by the disorienting sensation that the walls were moving in. Like I might somehow get trapped between them.

Theo's room—now the nursery—was rightfully across from Ren's, which I also avoided for its dizzying degree of chaos, and soon I found if I even neared that end of the hallway my chest would begin its boil.

At first I thought it was because Theo had left.

That I missed him or just disliked the forced change.

But I wasn't entirely sure.

On a Tuesday afternoon in mid-October I took Quincy to a three-bedroom twenty minutes up the coast. It was the first time I'd driven us to an appointment, and I was oddly aware of his hands resting on his knees with their large square fingernails.

The house was a decent size for a single dad.

Recently renovated.

Good wood.

But the ceilings were so low Quincy could place his palms flat against them, which he did, erect in the middle of the kitchen. "I feel like a giant in here."

"You are a giant," I said, and left the room.

The drive back felt too short.

I was overcome by an unexplainable resistance to returning to the office.

A precipitous urge to procrastinate though I wasn't sure what it was that I was procrastinating about. Out the window the ocean was so calm it looked like a sheet of plastic, and when we passed a sign for the botanical gardens I asked if he'd been yet. If he'd like to stop.

He looked at me for a long moment before nodding. "Yeah, alright."

The road to the gardens had a sign that read *Scenic Route.*

It was a wild, jungly thing.

Narrow and twisting with an umbrella of dense foliage over-head.

Halfway down we rounded a curve and nearly flattened two middle-aged tourists who had parked their rental along the weak suggestion of a shoulder. Out of the car, they stood in the middle of the pocked asphalt taking photos of the canopy above them.

I slammed on the brakes and the horn in concert. As we passed, the taller of the two pointed his camera directly at us and snapped the shutter.

We drove on a minute in silence before Quincy said, "It's weird to think we're stuck in a stranger's vacation photo now." He pressed his hand against the window. "Like bugs in amber."

I thought about the photos of Ren's belly I'd sent him over the last few weeks. Framed by the back of the couch. Pressing against the table. The bathroom counter. A disconnected sliver of her, and inside, a seed.

I refused to let Quincy pay the twenty-dollar admittance.

"I'll write it off anyway," I said, and he shoved his hands in his pockets as if he wasn't sure where else to put them.

The gardens stretched across several acres of lush jungle threaded with wooden walkways that groaned as you mounted them. Ankle-high signs named flowers and shrubs, and the light laced down through the trees, and together these elements lent the feeling that fairies weren't far off.

Quincy moved erratically through it all.

Stopping to carefully inspect the compact curl of a fern.

Bounding forward in a galvanic spurt as if through a door he'd been banging on.

Every so often he crouched low to take photos of tiny vulvic blossoms. I followed along behind, enjoying the wake of his excitement. It felt like a relief, somehow, to be out in the open.

In the center of the garden sat a cage the size of a two-car garage, inside of which lived a pair of large macaws feathered in cheerful blues and yellows.

When Quincy came near with his phone raised for a photo, the smaller bird bounced from one foot to the other. "Hey mister," the creature creaked, pausing dramatically before poking a stubbed tongue from its shelled beak.

Quincy laughed and took a photo.

"Hey mister," the bird called again, hopping in a tight circle on its prehistoric feet. "Mister, mister, mister."

"What a flirt," Quincy said, returning his phone to his pocket.

We walked on. The path before us was covered with soggy heart-shaped leaves the size of elephant ears and Quincy held one up to his face. *"Colocasia gigantea,"* he said, and I rolled my eyes and pushed ahead, where the path began to snake toward the coast.

"I've been thinking," Quincy started when he'd caught up, "how weird it is that Ren is having my baby, but I don't know her that well, when, you know her so well, right?"

I passed a small sign for a plant absurdly labeled the Wandering Jew. "And?"

"And, I don't know."

"Do you mean you, *the biologist*, think it's weird that nature doesn't give a crap about whether or not you know a person prior to reproduction?"

"I guess." He grinned sheepishly. "Yeah, I guess that's what I mean."

"I'm gonna leave that one alone."

He lifted his chin and laughed the same way he had that first night at the bar, and again I had that sense as if I'd won something.

"It's just kind of funny. From the outside, or even a legal standpoint, I would probably appear to be the more appropriate choice of parent, but that's really not the case at all."

"Honestly," I said, and then, before I could reel it back, "I'm terrified you *are* the more appropriate choice. That Ren'll decide I'm unnecessary." I surprised myself by saying this, and I seemed to have surprised Quincy too, because he stopped walking and turned to me with a look so serious I felt swiftly unmoored.

"But that's exactly how *I* feel," he said.

"What, terrified?"

"Of course. Generally and specifically. Ren doesn't need me. She has you."

This made me smile. "I'm glad we can commiserate, then." We began walking again. "Why didn't you want kids before? When you were married?"

"I did," he said, his voice quiet in a way that made me remember how I'd bullied him about his divorce that first night at dinner. "Oh, don't worry," he said. "It was eons ago."

"She's very pretty, you know."

"Who?"

"Your ex-wife."

"Jesus, let me guess, Facebook again?" Quincy laughed, and then, "She is, yes. I'll tell her you think so."

"She knows about all of this?"

"Oh yeah. We still talk. Hard to just turn that off."

"Not for some people."

"It is for me." He was a few steps ahead and looked back over his shoulder. "She was my friend first. We worked together. I think I asked her out like eleven times before she said yes."

"Persistent."

Quincy laughed. "Yeah, well. I tend to choose women who want nothing to do with me." He bent to the path and picked up a slim stick, which he began breaking into pieces. "I used to think I liked the challenge but now I think maybe I just hate myself." I looked at him to make sure he was joking but he just continued snapping his twig.

"What did you mean at dinner, when you said you didn't need to be married to get divorced?"

"You remember that?"

I remember everything, I wanted to say, but didn't.

"I guess I was thinking about common law. You and Ren are basically that by now, just, you know. Platonic." This made me smile. Quincy dropped the last bit of his twig onto the pathway and asked, "Are you nervous about it?"

"About what?"

His look was penetrating.

"I don't know, are *you* nervous about it?"

He smiled as if he'd caught on to a joke. "You really don't like to talk about yourself, do you?"

I shrugged.

"You must talk to Ren though."

"Well. Obviously."

"She's your person?"

I snorted. "My *person*?"

"You know. Everyone has that first person they tell when something happens. That first impulsive reach out."

"Ren's definitely that, yeah." I stepped over a rotting log that had fallen into the path.

Quincy stopped to drag it off to the side. "What about the things you can't tell her?"

"There isn't anything I can't tell her."

Quincy raised a brow.

"What?"

"Nothing," he said in a way that irritated me.

"Who's *your* person, then?"

"Well. It used to be Carrie." His ex. "My ex."

"And now?"

He thought for a moment and said, "Trees."

I sighed and walked faster.

"I'm serious," he called. "They never judge."

I was several yards ahead by then, so he had to run to catch up, and when he reached me he spoke a quiet, careful line: "So you'd tell Ren you're worried she'll prefer me to you?"

"That's not what I said."

"Close enough."

"Says the *scientist*."

He laughed like I wanted him to, but then his smile dropped. "Well, would you?"

"Of course I would."

This was a lie.

I would never tell Ren that.

I hadn't even realized I thought that until I'd said it.

Quincy reached out and touched my elbow and I startled. "Here. Come," he said, and pulled me toward the edge of the path.

"What? Where?"

"Just, come." He put his hands on my shoulders, stepping us off the pavement and around a thick patch of bamboo.

I glanced back, ferns shivering where our bodies had just passed through them.

"Oh, it's fine, no one's here." Quincy led us deeper into the thrush, past a dense row of rainbow eucalyptus, colors melting down like hot wax.

"I really don't think it is fine," I said, but inside me came a flicker of excitement.

Quincy stopped walking and released me.

The place where his hands had been felt warm.

We stood in a forest of spindly ʻōhiʻa trees, their lehua blooms sparking in needled red flares, like firecrackers. He pointed at the one closest to us. "Okay," he said. "Do you want to go first?"

I stared at him blankly.

"Go on. Tell the tree something."

His face was flat and open and earnest. I rolled my eyes.

"Come on, don't do that," he said. "Tell it something you can't tell anyone else."

"If I can't tell anyone else, then I certainly wouldn't say it in front of *you*."

Quincy grinned and held my gaze, and a small thrill striped my body from collarbone to belly button.

"Come on. One thing you can't say to anyone. Even Ren."

He stood only six inches away. If I dropped my eyes from his face I would be staring at the wall of his chest. I was abruptly overcome with a bizarre sensation. As if I were slowly filling with water. "There's nothing."

"You're so full of shit," he laughed. "I know there's something, we all have something."

My body felt engorged. "I don't."

"You do. Tell it about how you're scared I'll be a better parent than you. I like hearing about that."

I was so close to him that I could see the reddish-brown shadow of stubble above his lips, which were parted slightly and full in a way that was almost feminine. He was looking at me. His eyes were warm and eager.

My body began that staticky thrum. I had to remind myself to breathe.

"We shouldn't be back here," I said finally, and then I turned away before he could respond.

21

R

Jess helped me draft a resume so Quincy could put my name in with the university, looking over my shoulder as I typed, telling me the whole time not to get too excited, but they'd called me just a few days later to schedule an interview. I had no idea what it would be like, what kind of questions they would ask, and as I worked my way through a jar of kalamatas in the kitchen, spitting the pits into the sink, my fingers slippery with brine, I worried about seeming too pregnant, or too inexperienced, though I knew I was not inexperienced and there was nothing I could do about looking pregnant, because I was pregnant. I was overthinking it—it was just an interview after all, but I wished Jess was home so she could tell me these things, which was the only way I would believe them.

When the olives were gone I went into Theo's room, which I knew I should start calling the nursery now. I picked up a tangle of string and wood from the floor, a mobile with little hanging clouds meant to go above the crib, which we'd set by the window so light puddled onto its yellow sleeping mat.

The rocking chair Jess bought was still under the house in the carport, so I sat on the floor and worked on untangling the mobile, choosing one cloud and making my way down its thread. It was a meditative task, focusing on one knot at a time as I thought, not for the first time but with a new, staggering weight: Was I doing something stupid? The decision had felt so natural when I made it and because of that I felt, somehow, that pregnancy would feel natural as well.

But it did not feel natural. My body felt foreign, so much that I was constantly looking at pieces of myself and wondering who they belonged to, these puffed ankles, these striped hips. The sensation was nothing I could prepare for, as if someone I didn't know had moved into my house and convinced me that I was the one who did not belong. I was constantly googling the most insipid things—why were my gums bleeding, was it alright that my hands had started to bloat, would rubbing olive oil on my perineum actually reduce the risk of tearing, and if I did tear, what would recovery be like? These things felt so staggeringly intimate, yet there were entire forums dedicated to them, a whole rabbit hole of prenatal neurosis I could fall into whenever I liked, but none of these things actually answered my question, which was: Could I give this kid everything he would need? Was I even giving myself everything I needed? Had I ever?

It was dark when Jess got home, just after six, but I'd already taken a long bath in her tub and curled myself up in her bed. She called my name from the living room and immediately I felt soothed, then ashamed—how childish to feel so comforted by someone else's presence, as if I was the one who needed a mother and not the one about to be a mother herself. I didn't respond, just listened to the excited clack of Sookie's hello, the jangle of Jess's keys. I let her call my name all the way down the hall.

"Oh. Hi," she said when she finally found me, in her bed with the lights off. She looked lovely, a particular flush to her face, and I wanted to ask her where she'd been but didn't want to feel needy, so instead I told her she looked pretty and watched her turn away as she said, "Have you eaten?"

I shook my head, and she asked if I wanted her to make me something. We were suffering without Theo although neither of us wanted to admit it. I must've nodded yes because she left the room.

I lay in her bed feeling too warm, and when I kicked my feet out of the covers they were swollen, purplish, the magenta polish I'd put on my toes months ago ragged, half-grown-out. I couldn't even take care of my own feet, I thought. When Jess came back in with a plate of peanut butter toast, I sat up to eat it, carefully holding the plate to catch the crumbs, thinking how she would never have let me eat in her bed this time last year.

"Would you like to know what piece of produce he is this week?" she asked, opening up one of the baby books.

"A cauliflower," I said. I'd already checked.

She put the book down then, and I could feel her examining me, so I focused on my toast. I could take this piece of crisped bread, chew it up really small and then swallow it. I could do these things all by myself, and I knew what would happen before I did it, and after I did it.

"Is everything alright?" The concern in her voice made my throat clog up, and I stared at my plate as pressure began construction behind my eyes. Jess nudged me a bit with her shoulder then and said *hey*, softly.

I wanted to tell her how I couldn't stop thinking about my body splitting open, how I had no idea how I would manage this, how it had seemed so much simpler in theory, but instead I looked at her and said, "I can't even remember to paint my toenails," and immediately began to cry.

"Oh," she said with a sort of gentle surprise as I looked down at my inflamed feet with their chipped nails, those feet that looked like someone else's feet, and this made me cry even harder. I was still crying as Jess got up, disappearing into the bathroom and returning with a bottle of Cutex, a sleeve of cotton rounds, and a glass bottle of magenta polish, that same happy shade of berry I'd used on myself back in July. She got to work down at the end of the bed, turning those little cotton clouds bright pink, discarding them in a neat pile on the bedding as the room filled with the scent of acetone and I returned, toe by toe, to a feeling of warm, swaddled security.

J

On Sunday I drove Tatia Chen to a property thirty or so minutes toward Volcano. "Have you thought any more about the
book idea?" she asked as soon as she was buckled in.

I had not thought about it.

Actually, I had forgotten about it completely.

"Honestly I think we're both a bit too private for that."

"Ah," she said with a shrug. "You know yourself best."

I hadn't heard from Quincy since the botanical gardens days
earlier. This morning I'd sent him an article about city officials
in Melbourne who assigned email addresses to specific trees
around the city. They did this so citizens could report problems.
Instead everyone began to send love letters to their favorite trees.

In the body of the email, I'd written: *Guess you're not alone.*

That was six hours ago.

He had yet to respond.

It felt like a breach of some contract.

I had no idea what that contract would be.

The house I brought Tatia to was the last of a string of four
we looked at back-to-back. Two stories surrounded by jaca-
randa trees so purple they looked like an oil painting and when
we pulled up, she made a quiet purring noise in the back of her
throat.

We spent an hour inside. The floors were bamboo, and the
windows were wide, and on her third walk through the kitchen
Tatia clapped and said, "It's perfect."

I waited for that caffeinated jolt of victory.

It did not come.

Instead, I resisted the urge to check my phone, flipping
through my folder as if I were looking for the right paper though
I already had it pulled to the top. "They're asking five-ten, and

they want you to cover the closing costs. We could leverage that, aim for fifteen under, they'll likely counter for ten—"

"Don't ask for less."

I looked up. "No?"

"No. Offer the full."

"You're sure?"

Tatia didn't answer, just twirled around the room again with her head back.

I saw a flash of the girl in her then.

Years melting away, excitement softening her like spring.

She grabbed the back of a chair. "Let's celebrate."

"Too soon."

"Forget that," she said, waving a hand. "Let's celebrate me making a damn decision. Come on. Drinks on me."

We didn't celebrate though. A line of business cards had already taken residence on the kitchen counter. There could be other offers in the works, I told her. We needed to be swift.

In reality it took me less than twenty minutes to put the offer in.

I did this at the office, then picked up a pizza.

At home I found Ren on the couch in the same oversized tee she wore to bed the night before.

"Thank god," she said when she saw the pizza.

Sookie lifted her head from Ren's lap, and the sight of them snug together, Ren's stomach a perfect orb beneath her dirty T-shirt, made my heart throb.

It was similar to how I sometimes felt early in the morning when the sun had barely risen, and the air was soft and the doves cooed and my bones ached with a longing that made no sense because it was a longing for the moment I was already in.

We ate pizza straight from the box while watching a romantic comedy shot on Oʻahu starring a famous white actress playing a character meant to be part Chinese Hawaiian. I kept my phone next to me and checked it three times.

Midway through the film I asked Ren if she'd heard from Quincy lately, keeping my tone flat and disinterested.

She shook her head. The muscles in her jaw worked through a piece of crust. On-screen a bunch of actors rode a helicopter over the jungle.

"We're supposed to see a house tomorrow morning," I said. "But he hasn't confirmed."

Ren peeled a mushroom off her pizza and nodded. I could tell she wasn't listening, the TV mirrored in her eyes. I hid my phone beneath a couch cushion as if that might help.

Later, as I was getting ready for bed, it pinged from my bedside table, and I wandered out of the bathroom with my toothbrush tucked into my cheek.

His response was longer than I'd expected.

Dear Ohia, the email began. I sat down on the bed. I've been thinking about you all day, and how glad I am that I walked off the trail to find you there, looking so pretty. I've been feeling very sorry that I tried to push Jess to talk to you though; I'd seen a small crack and was trying to wiggle my way into it, but now I see that was bullish. I know, Ohia, that if you could talk yourself, you would tell Jess that there is no way Ren would ever prefer me, because I am an oafish idiot, whereas she is brilliant and caring and funny. I know you would also tell her that she will make the most wonderful other mother, and that her son, just like Ren, and just like me, will be lucky. With affection, (the other, less exciting) Quincy Jones.

I read the email three times with my toothbrush pressed against my gums as my mouth filled slowly with saliva.

On the morning of Ren's interview, Quincy and I visited a little house that had been stripped of its furniture. This was likely the listing agent's attempt at making the space feel larger, but it also made it seem more masculine, and in its stark vacancy, I could see Quincy.

"I like this one for you."

"Why? Because it's tall and empty?" He stood at the base of a staircase that zigzagged up to a narrow loft.

I smiled. "Do you like it?"

"I do."

I moved into the kitchen then. A window above the sink peeped into the yard, a bit wild around the edges, kudzu vines set to invade. "Plenty of room for a garden," I called.

Above my head a floorboard groaned. Then another. Another. As if the house were stretching while Quincy moved through it. A post and pier cat rising from a nap.

I turned back to the yard and pictured a child running across it. "You'd want to put in a fence," I said loud enough so he could hear. "Maybe a swing set."

Maybe Quincy could build a patio.

Maybe he'd get a dog. Smaller than Sookie.

One a child could hold.

I heard Quincy on the bottom of the stairs. "There isn't much around here at this price point, so we'd have to move fast if we want it."

He didn't answer, and when I looked over, he was standing there with a curious, soft gaze. I had the same disorienting sensation I felt at the gardens, as if my body was filling with liquid.

I turned my face away. "I can call Betsy as soon as we leave so she knows." I could feel his eyes on me. My mouth kept filling with words. "We could even be dealing with multiple offers."

"Jess."

"She said they had a couple in this morning who were really interested. Maybe we could write you a short letter pulling the soon-to-be-dad card, we might have a clear shot—"

"*Jess.*"

His expression was cottony. His eyes toured my face. I looked down at the tile floor and imagined all the things that could shatter across it. "You'll want plastic dishware." He said nothing. Our silence became so big and hollow I felt the urge to fill it. "Have you ever held a baby?"

His face twisted up in curious amusement. "Yes, my sister has three."

"Right, sorry, I knew that."

"Have you ever held one?"

"No."

"Just treat them like they're expensive."

The kitchen was not wide. The space between us could be crossed with just a stride of his tree limb legs.

"Are you nervous?" he asked, and I didn't know if he was asking again about the baby, or something else.

"No," I said, and he squinted as if he didn't believe me. "How about the cabinets? They used to be trees, right? Should I talk to them about it?"

He laughed and I felt reassured somehow. I checked my phone for the time. Just before eleven. Just before Ren's interview. I thought about us eating pizza on the couch. How the evening had felt so uneventful in the best kind of way. Moments to build a nest from.

Things would be alright. I understood that.

She would have a good interview, or she wouldn't.

She would get the job, or she wouldn't.

We would find a new normal.

Quincy could hold a baby and I would learn.

Quincy would buy a house, maybe even this house, and in the backyard, he would build a swing set. A treehouse. A clubhouse.

He would teach his son about trees.

Ren would show him how to dance.

Maybe when he was older, I could take him running.

I thought about this and felt safe.

I looked to Quincy and smiled.

And he smiled back.

And I smiled wider.

A laugh was born deep in the center of me then.

I felt it rise through my stomach and up into my throat and just as the sound began to travel up my throat, Quincy took one giant step across the room and put his mouth on mine.

From outside came the long singular cry of a crow.

His mouth was soft, and we stood there for what felt like a full minute but was probably one slow-moving second. Time was gelatinous. Our bodies in a bowl of Jell-O.

Then something clicked in my brain.

A fast pop like the shutter of a camera and time righted itself.

The buzzing began in my body with such immediate intensity I nearly gasped. My hand found his chest and shoved. "What are you doing?" My voice came coiled and hissing.

Quincy blinked, once, twice, surprised or confused or embarrassed or all three. "Sorry, I thought. Fuck. I'm sorry."

I put my hand against my sternum and pressed hard to steady my own painful vibration. Quincy stared at the floor. It felt unreal that his mouth had just been on mine.

Finally, he said, "But you're the one I talked to that night."

"What *night*?" Even though I knew.

Hearing the venom in my tone, he looked up. "At the bar."

I laughed though nothing was funny. "So, you're saying, what?" He didn't answer. He looked a bit scared. "You're saying Ren was your second choice."

"What? Jesus, no. I'm saying—"

"Your third? Fourth? You're very entitled, you know."

He swallowed. "No," he said slowly. "I didn't know that."

I could tell he was frustrated, and it felt like a wall between us, which was what I wanted. I looked at the tile floor and pictured broken glass.

"You know," he said, "Ren picked *me* up."

I laughed a hot bullish breath of air and turned away so he couldn't see my face. The wall in front of me was white and empty.

"She picked me up. She did. And that felt nice, alright? That felt really nice, to be chosen that way."

"Did it feel nice for your girlfriend?" I folded my arms tightly.

"I didn't even know Tavi when I met Ren." His voice was low and slightly strained. "Actually, the thing with Ren made me feel a lot better about myself. Encouraged me to get back online. Tavi was the first woman I matched with, okay? I..." He paused there. "I've been mostly single for a decade."

"*Mostly* single." I felt my mouth pull into a sneer and I let it.

He was quiet, and then, "I'm not some kind of womanizer, Jess. This year has been wildly abnormal, trust me."

It was an odd feeling, standing there with him behind me. He could see me, but I couldn't see him. I held my shoulders perfectly straight.

When he spoke again, his voice came soft and low. "What I am trying to say is, Ren and I had a drunken thing. We all know that's what it was." I started to challenge this, and his voice rose. "I'm not saying I regret it, I'm not saying that at all, what I'm saying is, it was you that I was interested in. Right from the beginning."

There was a strange pulse beneath my skin.

He went on. "I tried to ignore it, you have to know I've tried."

An electric pressure was building from somewhere inside of me.

The filling of a hose with its nozzle closed.

"But I don't think..." He stopped. I heard him inhale. Exhale. The walls of my body seemed to shiver and bend. "I don't think you actually want me to ignore it."

I knew then that if I stayed in the kitchen I would burst. There was no other way to articulate the clear sensation that my skin could not contain me.

I left him standing there. Moved dizzily through the empty dining room and into a narrow bathroom off the hall. I left the door open. I stared at my own reflection as if it could tell me how to feel, and after what could have been five seconds or five minutes Quincy stepped into the room behind me.

His eyes met mine in the mirror and my mouth went immediately dry.

I waited for him to say something, but he did not.

Just stood there. Looking at me.

And then he took a step forward.

The space between us hummed like a microwave. A box of radiating heat that was so distinctly whole I felt if I turned around, I could hold my palm against it and push. I did not turn. I did not blink. I focused on breathing to make sure I still was. I could see both of our reflections, layered, a mosaic—my body, his body, glass. Nothing moved but his Adam's apple, bobbing slowly on a swallow.

He stepped forward again.

There couldn't have been more than two inches between us.

If I drew my shoulders back, they might touch his chest, and the thought dropped like a hot stone into my body and stuck.

He said my name. In the mirror I watched his lips form the shape of the word that meant me, and the pain intensified and I closed my eyes.

With my eyes closed, it was easier.

He exhaled then and his breath hit the back of my neck and I stopped thinking.

I stopped thinking and I turned.

I turned and I lifted my face.

I lifted my face and invited him to kiss me.

I invited him to kiss me and when he did my knees seemed to liquify and heat spread across my body and that tight, busy feeling vanished completely and from somewhere inside of me I heard, clearly as if it had been whispered into my ear: *This is what it is to be wanted.*

I spun around, my back pressed against his chest. I opened my eyes and watched in the mirror as he ran his hands over a body that looked like mine.

The effect was nothing like it had ever been before.

It felt old and new at the same time.

Like we had touched a thousand times before and also never.

It made no sense, and it made every sense.

There must have been some time then.

A reconfiguration, or several, the rustle of plastic, but all I remember is this: he said my name as he entered me, and a warmth opened in my center and moved outward like a burst of sunlight.

I heard myself cry out and did not recognize my own sound.

His mouth pressed down on my neck, and he said my name into my own skin like it was a secret.

In the mirror, I watched one of his hands cup my breast. My shirt was fully buttoned but my pants were on the floor.

He moved down to touch me and the light in the room grew brighter, almost blinding, and I closed my eyes against it.

He said my name twice more and when I opened my eyes, they met his in the mirror and I came, hard and without warning, my breath fogging the glass and the counter cool and smooth and solid beneath me.

22

R

My interview was with a woman called Marta who oversaw the Arts department, forty or so, with high cheekbones and photos of two young hapa girls in various stages of toddle hung in thick silver frames on the wall behind her. An enormous box fan hummed from the corner, moving Marta's hair around her face as she spoke. "So you teach at Ralphie's gym?" She asked this with genuine interest, as if Ralphie's was a reputable institution and not a sweatbox stuffed with equipment from the nineties.

"Right, I used to teach three times a week but right now I'm just teaching a maternity class." I focused on keeping my hands clasped in my lap and stripping any inflection from the end of my sentences, like Jess had coached. I'd expected her to text before my interview, had been surprised when she hadn't. She was showing a house to Quincy, knowledge that comforted me, as the more time they spent together, the calmer Jess was about his general presence.

"Maternity dance?" Marta asked.

"It's been surprisingly popular."

Marta sat back into her chair. "God, I'll bet, I wish I'd gotten to take a dance class when I was pregnant."

"Apparently it's the only one on the island. Maternity dance, I mean."

"And are you liking it?"

"Very much." Marta nodded, her gaze calm and steady, as if waiting for me to continue. "It's oddly...comforting," I went on. "To be around so many pregnant women at once."

"I can imagine." Her questions continued, warm and earnest, not only about my dance history or when I was due but how I was feeling, and whether it was my first pregnancy, and which day care I was hoping for, and within moments I felt at ease, like she were Mei or ChaCha, like we were chatting after class or behind the bar with Kekoa guarding the door. I'd been nervous before and I'd expected to remain nervous throughout. In some ways I'd wanted the whole thing to be terrible, and if not terrible then at least forgettable, so that I could pretend it hadn't happened, shield myself from disappointment when I heard bad news or, more likely, no news at all. I told her about Crazy Palms and how I didn't want to go back to bartending after my son was born, those words still so large and alien in my mouth, *after my son is born, after my son is born.* I watched her face to see if she could tell how unreal it all felt but she just nodded encouragingly and said, "Yes, I understand that, yes."

The backs of my knees were damp as I drove home with all of the windows down. In the kitchen I opened the fridge, half expecting to be greeted by plastic containers of grilled vegetables, roasted chicken, cold spaghetti, like when Theo was around. Instead, I found only the same meager contents I'd been disappointed by that morning: a jar of peanut butter and half a loaf of sweetbread, almond milk, a bag of apples gone mealy. At some point I should learn to cook, I told myself. Jess certainly didn't have the time for it.

I took a grapefruit from the blue bowl on the counter and went out to the back lanai to peel it, tossing its pretty pink skins over the railing. The palms Quincy planted in August had gained a bit of height, their earthy beds compressed from weeks of hot sun and hard rain, grass sprouting from bald ground where the mulch pile once sat, and I saw all this and thought about how nature had the ability to adapt to almost any situation, and how I was a part of that, too. I ate my grapefruit section by section and thought about the afternoon Quincy had given me those two orchid stems, one for me and one for Jess, how thoughtful that had been and how I'd been so worried that she'd never warm to him but now, just a season later, everything was different. I imagined the four of us together in a few years, across the street at the beach, Quincy and Jess sparring over something they'd heard on the news, me watching our son play in the grass beneath a little floppy hat. He'd be walking by then. Running. Talking. He'd have a name.

Out in the yard, the light moved from white-hot to a gentle gold. Beside me, Sookie sighed as if her day had been hard, and as I wiped sticky nectar onto my leggings I circled back to my interview and there, for the first time, I let myself imagine it: returning to the place where Jess and I had met, to teach a body of students that I had once belonged to, with a son I would love who had a father I'd never loved, a rhythm forming that was natural and warm, and together we would all move forward like the bamboo in the yard that shot ambitiously for the top of the fence without ever asking where it was going, only knowing with certainty that it could do nothing but change.

J

On the drive home I thought about Quincy's mouth.

When I woke that morning, it had just been a regular mouth.
A set of lips over teeth.

Now it sent a triangle of heat through my body, connecting the
point of each breast to the cleft where my legs met. The change
was so large I had trouble comprehending it. Quincy yesterday
and Quincy today felt like two entirely different people. So did I.

When I arrived at the house Ren was in the living room
watching a show about decluttering.

"Hiya," she called, and smiled with weighted parturition.

As if expecting me to report on something specific.

I walked over and gave her fingers a brief squeeze. They were
sticky and smelled of citrus and I wondered if Quincy's mouth
had ever built a triangle of heat in her body.

She was still looking at me in a pointed way, so I asked if she
needed anything and she said no.

I did not glance in the direction of the nursery as I moved
down the hall. I went into my room and stayed there.

I took a shower that was hotter and longer than it needed to be.

I emerged a mottled angry red and it felt appropriate.

Quincy texted me twice and I didn't respond.

I thought about how the buzzing in my chest, the painful vibration that I felt often, had vanished when he'd touched me.

I got in bed and stared at the ceiling fan.

My hair was wet, and I let it soak through my pillow and pretended to be asleep when Ren crawled in next to me.

After a few soft silent moments she said, "I had my interview today."

I winced, the obviousness of her behavior slamming into place.
She had been waiting for me to ask.

"I'm sorry," I said, shifting to face her. "How was it?"

She started talking about the woman who interviewed her. The department chair of some sort. Mary or Margaret. I punctuated the dark with the appropriate *mmm* and *ahh* noises but kept thinking about Quincy's mouth on my shoulder. My neck. I put my hand on the spots where it had been.

Soon Ren stopped talking.

I listened to her breath go slow and steady.

Only then did I roll back over and look at her face.

Soft and familiar in the dark.

Her eyelashes trembled delicately.

I resisted an odd urge to take a photo of her.

I could send it to Quincy.

Look what I am looking at, the photo would say.

It felt important. Triumphant.

I watched Ren's eyelashes and at some point, I fell asleep.

In the morning there was another text from Quincy that I did not respond to. I went into the office early and stayed there late. I kept my door closed and when Theo popped his head in I pretended to be buried in paperwork. Kim ordered me lunch. I did not eat it.

Around three p.m. the seller accepted Tatia's offer on the house with the jacarandas and when I saw it come through I felt nothing. No pang of satisfied victory. No involuntary tallying of numbers in my head. I stared at my computer. I stared at the wall.

I ignored four messages and a phone call from Quincy. Not because I didn't want to talk to him. I did want to talk to him.

I could pretend I was punishing myself but that wasn't it.

In order to punish myself, I'd need to feel guilty.

I ignored him because I did *not* feel guilty.

Guilty was the right way to feel, and I did not feel the right way.

I had the sensation that I was watching myself through a window. A window into my own home where Ren was swollen and sleepy and walking into my room wearing mismatched socks to

ask if I wanted toast or cereal, which really meant she was asking me to make her toast or cereal, which I did.

I made her toast *and* cereal and when she was finished, I
washed her bowl and dried her bowl and put her bowl away,
the whole time wishing I felt guilty.

Instead, it felt like what had happened in the bathroom of
that empty house had nothing at all to do with what was happening in my own house.

Nothing to do with me and Ren. Or Ren and Quincy. All
of it felt completely segregated. Like lines connecting pins on a
map that never crossed.

I knew this was not the case. I knew it as I rubbed Ren's feet
while Quincy texted apologies to my silenced cell phone.

What I knew was the exact opposite of what I felt.

I felt that I could do anything I wanted, and it would have
no impact on anyone else.

I swished mouthwash beside Ren in the mirror and savored
the burn, and when her eyes met mine in playful challenge, I
thought about how I came while I was looking at Quincy, who
was looking right at me. I spat before she did though I could've
continued. As she crowed her victory, I thought about how I
had never come in front of anyone else before. Had never felt
that kind of good beneath anyone else's hands. With Quincy it
had felt different because he was not a stranger but someone I
already knew.

This felt both safe and reckless.

I wiped my mouth on the little blue towel that hung on the
hook and thought about how more than anything else I wanted
to feel that way again.

No one needed to tell me it was a bad idea.

I knew it was a bad idea.

Unfortunately, it was an idea I continued to have.

23

R

With Theo gone, the house became a much quieter adaptation of itself. It had always been quiet during the day, those hours before or after my classes a still life painting I could walk through, but in the evenings, it had been loud, and this was because of my brother. Pans clanging in the kitchen, music blasting from his room, his body stretched out in the living room with the TV on. I missed his constant noise. I missed Taylor too, his softness, the way Theo seemed a bit looser when he was in the room, as if drunk off his affection, the addition of another person changing his entire alchemy. *Our* entire alchemy.

And of course I missed his cooking. Two days after my interview, there were still no groceries in the house and the single grapefruit that remained in the blue bowl on the counter had grown a large spot of soft white fuzz overnight, its sudden presence reminding me of winters in Virginia when I would fall asleep to nude ground and wake to snow. It made me feel incapable, that empty refrigerator. I could keep a job and a room-

mate for fifteen years, I could make myself a baby, and if I could
do all of those things, then I could certainly cook myself a meal.
It was just before ten in the morning and my day held no plans,
a wide empty horizon line. On impulse, I sent Theo a message
asking for the recipe of that salmon dish I loved, one he baked
in some kind of creamy sauce alongside little red potatoes. He'd
made the dish for me early in my pregnancy and I'd been too
nauseated to eat it, but standing there in the kitchen, I realized I
wanted not only to eat the salmon but also to cook it. I wanted
to cook it for Jess, who'd been so consumed with work the last
few days she'd barely been home. She often got like that during
her busy season, although her busy season was typically not in
October, and I realized I both wanted to do something nice for
her, and to prove that I was a competent human being.

When Theo responded with a link to the recipe, I headed
out to the car before I could change my mind. In the driveway
I texted Jess telling her I was cooking dinner and asking when
she'd be home, imagining what sort of snarky comeback she'd
deliver. You? Cooking? Am I dead? I backed out of the driveway feeling an inchoate excitement. This would be my life for a
few months. Carry my saturated body around the house, make
a meal from scratch, prepare for the unpreparable.

This feeling withered in the produce section, where I realized
I should've organized the recipe into a list of ingredients to make
things easier, and also, that I did not know what a leek looked
like. I stood by the lettuce and Google image–searched *leek*. Jess
still hadn't responded to my text about dinner, but when I located the leeks, I let myself snap a photo and send it off to her
anyway. *Step one*, I wrote. *Produce scavenger hunt.*

In a frenzy of optimism, I got not only what I needed for the
meal but a dozen or so other things that looked fresh: a little
box of blackberries, a container of arugula, a package of ali'i
mushrooms. As I waited in the checkout line the tall, bony
woman in front of me glanced back with that specific moony

smile certain women had begun giving me, my body a sym-
bol for something else, hope or nostalgia or something in the
middle. I cradled my box of expensive mushrooms, wondering if I used to give this look to pregnant strangers before I became one myself, deciding that I probably had, realizing too
that I couldn't imagine Jess giving that look to anyone. Yearn-
ing wasn't in her emotional vocabulary. I put a carton of full-
fat yogurt on the belt and imagined the kind of thoughts the
spectacled woman in front of me must be having about my life,
who she might imagine I was going home to with my bag of
fancy onion grass, my thick pink pieces of fish, my tiny round
potatoes. Whatever she imagined, I knew she was wrong, and
this gave me a yank of petty satisfaction. My life was interesting and unique, and my experiences did not fit into any stupid
little boxes. As the woman finished checking out, I looked at
my phone again—still no response from Jess.

J

Two days after the incident, Quincy showed up at my office looking unkempt. His shirt was wrinkled, and his eyes seemed oddly sunken, and I wasn't surprised he was there. It was ten in the morning on a day we'd scheduled a showing, but we'd made this plan before and now everything was different.

Kim had called to let me know he'd arrived, addressing him formally the way she always did. *Mr. Jones is here*, and my head went light like I'd had too much coffee.

I could have had Kim tell him I was unavailable. I could have stood and shut my door. My office was visible from her desk. He would see me do this and it would mean something.

Those were things I could have done.

Instead, I told Kim to send him in and she did.

As soon as I saw his shape in the doorway, I realized I hadn't responded to any of his messages so he'd be forced to come to me and I could pretend I'd had nothing to do with it. "Hi," he said, and I told him hi back.

I actually said that. *Hi back.*

"Can I close this?" He motioned to the door, and I nodded.

He took a seat across from me wearing a muddy expression. Guilt polluted with want.

I understood then that I had been seeing this expression for weeks.

Maybe longer.

That I had maybe even known what it meant.

That I had submerged this understanding so that I didn't have to look at it.

Had he not come to my office I'd have been both immensely relieved and brutally disappointed. I had never felt that way before. Thrillingly ill.

"I'm sorry," he started, but I waved him off.

An apology felt like an admission of fault, but the fault was shared. Equal. If anything, it was more mine. I should've been the one to apologize.

But I didn't.

I leaned forward and said, "So you know, we can't do that again."

He nodded.

The moment seemed to expand and contract between us like lungs.

I wasn't quite sure how to break it, so I just stared at him. His shirt was white and long-sleeved. It looked incredibly soft.

"I really want," he started, and then took a breath. "I really want to be a good guy."

I pressed my fingernail into the faux leather of my chair and thought about our conversation in the botanical gardens. How he chose women who wanted nothing to do with him. "I know," I said. "So do I."

I stood then. Picked up my slim black folder.

Signaled it was time for us to do something else.

He looked out the window as I drove. Small talk would've felt false, so we just stayed silent, and as we moved through the bayfront neighborhood, the view was so picturesque it stung.

Leggy palms straight off a postcard.

The ocean rippling gently.

The morning's beauty seemed almost cruel. Like it was taunting us.

The property had been vacant for a few months and contained that signature empty house smell. Cleaning products and freshly stirred dust.

The picture frames had their stock photography still intact, and we stayed at least three feet away from each other at all times.

I didn't point out the new appliances.

I didn't talk about the good wood floors.

As soon as he entered a room, I would walk into a different one and not think about his mouth on me or how I would probably never feel that way again.

To be wanted by someone I knew and to want them in return.

I opened closets and windows and pictured Ren at home on the couch with her feet up watching reality TV trash. Ren eighteen years ago tying her hair up with a thin silk scarf before she left for class, her eyes on her own face in the mirror. I had never been this kind of friend to her. The kind who did things that could gouge. And if there ever was a time for me to behave that way it was definitely not now.

Quincy wanted to be a good guy.

I wanted to be a good guy, too.

I stood in one of the smaller bedrooms and stared out the window. The yard was wide and unfenced. I did not populate it with swing sets or garden beds. Instead, I listened to Quincy's footsteps move around the house.

It made me ache in a way that was similar to how I'd felt the last forty-eight hours. Thinking about him while ignoring his texts.

Wanting him to call me and yet not wanting to answer.

Wishing he might walk toward me so that I could move away.

It was an overwhelming way to feel.

Down the hall his footsteps grew louder as if in direct response to my own thoughts. My rib cage frothed with that tight, buzzing panic, and as he entered the room, I understood: the problem was that I wanted two things but one of them was easier.

We watched each other undress without touching. If we touched with our clothes still on maybe we would've changed our minds.

The buttons on my shirt were small, stubborn little teeth.

I undid them one by one with his eyes on me.

I felt as if I had no control over my body.

When the buttons were all undone, I watched his Adam's apple move up and then down.

There were no shades on the windows. Anyone could see us.

We folded our clothes and set them aside.

Something about the precision of this intensified the electricity in the room.

I felt like the wrong end of a battery.

When we were both fully undressed, we met near the foot of the bed. I tried not to think about the person who'd made it. These sheets had never been slept in. Never been washed. The whole house felt like an extended department store scene.

A scene we were invading.

When he brought his hand toward my face, I moved it to the place he'd last touched me. His fingers were cold, and my knees went soft as he took a small, surprised breath. He touched me until my brain went fuzzy and I murmured a string of vowels that made him reach for his wallet.

That shift of plastic. I tried not to think about what it meant.

That he'd come prepared.

He'd come prepared last time.

I had ignored it then, too.

He tried to press me down onto the bed, but I turned around and braced myself against it. His hands slid under my hips and lifted. The pressure as he moved into me was so immense, I flattened my face into the bedspread, which smelled of chemicals.

When he leaned forward so he could touch me I found I could float.

I could see us from above. From the side.

He put one large hand flat on the small of my back and when I looked over my shoulder his face was so twisted with want that I came, and as I did, he pulled my hips toward him, pushed himself as deep into me as he could and held himself there until I stopped shuddering and my tongue met the bedspread and it tasted toxic.

Afterward we lay side by side with six inches of space between us and I told him no one had ever made me come before. *No one other than myself.*

His smile spread itself open like legs.

He ran a finger over the upper half of my arm.

I shivered. I wasn't cold.

It felt impossible for the rest of the day to continue. Like the front door of the house had opened into some alternate reality we could step inside of. As if we could remain there for as long as we liked.

24

R

October disappeared as if something had swallowed it, one week, two weeks, three weeks, gone. Time seemed to both speed up and slow down simultaneously, the hours long but the weeks fast, twenty-two, twenty-three, twenty-four, my body hurtling toward February at warp speed while also somehow suspended, still. I could see the end, I could see myself being pushed toward it, not unlike how my son would feel as he moved from the inside of me to the out, but I felt as if I were motionless en route, flying forward without leaving the living room, doing nothing as I slid steadily toward big inevitable change.

Ten days after my interview with Marta, she asked me to come back for another one. I called Jess immediately and she picked up in that same breathless way she always did, as if I'd caught her right in the middle of something else. "That's great," she said, and then, downshifting, "but don't get too excited yet."

We'd gone back to eating cereal for dinner, the rest of the groceries I'd bought in that sanguine frenzy spoiled in the fridge, the mushrooms sliming and the arugula turning on itself until it was nothing more than a soggy green sludge at the bottom of a bag.

Jess had begun to come home later and later, but when she did, she came with gifts, wrapped bouquets of anthurium and 'awapuhi ginger, plastic containers of artisan olives from the deli and thick slices of cured ham. All I seemed to want was salt and she brought it to me dutifully, sitting with me on the couch, watching shows I knew she had no interest in. Even so, I'd begun to feel an abnormal distance between us, as if we were separated by something large and round and obvious. There had always been some level of sameness to us, a shared point of reference that we could tether ourselves to, starting with school, our similar family histories, then continuing with our proximity to one another, our lives placed in the same square diorama, but for the first time, I was experiencing something that was impossible to fully share with her. I could explain it using every word I knew, I could let her read me every baby book ever published, but none of them would ever fully make her understand what it felt like to be stuffed so full of someone else's life that you couldn't sit down comfortably. I knew she felt it too, which was why she was coming home late and coddling me from a distance, and I hoped that as soon as the baby arrived the job of loving him outside my body would unify us again, that it would be simpler and easier to share than the job of loving him while he was inside my body.

To pass the time in the afternoons I would wander across the street to the beach and sit in the shade or take Sookie for long walks. The dog seemed to regard me differently too, cautiously, as if I were her charge to care for and not the other way around, and when we walked, she moved slowly, looking back at me every few steps as if to make sure I was still there.

Quincy came for dinner again, just the three of us this time, and Jess managed a red sauce and I slathered garlic and butter on bread and broiled it, and afterward Quincy made tea and we video chatted with his parents. It was well after midnight in Montana and they'd clearly stayed up for us, asking questions from a tiny screen, about Hawai'i, the weather, if we'd thought of any names yet. Quincy's mom kept wiping at her eyes and saying *Quince, she's gorgeous,* then immediately apologizing and repeating the compliment to me directly, *Ren, you are gorgeous.* I wondered, but didn't ask, if they knew we weren't a couple, that we never had been. Jess asked questions about their bed-and-breakfast, which I didn't even know they had, and I felt strange then, like I could hear a conversation about me happening in another room.

Quincy'd brought over a DVD about two people who get pregnant after a one-night stand, and we watched it after we hung up, Jess making a joke about it being "a little on the nose," me falling asleep before the end, nestled between them on the couch with my feet on Jess's lap. I woke as the credits rolled with Quincy leaning over me to say goodbye. Jess said she'd walk him out to his car, and they stayed down there so long I fell back asleep, waking to Jess telling me to get up and brush my teeth.

Days began to cycle, nothing on my schedule but my doctor's appointments, the single hour I spent in the studio at Ralphie's. Sometimes in the afternoons I crawled into Jess's bed to make myself come. Her sheets were always clean, soft, pillowy, and my thoughts were easier in her room than my own. It took me much less time than usual, my body extra sensitive, like the blood was constantly pooled where I needed it, taking only the smallest touch to guide it in the proper direction. I developed a new thing to think about, a fantasy, and while it embarrassed me to call it that, that's exactly what it was. The scenario was Quincy standing at the edge of the bed watching me touch myself and wanting to touch me but not being able to because I wouldn't allow it, because only I could touch me, so he stood there at the end of the bed and touched himself, and I touched myself, and together we climbed. When I thought about this,

I wouldn't imagine myself as I was the time we slept together, twenty pounds lighter in a body that was mine alone, but as I was then, round and ripe and on the edge of something else. Sometimes I would try to imagine someone else, usually Ryan, the dimple on his chin and the swell of his chest from all the presses and push-ups he did after his shift ended, sometimes even Ryan and Mei together just to devastate myself into orgasm, but by the end I always returned, gasping and shaking, to Quincy, and my own unattainability. Afterward, I always felt a shallow flood of shame, not so much because I was in Jess's room or because she was working and I was there with nothing to do but pleasure myself, but because I never thought of Quincy that way when we were actually together, and the fantasy seemed to hang on this idea that I was *his* fantasy, something he had once and would never have again, and this unrequited want made me feel powerful, which was embarrassing after it was over. Wanting to be wanted just for the sake of it. What a small way to be.

I wished I could tell Jess about it, and if Quincy were someone else, maybe I would have. But it had been different with Quincy somehow, right from the beginning. Even the way we referred to him was different. Nohea had been *the Fighter* until his toothbrush took up residence in our bathroom, Ryan was *Juice Bar Ryan* or sometimes just *Juice*, and in college, my math tutor Jordan had been *Calc*, the nicknames we'd assigned to enforce the rule that these men were outsiders not consequential enough to be named. But Quincy had always been *Quincy*, right from the beginning, as if we knew even then how he would change things.

J

The houses were all that we had.

We made appointments at places he wasn't interested in.

At some point, we stopped evaluating them.

Quincy liked bedrooms but I preferred bathrooms. I liked to watch us both in the mirror. It felt like I was watching a stranger. I did not know that woman. That woman had no control over herself.

Three times we agreed to stop. Three times we continued. Eventually stopping stopped feeling like an option and with that came a release so staggering I felt dizzy. Like the rush I got after a run.

Twice the seller's agent met us unexpectedly, which was both disappointing and exciting. We walked around trading glances about what we'd be doing if we were alone.

In the bathroom of a duplex with warped floors Quincy smiled at me in the mirror and I smiled back and the seller's agent, a mousy woman named Pauline I'd worked with many times, leaned against the doorframe and asked us what was funny.

There is a certain type of person precariously drawn to high-risk investments. Until now, I had not realized I was one of them.

Quincy liked to talk after we were finished and we did, but not for very long. I liked to get back into our clothes just in case—although the "just in case" arguably made the whole thing more appealing.

He told me his parents had retired four years earlier and bought a five-bedroom Victorian he'd helped turn into a bed-and-breakfast.

He told me he'd applied for the UH gig on a whim and had been surprised when they'd called him. "I'm glad I did it, although it probably wasn't the smartest idea." We were in a dark bedroom set so close to the road I could smell exhaust fumes through the open window.

"Not smart how?"

"Well, I would've been eligible for tenure at UM next fall. Carrie certainly would've had something to say about that."

He talked about his ex frequently, always with affection, as if she were an old college friend.

"What happened there?"

"At UM?"

"No. With Carrie." I shifted, freeing a section of hair that had become trapped beneath his arm. "The pretty one."

"You mean why did my marriage fail?" Quincy pinched my arm gently and I felt bad then, remembering our conversation that first dinner. "I stopped trying, I guess. I got lazy. Eventually she got resentful and stopped trying too, and then, we just kind of, I don't know, *drifted*, until it was clear we wanted different things." There was sadness in his voice, but he laughed. "Well, I mean it was clear to *her*. I was pretty lost about it for a while but, I get it now."

I murmured something soft and sympathetic.

It was unimaginable. Quincy as someone else's husband. To me it was as if he popped into existence in April at the bar and there was nothing before that.

He sat up on his elbows and looked down at me, the shadow of his big body falling over mine. "She's married again, though, kids, big house, super successful, the whole thing."

"Really. What does she do?"

Quincy cringed.

"What?"

He put one pawish hand over his eyes as if afraid to look at me.

"What?" I prodded him in the ribs until he peeked through a slit in his fingers.

"She works in real estate."

"You're joking."

He dropped his hand from his face and playfully used it to shield himself, as if anticipating violence.

"Wow," I said, and then, louder, *"Wow."*

"Agent, though, not a broker." He nudged my shoulder with his head. "And that's new. When we were together, she was in retail, but yeah. Real estate."

I looked at him for a long moment. "Are you trying to tell me that I remind you of your ex-wife?"

"I'm not *not* saying that."

I laughed, lifting my shirt from the floor where I'd discarded it, but Quincy nipped it away from me, holding it out of reach.

"I take it back," he said, curling himself around my waist so I couldn't stand. "You're completely unique. Her, too. Both of you. Snowflakes."

Outside the houses, things stayed the same.

Quincy would send links to articles with innocuous comments like, *thought you might like.* He would send photos of sunsets or poke bowls or mixed pit breeds he met on the street with the same shark-toothed smile as Sookie.

The only difference was the unusual giddiness that sometimes overtook me when one of these messages arrived. A bubble of something a bit more effervescent than joy.

More feverish. Manic. A frothing sort of glee.

Sometimes in the evenings he would send these messages to both me and Ren in a group chat that we would enter side by side, talking to him and each other as we sat on the couch. The dining room. In bed.

During those weeks we chose a pediatrician and researched different formulas in case she had trouble breastfeeding. These things felt easier, somehow, with Quincy's presence a pleasant shadow in the back of my brain.

Life continued as it does. The days dayed on, one after another.

I brought home family-sized orders of coconut soup or bentos from KTA.

I ordered a breast pump on the internet and Ren tried it on and said it made her feel "rather bovine."

Her stomach stretched so large and round it was cartoonish.

I kept waiting for some colossal wave of guilt, but it never came.

Not in the hours when I was with Quincy.

Not in the hours when I was with Ren.

Sometimes, though, when he said my name in a certain way or put his mouth around some part of me, I would catch myself wondering if these were the things they'd done.

Had he touched her there and there and there?

Did it make her feel out of control and safe at the same time?

Could we do the same things and feel differently about them?

I thought about this as I observed her drinking juice from the small glass jar I'd soon rinse and dry and put away myself. She was watching something on the TV that I wasn't paying attention to, and she turned then and caught me staring. "What?"

I shook my head and she smiled and brought her gaze to the television and her smile lingered and I was glad.

Glad I could make her think good thoughts. Whatever they were.

We all went to Theo's for Halloween.

It was his first time hosting and he'd placed a glowing plastic jack-o'-lantern on the porch, which Ren rested on top of her belly so Quincy could take a photo. "Send that to me," she told him, "or Jess," as if it was the same.

We ordered Chinese food and sat around the near-empty living room taking turns with trick-or-treaters. Ren and I had dressed like two halves of an avocado, her bare belly protruding from her costume as the pit.

The costume was meant for couples.

Quincy'd found it online and sent us the link.

He sat on the couch drinking beer from a glass and wearing a headpiece modeled after a Venus flytrap. Little felt teeth framed either side of his cheekbones. He looked like some sort of villain on a kids' show, and I told him as much.

"How fitting," he said. "Actually, it's for a child." He turned his head so I could see the back. The zipper was fully undone, his hair and neck exposed. That morning he'd sent me a link to a baby-shaped piñata. "Too dark?" he'd written. We were two weeks from the surprise shower and the secret made me feel like I'd just stepped out of the ocean. Glittering and sharp.

Ren came into the room then with plates and cutlery we mostly did not use.

It was one of the first Halloweens in a decade she hadn't punched in at Crazy Palms and I knew she was feeling weird about it. It was amazing she'd been there that long.

In college we'd talk about our future selves as if they were real people. Already fully formed. Out there somewhere living a life. Calling our names. Beckoning us to join them. She'd had a plan. A backup dancer at first, maybe some music videos. LA was all opportunities, she'd said, and she'd be near Theo. When she talked about it her voice was full and heavy.

Like it could burst.

I'd been so envious then. Her clear vision. I was studying business because it made sense. I had no clue what I wanted to do with it until I saw the way Clem's house was sold.

But Ren knew.

Crazy Palms was just a short stop until she made her next move. Ralphie's, too. Then ten years passed. Then twelve. Thirteen. I didn't know why.

Or maybe I did.

I would never move to LA.

Theo's living room was full of boxes and the noxious fresh paint fumes.

The L-shaped couch from Kinkado's was the only assembled furniture and the cardboard from my costume made it difficult to sit fully, so I perched on the sofa's lip and picked at my fried rice.

Across from me, Theo was talking about what they planned to do with the house and while he spoke, he absently ran a hand along the back of Taylor's neck as if stroking a cat.

They wanted to renovate the kitchenette downstairs, Theo said. They wanted to rent that space out. Every now and then he would turn to Taylor for confirmation.

"We're thinking mango for the cabinets, right?"

And Taylor would nod and say, "Right, mango," and then, fortified, Theo would continue. They hadn't dressed up and their lack of costume made Quincy look even more ridiculous in his flytrap. The mouth gaped open around his face like he was in the process of being swallowed. He listened with interest to Theo's renovation plans as I watched his big muscular hands maneuver his chopsticks.

When the doorbell rang, Ren's turn, Quincy automatically raised one arm to spot her as she lifted herself from the couch, and a warmth spread across my body. Ren answered the door cradling the candy bowl. A little Moana stood on the front lanai holding a pillowcase and the hand of her mother.

She could've been three or six.

I had a hard time telling.

Ren held out her bowl of Laffy Taffy and Twix while Quincy asked Theo about countertops and tile, tugging on his earlobe the way he did when he was thinking. "You know, I could probably help," he said as Ren closed the front door.

"Yeah?" Theo asked.

"Sure. I mean, I'm not a contractor but I built the house my ex lives in from the ground up."

Ren wriggled her shoulders as she nestled back in beside me and I wriggled mine in response, a communication that made her smile and scrunch her nose. I returned this gesture as well.

"Here's a thought," Theo was saying. "What if you move into

one of the bedrooms downstairs and work on the kitchen. You know. Until you and Jess find the right spot."

My chopsticks froze.

Quincy flicked his gaze to me quickly, and then away. "Really?"

That painful purr began between my ribs. I looked to Ren, but she was staring at Theo, who glanced to Taylor again.

I recognized the exchange.

It was the same one couples used in my office before they made a decision.

Theo turned back to Quincy. "Yeah, I mean, it'd help us out."

"Please, it'd help *me* out," Quincy said. "Living with Jude is horrific." His costume wobbled ridiculously as he shook his head. "We share a bedroom wall, and the amount of porn that guy watches." Quincy made a face then like he'd eaten something sour. "He has headphones and he doesn't use them, it's almost like he wants me to hear."

Theo laughed. "Brutal."

I coughed as if a grain of rice had stuck in my throat but no one looked at me. The purr had heightened to a ferocious growl.

When I finally spoke, my words came unnaturally loud. "That feels a little unnecessary, don't you think?" Attention pivoted and I found my face was warm. "I mean, we're going to find a place soon."

There was a loaded pause before Quincy said, "Right, yeah, of course." He gave me a look that felt like a question I didn't know how to answer, so I stared at my lap.

My rice had started to congeal.

I could feel Ren watching me.

The smell of fresh paint was beginning to nauseate me, and my costume was making me sweat.

"Well, no pressure or anything," Theo said after a moment. "Take your time. Go home and think about it."

The doorbell rang then, and Quincy jumped to standing as if he'd been waiting for it.

The rest of us sat quietly as he picked up the candy bowl. Out on the lanai stood a tiny Tinkerbell.

At the sight of Quincy with his Venus flytrap head, the girl exploded into tears.

25

R

The trick-or-treaters dwindled by nine and Quincy left shortly after, leaving me to trail through the living room, filling a greasy takeout bag with used chopsticks and Laffy Taffy wrappers. Back in the kitchen, Jess stood at the sink rinsing grease from paper takeout cartons and talking to Theo over her shoulder, her voice thin and high. "Well, it just feels *incestuous*," she said, "for a lack of a better word."

Theo sighed dramatically. "It was just a suggestion. We don't have to turn it into a crisis scenario." Beside him, Taylor plucked at his ukulele, light bell-like sounds that felt too whimsical for the moment as I opened the trash and stuffed the oily bag inside.

"Well, I just wish you'd run it by Ren first." Jess turned to give me a pointed look. I didn't actually mind that Theo hadn't debriefed me about his invitation to Quincy, but I didn't want to betray Jess's sense of self-righteousness on my behalf, so I smiled at her in a way that I hoped appeared appreciative.

"Okay, fine, I'm *sorry*," Theo said.

"Don't say it to me, say it to Ren."

"Sorry, *Ren*." Theo held my gaze in jest, a look that told me he knew I didn't care, that this whole thing was a show for Jess, and that neither of us quite knew why the show was necessary, but somehow there we were.

Jess pumped soap onto her sponge with aggressive vigor. "And anyway, it doesn't make sense for him to move in and then right back out when we find him something."

"But that could take months, he shouldn't be stuck in that rental."

"Please," Jess said, turning from the sink. "You only invited him so he can renovate."

"So?"

"So, don't pretend you're acting in Quincy's best interests when it's blatantly self-serving."

"But I told him that," Theo said. "I don't get what the big issue is."

I tore a paper towel from the roll and ran it down the length of the countertop, picking up splotches of shoyu. Carefully, gently, I turned to Jess and said: "I don't know, it might be nice for him. For Quincy, I mean. He just moved across a literal ocean. Probably be good for him not to live alone."

Jess shut the faucet off. "He doesn't *live alone*."

"Okay, fine," I said. "Probably nice not to live with a porn addict."

Theo snorted and I shot him a smile, ignoring Jess as she crossed to the trash can and slammed her foot down on the lever with more force than necessary.

J

The day after Halloween, Quincy called my office line. It was just past three and I had lost a maddening hour trying to upload a listing video that kept stuttering out at seventy-five percent.

"Howdy," he said when I answered. Eight weeks earlier the corny greeting would have made me cringe, but instead I was relieved to hear his voice. Relieved, and a bit embarrassed. "So, that was awkward yesterday."

I slid my chair away from my desk. I knew my behavior at Theo's had been childish but didn't quite know how to talk about it. "Was it?"

Quincy said nothing then.

I listened to his breath on the other end of the line and tried to imagine where he was calling from. He had an office, but I'd never been there, or to the house he shared with internet Jude.

I couldn't picture either setting.

I could only visualize him floating in a blank white space, reading and responding to my messages.

"So, you'd be upset if I took Theo up?" he said finally.

"I don't know if I'd call it *upset*." I turned toward the window. The glass was beaded with moisture.

"What would you call it, then?"

"Nothing. I just wish Theo'd asked Ren first is all."

"Ren? Or you?"

"Both," I admitted. My door was open, and Lisa walked past, threading her arms through a raincoat. "How long would it take? The kitchen, I mean."

"Four weeks, tops." Now he sounded relieved. "No sweat, considering. Took me two years to build Carrie's place."

"So, she got to keep the house you built?"

"Well, yes, but actually she sold that one and used the money to buy a bigger one."

"Oh, she does remind me of me."

"Doesn't she?"

I looked up at the ceiling. "Theo loves to capitalize on free labor."

"Is that you granting permission?"

"I really don't think you need my permission." I said this but I knew it wasn't true. He wouldn't move in if I told him not to.

This thought gave me the sensation of being taller than I was. I remembered when we were camping how I'd been able to get a rare glimpse of the top of his head. How his hair had swirled delicately at his crown.

"You haven't sent me any listings lately," Quincy said, his voice low and thick with affection.

"Haven't I?"

"Not in ages." I could hear his smile through the line.

This was not true. We'd looked at a house three days earlier.

"Well, I guess I better get on it, then."

"I guess you should."

That night, while Ren took a bath in my bathroom, I sent him a dozen or so properties and he wrote back immediately: I like them all.

Surprisingly I did not think of Quincy as much as I imagined I might.

He did not consume my attention when we weren't together, and full hours often dissolved with no thought to him at all.

In some ways this was directly related to the childish elation I received when he resurfaced again. As if forgetting him increased the feverish delight that overtook me when I remembered again the way our dynamic had changed. Like a dream that returns to you hours after waking.

Sometimes when I came home to Ren and faced the swell that Quincy had co-created at her middle, I was hit with a paroxysm of importance.

Not that he was important, but that I myself was for choosing him.

Or more accurately, for letting myself be chosen.

After a showing on a Tuesday afternoon, the two of us stopped for lunch at the Thai place Ren liked over by Kalākaua Park.

Other than the botanical gardens, it was the only time we'd been anywhere alone together that wasn't an empty house. At one point, after we had ordered but before our meals came, he reached beneath the table to touch my knee and I felt an immediate slam of both giddiness and absolute horror.

These two feelings seemed directly in opposition and directly codependent. There was a symbiosis between them.

It was as if one was impossible without the other.

When our food arrived, I mentioned how, early on, I had told Ren I thought Quincy was taking the entire thing too easily. How it had seemed too simple, the way he showed up and just accepted things. "I actually asked her what the catch was."

"Jesus," he said, looking up toward the ceiling so that I could once again admire the thick muscle of his throat.

He was of course acknowledging that it was *this*.

This was the catch.

He looked down and said, "I guess I did take it easily, didn't I."

"Well. You're an easygoing guy." I remembered then what I'd said to Ren when we'd first had this conversation. I'd called Quincy a sociopath. "You're like a golden retriever."

"Ouch."

"I mean that affectionately."

"You? Affectionate?" He said this teasingly, but then his face dropped into seriousness. "I really don't see myself that way though."

"What, like a dog?"

He laughed. "Easygoing." He leaned back. "Honestly, I think I took to the idea because I felt so, I don't know." He searched. "Aimless?"

"Yes, well. I think that is why people have children."

"To acquire aim?"

"To acquire *purpose*. But really, you seemed far too happy to feel aimless."

"I was happy." He smiled. "I am now, too." His hand touched my knee again and heat climbed toward my center. "But you can feel happy and aimless at the same time."

I thought of Ren. Of the way she used to complain about the bar, the gym, though she clearly enjoyed working there.

Quincy's hand left my knee as I looked toward the door and said, "Well, I never have."

26

R

On a Thursday morning Mei brought her massage table to the house and set it up in the living room alongside a portable speaker cooing a soothing jazz playlist and a plug-in aromatherapy machine that periodically hissed rosemary-scented steam. I thought about the faces Jess might make if she walked in on us, but the sheets on Mei's table were good soft cotton and she massaged my body for ninety minutes, my face and scalp, my ankles and hands, and when she finished I felt as if I'd just emerged from a week of sleep, or had been fucked so good I had found myself momentarily paralyzed.

Before she left, Mei told me Ryan had given her his number on the pretense of taking her surfing. This was how she phrased it: taking her surfing. "I haven't written him yet," she said, folding her high-quality cotton in half once, and then again. "I feel like I should wait a few days, I don't want to seem overeager. Or maybe that's bullshit. Maybe I should be more forward. What do you think?" I of course could not tell her what I thought, which was: *This news has ruined my post-touch euphoria.* I considered how Mei texted in healthy, full sentences, and would never send Ryan a heinous string of emojis, and also that if I had just told her we'd gone out, instead of clutching this information to my chest, she might not be pursuing him at all, and this entire situation would be different, and therefore my misery was completely my fault.

"Fuck it, yeah, be forward," I said, and collapsed into a pile of dust.

My second interview went well, or, well enough, or at least, nothing went wrong. We'd met again in Marta's office, the two of us and a man called Kaipo who worked in HR, the box fan once again blowing a halo of hair around Marta's pleasant face. Afterward I walked over to Quincy's office, which was connected to the Arts building by a series of interwoven walkways. The campus was different than when Jess and I had been there, which shouldn't have been a surprise but of course it was, disorienting me as I walked along, as if I'd come home to find all the furniture rearranged.

I tried not to think about how this could be a path I would grow to know very well, Arts to Biology, Biology to Arts, but trying not to think about this only made me think about it more. It was just after eleven, bright and humid, the air smelling sweetly of plumeria although I couldn't see any growing as I moved along, sweating through my dress, feeling like a planet. I was seemingly too large for twenty-seven weeks, larger than the Google images of other women at the same stage, larger even than some of the women in my class who were further along, thirty weeks, or thirty-one. Early on, Jess had predicted I'd be the type of pregnant woman who only showed from the side, *like a beach ball shoved under your tank top.* She'd been wrong, obviously. It felt right, though, to take up so much space.

I wasn't ashamed of it, even if it was uncomfortable to live with.

Change was coming. Everyone should be able to see it.

By the time I found the Biology building the back of my dress was shellacked to my body. The door to Quincy's office was open and he was there, sitting behind a low desk the color of a walnut, tapping the end of a ballpoint pen to his lip as he stared at his laptop. "Hi," I said from the door, and he looked up and smiled.

"You found me."

"I did."

He stood then, which was his habit even though it felt too formal, considering. He offered to get me something to drink, and I sat in the chair across from his desk as he left the room. I felt fidgety, agitated. When Marta called for the second interview and Jess had told me not to get too excited, I'd wanted to explain I was not *excited*, I was *terrified*, but I never liked admitting to Jess when I was scared, since she was never scared of anything. Quincy came back then with two chilled bottles of Snapple.

He held them up. "Lemonade or Mango Madness?"

I chose the lemonade and when he handed it over, I pressed it gently to my face, enjoying the shiver it sent down the back of my neck. Quincy checked his phone as I twisted off the aluminum top and flipped it over.

"'Number twenty-nine,'" I read aloud. "'On average, a human will spend up to two weeks kissing in his or her lifetime.'"

To my surprise, Quincy blushed. He looked past me, toward the door. "I don't think I'm quite included in that average," he said.

"Me either, actually. What does yours say?"

He twisted the cap off his own bottle and shuddered.

"What?"

"'One hundred twenty-three. Beavers were once the size of bears.'"

"Yeesh, that is terrifying." I took a sip of my drink, the perfect blend of sweet and tart. "I can't remember the last time I had one of these."

"Ah, you're lucky. I'm completely addicted, we have a machine just around the corner." Quincy glanced at his phone again, then back at me. "So. How did it go?"

I groaned and wheeled my chair around, so I wasn't facing him anymore.

"Oh, come on, I'm sure it was fine."

"It *was* fine," I said, spinning back. "I just feel like it's not smart to focus on it."

"Why?"

I shrugged. Above me, water damage had left behind a dark mottled patch on the ceiling, like a bruise on a piece of fruit. "I don't know. I don't want them to hire me just because you work here."

"Ren, trust me, they won't. I'm new, they don't even like me that much, I swear."

I rolled my eyes. "You're infectiously likable. Just look how you won over Jess."

I watched his face flush for the second time in as many minutes. He brought his bottle to his lips and then lowered it again. "Well, anyway, it shouldn't matter. I didn't tell them that we were, that it's..." He looked away. "Ours."

"Oh," I said. *Oh.*

"Why?" he asked, looking slightly panicked. "Should I have?"

I waved a hand in front of my face, but I couldn't quite decide how I felt. Relief that nepotism was not likely now, but also a little bit wounded, as if Quincy viewed me as a walking display of his own reckless behavior. A walking display of my own.

"How are you liking it at Theo's?" I asked then. He'd moved in two days earlier, had already started sending Jess and me photos of the kitchen.

"It's a great space."

"Not too much work?"

Quincy shook his head. "I like working with my hands. Besides." He smiled. "He's been feeding me."

"I'm jealous. We've been surviving on cereal and toast."

Quincy frowned. "Well, that's not good." The concern in his voice made me smile. "How are you feeling?"

"Fine, I guess. He can hear now, you know."

Quincy drew his head back in surprise. "Like if I talk to him, he can hear me?"

"Uh-huh."

Quincy leaned across his desk. "Hello, little guy," he said, soft and low, a tone I'd never heard before, one that lifted the hair along my arms. "I can't wait to meet you."

I watched him, his eyes cloudy with affection, and felt a small, warm space open up in my body. Jess was right. He would be a good father. Quincy's phone pinged then, and he looked away. I watched his face brighten. "Sorry," he said, typing a response.

"You're good." I took a long sip of my lemonade, let its sweetness run down my throat and stay there.

I had assumed teaching my final class at Ralphie's would make me sad, considering that everything had been making me sad lately. I felt like a walking bucket so full with saline that even the slightest jostle, a throwback song on the radio, or a particularly sentimental Toyota commercial, could send me spilling over the sides of myself. But I knew, too, that the sadness was also happiness, they were the same feeling—a nostalgic joy, an emotionally simultaneous coming and going that was almost impossible to explain, and so mostly I didn't try. But my final class did not make me sad. Leading the group through our warm-up I realized: by the time I came back, every woman present would be a mother, or rather, every woman there was a mother already, each one of us experiencing our own form of the same transition, a graduating class moving energetically to the sound of our collective breath. This made me feel so elated that the hour dissolved into sweat and laughter and a collaborative whooping that poured out of the studio, too big to be contained by a room made of mirrors and glass.

This intense joy followed me into the locker room, where I emptied shoes, a hoodie, a few pairs of socks, and a tube of deodorant out of my locker. On my way out, I stopped out of habit by the communal jar of tampons, hovering for a moment as the mirrors above the sinks showed me my own unfamiliar shape. I studied myself, my cheeks bright, then turned and left without taking any.

Behind the juice bar, Ryan stood reading the back of a tub of protein powder, his brows pinched in such earnest concentration it looked like bad acting. I tapped my knuckles on the counter and when he saw me, he smiled and said, "Wow."

"*Wow?*"

"Wow, look at you."

"I can't see me," I said, although I had just seen myself, flushed and rotund, my belly burping over the top of my leggings. Ryan put the protein powder down and leaned onto the tips of his elbows.

"When my ex was in her third trimester, she'd piss a little every time she sneezed," he said. "We called it snissing." I laughed, though really I was entirely occupied by this mention of his ex, and what she might look like, where he'd met her, how long she'd been his wife or girlfriend before she became his ex, thinking how I couldn't even call Quincy my ex. Ryan didn't have a Facebook page, I knew because I'd looked several times, so I had no way to monitor his life from afar, which was probably a good thing. I wondered if he'd taken Mei surfing yet and tried not to think about them side by side in their bathing suits, and how close to naked that was. I understood that I had been wrong to interpret Ryan's flirtations with Mei as a display for my benefit, and that maybe he'd just figured out how to flirt sincerely with each of us at the same time without either of us noticing, or I had overestimated my ability to read people, or both.

J

Ren had begun to panic about names.

She brought it up constantly.

"Jonah?"

"Too biblical."

"But the Bible has so many of the good ones," she pouted, an open container of plain yogurt on her lap.

We were on the couch again with the TV on. We'd spent more evenings watching television in the past few months than we had in years. This was likely because Ren used to spend several evenings a week at Crazy and I never thought to turn on the TV by myself.

We didn't want anything trendy. No Atticus or Asher. Nothing that would be cute on a toddler but embarrassing on a man. Nothing location-based. Brooklyn or Kona or Lihue. Ren's phone pinged from her lap then and she looked down and snorted like something was funny.

"What?"

She held her screen out to show me a message from Quincy—he'd sent her a GIF of a baby puking all over a man's bare back. Seeing his name on her screen gave me the sensation that the room was tipping sideways.

"Gross," I said, and looked away.

The TV was set to a medical drama. I stared at the screen and thought of Quincy choosing the image across town. Saving it to his camera roll. Sending it.

We'd been together the day before in a large bathroom at a house Quincy could never afford. He'd whispered the word *please* into my ear over and over as if there were something else that I could give him.

"What does Quincy think about names?" I asked carefully.

Ren licked at her spoon. "You know, I haven't asked. Is that weird?"

Yes, I wanted to say. I didn't. "I'm sure he'd lobby for something botanical. Cypress or Sequoia. Some obscure orchid."

As I said this I thought of the slight hollow to Quincy's bare chest.

A subtle, inward curve. Like a platter for holding fruit.

Ren laughed and typed into her phone, and I wondered but did not ask if she'd written him what I'd said.

If she'd quoted me.

If she'd said it as herself.

Or maybe none of those things.

I took my own phone out.

My last exchange with Quincy had been logistics about yesterday's showing and, before that, a discussion about beverages for the baby shower and a meme of an infant strapped to the side of a dog that he'd sent with the note *think Sookie will be game?*

I wondered if he'd forwarded the same thing to Ren.

He'd been sending us progress photos of the renovation in a group chat with Theo. Slick new counters. The walls freshly painted gray.

On impulse I snapped a photo of Ren on the couch looking at her phone and sent it to him. My own socked feet were visible in the corner of the frame, resting against the bare skin of her leg.

I watched three little dots appear on the screen and then vanish.

A second later Ren's phone chirped, and she made a surprised *hmm*. "He said *Henry*."

"Henry?" I wrinkled my nose. "Of course." I wasn't even sure what I meant by that. It wasn't at all what I'd expected.

A message silently appeared on my own screen. A photo of Quincy's long feet at the end of the bed in one of the spare rooms at Theo's. Beyond the feet, an open closet revealed four hung shirts and a row of naked hangers.

I looked around our living room.

At our furniture and books and old magazines.

Paintings carefully selected and hung.

Almost twenty years of togetherness.

I looked back at his photo.

His bare feet and walls and closet.

I put my phone down without responding.

I asked Ren if she'd like a cup of tea and she said that she would.

Around this time, I saw Kuʻulei on the television.

There had been more arrests on the mountain, and while watching coverage over breakfast on a Saturday, camera passing face after face, there she was.

She appeared in two different news clips.

In the first, visible in the corner of a frame, she sat cross-legged on the ground wearing a puffed winter coat. In the second, she shuffled slowly past the camera, each elbow held by two men from the DLNR, her mouth pinched into a rigid line.

The way the men guided her was gentle, as if they were shepherding an injured party to safety.

I had never had a conversation with Kuʻulei about the telescopes. We avoided politics at the office for obvious reasons.

I found a clip of the video online, sent a screenshot to Theo.

She was back in the office on Monday, returning to her desk after lunch with a blue Zippy's cup, drinking soda through the plastic straw as if nothing had happened.

I didn't mention any of it to her. I didn't know how. That week, Lisa preordered fifty pies for pickup on Thanksgiving with the plan to drive them around town and leave them with former or potential clients. It was an expensive touch and it impressed me.

"Like a confectionary Santa Claus," Theo joked, but I could tell he was a bit bothered he hadn't thought of it.

The following weekend we went to a concert at one of the parks downtown where a temporary stage had been constructed and vendors sprouted beneath white tents.

Quincy and I came straight from a two-bedroom with a wood-paneled kitchen that hadn't been renovated since 1974.

We hadn't touched each other at all though we'd been there alone.

It seemed impossible when we had to meet Ren in thirty-five minutes, though neither of us brought it up.

The time constraint and the idea of Ren waiting for us could have made things more exciting but didn't. This was a relief.

I was glad to learn we weren't those types of people.

At this point, the shower was two days away and we spent most of the drive going over details. The menu and the guest list. How I would get Ren there. Where people would park their cars so as not to give it away.

"Whoa," Quincy said when we landed downtown.

Bayfront was bottlenecked with traffic. After ten minutes of stop-and-go I found a spot four blocks down. We lugged our beach chairs past the gallery with volcano footage on loop in its front window and the historic Palace Theater, its hundred-year-old awnings.

Suns of Aloha was the name of the band. Five snow-haired uncles who had been around so long it was impossible for them not to have amassed a following. We were twenty minutes early but already the grass was so thick with picnic blankets we had to walk single file as we searched for the others.

We found Theo and Taylor in low chairs beside a large patch of bamboo wearing V-neck T-shirts in complementary shades of blue. I asked if I missed the dress code memo as Theo lifted his legs so I could pass. Quincy hovered awkwardly then, as if deciding where to plant himself, before opening his chair next to Taylor and folding his long body into it.

I was oddly relieved with the two of them between us.

I didn't look at him.

I wanted to ask where Ren was, but Theo was already talking to Quincy about a bit of hardware he'd special-ordered on the internet.

Sandwiched between them, Taylor chewed on a toothpick, a signal he'd given up smoking again. His fingers drummed an antsy rhythm on the tops of his knees, and I watched as Theo reached over absently to still them.

Ren arrived out of breath and saying, "Holy hell, sorry I'm late." Quincy stood to kiss her on the cheek, and I looked away. "Bayfront is ridiculous." Ren propped her chair beside me. "Where did you park?"

"By the Palace," I told her.

Her hair was tucked into a yellow scarf with a single curl carefully pulled out by each temple. The color of the scarf and the way it drew attention to the stem of her neck lent her the graceful appearance of a tulip.

Quincy leaned over then to ask if we wanted anything from concessions.

I shook my head and busied myself taking my shoes off.

When he was gone Ren turned to me and in a quiet voice she said, "The woman from the university emailed. Just a thank-you for coming in again. She said I'd *hear from them soon.*" She bit at her bottom lip.

"That's great," I said, putting my hand to my sternum and pressing down.

The thought of Ren working at the university made me uncomfortable.

I knew it would be good for her. That I should be enthusiastic.

Instead, I was overcome with something like dread.

Quincy returned balancing a bottle of beer and two plastic cups of iced tea that he dispersed between me and Ren even though I hadn't asked for anything. "What service," she said.

Theo turned toward Quincy. "Remind me which of them you knocked up again?"

I kept my face from moving as Ren reached across me to jab her brother. "Both of us," she said, "I'm just the vessel."

"What does that make Jess, then?" Theo's tone was barbed.

I took a long gulp from my plastic cup. Ice pressed painfully against my teeth as Quincy asked, "What does that make *me*?"

"The sperm donor. They've been calling you that from the beginning."

There was a pause before Quincy asked, low and slow, "Is that right?"

I busied myself by crunching into an ice cube and studying my own feet.

Theo nudged me with his elbow and said, "Oh, calm down."

After the concert I drove Quincy to his car in the lot outside my office. When we stopped at a light, he turned the radio down and said, "Hey so, do you really refer to me as your sperm donor?"

"No. Well. We used to. Before."

I wasn't sure what I meant.

Before what?

Before he moved back on island?

Before we started sleeping together?

The car ahead of me had an *'A'ole TMT* sticker stuck to its bumper and I stared at it as if it could tell me something.

"At least I'm good for something, I guess." There was a forced levity to his tone and from the corner of my eye I could see his mouth was drawn. I remembered that time at lunch when he referred to himself as *aimless*.

The light blinked green and I moved us forward.

"Have you thought of any names for the baby?" I asked.

This was an obvious attempt at changing the subject, but also, I wanted to know if he'd give me the same answer he gave Ren.

He paused and said, "If it were up to me, I'd probably name him Henry."

The rush of satisfaction I felt seemed oddly oversized. "That's surprising," I said. I'd meant to sound genuine, but it came out stiff and oddly forced.

"It was my grandfather's name."

I felt bad then for making fun of it, though he hadn't been there and didn't know. "You should tell Ren that."

"I have."

I could feel him looking at me.

I stared at the road as it moved swiftly underneath us.

"Does it make you feel weird to talk about this?" he asked.

I drew my shoulders away from my ears. "Why would it make me feel weird?" My tone was thin and high. I tried to steady it. "We're planning his shower, we're going to raise him, we should be able to talk about his name."

Quincy was silent for a moment. "Have you come up with anything?"

"Not really."

"No?"

"I mean, I can think of names I like, but nothing feels connected to anything. I don't know."

I could see him nodding.

Then he asked, "What do you think it will be like, after?" He said this quietly. Almost a whisper.

We were approaching the office, which seemed comforting. As if we were nearing safety somehow. "I don't know," I said finally.

"I think she'd be okay with it." My body began to hum. "She said right away I should keep dating," he went on. "And you're her favorite person. I'm sure she'd commend my consistently excellent taste."

He'd attempted to joke on that last part, a smile threaded there.

I steadied my breathing and tried to imagine a universe in which what he said could be true. That Ren would be okay with this. With what we had been doing without telling her.

I duplicated an image of the concert we'd just attended, this time Quincy seated beside me, his hand on my knee like it had been at lunch.

It seemed preposterous.

I realized with a sharp push that I had never even considered telling Ren.

That there was no universe in which she would ever be okay with the way we had kept this from her.

I had assumed somehow that Quincy also understood this.

Clearly, I had been wrong.

I became dizzy then. Disoriented.

As if I were falling.

As if I'd stood up too fast.

It felt unsafe to be driving. I focused on the yellow line on the road as silence stretched nakedly between us. I was having trouble linking my inhalations and exhalations. "Maybe," I managed finally because I knew I had to say something.

When we reached the lot, I left the car running. Quincy studied me for a second and I thought he might say something, but he just kissed the side of my face and got out. When his mouth touched me I was not overcome with that normal wash of endorphins.

No feeling of fire unleashed upon dry grass. Just the frantic buzz in my center combined with a strange numbness to my limbs.

I drove myself home slowly and thought how he had kissed me in the same spot he had kissed Ren earlier.

I steadied my hands on the wheel and thought about how different the same moment could be for each of us.

27

R

Jess threw me a baby shower the Saturday before Thanksgiving. I'd thought we were just having brunch at Theo's, that's what she'd told me, getting herself up early to make a fruit salad, to ice a gallon of coffee, but when we pulled up to the house a line of familiar cars wound down the drive and onto the street, Cha-Cha's beat-up BMW, Kekoa's lifted Toyota with the *Free Hawai'i* decal on the back.

"Christ," Jess said under her breath, and then, "They were supposed to park around the corner." She parked and jerked her door open without looking at me. I felt disoriented as I followed her up the drive, as if I'd seen a movie in the middle of the afternoon and emerged from the dark theater into confusing, blinding daylight. A jumble of slippers lay by the front door, a dozen pairs or so, which Jess kicked out of her way. There was no organized holler when we entered, just Quincy at the door looking uncomfortable. "They were supposed to park around the corner," Jess repeated, pushing past him with her fruit salad held away from her body like something dangerous.

Quincy gave me an apologetic shrug. "Surprise," he said, and then, reaching for the pitcher of cold coffee I'd forgotten I was carrying, "Here, let me take that." Behind him ChaCha and Kekoa sat on the couch picking through a bowl of berries and looking out of place. I hadn't seen either of them before six p.m. the entire decade I'd known them, so the sight of them in bright midmorning sunshine felt like seeing a pair of nocturnal animals at noon. Mei was there too, folded into an armchair with a flute glass of something bubbly and pink, and I realized abruptly it was possible that Ryan had somehow been invited, that possibly they had even come together. Immediately I became aware of what I was wearing, old leggings and a cheap blouse I'd tugged from the discount bin in Ross's maternity section, hot-pink, a color I never normally wore, hadn't even considered when I got dressed. But Ryan wasn't there, which like always delivered that dichotomous swing of disappointment and relief, and as I moved through the house to make sure he was in fact not present, everyone touching me and commenting on how I looked, I began to wonder how long a baby shower lasted, exactly.

Theo stood alone in the kitchen slicing coffee cake into squares. "Maternity Barbie," he said when he saw me. "Can I get you a virginal beverage? Quincy designed one that he says is *reminiscent of your personality*." He pointed to a large bowl full of the same light pink liquid I'd seen Mei drinking.

I ladled some into a glass as she sidled up to me. "He's cute," she whispered, nodding toward the living room, where Quincy was installed on the back of a chair looking blankly into space. This irritated me, as if we had nothing better to talk about, which I guess we didn't. I was starting to sweat through the cheap polyester of my shirt. I excused myself on the pretense of using the restroom, but when I closed the bathroom door, I just stared at my own reflection for two minutes before flushing the toilet, running the tap, and exiting again. Quincy had disappeared from the living room, and I sat across from Jess in a bulky leather chair and let Mei rub my stomach.

"We were just talking about names," ChaCha said.

I groaned and Jess patted my knee. "We're having a bit of a block in that department."

"Don't worry," Mei said. "You'll know when he gets here." She smiled kindly and I wondered with surprising bitterness what experience she was speaking from, being twenty-eight and childless.

"So long as we don't spend the first two years calling him *Him*," Jess was saying. "He'll have a god complex before he can walk." She began talking then about the cultural specificity of names, of a study that examined whether our names could impact our expressions, *neuroscience, random chance, social cognition*, while over her shoulder I watched as Quincy exited the kitchen, glanced at the back of her head, then turned around again. I waited for him to reenter holding a drink or a piece of cake, but he didn't, and after a moment I got up to follow him, Jess behind me saying something about name-based identity crises as I wandered off. I found him leaning against the kitchen counter scrolling through his phone. He looked up when he saw me and said, "Oh, hey," sliding his phone into his pocket. He seemed vulnerable standing there alone in the kitchen, and I had a flash then of the fantasies I'd built by myself in Jess's bed in the middle of the afternoon. This felt uncomfortably embarrassing now that he was in front of me, as if he could know just by looking at me, the visuals playing across my forehead in a graphic projection. I must have made some face then, because his mouth crumpled a bit and he said, "Jesus, is this totally awkward for you?"

"What? No."

He gave me a long, stout stare. His brows corrugated.

"It's maybe just a little bit awkward."

"There it is," he laughed. "Hey, I heard good things about your second interview."

"God," I groaned. "From who?" and then, "Don't tell me. I'm trying not to think about it."

"No? How come?"

"Because. Whenever I think too hard about things they never happen."

"Funny." Quincy picked a crumb of coffee cake off the counter and deposited it into the sink. "Things seem to work the opposite for me."

"Great, maybe *you* can keep thinking about the interview, then."

"Alright, I will."

I was suddenly grateful for his presence, feeling at ease for the first time since we arrived. "So how are the renovations going?"

His face lit up. "Would you like to see?"

The lower half of the house was much darker, and it took a moment for my eyes to adjust, the only natural light coming in through a set of sliding doors, which projected a single bright rectangle onto the floor, like a portal you could jump into and disappear. "Now, I've only been working on this part for a week or so," Quincy was saying, pointing out a piece of cabinet that wasn't quite finished, then the box of yellow tiles for the back-splash he'd install behind the sink.

I looked at him there, proudly showing off his work, and imagined some other universe where he was more than just my baby's father, where Mei's comment about him being cute would please me instead of irritate me, a situation where I'd feel as proud of this kitchen as he did, because his work would also be an extension of me, some alternate party where we'd be sitting together upstairs, his fingers absently running along my neck and his arm vined along the back of the couch, the couch that matched the one we had at our house, which would be the house Quincy'd moved into instead of this one. In our house, he'd have been the one to repaint Theo's old room, to assemble the space into a nursery, to put together the cheap particleboard bookshelves and untangle the lines of the skinny blue cloud mobile. He'd have spent the last few months waiting for me outside the studio with a carrot juice as I wrapped up class, and when I looked up and saw him standing there our eyes would have a hasty dialogue that was deeply personal and private.

I waited for this to make me feel a certain way, happy or sad or bitter or anything, but nothing came, just a jab from an excited foot or arm inside me, these movements so frequent by then that I hardly gave them thought. I placed my hand on my center and watched Quincy open an empty drawer and explain what would go inside of it.

Jess and I were the last to leave, and as she loaded gifts into the back of the car, burping cloths and fuzzy blue onesies, knit caps barely bigger than my fist, I stood at the door and thanked Theo for the party.

"I didn't do anything really," he said in an almost bored fashion, looking over my head and out toward the drive. "Jess and Quincy arranged it all."

"Really?"

"I know, right?"

Through the open door to the kitchen, I could just make out the line of Quincy's shoulder as he loaded plates into the dishwasher, and behind me, Jess slammed down the back of her SUV. I thought of the two of them emailing ideas back and forth, going over the guest list, deciding on a menu and what ingredients should be purchased for Quincy's punch. It made sense then, the tension over the cars in the drive, Quincy hiding out in the kitchen, likely avoiding whatever smothering sensation Jess's affection-induced anxiety had created, and suddenly I didn't mind that the party had been forced on me, my annoyance replaced with the feeling I got when Jess drew me a bath or read things I already knew aloud from the baby book just so

I would know that she knew them, too: warm and taken care of and a tiny bit sleepy.

On the drive home, I thanked her.

"Please." She shrugged, as if I were applauding her for something as obvious and natural as breathing. I watched her drive, her focus unwavering, completely concentrated on transporting us—me—safely from one location to another, then reached over to touch her lightly on the knee.

"You're wonderful," I told her, and watched her wrinkle her nose in dismissal, her eyes stuck on the road, her knuckles slowly turning white against the wheel.

J

I couldn't stop replaying the conversation I'd had with Quincy after the concert. How he seemed to assume we'd eventually tell Ren about what was going on.

As if the unveiling of this information was inevitable.

Each time I thought about this I felt as I had then, swiftly and immediately dizzy, and the giddiness I'd experienced when Quincy would email me, would send me a text in the middle of the day, had been replaced with dread.

I was unprepared, I realized. This surprised me.

I couldn't remember the last time I started something without first examining how it would end.

The Monday after the shower I took Quincy to a house that he actually liked. One of Theo's listings, with a narrow front lanai and big square windows.

He'd come straight from class, so we met there, and when we entered he sprang ahead the way he did when he was excited. Like he was bursting from a box.

I closed the door softly behind us.

I did not follow him down the hall.

Instead, I slunk quietly into the kitchen.

Theo's card sat on the counter. I put mine above it, then changed my mind and slid it down below. "The light back here's great," Quincy called from somewhere else.

We were leaning toward the end of November. That morning I'd bought a fifteen-pound turkey and housed it in the freezer. It seemed outlandish when I thought about it. A huge frozen bird nesting in our refrigerator.

Three days until Thanksgiving.

Ten weeks until Ren was due.

A slight vibration began in my center as I tried to remember what was happening ten weeks ago. Ren was still working at

Crazy Palms. Theo was getting ready to move out. Quincy was still with his Craigslist roommate and had never touched me in any kind of way.

Out the kitchen window the yard was full of good thick grass. A perfect verdant rectangle.

I pressed my hand against the glass and thought how during Ren's shower I'd stood silently at the top of the basement steps and listened to her chat with Quincy about cabinets and drywall.

Ren asked appropriate, cordial questions and Quincy answered with enthusiasm. As if he couldn't tell she was being polite.

The voices they used alone together were entirely different than the voices they used alone with me and I had been pleased.

I knew a side of each of them that they kept from one another and this made me feel calm. Safe.

It was directly opposite from the sensation I'd had when Quincy asked what things would be like after the baby was born. I couldn't shake the sense that something was looming. A deadline I wasn't quite sure how to meet.

Quincy walked into the room then and said, "Well?"

It took me a second to realize he was talking about the house. That he liked it.

I stitched together the features of my face. Clicked myself into the proper gear. "We'll definitely want a termite inspection. It was treated in 2004."

This was exactly the type of information I would report to any client in this situation except that as I spoke, I thought how if he wanted to make an offer, and if that offer was accepted, there would be no more showings. No more houses for us to borrow. The end.

It seemed as feral as the beginning.

"What?" Quincy asked. I'd stopped speaking.

"Nothing. I'm just glad you like it."

I walked past him then. Brushed slightly against his shoulder and waited for a rush—for heat, for anything—but as I walked down the hall toward the bedrooms there came only the slow methodical clap of my own footsteps.

After, we lay on top of the bedspread.

I still wore my bra and camisole. Quincy was naked.

There were a few inches of space between us.

The sex had done nothing to calm me. I was antsy and voltaic. Quincy did not seem to notice.

He touched my arm and said in a soft voice: "Do you ever think about that night at the bar? Like, how different things would be if you hadn't left?" Quincy pressed his mouth against my shoulder then and I had an immediate, punishing urge to shove him away. "Or..." He smiled. "What if you'd been the one to take me home?"

My vision seemed to stutter then.

As if my brain had a glitch.

I thought of the flickering neon palm tree at the bar that night. *An arrhythmia.*

I closed my eyes and imagined Ren at home. Her body full of a life that was part Quincy's as she moved inside a house that was part mine. Walking slowly around the nursery. Touching the items we'd placed on the shelves.

I could imagine what she was doing at that exact moment, but it seemed highly unlikely she could ever imagine what *I* was doing.

Abruptly I became overwhelmed with injustice on her behalf.

A fierce, almost nauseating urge to protect her.

I knew it was ridiculous.

I was the one she needed protection from.

My feet swung heavily over the side of the bed. "I'd never have taken you home. You were a complete stranger." I grabbed my underwear and slid into them.

"Hey," Quincy said softly.

I kept my back to him as I stepped into my pants. "I don't want to do this anymore."

There was silence, long and steady, and then, "Okay."

He said it slowly. Like a swallow.

A furious heat erupted in the center of me. Like it had when the whole thing started. Like I might somehow explode out of my skin. *"Okay?"*

My clothes were entirely on by then. Quincy's penis lolled softly onto the bedspread like a tongue.

"If you want to stop, we can stop." His voice came quiet and compact. He looked so exposed and vulnerable it seemed like I should apologize.

Instead, I snorted as if he'd said something funny. "Well, what did you think would happen?"

I knew what he thought would happen, and the way I spat my question rendered it rhetorical. Quincy rubbed at the back of his head as if it were hurting him.

"What?" I pressed. "You thought we'd just tell her, and she'd be fine and the three of us would raise the baby together like some weird little family?"

I was aware of the animosity in my voice.

The sight of his soft penis made me want to scream.

"I don't know," he said finally, sounding tired. "I guess, yeah, maybe." I laughed and turned away from him again. "Jesus, Jess." I heard the clank of his belt. "I mean, wasn't that always the plan?"

"I don't think the plan ever included us fucking." The word was sharp in my mouth, and I wielded it like the weapon it was.

He exhaled then. A punctured, ragged breath. A noise so sad I left the room. Waited out by the front door for him to finish getting dressed alone. I was somehow both hot and cold at the same time. Sweating and shivering.

But mostly I was relieved.

It was over.

We had emerged unscathed on the other side.

Again, I imagined Ren at home. Drinking orange juice from the carton. Spinning the mobile above the crib.

As I imagined these things, I said Quincy's name over and over again in my head until the word lost its meaning.

I got back to the office around two o'clock.

Kim stopped me with a series of questions about a storage unit we kept across town to which I gave short, one-word answers before retreating to my office and shutting the door.

Theo knocked almost immediately, entering before I could say anything.

"How'd it go?" He closed the door.

It was then that I remembered the house had been his listing. I said something vague and noncommittal.

Theo frowned. "Too bad, I thought he'd be excited about it."

He was excited about it until I broke up with him in the master bedroom, I thought. I opened my email and clicked, hoping Theo would leave.

After a second of this he said, "Everything good?"

"Yeah. Why?" I feigned interest in an email thread about our SEO rankings. Theo watched me carefully. I tried to fix my face into something believably neutral. When it was clear he was not buying it I added, "We got into an argument."

"About what?" He leaned against the edge of the brown leather chair that Quincy had sat in when he asked me to be his broker and I said yes like an idiot. Like a puppet. Because Ren had wanted me to.

"Nothing, it's stupid, it doesn't matter." I could feel him looking at me, so I added, "Just. He can be really arrogant."

I didn't find Quincy arrogant.

I thought about his penis, slack and exposed on the bed.

"I thought you'd been getting along alright." I clicked around my screen until eventually he stood. "Maybe don't tell Ren about it," he said. "She doesn't need the stress right now."

I felt myself nod.

At the door he stopped. "Did you make a decision about the pie? I need to put an order in."

The pie. Of course. In just a few days I'd have to share a Thanksgiving table with Quincy and pretend everything was normal. Theo had been tasked with securing dessert. "Chocolate haupia," I said. Ren's favorite.

Theo gave me one final lingering look before he left the room.

On the drive home I listened to a news story covering a dengue fever outbreak. Entomologists had found a pocket of infected mosquitos in South Kona and were cautioning the entire island to take precautions.

At the house I spent an hour in the yard turning over buckets and empty flowerpots while keeping my back to the spot where our mulch pile had been. To the bamboo that now rose lustily above the fence. When I was done with the buckets I scheduled a handyman to come replace all our screens. I put bread in the toaster and lectured Ren about what dengue could do to a fetus.

Later, while she brushed her teeth, I deleted the thread of texts to Quincy from my phone. There was nothing incriminating in them aside from the letter he'd written to the 'ōhi'a tree back in October.

Still. I deleted them anyway.

The blank screen beneath his name offered a pretense of comfort.

28

R

There were a lot of ways to pass the day without going to work, it turned out. Eat a whole jar of peanut butter, or watch six straight hours of television, or lie in bed and imagine the skin between your vulva and asshole tearing open like a bag of potato chips. No Crazy Palms, no classes, just an occasional doctor's appointment and an endless string of hours in the house by myself.

The Tuesday after the shower, Quincy came by to talk about finances, or more specifically, what our future financial setup would be, which was a conversation I had been avoiding. I stayed in bed well past eleven, as if refusing to get up would mean the conversation didn't have to happen. He showed up on a break between classes, wearing pants that were too long and pooled around his sandals.

"When do you have to be back?" I asked at the door.

"An hour." His hair was unwashed, and when he came into the living room, he stood there a moment as if he were waiting for someone else.

"Everything okay?"

"Of course. Why?"

I shrugged. I was worried then he might ask about the university job, I still hadn't heard from them, but he didn't, just stared at the photo on our mail table of me and Jess at the beach with a peculiar look on his face. Something felt off, but I couldn't tell what it was, or if I was imagining it. My brain had been foggy for a few days, and the baby book said this was due to a *temporary shrinkage of brain cells*, which was disheartening.

In the kitchen I poured chilled pineapple tea into clean glasses, feeling quite domestic even though it was Jess who'd boiled and strained the fruit skins. I was proud anyway, carrying the drinks outside onto the lanai where we sat, the afternoon blue as a berry, the front walkway dolloped with the upside-down flowerpots Jess had overturned during a frenzied fixation on dengue fever.

The tea was sweet and cold, and Quincy drank his entire glass immediately. We agreed we'd prefer not to involve the state in any sort of official setup, which was a relief for both of us, and that he'd write me a check every month for half of everything—childcare and food, my portion of the mortgage. He'd contribute to the college fund. Like Jess, he seemed at ease talking about money, the way people who had access to it often did, as if it were a hobby, which I guess it was. The whole conversation felt surreal, like we were playing pretend, planning a vacation we'd never actually go on, some extravagant trip to Japan or Greece or Portugal. Except we were going. We were going in just ten weeks. Near the end of the conversation, Quincy told me the university would give him two weeks of paternity leave.

"A full two weeks? How progressive."

He smiled weakly and pressed his empty glass to his cheek. "I can help out however you need. Go to the store or, be here so you can sleep, or…" He seemed unusually flummoxed, as if he wasn't quite sure what I'd need and it embarrassed him.

"Thanks. I'm sure Jess will be in full helicopter mode at that point."

I'd meant it as a joke, but he frowned. "Right," he said, looking out into the street as a pickup rumbled by, and then repeating himself. "Right."

J

The day after I ended things with Quincy, I was on the phone with Tatia Chen when Theo came into my office and shut the door.

I moved to hold a finger up but the look on his face caught my hand down by my ribs.

Tatia yammered excitedly in my ear. Her closing date had been set twenty minutes prior. She'd asked me to celebrate with her and I wanted to say no but felt bad, her loneliness exposed like a bare throat.

All of that evaporated when I saw Theo's face. His eyes were hard little stones and his arms were folded efficiently across his body.

I cut Tatia off midsentence. Told her I'd call her back.

Off the phone, I waited for him to jump right in, but he did not.

"What's up?" I asked, hoping I sounded casual. My chest had filled with bees, and I resisted the urge to rest a calming hand there.

Theo studied me for an uncomfortably long moment. "There was a condom wrapper in the master bath of that two-bedroom on Lōihi."

Outside, a car door slammed.

I tried hard to keep my voice steady as I asked, "Which one is that?"

"The one you and Quincy were at yesterday." His teeth glinted as he spoke with slow, careful enunciation.

Quincy hadn't texted.

He hadn't emailed either.

He hadn't sent any kitchen photos or included me on any group messages.

I tried to coordinate a believable display of surprise, but Theo looked at me squarely and said, "It was cleaned right before and no one else has been there since."

"I—" I started but stopped. There was so much anger on Theo's face, so much force behind his words, I understood that he knew. Fully and without a doubt. That the tiny, jagged pieces he hadn't realized belonged to any sort of puzzle had clicked into place and he could see the full picture.

He could see how ugly it was.

I also understood how unethical my behavior had been. My clients trusted me inside their empty homes. Theo had trusted me. If this came out, I could lose my license.

Somewhere I must have realized this, but it hadn't surfaced and the brutality of my own dissonance was jarring. I wanted to ask who had found the wrapper but didn't dare.

Silence stretched between us like a tendon.

Out on the floor the phone rang, and Kim answered with her usual cheer. I had the sensation that my skin had been peeled back.

"Since when?"

"It isn't happening anymore."

Theo walked to the chair across from my desk and dropped into it. He cupped his face in his hands. "Since *when*?"

"Since yesterday, that was the last—"

"Since when did it *start*?"

I told him.

"Fuck, Jess." He said this without anger but with misery, which was worse. He peered out between spread fingers, the way Quincy had when he admitted his ex worked in real estate. I thought of how he'd called me a snowflake and curled his body around mine so I couldn't leave.

"But...you don't even like Quincy."

I shrugged and he laughed a hot, brittle laugh.

It was Ren's laugh.

The laugh she gave when she felt particularly self-righteous.

Hearing it kicked a hole in my chest.

All the angry little bees poured out.

Down into my arms and legs.

My whole body hummed with a sensation I had been unable to feel until this moment when Theo saw me as I was: guilt. And shame.

Guilt and shame. Shame and guilt.

They blossomed like spores all over my body and I found it hard to breathe.

It wasn't true that I hadn't liked Quincy.

I'd pretended not to like him as a form of preservation.

I wasn't sure anymore who or what I'd been trying to preserve.

I'd fucked Quincy then dismissed him like the asshole I'd accused him of being seven months earlier. It had been easy to pretend our behavior hadn't happened when no one else had witnessed it but now that there was a witness, I could see it the way they did, and it did not look good.

"Are you trying to be together, then?" Theo did not look at me as he asked this.

"No." I gripped the sides of my chair. "It was dumb and now it's over."

"So, what, was it a power move?"

"What? No."

"A mimetic thing?"

"A what? Theo, no, it was just a mistake. It should never have happened."

He was staring at me now. "Why didn't you tell her about it?" I laughed then, a laugh like *why do you think*, and he said, "No, really, if you didn't make it into some big secret, maybe it could've been, I don't know…"

Though the air-conditioning had long ago been fixed, the temperature of the room brusquely felt unbearable. Or maybe it was just what Theo was asking, and the way it aligned with how Quincy seemed to feel. I thought again of all of us at the park, of a world where Quincy could have touched me openly, publicly, where it could have made me happy, and how I had never wanted this, and how clearly something was wrong with me.

"What a fucking prick," he said, and it was then that I remembered with a slap that Quincy was living with him. I knew this, of course, but the information re-contextualized before me as Theo spat, "I'm going to murder him."

"Don't do that." I stopped myself from adding, *who will finish the kitchen?* I stared at the ground. Beneath my chair the carpet stretched its usual oaty color and I decided I didn't like it.

I could have it changed.

I could do that.

This made the bees in my body quiet down until Theo said, "You need to tell her."

"What? Why?"

He stared at me with so much disgust that I had to look away again.

"It's over now," I told the carpet. "And *you're* the one who said we shouldn't stress her out, right?"

"That is so unbelievably manipulative."

"It's also true."

Theo stood. I could feel him staring but didn't look up.

I waited a moment, and then another. "Who found the wrapper?"

"I did." My relief must have been apparent because Theo said, "You're one hundred times better than this."

"Clearly I'm not." It came out more sarcastic than I'd meant it.

The laugh came again, and I did look up.

He had his eyes closed and his palm pressed to the center of his forehead, and when he removed it, he turned toward the door and said, "I need to go tell Quincy to get the fuck out of my house."

"Wait," I said, and he stopped. I thought of Quincy, teaching his second class of the day. Oblivious to the chaos that was about to unfurl around him. "Don't do that, okay?"

"Are you serious? What am I supposed to do, cook him dinner?"

"I mean…"

"No." The muscle of Theo's jaw rippled. "I'm not going to be complicit in whatever the fuck this is."

I could see it then. The weight of what I was asking. The impossibility.

"Okay," I started. "Just. Don't say anything yet. I'll talk to Ren, okay?" I said this without thinking about it because I couldn't bear to think about it quite yet. "Don't kick him out until I talk to her."

He shook his head.

"Just avoid him tonight. Just until I figure it out, okay?"

There was something sort of vacant in Theo's expression. As if he were watching tourists at the beach. People he did not care to know and had no attachment to. Then he left the room.

Alone, I felt my guilt transform into a quiet rage. Quincy'd been packing the condom wrappers out. I knew he had. That he would forget now felt like a conscious betrayal. A passive *fuck you*.

But no. That didn't make sense.

Why would he purposely leave a land mine he knew would blow us both up?

After Theo left, I stared at my computer screen for nearly two hours.

I thought about calling Quincy.

It would be the fair thing to do.

I imagined him across town talking about microbes to a group of twenty-year-old students in a room Ren and I might have sat in ourselves sixteen years earlier.

I imagined him obliviously wiping chalk dust on the front of his pants.

I visualized calling him.

Interrupting his lecture with the savage reality of what was coming.

One moment, he might say when he saw my name on the screen.

I saw him answering right there in class.

How he might turn his back to his students for privacy.

But no. He would never do that.

His phone was likely on silent. Tucked away in that brown messenger bag he always carried.

He would see the missed call after class.

He would swallow a few times before returning it.

Maybe he wouldn't return it.

Maybe he would text me, *Everything alright?*

No, I would respond, and leave him to panic.

I sat very still at my desk and imagined this scenario and a few more.

I imagined them because it was easier than imagining whatever Ren was doing at home, and how slight the change to Quincy's reality would be compared to hers.

To mine.

I thought of the photo he sent last week of his bare feet in front of a blank wall. A half-empty closet.

In the end I did not call him. I stared at the void of my computer screen and did nothing at all.

29

R

I got the call from Marta in the Arts department just a few hours after Quincy left, and I held the phone away from my ear as if it might protect me from whatever she was about to say, which turned out to be: *part-time, jazz, hip-hop, intro to modern dance.* The semester began the following fall. I'd been lying on the floor working out a kink in my lumbar as the phone rang, and when I saw the name on the screen everything went still. *Three classes, two student showcases,* a hum in the background from that big boxy fan in her office. I imagined the hair moving around her face as if it were sentient. She told me I'd be getting an email with an official offer in a day or so. *Congratulations, Ren,* and, *We're all very excited.*

The call felt twenty minutes long, but when I hung up, I saw that it had been less than six. I stayed on the floor for a while, staring at the ceiling as a weightlessness rose up and held me, hovering a foot off the floor. I called Jess twice, but she didn't answer, then Theo, voice mail again. I sent Quincy a text because I knew he was teaching, then remained on the ground opening and closing my fists and thinking: soon I would also have texts to receive while I taught. I tried to visualize the students I might have, but their faces all looked like mine. I waited an hour and when no one got back to me, I leashed Sookie up and together we walked down the street to the truck that sold smoothies and acai bowls, because it was the only thing I could think of doing to celebrate.

It was six by the time I got there, and the woman working was just starting to slide the gridded metal gate down in front of her window, shoulders bare, nineteen or twenty with a high swinging ponytail. She looked between me and Sookie then pushed the gate back up, made me a bowl anyway, likely because of how pregnant I was, or how much I was sweating from the walk. The bowl was intensely purple, piled high with bananas and shredded coconut. It melted quite a bit on the way back to the house, where I ate only half of it, the coconut a little soapy but the fruit puree cool and sweet on my tongue, sitting on the front lanai, licking at my plastic spoon, holding my sticky fingers low for Sookie as we waited for Jess to come home, watching the sky shift from blue to pink to a mottled mulberry that became black so slowly I barely noticed. The temperature dropped, but I didn't go inside for a sweater. Instead, I closed my eyes and let myself feel it. Cool air, but also: joy.

I felt my son kick and I understood that things were just beginning. I had never quite felt that way before, or if I had, I couldn't remember it. Even after college, when the world should've felt big and bright and vernal, I slipped into things at Ralphie's and Crazy's on the pretext I'd be off to something else soon, which was still the truth if I could accept *soon* as relative, flexible, a sixteen-year soon, but finally soon had arrived, and this is what it felt like, crisp and exciting, like biting into a sturdy piece of chilled fruit. I wrapped my arms around myself and welcomed the little bumps that sprouted over my arms and legs, because I knew when I went inside, they would be gone, and this was clear proof that I was alive and changing, evidence borne by my own raised skin that good things were coming to me, and that I was ready for them.

J

Tatia wanted to go to Crazy Palms. Of course she did. I started to suggest somewhere else but stopped myself. It would be fitting, wouldn't it?

Seven months earlier I'd gone there and everything had changed. What could it do for me tonight?

I knew I needed to go home.

Ren'd called twice since Theo left my office and I hadn't answered. Theo couldn't keep any sort of secret, not that he'd even pretended he would.

But I didn't go home.

Maybe I wanted to hold on to a few more hours of normalcy. Maybe I was just a coward. Either way I justified the decision easily. It had taken six months to find Tatia a property. If she wanted me to celebrate, it was my job to oblige.

Happy hour was still underway. Ren's bouncer friend nodded as I passed and though I knew his name I did not use it. Inside I was enveloped by the same smoky beer smell Ren had carried home for years. Her spot was filled by a young kid with long hair tied at the nape of his neck in the same fashion Taylor wore his.

The sight of him stilled me. I stood until he looked up. Then I turned quickly away.

Tatia sat alone at a two-top. She said my name as if she hadn't seen me in years. I held my face forward so she could kiss my cheek the way she liked.

I don't have friends either, I fleetingly felt like telling her. I hadn't made a friend since I met Ren. Unless you counted Theo, which I did not. Unless you counted Quincy, which I definitely did not.

IZ's cover of "Over the Rainbow" played from the speakers at an obnoxious decibel that seemed counterintuitive to the general peace of the song. "I love this place before it gets crowded," Tatia half shouted. She had a drink already. Something dark with a little red straw. "Don't you want anything?"

I looked toward the bar. Two sunburned women in colorful shirts sipped unnaturally blue liquid out of what looked like a fishbowl and the sight of the kid cracking the tops off Coronas made me wince.

I had the stabbing understanding that his presence was like a window into a place that should contain Ren but did not, and this window terrified me.

My body began its painful hum, the familiar spasm that was inarguably linked to my inability to manipulate my own surroundings.

Quincy had quieted it for a while.

This wasn't something I wanted to look at.

How when he first showed up in our kitchen, I took it as a personal affront.

As if some part of me could see into the future.

But I knew that wasn't it.

The problem wasn't Quincy.

The problem had probably never been Quincy.

"What d'ya think?" Tatia asked then.

"About what?"

She pointed a fingernail toward the women at the bar. Their necks were the color of raw salmon save for two matching ribbons of white skin, the telltale track of a swimsuit. She motioned toward their goblet of blue slush and smiled wickedly. "Should we get one of *those*?"

I managed to wait until the rideshare pulled out of the driveway to vomit. Bright blue liquid splashed on the asphalt. Above me, palms swayed like long-necked dinosaurs.

It was early. Just after eight. And yet there I was, puking a puddle of pool-colored liquid by the front steps.

In the living room Sookie lifted her head from the couch but did not move. Just a watchful stare. Tail wagging cautiously. Like she was making up her mind.

I placed my palm flat against the wall to steady myself as I moved down the hall. Past the nursery. Ren's door was open. Her TV was on.

Blue light flickered and beneath it she lay on the bed with her back to me and her body curled like a kidney bean.

As I approached, she turned and smiled. "Hiya," she said, scooting over and patting the space where she'd been.

I moved into it. The stretch where she had lain was warm and I felt paralyzed, marinating in a patch of her heat.

"Where were you?" Her voice was heavy with sleep. "I called."

I moved closer to her. Murmured something about going to celebrate.

"Celebrate what?"

I nuzzled into her back.

It felt like nuzzling into myself.

I walked my fingers down one of her shoulders. The soft fabric of her shirt. It felt so good I could cry.

She rolled to face me then, grunting lightly with the effort. The TV illuminated the curve of her cheekbone in a chilly blue. "Celebrate what?" she asked again.

I placed my hand against the warm globe of her stomach which felt solid and still, but I knew that inside it, life moved. "Magic," I said.

"Wait," she said. "Are you drunk?" There was a smile in her voice.

I must've nodded because she laughed, and the room swam and I tried to close my eyes but when I did I saw Theo in my office staring at me with disgust so I opened them again and said, "I did something stupid."

The corners of her mouth tugged upward as if something good were coming. "What's that?" Her fist was tucked by her cheek. I poked a finger into the center of it and when she squeezed, a million warm shivers surged throughout my body.

I thought of Quincy's story about the fish not noticing their own water.

I thought about the second life living inside Ren.

Moving all the time beneath her skin.

He moved, too.

Our hearts hammered out blood in gallons as the earth spun and we tried to steady ourselves inside it. To lie to ourselves. To tell ourselves that we were still.

That we knew what was happening around us.

That we were in control.

"What," she asked again, giving my finger another squeeze.

Her face hung before me, big like the moon. The face I always found in a room full of strangers, and always, every time, it felt like coming home.

"Why are you being so weird?" she asked, and I leaned in and pressed my mouth against hers.

Her belly stood firm between us and then her hands were on my shoulders, and I touched my tongue against the soft skin of her lip and she pulled back slightly, a curtain of air between us.

"It's okay," I said, and closed the space. Found her mouth again.

One of my hands moved up toward her hair, moving moving moving and then, she pushed.

Her palms were solid against my shoulders, and I realized they may have been pushing the whole time, what felt like a minute only a second, and as cool air came between us again Ren backed away with a look that was unfamiliar.

She sat up.

Blinked as if she couldn't quite see me. "What is happening?" she asked.

"Nothing." An ache had begun at the base of my tongue. "Nothing," I repeated.

Her eyes were wide and full of something I couldn't read as she shook her head.

Just one gentle shake.

No.

I felt acutely as if I might vomit again. Blue bile rose. I swallowed.

Shut my eyes against some understanding screaming from the center of me.

Some disorienting sensation.

Like walking into a room you recognized though you'd never been there. A feeling that told me. Made me understand. There had always been a line between us, invisible yet solid, and I had just crossed it.

Bile rose now in the form of words. As if I might say anything to escape the moment I had created. "Quincy and I slept together."

Ren's mouth opened.

I thought about the lonely vulnerability of Quincy's body laid bare on a stranger's bed.

"A few times." The room was incredibly warm. "But we stopped."

Silence hung heavy and then she said, "Fuck."

The sharp consonant digraph slammed against my ribs.

She was out of the bed then. "What the fuck." A muscle rippled across her jaw and the look on her face was like a door slamming. Her voice came again. Thin and shaky and full of jagged accusation. "Oh my god. While you looked at all those houses?" And then, with fresh understanding, "Is that why you were so fucking weird at my shower?"

Had we been weird at her shower? My vision was spotting. I shook my head.

"I know," I tried. "I don't know what I was thinking."

Then it came.

That hot little laugh Theo'd given me in my office. "You don't know what you were thinking?" Her voice had an edge. Accusatory. Demanding.

It was an edge I recognized.

It was an edge I'd heard coming from me.

"You *don't* know *what* you were *thinking*?" she said again, weaponizing every other word.

Distrust, disbelief, rage, anguish. These flashed in symphony over her face, expressions I'd seen before, but never, not once, directed toward me.

My voice was pinned to the back of my throat. I said her name finally, with effort, and with her eyes on the floor she said, "I need you to leave."

"Ren—" It came out choked.

"You need to leave."

I rose to kneeling, my body small in the tangled knot of her sheets. "But—"

"Out," she said, backing away with a barbarous finality that seemed to puncture something deep within me. "Out of the house."

"But where—"

She backed to her own door and flung it wide open. "Get out."

A version of sobriety had descended by the time Theo's car pulled into the drive, accompanied by a throb between my temples. The overnight bag by my feet was the same one I'd taken camping just two months earlier.

I couldn't remember what I'd packed.

Only the sound of Ren's door as it closed behind me.

When Theo'd answered the phone, I'd apologized for calling so late though it wasn't late at all. Barely even nine.

While I waited for him, I'd forced myself to open the door to the nursery.

To stand inside it and observe its tidiness.

The hours Ren had spent lovingly arranging it.

It was the only room I had ever seen her clean voluntarily and its order made me claustrophobic. I spent a solid minute staring at that crib before I closed the door.

Theo said nothing when I got into the car.

His seats smelled of orange oil, and as we drove down Kalaniana'ole I inhaled the comfort of clean upholstery and stared into the windows of houses, their yellow light fleeing into the dark.

I hadn't wanted to call Theo.

I hadn't wanted to call anyone.

I had thought about ignoring Ren's order entirely and crawling into my own bed to deal with things in the morning.

But she'd rattled me. Not so much her demand for me to leave but the look on her face while she made it.

Theo's jaw worked tightly back and forth. I knew he'd have talked to Ren in some form before retrieving me. A call or a text. I wanted to ask him what she said. I wanted to know if she told him about the kiss or just the confession. I wanted to ask if he'd spoken to Quincy. If he'd kicked him out. If he'd be at the house when I arrived.

I didn't ask any of these things.

"Thanks for picking me up," I said weakly.

He nodded. I could see him chewing on the inside of his lip.

"Are we not speaking?"

"I don't know."

We lapsed into silence until finally I said, "Well. You were right."

He didn't ask me what I meant, and I wasn't quite sure if I even knew.

There was a light on downstairs when we arrived at the house.

I waited to feel something, but nothing came.

Theo led me around the side and through the sliders on the lower floor. I got the impression he was trying not to look at me.

From beneath Quincy's door a blade of light sliced the dark room.

I studied it and thought of Ren's face as she told me to get out.

Following my gaze, Theo flipped the overhead light and I winced.

"Sorry," he said without sounding it.

Lit, I could see the kitchen had a gaping hole where the sink should've been, the guts of its piping on full display.

Theo began moving neat piles of laundry off the futon against the far wall. "Third bedroom is full of boxes so this'll have to do." He kept his back to me. "Sorry it isn't more comfortable."

I told him it was fine, great, even though of course nothing was great. I was aware of the stillness behind Quincy's door and that he could hear us.

The hinge of the futon caught, and I put my bag down to help. We stood on either end and jiggled things around without making eye contact. Inside my mouth my tongue felt thick and molluscan.

Finally, we got the futon down and Theo went into the spare room and returned with linen sheets and a thick quilted blanket.

I was struck by the full circle we'd taken. Me a guest in his home. I thought, too, that if Ren hadn't gotten pregnant, Theo'd still be living with us and then who would I have called?

But of course, if Ren hadn't gotten pregnant Quincy would've just been some stranger she'd brought home from the bar and then promptly forgotten about.

Theo shrugged then, though neither of us had said anything. "We can talk tomorrow, just…" He paused. Shook his head as if changing his mind. "Lights are by the stairs."

"Great." I cringed. I wished I would stop using that word.

After he left I forced myself to put the sheets on the futon. To spread the quilted blanket. When the bed was made, I sat and thought about how Ren and Quincy had stood in this room three days earlier and made small talk as I listened from upstairs and felt relieved.

Raw wires tentacled from the kitchen ceiling where a light fixture had been removed. The mess felt appropriate. Like I belonged in it.

The floor creaked in Quincy's room then, and a shadow passed the sliver of light beneath his door. I could tell that he was aware of me.

I was curiously removed from my body. As if none of this was happening.

I'd felt that way the whole time we'd been doing what we did.

As if I were operating in a space that didn't really exist.

As if it didn't matter.

But of course it mattered.

Everything mattered.

Quincy opened his door. He wore gym shorts and a plain white shirt and there was a deep groove between his eyebrows. Like he'd aged years in two days. "Hey," he said, as if it were normal for me to be there.

I just looked at him. My presence, the bag by my feet. My embarrassment was ferocious.

He hovered in the open door. It seemed impossible that he was the same person who'd so recently stretched naked beside me. "I talked to Theo," he said finally.

"Ah."

"He's not very happy with me, obviously." A pause stretched, and when I looked up at him, he was giving me a warm, almost affectionate look. This surprised me.

"Are you leaving, then?"

He nodded. "Tomorrow."

I didn't ask where he was going.

I didn't know where he could go.

I had never really thought too heavily about Quincy's existence outside of my own and the question reminded me of how much he'd liked the house we saw the day before and how in another universe where we'd never slept together maybe we'd have made an offer on it and I'd be at home.

"How is Ren?" he asked.

"Not happy."

His mouth pulled to one side. "I'm sorry, Jess." His face strained as if he were in pain. "I don't know how I left that wrapper. Honestly, I don't remember doing it. I was a bit out of it."

It would've been nice to be able to blame him for everything, but I knew that was unfair, and I told him as much.

"Yeah, I know," he said, "but I still feel like I hold the lion's share of responsibility."

"Why's that?"

He lifted his shoulders then let them drop. "I guess because I'm the interloper."

I wanted to say that gave him less responsibility. He was the dispensable one. Instead, I shrugged and said, "Next time you knock someone up try not to start fucking her roommate."

He smiled then. A sad sort of smile. His eyes met mine with the look he used to give me before things started. As if he knew what I was thinking and thought the same thing, too. "You're not just her roommate."

I picked at a thread on my bedding. "I'm surprised Theo didn't try to kick your ass." I'd meant it to be a joke, but his face went slack.

"I'd have let him, too."

I didn't say anything else, and after a moment he told me he'd probably just go to bed. He paused slightly after he said it. Held my gaze.

An invitation.

Over his shoulder his sheets were already thrown back as if he'd been in bed when we arrived. For a second I allowed myself to imagine a scenario where I could climb into his bed and let him curl around me. We'd never slept together in the actual sleeping way of things.

It would not be the comfort I was looking for.

I told him to get some rest and he nodded as if that's what he expected me to say. Before he closed his door, he looked back at me and said, "Jess?"

I waited.

"I am sorry though."

"Yeah." I shrugged. "Me, too." His door closed with a gentle click.

I called Ren twice before I got into bed.

There was a flickering hope that she'd answer and I could apologize and she would let me come home. Pick me up even. I could make a pot of jasmine tea. I could tell her I was sorry. That I hadn't meant to kiss her. Or, more accurately, that I hadn't known what I meant when I did. That I didn't understand my own feelings.

She didn't answer, of course.

I changed into the sleeping shirt I'd managed to shove into my duffel and used the little bathroom to brush my teeth.

Quincy's lights were off when I came out.

I thought how I could still knock on his door and open it and enter and walk the few feet across the floor and climb into his bed where he'd open his arms and let me.

I could do that if I wanted.

But I did not want to.

I crawled onto the futon and waited impatiently for sleep.

30

R

I woke with the birds, light filtering into the room in bruised purples and blues, daylight still an hour off, with a hollow in my chest, a tightness behind my eyes that I couldn't immediately place. The baby kicked and I rolled onto my back, imagining—as I often did—his tiny limbs moving inside me, and what he would look like when he arrived, the shape of his nose, the color of his hair, his skin.

I had about sixty seconds of this until, like a douse of frigid water, I placed the source of the cavernous ache above my ribs: Jess, and her drunken, devastating, left-field confession. I sat up sharply, nearly gasping as embarrassed, curdled fury landed hot in my throat. It sprang front and center, the things that had been kept from me, had gone on behind my back. Humiliation washed in then, shame over my own idiotic oblivion, thick and rancid and cruelly unfair. *Be nice, try harder.* It felt as if a hole had been punched into the wall of my life, and through it, everything that had seemed one way now looked entirely differ-

ent. Interactions ran through my brain like slides: the ebb and
flow of Jess's warmth toward Quincy, her behavior on Halloween, the time after dinner she walked him to his car and stayed
down there so long I fell asleep.

And the kiss! I couldn't decide which was more disorienting—
the kiss or the confession, and how the two were related, or if
they were related at all. I thought of the look on Jess's face when
I told her to get out, as if I'd slapped her, as if she might cry.

I had never, not once in seventeen years, seen Jess cry.

Good, I thought, she should cry. She deserved to cry. But
even as I thought it, I felt my own tears building in response,
that hot pressure from the front of my skull. I'd fallen asleep to
my own choked noise, thinking of all the hours I'd spent putter-
ing around, hopeful, lonely, terrified, excited, a whole range of
oblivious mental states, thinking I knew where I was and what
was happening as Jess fucked Quincy instead of showing him
houses, or fucked him while she showed him houses, or showed
him which houses were fun to be fucked in. Had she gone to
the shitty rental he'd shared with that Craigslist roommate?
Had he ever come here? Jess didn't even like sex! She described
it as clinical, something done to her, something she didn't feel
like she was participating in. And that party they'd thrown me,
that fucking awkward party. Rage curled inside me like a fist,
and I cradled it.

Theo'd called to tell me she was sleeping downstairs on the
futon, as if she would stay there, as if it would make me feel better if she did. I lay completely still and pictured her and Quincy
waking up together, having coffee, coming up with a plan for
the mess they'd made—Jess was great with contingency plans,
and Quincy, he'd surely do whatever she wanted. They would
be closer now, unified by my anger. Maybe they'd find their
own place, and ten years from now I'd just be a diluted memory, the person that brought them together, the means to their
end. I lifted my hand in front of my face and imagined it noth-

ing but a bundle of bones belonging to someone else, but immediately that someone else became Jess and the hand rested on Quincy's chest.

What would have happened if they'd told me earlier? Before they acted on it? Would it still have felt like a betrayal? Neither of them had ever really belonged to me in any definitive way. So why did it feel like treason?

In the kitchen, I opened the slider door for Sookie and drank the last of the juice straight from the carton, leaving it empty on the counter in an act of pointless defiance considering that Jess wasn't there to clean it up. I forced myself to check my phone, four missed calls, a text, a voice mail, and deleted them without looking, without listening. I spotted a sticky note she'd left on the fridge earlier in the week about thawing the turkey and I remembered—Thanksgiving. We were supposed to have it at our house, Jess had brought home humongous sweet potatoes to turn into a casserole. That had been the day before yesterday—*yesterday*. And now everything was entirely different. I peeled the note off the fridge, crumpled it, threw it in the sink, ran the tap, and let the garbage disposal rip. I sat that way for a minute, the water running, the gears grinding. When I turned it off the house was so quiet and still that I felt like breaking glass just for the sound of it.

Instead, I circled back to our fridge, the scrapbook of our life stuck all over its face, receipts of taunting normalcy pinned atop one another, Jess's digitally whitened smile on her promo magnet. I dragged the trash can over and cleared the entire thing, the scan from our first ultrasound, the graduation snapshot, everything shoved in the can until nothing was left but a shiny plane of stainless steel and a distorted, fun house construction of my own reflection. I looked at the wobbly line of my face, my hair a wild shadow around my head, and pretended that I did not know that woman. Somehow, this was less painful than the idea that it was Jess I didn't know.

★ ★ ★

Later that morning I received the official offer from the university. I opened the attachment and skimmed it until my eye
hit a number and stopped. The start salary, though much less
than what Jess made annually, was nearly twice my combined
pull from the bar and Ralphie's. I accepted it immediately, my
hands shaking, proud of myself for not calling anyone to con-
fer, which really meant I felt gratified that Jess might find out
about this from someone else.

I was forcing down a bowl of cereal, imagining the nutrients
bypassing my own stomach and entering directly into my son's,
when a car pulled into the driveway. I froze at the sound of the
wheels crunching, then pushed my bowl away dramatically. I
didn't want to talk to her, but at the same time, I wanted her to
see how devastated I was, to know what she had done, which
made me feel small and hot and embarrassed. In the living room
I pulled back the blinds, my heart beating so hard I could hear
it in my ears. Quincy's white Element sat in the drive, and at
first I'd thought they'd come together—what nerve—but no,
it was just Quincy, moving toward the steps with his odd, lop-
ing gait, his feet turned slightly out, and I thought: Will my son
walk like that? Will he have those narrow shoulders? Those long,
orangutan arms? Will he be a total fucking asshole?

I was shaking by the time he made it to the top of the steps,
my insides egg-yolked. He looked pale, his shirt wrinkled, and
I wondered whether Jess's head had rested on that bit of cotton.
"Hey," he said, then a pause, room for me to return the greeting.
When I didn't, he took a long, slow swallow. "Can we talk?"

I did not invite him inside, I'd done enough of that. Instead,
I stepped out into the bright morning, closing the door behind
me. It was early still, my feet bare, the wood dry beneath them.
I knew I needed a shower but somehow I felt proud to be raw
and exposed and smelling entirely of myself, or maybe I just
wanted my appearance on the outside to match how I felt on

the inside in hopes it would make him feel terrible. I folded my arms atop the shelf of my stomach and gave him an expectant look, a look I hoped said *you have one minute*, a look I hoped said *go fuck yourself.* I gave him this look and wondered if this is what the next eighteen years would be like: me on the porch with my arms crossed staring at the father of my child, a man I had never loved and now refused to like. This couldn't be more opposite from the way I had felt yesterday, outside on the exact same piece of wood, feeling as if the world was opening just for me, and I shoved my hands in the pockets of my sweatpants to hide my trembling fists.

He told me he was sorry, pulling idly on his own earlobe. "I want you to know that and, to hear that from me." He stopped then, as if I might speak, but all I did was remove my hands from my pockets and cross my arms again. "I don't know what Jess told you, she's not really telling me much—"

I laughed then, over how distressed he sounded. I'd meant to sound incredulous, but in actuality I was immensely relieved to know this, that maybe we were all alone on our own little emotional islands. These unspoken lines of unity made me dizzy, how they'd shifted continuously without me even realizing it— Jess and me, me and Quincy, Quincy and Jess, now none.

He gave me a miserable look. "I feel like you should know that I started it, and that she ended it, and I'm sorry."

"Sorry for what? That you started it? Or that she ended it?" It was the first thing I'd said, and even I was surprised by the hissing, snarling way it came out, the sound of an animal you had to coax from a pit with a long stick.

But Quincy's gaze went soft, as if he was grateful I'd spoken at all. "All of it. I feel like I dropped a bomb on your life, I feel like—" He closed his eyes and paused before saying, "I want you to know how excited I was, how excited I *am*, to be a dad." He looked at me then. "To do this thing with you, and with Jess—" I winced on her name and his face collapsed as he stared up at the roofline, swallowing hard, and when he looked back down his eyes shone in a way that made my throat close. I tried to hold on to the kite of my anger before it floated away. He looked at me with large, wet eyes. "You two had such a cool thing going and then I came along and..." He touched his throat, then ran a distressed hand through his hair. "I do this thing, Ren, where I fuck everything up. It's, it's a pattern of mine. I always fuck everything up."

"I'm not going to feel bad for you."

"No, I know, I'm not trying to make you feel bad for me."

"Good, because I don't."

He rubbed his jaw. "I just want you to know that nothing was..." He paused as if searching for the right word. "*Calculated.* If that makes sense."

Quincy, I realized abruptly, could move back to Missoula if he wanted. He could get his old job back, and his old girlfriend with her mountain bike and big hat, and his life would be exactly as it was before he came here. Jess had more to lose than he did, she was the one who'd take the brunt of this. And me. "Are there feelings, then?"

"I have those, if that's what you mean." This was a joke, though of course I did not laugh. He seemed to deflate further. "I have feelings for Jess, yes. But Jess, she, she wasn't ever... I think she felt..." I bristled. Even though I'd asked, I didn't like him telling me how Jess felt. If she wanted me to know how she felt she should tell me herself, although I knew this wasn't fair, because I was actively ignoring her calls. I found myself experiencing two opposing feelings that each made sense individually but no sense at all when combined. "I don't know how she felt, I guess," Quincy finished.

"You know what I keep thinking about?" I said, not caring about the bitterness oiling my words, my breath. "When all this started Jess complained about how *easy* you were taking this. She asked what the *catch* was."

Quincy studied me for a moment. "She told me that."

I felt a surge of intense, maddening fury then, that Quincy already knew this, that the two of them would have talked about this together. "Did she tell you she thought you were a sociopath?"

He swallowed. "She did not."

"Well, she did. And last night, she came in drunk. She said she'd been *celebrating*." Quincy frowned. I could tell this bothered him, and that made me feel a bit better. "And then she kissed me."

Quincy's mouth opened like a dying fish. He took a full inhale and exhale. "Was that... Had you... Had you ever..."

"No."

I could see him trying to push this new information around, trying to make things come together into some shape that made sense. I felt a bit of anger drain out of me then. "I know you and I were never really a thing, other than that one night," I said, and he looked away then as if he were ashamed, as if the memory alone made him uncomfortable. "I know technically that means you can fuck whoever you like. I just think your selection and timing are terrible."

"Right, well, my selection and timing are usually terrible." I didn't laugh, and he grimaced. "Sorry. I *am* sorry, Ren."

I shrugged. The day was unrolling into its full beauty, sunnied and crisp, and I felt robbed.

"I got the job, by the way," I said then.

His face brightened. "You did? Of course you did. I knew you would."

"Well, I didn't."

Inside, the landline began to ring, shrill and sharp. Once, twice, I didn't move.

"Do you need to—" Quincy started, but I cut him off with a shake of the head. He held my gaze then, both of us there on the lanai, staring at each other, listening to the phone ring, neither of us moving, because neither of us knew quite where to go.

J

Quincy was gone when I woke.

His door had been left wide open and his bed was made with military precision.

I poked my head into the room. His clothes hung neatly in the closet.

Upstairs, Taylor sat shirtless at the kitchen table with his hair loose around his shoulders. An empty cereal bowl rested by his elbow and his laptop was open.

He smiled when he saw me. "Morning," he said. My mouth held a sharp acidic taste. "Sleep okay?" His eyes were soft and warm, and I wondered what exactly Theo had told him. Not that it mattered anyway.

I said yes, I'd slept great. I knew my face couldn't be convincing.

"Sorry. I know that futon isn't very comfortable..."

"It was fine, really."

I realized then how little I'd been alone with Taylor. How we were usually buffered by Theo's presence. He shifted awkwardly, as if he were thinking the same thing. "Can I get you anything? We have cereal, eggs..."

"Coffee?"

He pointed to a French press on the counter by the fridge. It was half-full. I moved to it. Placed my palm on the glass. Still warm. "Is Theo up?"

Taylor's eyes were back on his laptop. "He headed into the office about twenty minutes ago."

I chose a heavy yellow mug from the cupboard. It wasn't even eight yet. Theo was never at the office this early. Avoiding me, most likely.

I watched Taylor move a finger over his track pad and wondered what his life was like this time last year. Certainly nothing close to this. He was lucky to have found Theo.

To be in this bright, quiet kitchen.

No more noisy roommates.

No one else's leftovers growing mold in the fridge. Stability. Space.

Theo's party had sent him in a new direction completely. How unnerving to think that one person could come in and change everything for you.

I was turning away when he began to speak. "You know, I think Theo is making a bigger deal of this than it needs to be."

When I looked back, Taylor's eyes were on his screen and for a moment I thought I had hallucinated, but then he lifted his face, which was not washed in the timidity I had come to expect but something almost detached.

"I thought something was going on. With you and Quincy, I mean." I just looked at him. This was the first assertive observation he had ever volunteered to me, and the fact that it was about my own behavior was startling. "When we all went camping. And definitely by Halloween."

This time, when his smile came it was not the timorous crescent I had grown accustomed to but one of calm self-regulation and I understood then how much I'd underestimated him.

His presence in our group. His ability to govern himself.

That what I had taken to be an adolescent meekness may actually have been a proclivity for nonpartisan surveillance.

A keen, sharpened knack for deduction.

I cleared a discomfited lump from my throat. "You didn't mention it to Theo?"

He shrugged, looked back at his screen. "I figured you'd work it out."

Back downstairs with my mug of coffee I found a text from Theo letting me know he'd come home at lunch to take me to my car. Nothing, I noted, from Ren.

I dug around in my bag to see what I'd managed to bring with me. Socks. A pair of jeans. A balled-up blouse now matted with wrinkles. Fresh underwear. Not enough to last more than a day.

Out in the yard, the sun was covered by a field of clouds, and I sat at the shaded patio table and listened to the doves and messaged Kim to tell her I wouldn't be in until the afternoon.

Asked her to field my calls and cancel my eleven a.m.

Overhead, the clouds glowed in their effort to mask the sun. I stared without blinking until my eyes began to ache.

Then I dialed the house. Closed my eyes and imagined the phone in the kitchen ringing. Once, twice, three times. This time, I did not hang up.

In my mind, I summoned Ren.

Watched her walk out of her room and down the hall.

Through the living room.

I saw her socked feet move across the floor.

I saw her bring her hand to the ringing phone.

I heard a click and held my breath for her voice, but no. Just my own, reaching me through the answering machine. I hung up. Took a sip of my coffee, the bitter liquid easing the throb between my temples.

I drank most of the cup and then tried Ren's cell.

Her voice mail kicked on immediately. The same one she'd had for over ten years. I did not leave a message. Instead, I sent an email to Lisa asking her if she had time to take over one of my clients, and she wrote back almost immediately.

I sent her Quincy's contact and a list of the properties we'd already seen.

There were fourteen of them.

A list of the locations for our bad behavior.

I blinked that thought away and tried the house again.

I was still out back when Quincy showed up. I tried not to wonder where he'd been, up and out so early.

"Hey," he said, then sat across from me and drummed his fingers against the tabletop.

He wore the same shirt he'd had on the day I ended things. Eight buttons. A pale gray.

I wanted to ask if he had spoken to Ren but instead I said, "Not teaching today?"

"Called out."

His fingernails rested atop the glass. They looked clean and red around the edges as if recently scrubbed.

I told him then that Lisa would be taking over his account. That he would hear from her soon. He gave me another sad, sleepy smile and I looked away. Swallowed the lump in my throat. "Have you heard from Ren?"

"Actually, yeah."

He was staring out at the yard, morning light tracing the profile of his face. The buzzing began behind my sternum. "When?"

He looked over. "Just now. I went over there."

"You went to the house?"

He paused as if considering something. "Yeah."

"And?"

That Ren would talk to Quincy and not me felt so unfair my vision went spotty.

I had called the house six times since I woke up.

I imagined them sitting in the living room as the phone rang endlessly in the kitchen.

My cheeks began to burn.

Quincy was speaking. "I told her that all of it was my idea, and that you're the one who called it off."

I knew he was trying to put me at ease, but I felt the opposite of at ease. Of course Ren would be angrier at me than she would be at Quincy. Even if it was his idea. Even if I did end it. He could afford to be an asshole. The real transgression had been mine.

His voice dropped an octave, and he peered up at me through the hedge of his eyelashes. "She told me that you kissed her."

Right. That.

I could feel him watching me. Waiting for me to explain myself. I picked my mug up as if there were still something inside of it.

After a moment he placed his palm on the glass of the tabletop. "Well, I guess I'll go pack up, then." I didn't respond and eventually he stood and added, "I'm a little bummed I won't get to finish that kitchen."

He had the collar of his shirt pinched between two fingers and was staring at me like he wasn't talking about the kitchen at all.

I stayed at the table for a few minutes longer and then followed him inside. Leaned against the door to his room as he pulled his shirts from their hangers. It was odd, but now that he was leaving, I felt a hard push of panic. This man, who I had spent months wishing away. Now I was getting what I'd wanted and all I felt was a frenzied dread.

"Where will you go?"

"Sublet on the other side of campus." He opened the top drawer of the dresser. Scooped out a dozen or so pairs of white socks rolled into neat packages the size and shape of dinner rolls. Crossed over to the suitcase that lay open on his bed and snuggled the pairs inside one by one with a precision that surprised me.

He and Theo made great roommates after all.

He zipped the bag.

Lifted the massive thing with one easy swoop and set it by the door not far from my feet.

I stared at the luggage so I didn't have to look at him. Navy nylon monogrammed with his initials in thick white stitching. I couldn't imagine him ordering that bag for himself. Probably a gift. Received on a Christmas morning somewhere it snows. Steaming cups of coffee. The ex-wife. Maybe they had matching sets. Maybe she was off in the world somewhere with the other half.

I'd only packed enough clothes for one night away.

I couldn't stop focusing on this.

On all the things I needed at home.

When I looked back up Quincy was removing the sheets from the bed. I felt like I should say something, but I wasn't sure what. I finally came up with, "Lisa's good. Everything should be smooth."

He glanced up and threw me a half smile. "I have no doubts."

The room was empty then. A bald mattress. Closet open. A few hangers still swaying softly.

Quincy moved toward me suddenly. No, not toward me. Toward his suitcase.

I backed out of the doorway to create a wider berth between us. The movement was awkward and he looked at me for a long moment.

"You know—" he started, then stopped. His gaze dropped to the floor. He wore those sandals, the ones from the night we met. They didn't seem as hideous as they used to.

Quincy started again. "The last couple months..." He trailed off. I kept my gaze on his feet. His toenails were trim and square. "I guess it felt like something really good was starting." There was a tremor to his voice I'd never heard before. "Not just you and me, but also Ren, even Theo. All of us. I was really...just... *excited.*"

I forced myself to look up at him. He seemed tired. Older. His shoulders hung lower than I remembered. I stood there quietly and thought of Ren. Of how she, too, had seemed so excited. Bright.

"What I mean is, I don't remember the last time I felt that way. Like there was really something to look forward to."

"I know," I said finally.

We stood facing one another for a long moment. I could sense he wanted me to say more, but I wasn't sure what. He leaned forward and kissed me on the cheek. "Have a good Thanksgiving, Jess," he said, and moved for the slider doors.

Thanksgiving. It seemed unimaginable. Like today existed in some sort of vacuum. Some nightmarish rabbit hole I'd fallen into. Except I'd dug the hole myself.

I watched him go. The tall, oversized stretch of his body dipped through the doorway and then with a wave he was gone.

Alone, I stared at the slider he'd just exited through. A rectangle of morning light like the entrance to the afterlife.

From the driveway came the noisy first breath of Quincy's car, then the zippy vroom of it backing up and away. I waited a few more moments. My hands hung empty at my sides.

31

R

Theo tried hard to bully his way over for Thanksgiving, but the idea of sitting around with him and Taylor was exhausting, and even though he tried to assure me we didn't have to talk about "it," the idea of talking around the issue felt just as tiring as talking about the issue itself. I was irritated, too, that he'd taken her side so immediately. "I'm not *taking her side*," he'd said on the phone. "I just think you have twenty years of friendship on the line and now may not be the best time for radical change."

"*I'm* not the one who made a *radical change*," I snapped, though of course it wasn't true, considering the pregnancy was the biggest change I'd ever made.

I heard him sigh. "You should at least talk to her."

"I don't want to talk to her."

It was true, I didn't want to talk to her, was ignoring her calls, but every time I heard the whack of a car door outside, my pulse quickened. I was trying not to think about how long I could avoid her. It was easier if I focused only on the present moment, the next few hours, if I told myself I didn't have to talk to her *this morning*, which turned into *this afternoon, this evening*.

"Just let us come over. We can bring takeout, there won't even be any dishes."

I thought about the massive frozen turkey in our freezer and felt a stab of longing for the day we'd planned. Jess had always dismissed Thanksgiving as *a celebration of colonization*, but still, she'd bought the bird. Hypocrisy seemed to be her style, I mused.

I managed to get him to drop the subject by lying about plans with old coworkers from the gym. I could tell he didn't believe me, but I didn't care.

I spent Thanksgiving morning in bed, ignoring the house phone, listening to the rain and feeling sorry for myself. I got up once to pee and let Sookie out so she could do the same. Outside the bedroom window the rain came down, palm fronds rippling like long fingers.

Around eleven I received an email from Quincy, a follow-up to our conversation out on the lanai, mostly about how sorry he was for not being forthright about his feelings for Jess before anything happened, how he knew he'd been selfish and cowardly, how he thought in a way it could've been a response to his fear over becoming a dad. But he'd told me he'd been excited to be a dad. Could he be excited and scared at the same time? I knew, of course, that the answer was yes.

I didn't respond. Instead, I lay there and thought about the months I'd spent stalking his social media and not telling Jess about it. How I hadn't wanted to tell her when I'd reached out to him either. The impulse had made less sense the more I thought about it, not that I could really compare the two behaviors, considering mine was minor and hers was monstrous, but they seemed born from the same desire to keep things separate and under control.

My phone dinged, a message from Mei. When I opened it I

saw a photo taken selfie-style of her and Ryan at the beach, their torsos pearled with water, Mei grinning, her dark bangs pushed back to reveal the seldom seen dual hyphen of her eyebrows, Ryan throwing a shaka. *!!!!!* she wrote beneath it, followed by, *Happy freaking Thanksgiving!* I saved the photo to my camera roll, clicked on it, reverse-pinched my fingers to zoom in, Mei's eyes bright with a near-cultish joy, Ryan's five-day Clooney shadow speckled an attractive silver. I zoomed back out. Their shoulders were touching. I threw the phone across the bed.

At one o'clock I finally got up and made myself tea, ignoring the heap of dirty dishes that had somehow accumulated in the past forty-eight hours though I barely remembered eating. I sat out on the front lanai watching cars pass, none of which were Jess's, as the house phone rang off and on, and by four p.m. I was so hungry I drove myself over to one of the hotels and paid forty-five dollars for a mediocre prix fixe meal.

The dining room overlooked the ocean and was full of families and couples, all likely disappointed to learn it could rain on a holiday in paradise. I ate turkey and Okinawan sweet potatoes and paid special mind to the way the children in the room interacted with their mothers, trying to ignore the fathers while I did it. There was a young couple at the table across from mine with a fat brown cherub of a baby, so chubby it had dimples on its elbows, even its legs. There was nothing more comforting than a fat baby, and as the child's mom doled out individual peas one by one with her fingers, I wondered why it was that society celebrated chubby babies but stigmatized chubby adults, wincing over my instinct to wish Jess was there so I could make this observation to her, so she could deliver some serrated commentary on the patriarchy.

As I finished an underwhelming slice of liliko'i cheesecake two women in their thirties sat down three tables away, both slim and pale in strappy floral sundresses. One put her hand on the other's shoulder and said something that made them both erupt into loud, rowdy laughter. I watched them for a bit, trying to determine whether they were friends or partners, sisters, maybe cousins, before deciding it didn't really matter, because there they were, enjoying one another.

Traffic was particularly hellish on the way home, rain coming down with manic vigor. All the stoplights felt longer than usual, and as I sat there with the AC pumping, my windshield wipers a comforting metronome, I thought how in the beginning I'd assumed Jess disliked Quincy because she was being protective, if not a bit possessive. It hit me then, the narcissistic naivety of my assumption. I thought about how I used to ignore Ryan at the gym, trying to suppress a want that scared me, a want I didn't know what to do with, all of it to ensure I wouldn't have to feel a specific way that was big and consuming and slightly too real. Had she ever felt this way? I had never even asked Jess why she didn't want Quincy around. I'd just assumed, and continued to assume, and I'd been wrong. I had repositioned their interactions into a narrative revolving solely around myself, and the life growing inside of me. No one else's experience mattered. This clarity brought with it a sadness so acute I wanted to reject it outright, to return to the comfort of rage.

At home I sat in the driveway for twenty minutes trying not to think about how vacant the house now felt, how much I did not want to go inside and lose myself in that emptiness. I could've pulled the car underneath the house where Jess used to park, but it felt wrong somehow, and so I just sat there, exposed in the drive, rain pounding the roof like it had during Hurricane Zane, when Jess and I had boarded up the windows, when the house had smelled like jasmine, when we sat in the living room and I had felt him kick while Jess had not. I began to cry—not some delicate, leaky faucet cry, but an ugly, heaving cry, a busted waterway cry, a cry that matched the sound of the rain, that made my throat raw and my ribs ache, and this gagging, gasping kind of cry is exactly what I was doing when Theo pulled in behind me, his headlights filling the inside of my car with light.

"I'm not playing go-between," he said, opening a drawer.

"Then what do you call this?"

I stood in the mouth of Jess's bedroom, chewing my thumbnail as Theo emptied the contents of her sock drawer into an old duffel bag I hadn't seen Jess use since college.

"What, did you want her to come do this?"

No, I didn't, but the fact that she was calling incessantly while too cowardly to show her face made me feel further incensed. I'd unplugged the kitchen phone and I thought of it then, disconnected and silent. "Just, tell her to stop calling." The skin of my face was tight from crying, which Theo had graciously not mentioned, although he'd stared at me for an uncomfortably long moment in the living room after we'd both toweled off.

"So, what then," he said. "You're just never going to talk to her?"

I removed my thumbnail from my mouth. I'd chewed it nearly to the quick, something I hadn't done in years. "I don't know."

Theo shook his head and said in a small, hard voice: "Now is not the time to be proud, Ren." He opened Jess's underwear drawer, then paused and made a soft sighing noise, like he couldn't believe what was being asked of him. It was the first time I'd been in Jess's room since she left, and as he shoved a stack of white cotton into a bag, I looked around her regulated collection of belongings and tried to pretend I'd never seen them before, as if they could help me assess the type of person she really was: bed made, chair tucked neatly into her desk, loose change on the dresser top divided into their proper categories—quarters, nickels, dimes—and stacked into columns.

"Can I ask you something?"

I rolled my eyes. I hated when he asked permission to ask a

question, as if I had the ability to say no. I made a lazy vertical gesture with my shoulders to indicate reluctant consent.

"Why do you think Jess takes care of you the way she does?"

"She does not *take care* of—"

"Just. Answer."

I looked at the floor. This Theo had pointed out many times. The way Jess made sure I got the oil changed in my car, that I had my teeth cleaned twice a year, paid my credit card bill. Her hovering never irritated me the way I might expect it to. Mostly, it was comforting. I knew Theo wanted a larger answer, something more dramatic, something that pointed to an under-standing of a hidden meaning behind Jess's devotion. I hadn't told him about the kiss. The Quincy issue had enough gossipy marrow for him to suck on. He didn't need another bone. But he was looking at me, waiting for an answer. "I don't know," I said finally. "It's always felt like a good thing, so I never really thought about it."

He closed a drawer harder than he needed to. A stack of quar-ters teetered on the dresser, and as they tumbled, I resisted the urge to step forward and stop them. Instead, I lingered ghost-like on the periphery. I'd always liked being in Jess's room, the sense of order comforted me, the way Jess thought of things I never did. Columns of quarters, for instance. In a way, too, it never really felt like I was in Jess's room at all, but a room in our house as communal and open as the living room. When we'd met, her room had been my own, and it had never stopped feel-ing that way. Her space was also always cleaner, and so sleeping there, showering in her shower, was an easy way to avoid the reality of my own chaos, like a vacation from myself. And she made it comfortable for me to be there, kept my conditioner in her shower, a clean water glass by my side of the bed, and tucked into her dresser mirror was that photo of me smiling. Not me and Jess or me and Sookie, just me, taken from right above the shoulders, the lighting awful, one of my eyelids drooping lower than the other, midlaugh, undeniably happy. I couldn't remember when or where the photo was taken, but I knew Jess took it, and I knew it had been stuck to her dresser mirror since we moved into this house. Ten years, she'd looked at that photo, that captured moment of my own oblivious joy. My throat cottoned then as I understood: I liked to be in Jess's room because I felt loved there.

It had never occurred to me to ask in what way I was loved, or why. This had never seemed relevant. I thought about the phone, unplugged in the kitchen, and wondered if she was still trying to call it, and even as I wished she wouldn't, there was a piece of me that felt comforted to know she was.

Theo moved to the closet and drew back the doors. Jess's clothes hung in a neat line, like color-coordinated commuters on a crowded bus. I felt a current of longing then, and as a distraction, I slid my hand under my shirt, pressed my palm hard into my skin, and willed the baby to kick. Sometimes that worked, as if he could read my mind, as if we were already communicating. But he did not kick, and I felt nothing but the warmth of my own body. At the closet, Theo slid a single hanger left to right, then dropped his hand, defeated. "I really have no idea what she wants here."

I left the doorway and entered the space. I took my hand off my stomach, moved to stand beside my brother, and began pulling clothes from the hangers.

J

I spent Thanksgiving morning at the office, grateful no one else had come in.

I could breathe easier there. The consistent glow of my desktop provided a sense of safety. An anchor.

Outside, the sky dumped rain like someone had torn a hole in it.

Intermittently I called Ren. The cell went straight to voice mail, but the house phone rang and rang. That made me feel better somehow. To know that I could call, and she would hear it. That I could still have that one thing.

It had been forty-eight hours. I couldn't remember the last time we went forty-eight hours without speaking to each other. Not since we met. Our lives were a constant thread of communication, our hours apart routinely punctuated by messages. Emails. Texts. Photos of the dog. In the middle of the afternoon I might receive a snapshot of the remnants of her lunch. The grainy crust of a sandwich. A half-eaten container of yogurt. *Killed it*, the note would read.

We'd had this type of exchange a thousand times.

Two thousand.

Unexceptional. Ordinary. The way truly intimate things usually are. Her fingernail clippings scattered around the base of the toilet. She'd never had very good aim.

I'd stopped texting her. I couldn't bear to open our chat exchange. To scroll through the blue wall of one-sided conversation. The panicked messages leaning more and more desperate. At least phone calls disappeared after I made them. Their proof was only visible if I checked my outgoing calls, which I didn't.

My overnight bag was in my car. I'd brought this to work hoping I'd hear from her and go home but by two o'clock I could see I'd been naive.

I was enticed by the concept of kicking a hole into the taupe-painted drywall across from my desk. I exhaled. Refocused on the comforting face of my computer.

In the late afternoon I showed an ugly slab home to a newly transplanted couple from Ohio who thanked me repeatedly for *taking the time on a holiday.*

I kept my smile pinned like a dead butterfly to my face.

We finished around four and I decided to drive home.

There was a break in the rain and, through it, the house looked the same as ever. The lanai wide and white and the spot where Ren normally parked her Corolla gaped like a missing tooth. I considered going in. Waiting for her to return. In the end I just kept driving.

I wasn't scared to talk to her. That, I wanted to do. I was scared she would refuse me. That I would be demoted to a rank even lower than Quincy.

That I already was a rank lower than Quincy.

I wondered if they'd had any more contact. He'd probably texted her a nice follow-up. She'd probably answered with something cool but polite. Something to show him he was still on her shit list, but a response nonetheless.

This made me feel so sorry for myself I twisted the radio on. Found a bubblegum sort of pop song and blasted it so loud it was almost painful.

Taylor and I were in the kitchen boiling water for pasta.

The two of us had hit a comfortable stride chopping olives and anchovies and garlic. Theo'd been teaching him how to cook, he told me. Had showed him what we needed for the puttanesca. How small to chop everything so that it came together evenly.

It was the meal Theo'd made for Quincy the first night he came over and I thought about this as I hacked ingredients into tiny pieces.

Taylor had finals in three weeks and I asked about his course load, his professors. We didn't talk about how it was Thanksgiving or what our plans had been until forty-eight hours earlier. How carefully those plans had been made. Who would bring what and what time and how long I should cook that damn turkey.

To solve the problem of my terribly packed overnight bag, I'd asked Theo to stop by the house for clothes. The request took so much strength I'd considered going to Macy's to buy whatever I needed. Socks and underwear and a few shirts.

When he came back, he dropped my bag with more intensity than needed. It hit the floor like a body. "Well, this is cozy," he said, nodding at the pasta pot and our neat piles of minced garlic and fish.

I thanked him for getting my things but couldn't look at him while I did it.

I wanted to ask him if he saw Ren. How she was. What they'd talked about. If she'd asked after me. To milk every detail of their interaction until it felt like I had been there. Instead, I asked, "Did you remember my phone charger?"

"Yeah, Jess, I did."

Taylor poured wine into a stemless glass and slid it across the counter unprompted.

"It was probably unnecessary, honestly," I said as Theo took a grateful sip. "I'll probably just go over there tomorrow."

Taylor and Theo exchanged a long glance that made me feel particularly childish. As if they were my parents joining forces to break bad news.

Theo lowered his glass. "I don't think Ren's ready to see you."

"She saw Quincy."

"You're not Quincy. And you should stop calling her every five minutes."

"I'm not."

Theo's gaze was kind then. Soft. This only irritated me. I

felt patronized. I rolled a kalamata olive around the countertop with my index finger and thought about how Ren had eaten them by the jar during her second trimester. I applied pressure. Flattened it like roadkill.

Theo sighed. "You're not making things any better for yourself." He walked around the counter and started to wash his hands, resting his chin on Taylor's shoulder for a moment as he passed. This felt like a dismissal of a subject I was not ready to let go of.

"It's my house, too." I moved to the window and cracked it open.

"I don't think this is really about the house, Jess."

Obviously, I knew this.

Out the window, the lawn was a dark mossy carpet. It looked misleadingly plush. Something I could sink my feet into.

"She got that job at the university," Theo said then.

I stood absolutely still as if I hadn't heard him. I stayed like this for a long moment. When I turned back around Taylor was at the sink draining pasta and Theo was pulling arugula from the fridge and I had the bizarre sensation of being invisible.

An apparition by a window watching a snapshot of their lives.

One I had no business being inside of.

I told them I wasn't feeling very hungry and would probably just go to bed. It was a few minutes after seven. I didn't look at them as I left the room. I didn't want to see their faces.

Per Theo's suggestion, I stopped calling Ren.

Even though I wasn't calling her I was still painfully conscious that she could be calling me.

I checked my phone constantly. Was aware of its presence all the time.

A little electronic lighthouse amidst the dark night of my anxiety.

On Friday Lisa brought Kayson to the office.

There'd been an uku outbreak in his preschool. He didn't have them, but she was keeping him home while they took care of it, her mother out for jury duty. She told me this with a certain degree of apology. As if I'd be irritated.

I didn't want to be the kind of boss who was irritated when you had to bring your kid in.

I assured her it was fine. Not to worry.

That it was nice to have him around.

She smiled as if she didn't believe me. The front of her blouse had a small brown spot on it. Coffee or tea. I tried not to look at it as Kayson raced up and down the strip of carpet that spined our two rows of desks.

He wore bright red sneakers and made soft whirring noises with his lips as if he were a plane or a car. He must've been six or seven but when I asked, Lisa said he'd just turned four. I knew that, I realized. I'd gone to his shower.

Ku'ulei came in then with hot malasadas and I retreated into my office and shut the door. Sat at my desk and listened to Kayson zoom up and down outside and imagined what this would sound like in our house.

Little feet on the hard wood.

Sticky malasada fingers on the walls.

I realized no one in the office knew about Ren's pregnancy. I'd never mentioned it. Despite all our plans. Despite the fact that all three of the women in the office had their own children. It hadn't occurred to me to tell them. To invite any of them to the shower.

I hadn't approached that shower like it had been any part mine at all.

I thought about what Quincy had said about himself. His marriage. How he moved on a whim just as he was nearing tenure. How these last few months had been so exciting for him, and yet he'd been the one to unwind it. I wondered if that sort of self-destruction could be contagious.

★ ★ ★

In the afternoon I had coffee with Tatia Chen just to get outside of myself. To distract myself from my phone, which pinged and hummed with a dozen messages an hour, none of them from Ren. The idea of going back to Theo's basement was nauseating.

I still hadn't unpacked any of my things.

Tatia was already at Lava Java though I arrived several minutes early, and when I sat down, she immediately asked if I was alright.

I told her all the rain had triggered my allergies.

I could tell she didn't believe me, but she nodded and made a joke about a free car wash.

I liked that about Tatia. She knew when to drop a subject.

We spent the better part of an hour talking about furniture motifs and color palettes.

She closed in three weeks.

"Country beach house" was what she called her intended decor vibe.

An oxymoron. But I knew what she meant.

White ceilings. Wood floors. Accents in beiges and soft blues.

Talking about this was like slipping sweetly into sleep.

At some point she stopped in the middle of a sentence about distressed wood and said, "It's important to get these details right, you know. This will be the house I die in."

I'd had my coffee halfway to my mouth and stopped short, which made her laugh.

"I know that sounds morbid." She touched a knuckle to the tip of her nose. "I think it's healthy to consider these things. To come to terms with them."

I pictured our house on Kalaniana'ole and the way the light bounced around the kitchen in the morning. I wondered whether I'd ever hoped to die in that house. I'm sure I had even if I'd never thought that directly. Now I couldn't even enter without permission.

"You should start using that line with clients," Tatia said.

"What? Is this the house you want to die in?"

She took a small sip of tea. "Why not? Most people appreciate that kind of honesty, I've found."

I thought about Tatia living on her own with her good job and the house she wanted to die in.

Her family grown and gone.

Loneliness leaching out of her pores like sebum.

Or maybe I was wrong.

Maybe she wasn't lonely.

Her divorce, after all, had seemed to be her own idea.

Maybe Tatia looked forward to coming home to an empty house.

A glass of wine and the sunset by herself.

Distressed wood and white ceilings.

What did I know?

I had never enjoyed returning to an empty house. Ren had always been there, if not in person, then in spirit. It had been the greatest comfort of my adult life, and as far as I knew, she had felt the same. I thought then about Theo telling me to give her space.

What if she didn't want space?

She'd seen Quincy because he hadn't asked for permission.

He'd just shown up.

What if she wanted me to just show up?

What if she was waiting?

32

R

The Monday after Thanksgiving I drove to the university to meet again with Marta and Kaipo from HR, trying the entire time to conjure the same excitement I'd had the day she called, when I'd sat out on the porch feeling like ripe fruit, but all I could muster was exhaustion. I wandered around looking for the HR office, trying to imagine myself comfortable there, the hallways as familiar as my own, but instead kept worrying I'd run into Quincy. I hadn't responded to his email yet and didn't feel like making polite talk, or any kind of talk, really.

Jess's car was in the drive when I got home.

The sight of it beneath the house was so familiar, for a moment I forgot it wasn't supposed to be there and so my anger came delayed, an emotional double take. I could see her from the drive, sitting on the lanai with Sookie, scratching the dog's ears and looking down at me. I turned the engine off but didn't get out, just sat there with the doors closed, my heart beating too fast. Even from a distance I could see she looked tired, and I felt a small, satisfied pull from my center. But Sookie's presence meant she'd gone inside the house, and this realization shrank my self-righteousness down to a tight nut as I remembered the dishes in the sink, the kitchen trash that had begun to stink, the tufts of Sookie's hair collecting in corners, domestic tumbleweeds in a living room Western. I felt infuriated and embarrassed, simultaneously hot with both superiority and shame, and I carried all of this with me as I climbed slowly from the car. Sookie's tail beat the top step as I approached, the hollow thud-thud-thud drifting down to greet me, and I was conscious of the ragged sound my own breath made from the effort of moving.

"You wouldn't answer your phone," she said when I reached her. Her words had a familiar softness to them, the tone she took out when she was being gentle with me.

"I didn't want to talk to you." My own voice was narrow and cold.

She stroked the dog's crown. "Didn't? Or don't?"

I said nothing as Sookie squirmed, straining in my direction, Jess gripping her by the collar to keep her from lunging, from knocking me down the stairs. This bothered me, Jess trying to protect me when she had so recently done the precise opposite. The adrenaline I'd felt pulling into the drive was gone, leaving me worn and a bit sticky, like something discarded, a wet clog of hair at the bottom of a shower drain.

"Theo said you got the university job," Jess said. "That's exciting."

I swallowed hard, refusing to give in to menial small talk, both because Jess was excellent at it, and because I didn't want to pretend for even a few seconds that things were normal. Near the ground I could just make out the tops of my toes beyond the curve of my stomach, still that bright berry color she'd painted them weeks before when everything was different.

"How was your Thanksgiving?" she asked. "How was that turkey?"

I squinted at her. She knew I did not cook that turkey, that I'd never cooked a turkey in my life. I was overcome with a violent urge to grab her shoulders and shake her. "Is that what you came here to do? Ask about my holiday?"

She stared at me a moment, then screwed her eyes shut. When she spoke again her voice was thick. "Can we go inside?"

"I'd rather we didn't."

She nodded as if I'd asked her a question.

Silence bled and I stared at her, willing her to speak, and when she didn't, I asked: "What are you doing here?"

"I came to…" She wiped the tip of her nose with one knuckle. "To tell you that I'm sorry."

I waited for her to continue, to explain herself, to clarify what exactly she was sorry for, but as I watched her take little sips of air, her eyelids flickering, a renewed sense of rage blistered. She'd clearly come all the way over here without any sort of plan, thinking what? That I would roll over just because she said she's sorry? "I didn't think…" she started again, then stopped. "I didn't think you were interested in Quincy."

"This isn't about *Quincy*, Jess."

I pushed past her then, which took some effort given how large I was. She'd left the front door unlocked and I swung it open and called for Sookie, who looked uncertainly at Jess and then back at me with a timid, conflicted wag. "Sookie, *come*," I said, conjuring vocal steel. The dog cast what appeared to be an apologetic glance at Jess, who released her collar so she could click-clack past me into the house, tail tucked.

Jess said my name then, was still speaking when the door slammed.

In the kitchen I dragged out our largest cooking pot, removed a pile of dishes from the sink but did not wash them, just stacked the bowls and cups on the counter, put the pot in the basin, turned on the tap, the ferocious sound of water mashing against metal oddly satisfying. When the pot was half-full, I opened the freezer, pulled out the massive frozen turkey, and plunged it inside. I'd underestimated how big the bird was and water spilled over the edges, sloshing out onto the counter and floor. I threw a dish towel over the largest of the puddles, then went into my bedroom and shut the door.

I slept in short, intermittent flares, waking early in the morning to two missed calls from Theo that I did not return. The internet said to cook a turkey for thirteen minutes per pound, but I wasn't sure the weight of the bird and guessed, keeping it in the oven for three solid hours until the house smelled heavenly, checking on it every forty-five minutes to spoon pan liquid over the top the way the internet instructed. It felt nice, moving from the couch to the stove once an hour to tend to the roasting thing, a happy, productive hover. When I finally pulled the bird from the oven the skin had transformed into a lustrous caramel brown. I waited twenty minutes, then pulled bits of it apart with my fingers, eating them right over the stove. The outer pieces were a bit dry, but toward the center the meat was rich and warm, buttery grease making my fingers obscenely slippery. Sookie sat patiently by my feet, and I fed her morsels of flesh and skin, the two of us hunkered at the stove in the too-warm kitchen, just past noon, eating richly as the day floated bizarrely by, bright and airy as a parade blimp.

J

Two days passed the way days do.

One hour and then another and then another. I did not call Ren.

Lisa closed on a million-dollar property, her biggest sale.

I brought in champagne and a sleeve of paper cups.

I started running around Theo's neighborhood. Short residential circles. Mailbox after mailbox, my muscles lengthening then contracting. My rib cage pushing. The effort a familiar comfort.

I missed Sookie. Her jaunty motivational gate. Our route to the old manele tree. A quieter run than this.

My third time out I stopped at a graveyard a mile or so from Theo's house. I must have passed it a thousand times in the car but had never really seen it. Inside, shy morning sun slanted through rows of squat stones and in the center grew a massive monkeypod, its branches fat and low.

A crosshatch of trim walkways gridded the yard. I looped them five times as sweat gathered in the folds of my elbows before stopping to catch my breath beneath the ancient tree.

Two female cardinals called to each other from the branches above, their feathers a muted gray with a shadow of sunset orange. The delicacy of their song seemed odd for such a somber place.

The harsh caw of a crow would be more fitting.

I knew I'd panicked out on the lanai. Had been unable to explain what I was sorry for. I hadn't known what to lead with. That I'd slept with Quincy? That I'd hidden it from her? That I'd kissed her while I tried to confess?

I wasn't even sure if that last bit was something I should apologize for.

I didn't know why I'd kissed her other than that I'd wanted to, which was so moronically hedonistic I was ashamed to say it.

In college Asha had made a jab about me being "half in love with a straight woman." It was one of the last things she ever said to me. Theo certainly would have agreed. But I wasn't in love with Ren. Hadn't been mooning over her for two decades. The only time I'd ever had the urge to kiss her, I'd done it.

Did it matter if I knew why?

Did it matter how I loved her? Or simply that I did?

Admittedly I'd never been in love with anyone so maybe I didn't really know.

I certainly wasn't in love with Quincy.

Cruelly it would've been better if I was.

At least I'd have a proper excuse for my poor behavior. I should have said all of this to Ren.

Instead, I said none of it.

I'd thought for sure she'd let me back in. That once she saw me, she'd want to talk. That she'd been missing me. It was unbearable to know she didn't feel that way.

That she could be ignoring her phone instead of checking it constantly.

That we could be having such separate variants of the same experience.

It felt as if I were living through an anxiety dream. One where I'd put something important down in the next room and couldn't get to it.

I pressed my hand against the monkeypod. Its trunk was twisted and cool under my hot palm. Light needled through the gaps in the leaves above me and I thought, maybe Ren and Quincy would return to their portion of the plan.

Maybe this whole ordeal would bring them closer.

Maybe they'd end up together after all.

Maybe he'd say her name in that hushed tone like the word itself was a secret and in ten years I'd be someone they talked about in jest or worse, not at all.

Thinking about it made the fizzing in my chest start. But somehow even in my anxiety I found comfort, too.

A safety knowing that even if Ren wouldn't forgive me, she could still choose not to be alone. It was jarring that I could feel two completely conflicting emotions at the exact same time.

Devastation, and there, lodged behind my rib cage, relief.

I glimpsed something then. The edges of an understanding that had always been present but out of focus. As fixated as I was on being allowed back into our house, for as often as I called, when I imagined myself back home it was with Ren alone.

I wanted to return to our life together as it was.

Not our life together as it was about to become.

Overhead, the two cardinals looked down at me and I made a soft chirping sound. They cocked their heads. The larger of the two gave a dainty hop, her pronged feet a tender pink.

Then she flew off, giving me one last curious glance before leaving me behind.

Back at Theo's I carried my bag into Quincy's old room. Someone, probably Taylor, had made the bed with fresh sheets. Had put a single hibiscus in a votive on the nightstand.

The lonely blossom made my throat constrict. Breathing became laborious.

I opened the bag Theo had packed for me. Unpacked the jumble as sweat cooled on my skin. My dress shirts and camisoles. Silk tops, jeans, tees. My one pair of heels.

When the bag was empty, I fingered my way along a slim interior pocket. Inside I touched a sturdy, polished square of paper. I tugged it out and froze.

Ren.

The photo I took of her back in our first apartment, smiling with one eye half-shut. The faded image I'd had wedged into the edge of my dresser mirror for nearly ten years.

Why had Theo packed this?

I lay down on the bed with my belongings spread around me.

Looked down at my feet, still wrapped in my sweaty socks. Past them, the open closet exposed a row of bare hangers.

My feet, with the closet behind them. It was the same perspective that Quincy'd sent me in a photo a month earlier. I'd been sorry for him then.

For his half-empty closet. His borrowed bedroom.

Those things which were mine now.

I wrapped my arms around myself then, and I let myself cry.

33

R

The second week of December two repairmen came to replace our screens. Jess had hired them during her dengue fever fixation just before everything imploded, and I found their presence rankling, mostly because it pointed to how Jess could be so neurotic about protecting me in some ways while entirely overlooking the most basic example of care. It took the men all afternoon to get through the house and at the end of it they wrote me a bill, which I paid, because I didn't know what else to do. I'd all but stopped sleeping by then.

Four a.m., morning light still hours away, I lay listening to the waves slam across the street and tried to concentrate on synching my breath to their rhythm, to imagine water crashing with every exhale, retreating with a sigh on the inhale. The lack of sleep had me walking around zombielike during the day, dazed, forgetting things, rice left on the stove until the house smelled of fire, and when I rushed back into the kitchen, I found the contents of the pot completely black. There in bed, it occurred to me that the thing was still soaking by the sink. I'd forgotten that, too.

I left my bed at quarter to five. The failed attempt at marrying my breath to the sea had me longing for water, not our protected beach across the way, but somewhere with real waves. I dressed warm, sweats and one of Theo's old hoodies abandoned in the back of our front closet. Sookie was beside herself as I loaded her in the car, mouth open, tail full helicopter, and drove us to the surf spot I took Quincy to during the summer when he listened to Bruce Springsteen and I pretended to like it. It was still dark but already the lot had a dozen or so pickups, the surfers always so impressive with their commitment. I'd never had that kind of dedication to anything, really.

I parked near the bathrooms and let Sookie out with no leash, watched as she bounded down the craggy strip of shore, a sad excuse for a beach, but you didn't come for that. You came for the waves. I found a dry spot, kicked off my slippers, rolled my swollen feet over the stones, and waited for the sun. Up ahead Sookie ran along the break, barking as she charged a wave then shrank from it, a noisy game of chase-retreat, and further out, two dozen sets of shoulders bobbed above their boards, waiting. It was hard to imagine that in August, Quincy and I'd stood just a few yards away, drinking brightly colored tapioca tea and talking about the future.

We'd recently begun exchanging emails. His were longer, rambling, confessional, and mine shorter, guarded. He'd written about the end of his marriage, how it hadn't been his decision, yet he'd let it happen, slowly, by not paying attention, not listening, focusing only on himself. *This feels a lot like that*, he'd written. *Maybe that's awkward to say, but it does.* He wrote how he'd been relieved early on when it was clear there was nothing between us; he'd told himself that meant he couldn't mess things up. *Ha*, he'd written. Ha.

I'd told him how I'd let Jess do too much for me, the things Theo always pointed out, how she could be controlling, even cruel. How our devotion to each other had naturally made us less interested in romantic relationships, how I wondered what the last few decades would've been like for me if we hadn't been so close. It was unnerving to think that way, about how a single person could change the track of your life, but they can, and she had, and I knew that Quincy was doing it now too, even if I was angry with him. It felt weird to be writing about Jess without her knowing it, but everything I shared about her felt equally my own, my experience in her orbit, and so even though some of these things were intimate, they felt like they were mine, and I wondered if this was at all how she felt, being with Quincy without me knowing. In one of the emails, Quincy asked if I thought that maybe Jess had romantic feelings for me, and I told him that I didn't really think it mattered, because it didn't change anything.

These emails felt easier than talking in person, though I typically took a day or two to respond. I knew if Jess had written me an email, I doubt I would have been able to open it, which made me feel guilty, a response that then infuriated me. But it was easier with Quincy, the wound smaller, easier to lick, and if this was unfair of me then so be it.

It would be easier for me to just forgive her. I knew this. What would happen otherwise? I couldn't experience time in a vacuum for much longer. But still, I couldn't smother the coiled, wounded rage that lifted its daggered head whenever I thought of her. This anger was confusing because I had a hard time pinpointing its source. The sneaking around, obviously, and the dishonesty, but mostly the humiliating way she had trapped me, for a stretch of time—a month? two?—on the wrong side of a two-way mirror, had forced me to walk around like an idiot without the slightest idea of what was actually going on, and to do that anytime would be horrendous, but to do it now, when I was this vulnerable. No. Their audacity—*her* audacity—was outrageous.

I knew, too, that part of my fury stemmed from the massive slam to my ego. Quincy'd knocked me up but fallen for Jess, and it stung. I hated looking at myself that way, so basic in my own reactions. Leave it to Jess not to sleep with anyone for years and then create some novelistic scandal. In the book edition I'd forgive them both, they'd get married, and we'd all raise the baby together like we'd planned. I could just see the cover—pink, with a massively pregnant woman silhouetted in black, some scattered palms to sell the tropical setting. It would be a bestseller with middle-aged women in the doldrums of their marriages. Someone in Hollywood would buy the rights and turn it into a made-for-TV movie, Jess and me played by two pretty white women a decade younger than us, Theo a caricature of himself, queeny and full of cheeky one-liners, and Quincy of course would be brooding and chiseled instead of excitable and gangly. In some ways it felt backward. Historically, I was the irresponsible one, I should've been the one to sleep with Jess's baby daddy while she was seven months pregnant. Except I would never do that because I was not that person. Was I?

Up ahead, a set was coming in, and I watched as the surfers paddled with frantic strength to greet it, to ride it ashore. I rolled my feet over the smooth stones and made myself consider something: I could never have slept with Jess's baby daddy while she was seven months pregnant, because Jess would never have been seven months pregnant, because Jess had never really wanted to be a mother, and I knew this. I felt it to my core even if I had spent months refusing to look at it, and there on the beach, I couldn't help but wonder if she'd behaved this way in an attempt, albeit a subconscious one, to get out of her commitment to me. She couldn't help me raise a child if I no longer wanted her to.

I felt something loosen inside of me then, like the turning of a bolt, and with it came a disorienting twisting and clicking as the last few seasons resettled around me. What might it have been like for Jess, if it were true she hadn't wanted what I did. If she was only trying to suit me. So much of what she always did, really, was to try and suit me. And what had I ever done, really, for her?

A surfer emerged then from the water with his board under one strong arm. I watched his body move, different from the others, not long and lean like a stray dog but thicker, and as he walked up the rocky shoreline, there was a familiar swing to his step, the way he held his head. I recognized him just as he must have recognized me, because he veered suddenly in my direction.

"Hey, stranger," Ryan called as soon as he was in range, swinging wet hair from his eyes. I lifted my arm in a wave, trying to hide my shock.

He came to a halt a foot or so in front of me, water brailled along the curve of his chest. My belly pushed against the thick, worn cotton of my sweatshirt. I hadn't even washed my face. "You're up early," he said.

"Sleep isn't really a thing right now."

"Ah yes."

Sookie bounded over then, barking and shaking, spraying us with salt and sand. Ryan laughed, shielding himself with an elbow.

"This is Sookie," I said. "She's very rude."

Ryan squatted down to her level. "Hello there, Sookie," he said, suddenly serious and matter-of-fact. He scratched her wet head, then turned back to me. He asked me how I'd been, and I told him fine.

"I heard you had a shower that I didn't get an invite to." *Mei*, I thought immediately.

"Sorry. It was a surprise, I had nothing to do with the guest list."

"Sure, sure." Ryan wiped the back of his hand across his forehead. The sun was coming up just behind him, creating a halo of light around his upper half. "So, when will I get to meet your guy?"

I shielded my eyes to see him better. "I'm about seven weeks out."

"Right, but, I meant, your *guy*."

"Oh." I dropped my hand, picked up a small black rock and pressed it between my fingers. "Yeah. I don't know. We're…" I stopped, trying to figure out the simplest way to put it. "We're not together."

Ryan laid his board down gently. "I'm sorry to hear that." His eyes were so sincerely concerned I looked away.

"It's fine. We were never really together actually. One of those recklessly irresponsible moments, you know."

I was trying to be funny, but he didn't laugh. Just nodded. Sookie was back in the surf then, snapping at the spray as if it had insulted her. "It's a scary thing, huh?"

"You have no idea."

He wobbled his head. "Ehhh, I have some idea."

I cringed. "Of course. Sorry."

He smiled kindly and we dipped into an easy silence. I trained my eyes on the coastline but remained aware of the shape of him, the droplets of water slowly drying on his shoulders and chest, the salt quilting sections of his hair.

"Hey," he said abruptly. "Will Sookie ride in a pickup? We could grab an acai bowl. Breakers has the best, they open at seven."

I hesitated. I liked the idea of a further distraction, something to take me away from everything that was happening, everything that would soon happen, the emptiness of the house that awaited me, the choices I would soon have to make. But Sookie had never ridden in a truck, and I felt tethered, somehow, to the beach, and if I was being honest, I was nervous about being alone with him. I had always been nervous about being alone with him.

"I think I'll just hang here for a bit." Immediately, I was disappointed in myself.

Ryan just nodded. "Fair enough."

And then, before I could chicken out: "Rain check?"

He smiled. "Yeah, alright." He hitched his board under one arm and began walking backward, holding my gaze. "I'm gonna hold you to that though." He turned away then, and from inside came three sharp kicks in rapid succession, like someone knocking on a door.

Stepping out of the shower I picked an old towel off the floor even though it smelled of mildew, wringing my hair out and clenching my eyes shut until bright white sparks freckled my vision, and when I opened them, it felt like I was seeing the room for the first time. Not the tub and sink, the small watercolor beachscape hung across from the toilet, but the mess—my mess, the stamp I left across the house. My own clutter had never bothered me before, sometimes it even felt like a comfort, like the smell of your own sweat, but looking around the room, I felt only shame. Two pairs of discarded underwear lay rumpled on the tile, an old tub of cocoa butter sat on the edge of the sink, lid off, various pieces of my own hair spider-legging over the edge. The trash had long since overflown, toilet paper tubes and waxy Q-tips spilling out, cotton balls dark with eye makeup. Mildew claimed the cracks between the tiles in the shower. A slug of my own hair curled around the drain.

In my bedroom, the wreckage was worse. I imagined a toddler moving through here, growing up in this. He'd be used to it, think it was normal, until eventually he would visit a friend's house and notice their bare counters, their dishes washed and put away, laundry folded into drawers. He'd realize my shortcomings then, his opinion of me tarnishing. But it wouldn't even take that long, I realized. All we'd have to do was go to Theo's.

I grabbed a half-full laundry basket and began scooping up mounds of clothes, sleeping tees and maternity bras, my old university shirt. I carried the heaping basket out into the hall. When I got to the living room, I stopped short. The mess in my own room was to be expected, but Jess had always cleaned our communal spaces, setting my dirty dishes in the sink, plucking my socks off the floor. She never complained about doing these things, and so I stopped noticing it was even happening, but now, three weeks since she'd been in the house, I could see how I had overtaken it. The coffee table littered with potato chip bags, three half-empty water glasses, Theo's hoodie—the one I'd just worn to the beach—already draped across the back of the couch. The potted fern in the corner by the TV had yellowed, its leaves curling with the injustice of thirst. I picked up two of the forgotten glasses of water and emptied them into the plant's dry dirt. Immediately, I felt a little release.

The kitchen smelled of decomposing fruit, the sink fat with cereal bowls, plates smeared with jam, my burned rice pot on the counter where I'd left it to soak, a dead blister beetle floating among the charred grains. On the counter, a vivid green gecko curled around a topless peanut butter jar. I watched his pink tongue flick out to touch the plastic and retreat, again and again, his eyes on me the whole time. The countertop, I noticed, was beaded with gecko shit.

From under the sink, I grabbed a trash bag, snapped it open, began to fill it. The peanut butter jar first, gecko scuttling off to safety, then the produce that had collapsed in the blue ceramic bowl, a saggy hand of brown bananas. I swept the floor, scoured the counters with a Brillo pad. It was time-consuming but not difficult, and I avoided asking myself why I never did this, because I knew the answer clearly: I never needed to.

After an hour my body whined, my eye sockets felt as if someone had packed them full of sand, but the kitchen shone. Before I left it, I plugged the phone back in. I half expected it to ring immediately, even stood there for a moment just in case, but the phone remained quiet and still, slumbering soundly in its cradle, and I felt a set of twinned pricks, needled jabs of both relief and disappointment. It was well into the afternoon when I scrubbed the planetary ring of grime that circled my bathtub. Afterward, the house seemed calmer somehow, and I felt lighter. I took a load of fresh towels from the dryer, showered again in my newly bleached tub, and emerged accomplished, clean, and entirely exhausted.

In the hallway, I paused by Jess's room for a long moment, then opened the door and entered. Inside, I stood very still. Save for what Theo had taken, her things were as she'd left them: navy robe on the back of the bathroom door, the boar bristle brush on her dresser that made dry, grassy noises in the morning when she pulled it through her hair. From my center came an ache, a slow longing like the stretch of a tender muscle. This time, I did not push it away but let it wrap itself around me and hold on. I stared at the empty spot on her mirror where my picture had been and wondered if she'd found it yet. It was cruel, to tell her she couldn't be here, to demand that she leave, but then, in a way, to insist that she take a bit of me with her.

I'd shrugged Theo off when he'd asked why I thought Jess took care of me, told him I hadn't thought about it, but I realized then, standing among her belongings, random fragments that she'd chosen to represent herself—ChapStick, bracelet, shoestring, watch— that maybe what he was asking me was *why* I hadn't thought about it. Jess had always made things easier for me, her presence a comfort I'd never questioned because it felt like a good thing, and in many ways, it *was* a good thing, but maybe if I'd made myself look a bit harder, I'd have seen the way I let her pin me firmly in place.

I took one deep inhale, exhaled long and slow, then moved to her bed, pulled back her comforter and slid in. On my side, I curled into myself, Jess's smell all around me, and immediately, I fell asleep.

J

By the middle of December, I'd begun to fall into a bit of a routine.

In the mornings after my run I would sit with Taylor in their sunny kitchen and have coffee and check my email while he studied. In the evenings Theo would cook or I might pick up Thai or sushi to feel like I was contributing.

They refused to let me pay rent.

At night we'd stay up watching TV or playing Spite and Malice. Taylor was a surprisingly terrible loser. Pouty and defiant. "An only child, can you tell?" Theo'd said with affection as Taylor stomped off to put on water for tea.

He seemed to have forgotten that I too was an only child.

Theo'd told me then that Ren had taken Quincy with her to a doctor's appointment, and I'd tried not to move a single muscle in my face. "Maybe you should call her," he'd said quietly.

"You told me not to call her."

"Well, it's been a bit now."

One month.

It had been one month.

Two days earlier Lisa had found a property for Quincy. When I saw his name come through on the paperwork I'd gotten up from my desk and walked over to the window, where I stood for a long time without really looking at anything.

I'd resisted the urge to check the property on the listing server. To hover over photos of the kitchen and imagine Ren sitting there with a glass of wine as their child played on the floor. To sift through shots of the bathrooms and envision what we might have done there if things had gone on longer.

To ask myself again why they'd gone on in the first place.

Toward the end of the month, I did a final walk-through with Tatia on the property up the coast. The selling agent, Betsy, trailed behind us commenting on how gorgeous everything was as if we didn't already know.

The space did look even more beautiful without furniture.

Stripped down to the bones of its own walls and wood.

Warmth pooled in my chest as I watched Tatia move through it. Flipping light switches. Raising blinds.

It was a very specific type of pride.

My job had been to help her, and I'd done it and now her life was better for it.

It was a relief to feel this way when I'd felt nothing but anxiety for weeks.

Before we got in our cars, she gave me a small wrapped box, kissed both my cheeks, and told me she'd call me. I wasn't quite sure if she would, or if I wanted her to.

The box had been wrapped neatly in gold foil and I waited for her to drive off before opening it.

Inside was a pair of earrings. Simple, austere silver studs. Nothing like the gaudy costume pieces Tatia herself wore. They were exactly something I would have chosen for myself, and I was surprised at how closely she must have studied me to know this.

I wondered then if we'd really started some sort of friendship or if it had been an extension of the close correspondence we'd had to keep over the past few months.

Maybe it could be both.

A friendship with a clear expiration date. I took the long route back to the office.

HPR was covering the telescope again. A Supreme Court ruling had invalidated the construction permit. Forward motion was paused, and I tried to feel hopeful about it.

I realized that for how closely I'd been following this case, for as feverishly as I argued on its behalf, I had never once gone to one of the protests downtown. Never driven up the mountain to stand with the protectors.

Instead I had watched and complained and argued self-righteously and done absolutely nothing. This filled me with such bloated shame I found it difficult to breathe. As I sat there, taking uneven sucks of air, I thought not only of the mountain but of Ren. Of all that I had jeopardized, and the scopious chasm between self-sacrifice and self-destruction.

I did call Ren then. I called the house and held my breath.

The voice mail kicked on. A good sign. Weeks earlier it had done nothing but infinity ring. My own voice still spoke from the machine. It was a challenge not to hang up. I held on. I waited for the beep. "Hi," I started stupidly. I imagined Ren standing by the phone listening, wondering whether she should pick up, though I knew that wasn't how voice mails worked anymore.

My words were being delivered into a void she could check later, or not.

Still. I let myself imagine I was speaking to her in real time. It was easier that way.

"I don't even know if you will listen to this," I started again, "but I don't know what else to do." I inhaled. Placed a hand to my chest. "I am so sorry, Ren. I wish I could tell you why I behaved so horribly, but honestly, I don't know. I do know that I was terrified. Am terrified. Of the way everything is changing. Of how little I seemed to have to do with any of it." I paused. My throat was dry and scratchy.

"Maybe on some level I thought by sleeping with Quincy I could sort of…keep him in a corner that felt safe. But obviously I see now that space was only safe for me, and not even. There is also a part of me that thinks I slept with him because he wanted me and I liked how it felt. Being wanted, but not needed."

I stopped. Breathed into the receiver. Began again.

"And I'm sorry about kissing you." I closed my eyes. "I know Theo thinks I'm in love with you, and honestly maybe it'd be easier if I was, but I'm not. Or, I don't think I am, which I'm pretty sure you know. I do love you though. I think in a lot of ways I behaved this way because I love you. I know that doesn't really make sense, and it's a pretty terrible justification anyway."

I stopped again. Considered hanging up. Made myself keep going.

"Look," I said. "I know things can't go back to the way they were. I do understand that. I also understand that maybe they shouldn't. Maybe that's what all of this is about. But I'd like to be able to talk to you. Nothing feels like anything without that."

Back at the office I checked my emails. Tomorrow would be Kim's birthday, so I left a card and a potted succulent on her desk for her to find when she came in.

It was just before six when I left for Theo's.

The cars parked along his street were washed in warm gilded light, and when I turned into the drive, there was Ren's car.

Blood pumped in my ears.

She might not be here for you, I told myself. *Maybe she came because she knew you weren't home.*

But no one was home. Hers was the only car in the drive.

I remembered the voice message then.

Watched my knuckles go white.

Waited for the anxious buzz to begin.

It did not.

There was nothing I could do that would impact whatever would come next. She would either be there to see me or not. She would speak to me or not.

All I could do was tell her again that I was sorry and hope that she believed me.

She sat out back at the round glass table with her feet up on the chair in front of her. The sight of her was both familiar and alien—her belly almost comically large, a massive boulder lodged between her breasts and the fold of her lap, which she rubbed with both hands in a slow circular motion. Her face was turned out to the yard so that her eyelashes cast spidery shadows along the tops of her cheeks.

I thought about that photo those tourists had taken of me and Quincy, back before things had started to turn.

How we were trapped in that image forever. Preserved. How they'd forced a hold on something that never belonged to them.

"Hey," I called to Ren, and when she saw me, she smiled.

EPILOGUE

J

Spring in Hawai'i is full of subtle change.

A quiet surge of new growth.

Plumerias opening in preppy pink clusters.

Orange blossoms slowly surrendering their sweetness into the air.

It's easy to miss if you aren't looking for it.

I sat in Theo's backyard in early April with my hair damp from the shower and my coffee cooling slowly in front of me. A few yards away, Sookie snuffled through her morning yard patrol.

That had been our deal.

Ren got the house.

I got the dog.

From inside came the comforting clatter of Taylor and Theo moving around the kitchen. The dishwasher being unloaded. Plates and cups returning to their homes.

I missed the place on Kalaniana'ole. The creak of the old wood and the constant sound of the ocean. The smell of it.

Mostly I missed having a place that felt like mine.

I'd find another one.

When I was ready for it.

I checked my phone. It was almost time to leave.

Sookie came to the double click of my tongue and together we moved toward the house.

Zane Henry Kelly was born on February 9 at 4:27 a.m. Seven pounds eight ounces. His birth announcement was pinned to the mirror in my bedroom at Theo's.

I had known it was happening.

Had heard the frantic movement overhead around ten.

The sudden scramble of feet.

That night was the worst of it. As bad as it'd been when she'd first told me to leave. I'd lain in bed and cried for hours. Cried for both of us.

Cried for my behavior and the places it had taken us.

I cried for Zane, though I wouldn't know his name for several hours.

I cried for the way he would not be any part mine after all.

I cried because I was relieved.

I cried because I hated myself for it.

By early morning I felt so drained it was an effort to roll over. As the sun rose slowly outside my window my phone pinged. A hopeful note in the semi-dark. Theo, letting me know she'd delivered. *He's beautiful*, he wrote.

Just like his mama, I'd thought, before drifting, finally, gratefully, to sleep.

We piled into Theo's green machine, Sookie and I in the back with a mushroom frittata Theo made that morning. Up front, he rubbed Taylor's leg softly before starting up the car. They had their first real fight the week before and there was a fragile tenderness between them. One that I found both painful and beautiful to be around.

The care with which they navigated each other's space.

Their gentle, intentional movements.

A hand on the back of the neck. The unprompted refilling of a water glass. These little intimacies that silently said, *I am sorry that I hurt you*, and, *here I am, here I am*.

When we turned down Kalaniana'ole, Sookie began to whine, her tail thumping away at the leather.

There was a handful of cars already parked out front of the house. Quincy's Element and that big pickup that belonged to the juice guy from Ren's old gym.

"You know his name," Theo reminded me at dinner last week when I'd called him that. He was right, of course.

Ryan was there in the backyard when we entered through the side gate. He sat crisscross in the grass blowing large bubbles through a flower-shaped wand. In his lap laughed a little girl with a lavender dress and pigtails.

His daughter, Theo'd told me. I'd been surprised.

During the two years Ren had obsessed over him, she'd never mentioned that.

The palms Quincy planted last August had grown at least a foot in my absence, and in the corner where our mulch pile once sat was a folding table and a big white tent. Quincy stood beneath it, arranging a centerpiece of ferns and birds of paradise.

I walked over to him and set the frittata next to a bowl of sliced pineapple.

"Howdy," he said, glancing at me and then immediately away.

He was distant with me still. Refusing to let his gaze linger.

As if he were exercising some sort of self-control.

We'd met for coffee once to talk about it. *It.* But once we got there, we found there was actually little left to say.

Instead we'd talked about work, the baby, and Ren.

I had waited to feel even an echo of the rush I used to get when I saw him, but nothing came. The rush, I realized, had never been about him.

"She's upstairs," he said then, though I hadn't asked.

★ ★ ★

I found her in the living room nursing on the couch I'd picked out. She'd rearranged it so it sat in the center of the room, facing the only wall without windows.

"Hiya," she called when I came in. She'd put down a fluffy white rug on the floor. Not so sensible with an infant but I said nothing.

It was hard, to be inside the house.

It contained anomalous smells now. Baby wipes and powder.

Theo came twice a week to cook batches of curry or pans of lasagna that he stocked in the freezer. He'd hired a woman to scrub the toilets and the stove. To do the laundry. The things that I might've done.

The leather gave softly as I sat, and Zane detached for a moment to eye me, one round fist curling up by his cheek.

"Can we say hi to Auntie Jess?" Ren said to him. "Mmm?" Her voice was low and soft but held none of that syrupy sweetness.

She talked to him like he was. A person, only small.

"Hi, baby Z." I tried to match her tone.

His eyes latched on to mine for a moment. Ren's eyes. Theo's. That impossibly rich brown. He had their warm skin too, their dark curling hair.

I hadn't seen Quincy in him at all, and I'd been looking.

Satisfied with his inspection of me, Zane uncurled his fist and snuggled back into his mother. "How're things with them?" Ren asked, brushing Zane's forehead with the pad of her thumb. I knew by her hushed delivery that she meant Theo and Taylor.

"Oh, I think they're working it out."

"Good." We sat in near silence for a moment. Just us and Zane's tiny, satisfied suckling noises.

On the wall across from the couch Ren had hung a large black-and-white painting. Splotches of pigment splattered around a big square canvas. The beachscapes I'd collected over the years were stacked in Theo's garage. Ren'd replaced them all with these abstract things.

It was a surprising transformation, what she'd done with the place.

Streamlined and mod.

Spare.

Stripped of clutter. As if she couldn't trust herself with it. As if she, too, were exercising self-control.

But the painting was an ugly, aggressive thing. "I don't know if I quite get it," I said, nodding toward it.

"I think what everyone gets from it will be a little different."

"Like a Rorschach test." I gave her a smile, and she returned it.

We were gentle with each other, too. Tender, careful. Like Theo and Taylor.

Long silences filled with apology. With gratitude. *I am sorry that I hurt you*, and, *here I am, here I am.*

Zane released his hold with a loud smack and Ren moved him to her shoulder. Bounced him a bit. Patted his back.

The weight she'd put on to carry him was almost gone. Just a subtle softness left around her arms and face. Something you'd notice only if you'd memorized those pieces of her.

"You wanna put him down?" she asked then, offering him out to me.

Holding him still made me nervous. I took him and stood very slowly, each movement drawn as if I were carrying an armful of fragile china. I remembered what Quincy'd said to me months ago. Just pretend he's expensive.

Of course, he was.

The week Zane was born I had gone to the bank and opened a separate savings account. Since then, I'd been putting three hundred dollars a month inside it, the way we had once planned.

I hadn't told Ren about this yet.

Still, it gave me comfort to know it was there for her. For him.

I carried Zane into Theo's old room, which was his room now. He was warm and dry and smelled like fresh bread. I rested my nose on the top of his head where his dark hair swirled out from the center, and inhaled.

Leaning carefully over the crib I'd chosen, I lowered him down. Just as his small body met the mat below, his eyes opened and there in front of me stretched Quincy's wide, crooked smile, such an identical iteration I gasped.

This child. The sum of so many decisions. Some made, some stumbled into. Named for the storm we sat through together.

I called out to Ren then, an instinct still.

In another room, she lifted her body from the couch. The house creaked in one spot and then another. I stood, quiet in a warm expanse of sunlight, as she moved herself toward me.

★ ★ ★ ★ ★

ACKNOWLEDGMENTS

I'd first like to acknowledge my home on Hawai'i island, where I wrote this book and where this book is set, as an Indigenous space whose original people are today identified as Kānaka Maoli, and my support of the sovereignty movement on their occupied land.

I'd like to thank Abby Walters for believing in this book, Meredith Clark for lovingly shaping its final form, and everyone at the CAA and MIRA/HarperCollins families.

Thank you to Laura Mendoza and Ivy Torres for being the original champions of this story. Thanks to my parents Annie, Dana and Mark, and my brother, Zachariah, for encouraging a career in creativity, and my grandmother Jean for showing me how to fall asleep while reading.

Thank you to Bella O'Toole, my own significant other, for raising our business baby so I could write.

Endless gratitude to the Creative Writing department at the University of Lynchburg, specifically those reigning between 2006 and 2010.

Thanks to Stefanie Bivona, Meg Sunshine Roberts, and Jaleen

Francois for reading adolescent drafts. Thank you to Kristiana Kahakauwila for your insight and intuition in the final days, to Ty Sana for your warmth and wisdom, David Singh for your demented humor and bottomless belief in me, to Helen and Rita Chen for the delicious depth of friendship, to my favorite grammarian, Chris Gibbon, and to Aaron Kandell for always getting in my corner (even on a school day).

Last but never least, thank you to Phillips, for absolutely everything else.